WESTERN

Rugged men looking for love...

A Lullaby For The Maverick
Melissa Senate

The Rancher's Reunion
Lisa Childs

MILLS & BOON

Melissa Senate is acknowledged as the author of this work
A LULLABY FOR THE MAVERICK
© 2024 by Harlequin Enterprises ULC
Philippine Copyright 2024
Australian Copyright 2024
New Zealand Copyright 2024

First Published 2024
First Australian Paperback Edition 2024
ISBN 978 1 038 91077 6

THE RANCHER'S REUNION
© 2024 by Lisa Childs
Philippine Copyright 2024
Australian Copyright 2024
New Zealand Copyright 2024

First Published 2024
First Australian Paperback Edition 2024
ISBN 978 1 038 91077 6

MIX
Paper | Supporting
responsible forestry
FSC® C001695

Published by
Harlequin Mills & Boon
An imprint of Harlequin Enterprises (Australia) Pty Limited
(ABN 47 001 180 918), a subsidiary of HarperCollins
Publishers Australia Pty Limited
(ABN 36 009 913 517)
Level 19, 201 Elizabeth Street
SYDNEY NSW 2000 AUSTRALIA

Cover art used by arrangement with Harlequin Books S.A.. All rights reserved.

Printed and bound in Australia by McPherson's Printing Group

A Lullaby For The Maverick
Melissa Senate

MILLS & BOON

Melissa Senate has written many novels for Harlequin and other publishers, including her debut, *See Jane Date*, which was made into a TV movie. She also wrote seven books for Harlequin Heart under the pen name Meg Maxwell. Her novels have been published in over twenty-five countries. Melissa lives on the coast of Maine with her teenage son; their rescue shepherd mix, Flash; and a lap cat named Cleo. For more information, please visit her website, melissasenate.com.

Visit the Author Profile page
at millsandboon.com.au for more titles.

Dear Reader,

At thirty-five, wealthy rancher Theo Abernathy is finally ready to settle down and find himself a wife. Problem is, all his dates seem to bring up babies and children and families, and Theo is far from ready to be a father. So when he finds himself inexplicably smitten with a four-months-pregnant wedding singer, Theo does his best to ignore his blazing attraction to Bethany McCreery.

About to be a single mother, Bethany can't afford to fall for a man who doesn't want children *now*. They shake on friendship, but Bethany longs for more... Little do they both know that many surprises are in store for them in Bronco this summer.

I hope you enjoy Theo and Bethany's romance. I love to hear from readers, so feel free to email me at MelissaSenate@yahoo.com and check out my website for information on new books coming up.

Happy reading!

Melissa Senate

CHAPTER ONE

As a WEDDING SINGER, Bethany McCreery had performed at many June weddings—it was her band's busiest month. From the fanciest Saturday night shindigs to casual afternoon backyard ceremonies, Bethany and her band performed her slow ballads and dance numbers in the midst of all that love, all that happiness and hope for the future. But tonight, June 28, was her favorite wedding of all: her brother Jake's. After all he'd been through, she was so happy that he'd found his forever love. The ceremony had been so touching, and now Bethany stood on the makeshift stage at the reception, held in the beautifully decorated backyard of the bride's grandmother's house.

As Bethany sang a ballad, one of Jake's favorite songs, she watched her brother and his new wife, Elizabeth Hawkins, slow dance. The newlyweds were gazing at each other with such tenderness that Bethany felt her eyes get misty. And she'd cried plenty already during the ceremony. The couple, both widowed, had five children between them, from five to ten years old, and they were now one very big, very happy family.

As she watched her nieces and nephews do an adorable line dance to their own beat, robot moves and ballerina twirls among them, all she could think was, *The five of you will soon have a new cousin.* A baby cousin.

Bethany's baby.

She was four months pregnant.

And no one knew.

Not her mother, with whom she was very close.

Not her brother, who'd always been her best friend.

Not her two close girlfriends, Suzanna and Dana, who she usually told *everything*.

Not even the baby's father, whom she'd intended to tell. Rexx had quit the band not long after their unexpected one-night stand, and when she'd called to tell him about the pregnancy, he'd interrupted her to remind her he was now engaged, so it was best that Bethany not call again. *Click*.

Given her hormones, her nerves, and all the happily-ever-after in the air, no wonder she was extra emotional.

Bethany sang on, gripping the microphone, and moved across the stage, once again noticing the very handsome man who'd been watching her—intently—all night. He stood by the bar, nursing what looked like whiskey. He was looking straight at her. With interest in his eyes. *Yeah, that'll last*, she thought with bittersweet cynicism. *Once you find out I'm pregnant, you won't look my way again.*

Which was fine with her.

Bethany, thirty-five years old, was done with romance, done with love, done with wishing and hoping and wanting.

And she knew who the man was—a very wealthy rancher from a big and influential family here in Bronco, Montana. Theo Abernathy. He was the same age she was, so she'd grown up with him. Theo had had a lot of gorgeous, busty girlfriends with amazing bodies over the years.

Bethany had the busty part down—she'd gone up a cup size already—but her once-svelte figure was changing before her eyes, Bethany marveling at it in the mirror every morning. She loved her new curves, particularly the one on her belly. She was just starting to show, but her penchant for flowy dresses had kept her secret safe. Even her bridesmaid dress had helpful tiers.

Where were you five months ago, Theo Abernathy? she thought with more of that bittersweet cynicism, the yearning and passion in her voice as she sang reminding her what she'd wanted so badly.

A man in her life. A husband. A family.

Now she'd have the family. Just not the man. Or the husband.

Love had passed her by. That was mostly her fault too.

As she sang the closing note, she noticed Theo finishing his drink and setting the glass on a passing waiter's tray. He was moving now—closer to the stage. And closer still, his gaze not leaving hers.

A line of goose bumps broke out on her neck.

She swallowed and put the microphone back on its stand and thanked the audience, sweeping a hand toward the men guys who made up her band, Bethany and the Belters. The guests heartily clapped, and there were even a few wolf whistles, including from the groom.

Theo was still watching her, still inching closer.

Oh, yes, Theo Abernathy had *I'm very interested in you* written all over his handsome face.

Even if he didn't run for the hills when he found out she was pregnant, this was hardly the time to start a romance. She needed to focus on the fact that her life was about to change. Dramatically. She needed to prepare—mentally and emotionally—which for her meant making a lot of lists. Such as people in her life she could count on—and thankfully, there were many. And things she needed from the get-go, like a bassinet, an infant car seat, a stroller, baby bottles, a bath contraption, and *a lot* of diapers. Tiny pajamas and ever tinier socks. Depending on what she was reading, she also needed everything from a baby bouncer to a wipes warmer. And since she'd be a single mother, she'd have to make a new budget and be very careful.

She wouldn't speak for all wedding singers, but Bethany wasn't exactly rolling in dough. She earned enough to pay her bills and had a very small nest egg that would get smaller and smaller even if she spent on just the necessities.

In other words, she was busy, preoccupied, and a bundle of nerves.

And she was something else: deeply happy and fulfilled that she was going to be a mother. When she got scared about the unknown, she'd focus on that. The baby coming.

Bethany forced her gaze off the very hot rancher. She again thanked the clapping guests, announced that the band would be taking a half-hour break, and then headed to the bar—for cranberry juice. With a lime twist that she'd been inexplicably craving for the past few songs.

"You sing like an angel," a male voice said from behind her.

Her drink in hand, she turned to find Theo Abernathy looking at her with that same interest in his green eyes. Ooh boy, was he good-looking. He was very tall, rancher muscular—though as part of the wealthy Abernathy family, did he actually lift bales of hay? She doubted that. His thick, dark hair was tousled back. And his gray suit fit the way expensive custom suits did.

"I felt that last song right here," he added, tapping his well-muscled chest over his heart.

Wow, did he know how to lay it on. And it was working. She felt his compliment in that exact spot in her *own* chest.

Hormones.

"Bethany McCreery, right?" he asked with a sexy smile.

That he knew her name was no surprise, even though they'd never run in the same circles, starting with kindergarten, when he'd sat behind her. But in Bronco, everyone knew everyone.

She eyed his Stetson and smiled at a memory, of Theo being sent to the principal's office the first day of kindergarten because he'd come wearing a cowboy hat—yes, a pricey Stetson at five years old—and had refused to take it off.

"Right," she said. "And you're Theo Abernathy."

"We were in a lot of classes together over the years," he said. "I wonder why we never dated."

She almost snorted. *I'll tell you why. You were a golden boy from one of the richest families in town, and my dad was a truck driver and my mom a secretary at Bronco Bank and Trust for thirty-five years.* Very different circles.

"I wasn't much of a dater back then," she said instead.

She took a sip of her cranberry juice to break eye contact with the man. Way too intense.

"What about now?" he asked, those green eyes twinkling—and intent on her.

She almost spit out her juice. She hadn't expected that.

"I'm taking a break from men," she blurted, feeling her cheeks warm. She hadn't exactly meant to say that. But it was better than the truth: *I'm unlucky in love. And pregnant.*

"Yeah, I've had those breaks. The last woman I dated gave me an ultimatum on our third date—exclusivity *and* assurance that I wanted two children, as she did."

Well, that had her ears perked. "And neither was in your plans?" Bethany asked.

"Honestly, I'm all for exclusivity. I'm thirty-five and have been ready to settle down for a while now. But the children part…that's less a sure thing."

She stared at him. "You don't want kids?"

"I'm sure I do, *someday*. I just don't feel ready yet. That's a lot of responsibility, a lot of sacrifice."

Ah, the thirty-five-year-old man not having to worry about his biological clock. Humph.

And she noticed he didn't mention money—how *expensive* kids were. Because he didn't have to give the cost of raising children a second thought.

"Commitment, yes," he continued with a firm nod. "But a family, the whole shebang? No." He gave his head a shake for emphasis.

Despite Theo's insistence that he was not open to romance, something inside her deflated.

So they were opposites. She was closed to romance but open to children. He was open to romance but closed to children—for now, anyway. And now was key for Bethany.

Wasn't that always the way?

Maybe just in her world.

Luckily, the bartender came over to take Theo's order, which gave her a minute to compose herself, get back to neutral.

His top-shelf scotch in hand, he held it up to her. "To your beautiful voice," he said. "I could listen to you sing all day."

Well, that was nice. She smiled and clinked her glass with his, then took a sip of her cranberry juice.

She was about to make an excuse to slip away, but a group of guests coming to the bar forced him to move closer to her—and he'd been just inches away to start with. They were *so* close that she could smell his cologne or aftershave—faint but spicy. And intoxicating. She was mesmerized.

"As a wedding singer," he said, "this must be your busy season—summer."

She nodded. "The band and I have performed at fourteen weddings this month alone. Everything from Bronco's fanciest venues to barns and even a mountain cave. That was some schlep getting our mikes and drum kit there."

He chuckled. "How were the acoustics?"

"Terrible. But the bride and groom met on a cave exploration trip for singles, so…" She smiled, recalling how dressed up they'd been too—a tux and a ball gown. She'd half expected them to turn up in cargo pants and hiking boots to say their I dos.

She was about to tell him that she had two more weddings booked—one in a restaurant and one outdoors on a ranch—which would end June on a very good financial note, when she felt a flutter on the side of her belly.

She almost gasped as her hand flew to the spot. Could it be her baby's first kick? She'd asked her ob-gyn when she could expect that and was told closer to twenty-five weeks with a first pregnancy, but her little one gave her an early little kick.

And reminded her that chatting flirtatiously with Theo Abernathy wasn't how she should be spending her thirty-minute break. The last thing she needed to add to her plate was a silly crush on a man who didn't want kids *now*.

It was bad enough she was charmed by the way his crow's-feet crinkled at the corners of his eyes when he smiled. How broad his shoulders were. The warm intensity of his green eyes.

Plus, she was aware that he was checking her out the way people did when they were definitely interested. The way she was checking *him* out. And what if he noticed her baby bump? She moved her hand, lest she draw attention to her belly.

Not that he'd say, *Oh, you're pregnant.*

So far, no one had. But she knew the town's nosy Nellies would soon enough. Her own family included. She'd tell them before they could notice, of course.

That day was coming up fast. She just hadn't been ready to share the big news yet.

It was definitely time to slip away from Theo. He'd surely feel funny for flirting with a pregnant woman whom he'd just told he didn't want kids in the near future.

"Well," she said, clearing her throat, "I, um, should get back to the stage."

"You have at least fifteen minutes till you're due back on," he pointed out. "I was hoping for a dance—or two or three."

Whoa. If she'd been flattering herself that he was interested, she knew without a doubt now that he was.

The music, via Bluetooth speaker, was another slow love song. A little too romantic. She couldn't be in this man's arms for a minute and a half.

Besides, she needed a chair, pronto. And a back rub that she'd have to provide herself.

"Actually," she said, "I was hoping to find the waiter carrying around the tray of those delicious-looking hors d'oeuvres, the little mushroom tarts. I'm starving, and I've got another two hours of singing ahead of me."

He tilted his head slightly, as if he wasn't used to a woman turning him down for anything, let alone a slow dance.

Trust me, she thought. *I'm saving you.*

Just then, that very waiter happened to be walking by, and Theo stopped him so that they could both put a few of the tiny tarts onto little plates. Two seats at the bar suddenly became vacant, and he gestured toward them. She gave an inward sigh and sat down. He sat beside her and popped a tart in his mouth.

Well, if they were going to talk, she had to steer the conversation to less personal topics. She took a long sip of her juice to give her a few seconds to come up with something.

Ah. Got it, she thought.

"I heard your podcast the other day," she said. "My brother picked me up to go cummerbund shopping, and he was listening to *This Ranching Life*. It was so interesting—and I've never been part of the ranching world. I was hanging on your every word."

The episode had been "a day in the life of a rancher," but wasn't about Theo or the Abernathys or their ranch, the Bonnie B. He'd had a guest, a young cowgirl who'd struggled to get her start on a big cattle ranch, having been turned down for the job by six ranches. "The last foreman told me I'd have to take up bodybuilding before he'd let me step foot on his operation," she'd said. "And then I picked up a hay bale and lifted it over my head. I got the job." Bethany had actually clapped right there in her brother's pickup.

The podcast, which aired weekly, was very popular, not just in town but across the Northwest. Theo had some major sponsors, which she knew from the commercials—rodeos, a chain of feed stores, and some dude ranches, to name a few. Her brother had told her that Theo actually donated all revenue from *This Ranching Life* to a fund for ranchers in need. That sure was nice of him, despite the fact that he was super rich and didn't need the money.

"Wow, that's quite the compliment," Theo said with a smile. "Thanks."

"After listening, I even told my brother I wished I could buy a couple of goats or some chickens," she said with a chuckle. "But I live in a small two-bedroom apartment above a hair salon in Bronco Valley, and *one* goat wouldn't even fit on my tiny balcony. And the chickens would fly away."

He studied her for a moment, and she wondered what he thought about where she lived. She knew he and most of his many siblings lived in luxe cabins at the Bonnie B ranch. His kitchen was probably bigger than her entire apartment.

"It's odd that we've known each other our whole lives but have never really talked," he said. "I've seen you perform at a few other weddings over the years. But this is the first time I've been able to approach you."

Interesting. "Oh? Why is that?"

"Either I had a date or I was on one of my own breaks from anything to do with romance," he said. "But now, neither is the case."

"It is for me," she reminded him.

He tilted his head again. "Ah, right—you're not dating now. Maybe I can change your mind," he added with a sexy smile.

I doubt I could change yours about children in the next five months, she thought with a sigh.

It was beyond time to make that getaway. She made a show of glancing at her delicate gold watch, a gift from her late grandmother for her sixteenth birthday. "Oh—I'd better get back on stage. Nice to talk to you, Theo." She gave him a tight smile and then hurried toward the stage.

One of two things would happen: either Theo Abernathy would consider her a challenge and wait for her next break to flirt some more and up his game. Or he'd be dancing with another woman by the time her next set started.

She had a feeling it would be the latter. And that was fine with her.

Because Theo Abernathy *definitely* wasn't the guy for her.

CHAPTER TWO

As Theo sat at his table at the wedding—he was friends with both the rodeo-star bride and the rancher groom—he tried to stop staring at the beautiful woman on stage with her band. He'd struck out with Bethany, something he wasn't used to.

"Get her number?" his brother Jace, sitting next to him, asked. "Saw you two chatting it up at the bar."

Theo scowled. "Actually, no. She made an excuse to stop talking to me."

Jace's eyes practically bugged out. He laughed—heartily. "First time?"

Theo actually thought about that. "Yes, it was. I can't help it if I'm the good-looking Abernathy."

Jace's fiancée, Tamara, grinned. "Um, I take issue with that."

Theo laughed. Jace—younger by two years—was engaged and raising one-year-old Frankie, who'd recently had a big first-birthday party, with Tamara. His brother Billy, on the other side of him, the eldest at thirty-eight and the divorced dad of three teenagers, seemed even happier than usual tonight, his fiancée Charlotte beside him. And now Theo's younger sister Robin was engaged too. That was three out of the five Abernathys—all planning weddings. The youngest, Stacy, was the only one besides Theo without a significant other.

Suddenly, Billy lightly clinked his water glass with a spoon, and all eyes at their table turned to him.

"Charlotte and I have an announcement," Billy said. "We told the kids and mom and dad earlier today, so you all are the last to know," he added with a sly smile.

"Know what?" Theo asked, wondering what the big news was.

"We're expecting!" Charlotte said. "I'm pregnant!"

Theo bolted up and pulled his brother and Charlotte into a hug. "I'm gonna be an uncle again! Very happy for you guys."

"The kids are so excited to have a baby sibling," Billy said.

Theo, Jace and Tamara toasted the couple, Billy drinking cranberry juice in solidarity with Charlotte. Theo made a mental note to pick up a gift for them in Hey Baby this week.

He returned his attention to Bethany on stage, and for a few moments he was so mesmerized by that angelic voice, the passion in it, that he barely heard his brother asking him something.

"Don't take it personally, Jace," Tamara said to her fiancé. "Theo's lost to us. He's been *challenged*. And you know how he reacts to a challenge."

Jace laughed. "Oh, yeah. Gives it all he's got until he conquers it."

Thing was, Theo thought, as he took in Bethany McCreery's long, silky, light brown hair, her curvy body so sexy, even in that puffy bridesmaid dress, this wasn't about a challenge. It wasn't about a woman turning down a dance. Or walking away. He'd felt a real connection to Bethany when they'd been talking. Yes, he'd been unable to take his eyes off her, but it was much more than that. He'd rarely felt a connection so quickly.

Which was why when his dates invariably brought up the subject of children, casually mentioning they wanted two or four or *twins*, he made a quick getaway.

He really did want kids—someday. All he knew for sure was that he wasn't ready yet. He loved children—*other* people's. But Theo had lived on his own terms for a long time, and he liked that.

Maybe Bethany was the same. He'd immediately noticed she hadn't been wearing a wedding ring. Single. Like him. And the few times he'd seen her around town, she'd never been with a baby stroller or a kid. Maybe she felt the same way he did about the *not yet*. He tried to remember what she'd said when he mentioned he wasn't ready for children. He drew a blank. Too focused on how pretty she was, her big blue eyes, and that feeling he had when they'd been flirting—when *he'd* been flirting, he realized now.

Hmm. Maybe she just wasn't interested?

Duh, hotshot, she's probably in a serious relationship.

Except she wasn't just the wedding singer at this particular event; she was the groom's sister and a bridesmaid. She surely had been invited with a plus-one. And if she'd come with a date, he would have muscled his way over when Theo had been standing a half inch from her at the bar and clearly going for it.

She just wasn't interested, he thought, which *did* send up challenge signals. Challenges were exciting; his brother and Tamara had that right about him.

Theo would find Bethany after the last song of the night, when the guests were leaving, and...what? Ask her for her number, which he hadn't even had the chance to do? Yes, he'd start there. If she didn't want to give it to him, he'd take no for an answer. He was a gentleman, after all. The code of the West called for it.

For the first time in Theo Abernathy's life, since he was,

say, twelve, he didn't dance a single dance with a woman at a wedding. And he'd been to plenty in the past few years.

As the night went on, Theo tried to stop being so aware of Bethany—on stage or off, when he'd catch her mingling. She danced with her brother, with her parents, with the other bridesmaids. Once he saw a guy he vaguely knew through the ranching community approach her and then walk away after five seconds. *Strikeout*, he thought happily. So it wasn't just him. She wasn't dancing with any man.

He himself had been approached at least ten times by single women during the course of the night, and he had made kind excuses. He didn't want to dance with anyone but Bethany McCreery.

Finally, the wedding was winding down. The band was collecting their instruments. He watched Bethany hug the three guys—guitarist, keyboardist, and drummer—and then come down the stage steps. Her parents hugged her, the bride hugged her, a bunch of other people hugged her. Finally, she was alone.

It's now or never, he told himself.

He caught her eye as he was heading toward her. Unless he was flattering himself—something he did probably a little too often—she seemed excited to see him. Something in the way her eyes sparkled. But as he stepped up to her, she seemed...wary.

Hmm. Challenge part two: figuring her out.

"I just wanted to say again how much I loved listening to you sing," he said. "You're so talented." Every word was true. Even if he wasn't romantically interested, he'd say all this.

She gave him a warm smile that reached right inside him. "I really appreciate that. Thank you."

"I can't leave without at least trying to get your number," he said. The flirtation had gone out of his voice, he realized. He wanted her number—badly.

She looked away for a second, then started talking really fast about how her life was very complicated right now, a lot going on, booked weekends, some family events.

Wow. She really didn't want to go out with him. Or get to know him better.

Disappointment socked him in the stomach. He wanted to save them both from this uncomfortable moment, so he said, "I, uh, was asking because three of my siblings are engaged and will be getting married in the coming months, and I can pass along your contact info—as a wedding singer."

Her face flushed for a moment. Great. Now he'd made her feel foolish for thinking he was asking her out—when he was.

He sighed. "Full disclosure, Bethany. I asked for your number because I was hoping we could get to know each other. I'd love to take you out to dinner. Or a walk on my ranch—it has some gorgeous spots to watch the sunset over the mountains. I know you said you were taking a break from dating, but you can't blame a guy for trying, right?"

She gave him something of a smile. "I really like your honesty, Theo. That's the second thing you were very open about."

"What was the first?"

"Not wanting children in the near future," she said.

He raised an eyebrow. "You do?" he asked. He didn't know a thing about her, he realized. Maybe she did and *that* was the problem.

"I definitely do," she said.

"Oh" was what stupidly came out of his mouth.

"If you give me your phone," she said, "I'll put in my

contact info for you to pass to your siblings. Networking is everything," she added with a kind of fake cheer.

He handed over his phone, and she entered her info, then gave his phone back.

He texted her a Hi so that she'd have his number too. Not that she'd ever use it.

"Well, bye!" she said and then fled.

He let out a hard sigh. He'd mangled that.

But as he watched her catch up with a couple of other bridesmaids at the door, he was aware of how much he already wanted to see her again.

BETHANY WAS ON her way home from the wedding when she found herself passing right by her apartment building and making a right at the next street instead. Her parents' house was a few miles away, and that was where she wanted to be.

She'd come so close to blurting out to Theo that she was pregnant. *Not only do I want children in the near future, but I'll be having a baby in five months!*

But no way would she tell anyone before her mother.

It was late, but the news couldn't wait. Besides, her mom would be awake, too excited to go to bed now that her firstborn was married. She'd be up and in the kitchen, making tea and having a little bit more of the wedding cake the bride and groom had insisted she take home, and looking through the hundreds of photos and videos she'd no doubt taken with her cell phone.

When Bethany pulled into her parents' driveway, the kitchen lights were on.

She texted her mom that she was here. Her mom responded immediately.

Wide-awake and in the kitchen making tea. Come on in.

Ha, called that one, she thought with relief that she could talk to her mom right now. But butterflies let loose in her belly at actually sharing the news. She was the only one who knew her secret since she'd been surprised with the discovery at seven weeks along.

She tapped on the door, and her mom opened it, tears in her blue eyes.

"Aww, emotional?" Bethany said, her own eyes misting.

"My baby got married," Raye McCreery said, opening her arms for a hug. She still wore her lacy, pale pink mother-of-the-groom dress, her ash-brown hair in an elegant updo.

Bethany flew into her mom's arms. Best feeling in the world.

"Dad dozing in the recliner in the living room?" Bethany asked as she sat down at the kitchen table.

"You know it." Her mom poured two cups of herbal tea and set out the big hunk of wedding cake.

"I barely got to try it," Bethany said, digging her fork into a piece. "Yum," she said. "Both rich and light at the same time. Magical."

She really had no appetite. She was just stalling. Bethany looked out the window, the moon almost a perfect crescent.

"You okay?" her mom asked, eyeing her. "Did the wedding bring up some stuff for you?"

Bethany wasn't surprised by the question. She and her mom had always been close, and Bethany had shared her worry that she'd let love pass her by. And had suddenly woken up one day thirty-five and single.

With a serious case of baby fever.

"Well, it did," Bethany said, "but the reason I'm very emotional right now—and have been the past few months—is because of something else."

Her mother paused, fork midway to her mouth. She set it down. "What, honey?"

Bethany bit her lip. *Here goes. The cat out of the ole bag.* "Let me start from the beginning."

Raye nodded and sipped her tea.

"You know I've always enjoyed being single, living the life of a wedding singer, constantly on the road, traveling from wedding to wedding," Bethany said. "And I always believed that eventually, I'd find my Mr. Right and get married. Well, eventually never came, but thirty-five did. My biological clock has been ticking really loudly."

Her mom was listening intently, and Bethany could tell she was forcing herself not to interject or interrupt. Raye McCreery was already a grandmother times three—and now five, counting Elizabeth's twin five-year-old girls— but she was excited for Bethany to add to the brood.

She took a long sip of her tea, the chamomile scent and warmth so comforting. "Back in January," she said, "with the new year, I started exploring my options, particularly single motherhood via a sperm bank and in vitro fertilization."

Her mom's eyes widened, and she quickly ate a bite of cake so she'd stay quiet. Bethany had to smile at how well she knew her mother.

"But in the midst of reading brochures and websites and even visiting a clinic," she continued, "I had a very unexpected…encounter with Rexx Winters. You remember him, right? He used to be the bassist in my band?"

Her mom nodded. "Nice guy. Handsome too. Could use a haircut, in my opinion."

Bethany smiled. Rexx had always been in need of a haircut with that floppy mop of his.

"Well, one night, after a wedding at a ridiculously over-the-top country club in Billings, Rexx and I ended up kissing. We'd both had a little too much champagne. And one kiss led to another and suddenly we were in my hotel room. In the morning, we were both a little embarrassed and agreed it was a onetime thing, that aside from the basic attraction and the band, we had little in common and not much chemistry."

Raye was hanging on her every word, clearly wondering where this was going.

"Well, I was hard on myself afterward," Bethany said, "thinking that was exactly why I was still single at thirty-five. Something brought me and Rexx together, and immediately afterward, there I was saying no, writing it off, not even giving the idea of a relationship with him a chance. So I was thinking about that, and a week later, we performed at another wedding, this one on a lake with such a beautiful setting, and it was so romantic and the ceremony so emotional that I got wistful. I decided I'd talk to Rexx about giving us a try."

"And he said?" her mom prompted.

"Well, I couldn't find him that night. But in the morning, the band met for breakfast, and I pulled him aside after so we could talk, and before I could say anything, he told me he finally understood what all these weddings were about, that he'd fallen head over heels for a bridesmaid last night and knew immediately she was The One and that he'd marry her. After knowing her a few hours!"

"Oh, Bethany, I'm so sorry," her mom said.

Bethany sighed. "Two weeks later, he called a meeting of the band, told us he was engaged and was quitting to follow his fiancée to her home in Colorado. I thought wow, I was really going to try to work at a relationship with a man I don't have feelings for. That's not good. So right then and there, I decided to pursue in vitro fertilization and make my dream of a family—a child—come true."

"Wow!" her mother said. "So you're going ahead with it now?"

"There's more to the story," Bethany said, quickly having another bite of cake. "At my appointment, I was examined by the doctor, and about ten minutes later, the doctor and nurse returned to the exam room to say, 'Surprise, you're *already* pregnant.'"

Her mother gasped.

"Yup, that was my reaction," Bethany said.

"What did Rexx say?" her mom asked.

Bethany sighed. "I debated telling him at all because of the situation with his new love—throwing a monkey wrench into that. But I decided of course I had to tell him. He deserved to know. And the baby deserved the father to know about him or her. But when I called him, he immediately cut me off and said he was engaged and very happy and needed to leave his past in the past. He disconnected the call before I could tell him the big news."

"So he doesn't know?"

Bethany shook her head. "You're the only one who does."

"And me," came a voice from the doorway. Her father stood there, holding out his arms. Mack McCreery was still in his suit, now a bit rumpled like his graying brown hair.

Bethany got up and flew into her dad's embrace. Her mom came over, and they had a family hug.

"We're gonna be grandparents again, Raye!" her dad said excitedly. "Where are my cigars?"

Bethany absolutely loved that that was his takeaway from that whole story. "You two will the best grandparents in the world." Doting, loving, and *there*. She could always count on her parents.

"Doesn't it just figure that both Jake and Elizabeth either sold or gave away all their baby stuff from five kiddos?" her mom said. "I've been to your apartment and know you haven't bought anything for the baby—unless you've been hiding things in the closet."

Bethany shook her head. "The day I found out I was pregnant, it didn't feel quite real. So I went to the baby section of a store outside Bronco where I wouldn't run into anyone I knew and bought two things—adorable yellow fleece pj's, since the baby will be born in November, when it's chilly. And a floppy stuffed rabbit with long ears. But that's it so far."

The pj's were in the dresser in Bethany's spare bedroom. She'd moved to the apartment just last year, when she'd started thinking about her future, about wanting a baby. Her lease had come up for renewal on the tiny one-bedroom she'd lived in for the past decade, and she hadn't been able to bear signing it again—signing up for another year of not moving forward on her dreams. Every now and then, she'd go into the spare room she envisioned as a nursery and look at the bunny sitting on the dresser. She'd open the drawer and take out the yellow pj's and hold them, and she'd feel such hope, that her dream of having a baby would happen.

"You can count on us to help, honey," her dad said. "We'll get what you need before the baby comes. Don't you worry about anything, okay?"

Her eyes did mist up then. "I love you two so much," Bethany said. "I don't know what I'd do without you."

They had another group hug, then sat down at the table. Her dad poured himself a mug of tea and dug into the cake, instantly getting a little chocolate icing on his tie.

"Eh," he said, taking another bite.

Bethany and her mom laughed. She might be facing single motherhood, but she was doing it with the best parents in Montana.

CHAPTER THREE

COFFEE THERMOS IN HAND, Theo left his cabin on the property of the Bonnie B and walked the half mile to the ranch office to meet his brothers. He breathed in the fresh summer air, the family ranch with its majestic evergreens, the mountains in the distance, and the cattle dotting the pastures and ridges of the ranch never failing to rejuvenate him. The Bonnie B was truly a family affair and not too far from his aunt and uncle's ranch, the Flying A. Except for Theo's youngest sibling, Stacy, a teacher, all the Abernathys worked for the ranch in some capacity. Theo focused on cattle management, but at heart he was a cowboy.

He let out a yawn, which was unlike him. Theo usually slept like a rock. Not last night. He'd been unable to stop thinking about Bethany McCreery. Or her voice.

His grandmother had had a favorite phrase, and it came to him right then: *Don't court trouble.*

He'd be doing just that by pursuing Bethany. He could see it now—they'd be dating three months, getting serious, and she'd bring up the subject of starting a family. At thirty-five, her biological clock had to be a major factor in the timeline. He understood that.

But a first baby at *forty* sounded right to Theo. Maybe even forty-two.

When you knew you had different wants, different goals *before* the first date, there shouldn't *be* a first date.

That was Basic Life Skills 101. And because he *was* thirty-five, Theo should know better.

Don't court trouble...

Except he couldn't stop thinking about her. Dang it.

He drank some coffee, waved at the two cowboys on horseback who were heading past him out into the far pastures, and tried to focus on this morning's meeting. Usually, Theo and his brothers didn't schedule meetings on Saturdays, let alone after a wedding that had kept them out late. But they all had packed schedules, particularly with family commitments, so this morning was the only time they could get together to talk about the upcoming cattle auctions.

In the office, which was attached to the main house where his parents lived, he found his brothers at the coffee station. The three Abernathys looked alike, as everyone said, tall with green eyes.

"Third cup," Jace said, holding up his mug. "And it's only 9:00 a.m." He took a sip and then sat down on his desk chair, facing out. "Frankie's teething and woke up a couple times, including just past 3:00 a.m."

Theo didn't know how his brother was standing. Back when just-turned-a-year-old Frankie woke multiple times a night, there was Jace with the baby bottle, rubbing the boy's little back, or walking the house with him to soothe his cries. Theo knew this because his fiancée, Tamara, often talked about what a great dad Jace was.

How was his younger brother so ready to be a dad when Theo wasn't? Then again, Frankie had come into Jace's life as a foster baby. A volunteer firefighter, Jace had rescued the baby's pregnant mother from a house fire and delivered the child before the mother unfortunately died of smoke inhalation. Distraught at the experience, Jace had surprised everyone—himself included—by insisting on taking responsibility for the infant. Tamara, an ER nurse, had helped him care for Frankie, and they'd started forming a family without even realizing it.

"Second for me," Billy said, refilling his own mug. "I've got a busy day." He glanced at his phone, which was balanced on his knee. "And about fifteen minutes before I need to drop off all three teens at different places. I veer between dreaming of them getting their driver's licenses and realizing Charlotte and I will actually have to *teach* them to drive. Sitting in the passenger seat without a foot on the brake? No, thanks."

Jace laughed. "Yeah, I'm glad I've got a good fifteen years till permit time." He pulled up the cattle auction website on his desktop. The three of them had already made their decisions on the additions for the ranch; it was more a matter of timing. The auctions would be ongoing for three days but were a good forty-five minutes away from Bronco. It was looking like the three of them would need to attend separately.

Jace eyed the screen and shook his head as he relayed the days and times for the auctions. "Monday's not good for me. I take care of Frankie solo on Monday. I can go to the Tuesday auction."

"That works, since Tuesday's out for me," Billy said. "I'm volunteering as a camp chaperone for a hiking expedition. I can go Wednesday morning."

"Not for me," Jace said. "Frankie has a well-baby checkup that morning."

Just the usual meeting among the brothers. Trying to plan anything when Jace and Billy had such busy lives was often impossible.

"I'll take the other day," Theo said. "My only responsibility is the ranch."

"I can't even remember when that was my life," Billy said with a smile.

Jace nodded and sipped his coffee. "*I* can barely remember, and it's only been a year since I became a dad."

Case in point, Theo thought. He could attend a cattle auction any day of the week he damn well pleased.

"Okay, now that that's settled," Billy said, taking a sip of his coffee, "let's move to very important matters—like your love life, Theo. Did you get Bethany's number last night?"

Wasn't he trying not to think about the beautiful wedding singer?

Especially after this? The woman wanted kids right away. She'd said so.

"Actually, I did," Theo said, dropping down in a chair across from the desks. "But I don't know if we want the same things right now."

Billy raised an eyebrow. "You could tell that after talking for, like, all of fifteen minutes during her break?"

Well, yeah. Because he'd been up front. And she'd been up front.

"Go on a date," Jace said. "Then decide."

That was a problem. He barely knew Bethany McCreery and couldn't manage to get her off his mind. Two, three hours on a date, just them, sitting across from each other at a romantic restaurant, and he'd be a goner.

He knew it.

And then what? He was nowhere near ready for kids. She was.

So why start something?

Just then Tamara came in holding baby Frankie, her son's little fist wrapped around a hank of Tamara's long brown hair. Theo watched Jace's eyes light up at the sight of both of them. His brother bolted up to give his fiancée a kiss, and Theo didn't miss the passion in the three-second kiss on the lips, the tenderness in Jace's gaze as he looked at the baby, cupped his little cheek.

I can't see it for me, Theo thought, sipping his coffee.

He got up to greet Tamara and to play a round of peek-aboo with his nephew. Frankie's big eyes locked on Theo as he moved his hands away his face with a "Peekaboo! I see you!"

The baby laughed, the sound going right into Theo's heart. Both his brothers often said there was no greater sound on earth than a baby's laughter. Theo had to agree.

"Hold him for a second?" Tamara asked Theo. "I need to get all this hair into a ponytail. You'd think I'd have learned to do that before I carry Frankie anywhere, but nope." She laughed. "Theo, try to free me from the iron grip, will ya?"

Theo laughed too and gave Frankie's tummy a tickle. The baby let go of his mom's hair.

"Ah," she said, handing the baby over to Theo.

He held Frankie out and studied him. "Good grip, little man," he said. "That's the way you'll be holding the reins in a few years when you get on your first pony."

"Hey, maybe he'll take after me and go into the medical field," Tamara said. She smiled and shook her head. "Eh, who am I kidding? He'll be a rancher like most Abernathys."

Theo cuddled his baby nephew against him and gave him a gentle pat on his back.

Which was when a big glop of baby spit-up landed on his favorite faded denim shirt.

Jace and Billy burst out laughing.

"Good aim, Frankie ole boy," Jace said when he recovered from his laughing fit.

"Yeah, you chose well, kiddo," Billy added. "Better Uncle Theo than me."

Theo mock narrowed his eyes at his adorable nephew. "You can spit up on me anytime, Frankie."

Because I get to give you back. Getting thrown up on was a novelty.

"Well, *I'm* sorry," Tamara said with a smile, her hair now safely in a ponytail. "Here, I'll take him."

Theo happily handed over the drooler.

Maybe he *wouldn't* call Bethany.

AS A WEDDING SINGER, Bethany always held meetings with potential clients in their homes, because they invariably wanted to hear a live a cappella performance, and she couldn't belt out Celine Dion or Frank Sinatra or the bride-to-be's favorite song in the middle of the Gemstone Diner or Kendra's Cupcakes. On Saturday morning at ten, Bethany sat in the kind of living room she'd only seen in very fancy home decor magazines and websites devoted to interior design. The sofas were white and pristine and looked like they'd been delivered that morning. Bethany didn't yet have a child or a pet, and she'd *still* had to turn over the cushions on her nubby textured sofa from a thrift store because of a juice spill when she'd been spooked during a thunderstorm.

Sitting across from Bethany was Laurene Fields, a bride-to-be whose wedding Bethany *had* to secure because she needed the deposit to allow her to take a solid three months for maternity leave. Laurene had already said she'd double the band's usual fee because she was getting married on Valentine's Day night.

Like I'd have a date to cancel because of work. No problem there.

Laurene and her fiancé were both mega wealthy and

were having a "sky's the limit" wedding. Bethany knew this because Laurene had told her so—at least three times since she'd arrived at Laurene's huge house in Bronco Heights. Bethany used to occasionally babysit Laurene, who was seven years younger, but Laurene claimed not to remember her. Bethany and her band were on Laurene's radar because they'd performed at her cousin's wedding and had apparently made quite an impression on Laurene. That was one of the perks of being part of a wedding band—so many potential clients among the guests.

Laurene had gotten engaged only last night and had called Bethany early this morning for the meeting. *I'm hoping you can meet before noon,* Laurene had said. *I have a million calls to make.* Bethany had dropped everything to squeeze it in—she had an afternoon wedding to get ready for and would have liked to just spend the morning resting since she got tired easily these days, like now.

But she would not let one yawn escape her while with Laurene.

Her other plans for the morning had involved coming up with ways to get Theo Abernathy off her mind. Nothing worked. She'd woken up thinking about him, and had tried to keep their conversation about children on a running loop.

Her: *You don't want kids?*

Him: *I'm sure I do,* someday. *But I just don't feel ready yet. That's a lot of responsibility, a lot of sacrifice.*

His face kept creeping into her thoughts. His long, muscular body. And the past month, she'd thought she'd lost her sex drive. Turned out she was wrong.

She'd tried telling herself that he had a new girlfriend

every week. She didn't know if that was even true, but it probably was. Then again, he hadn't gone to Jake and Elizabeth's wedding with a date. Interesting. Or maybe not. Maybe weddings were among his favorite places to meet someone.

He had met someone. Her. It just hadn't gone anywhere—and couldn't.

"Can you sing the first few lines of these songs?" Laurene asked, handing her a list and breaking into her renegade thoughts.

Bethany took the piece of paper and smiled. All classic wedding songs.

Bethany sang away, and Laurene surprised her by holding a hand over her heart.

"I just love your voice," Laurene gushed. "You sound like you mean it."

Bethany smiled. Yes! This gig just might be hers and the band's. They could all use double their usual fee. They'd get half up front, half on the wedding day. "I appreciate that."

"I can tell you right now that you're hired," Laurene said. "I knew at my cousin Tara's wedding that when I got married, I'd have to have you as the singer. My fiancé, CJ, agreed—he was my plus-one."

"Count on us, then," Bethany said, relief flooding her. She could take off those three months and not rely on her parents so much for babysitting—particularly for weddings that ran till well after midnight.

"I'm so excited to be engaged!" Laurene trilled, holding out her engagement ring. "The proposal was everything! He hired a skywriter to propose over our picnic spot at my family's ranch."

"That's so romantic," Bethany said and could hear the wistful edge in her voice.

"Our wedding will be on Valentine's Day, and we'll have our first baby by Christmas. Then our second, third and fourth every three years thereafter. Of course, I'm hoping for twins—they do run in our family." She slid a glance at Bethany's left hand. At her blank ring finger. "Not married?" she asked, surprise in her expression.

"No," Bethany said, biting her lip. "Just haven't found my Mr. Right."

"And no children, then?" Laurene continued. "Wow, aren't you like *thirty-five*?"

Bethany wanted to say, *Well, I am pregnant*, but she was sure she'd only gets look of pity at having to be a single mother. And no doubt Laurene would say something like *Maybe you'll meet someone at my wedding*.

Bethany's phone vibrated. She glanced at it on the coffee table. Theo Abernathy's name popped up on the screen.

Her heart lifted. She needed to feel like she had a prospect in that moment.

Wait a minute. Theo was *not* a prospect.

She certainly couldn't answer the call during a work meeting, especially when Laurene was going on and on about how much CJ loved her.

Just when Bethany was bursting with envy over the bride-to-be's stories of how sweet her fiancé was, Laurene's phone rang with a hopeful caterer needing to meet earlier, so she had to run.

Outside the swanky apartment complex with its indoor and outdoor pools and a view of the mountains, Bethany texted her bandmates that the gig was theirs. They all sent back dollar and heart emojis.

It wasn't until Bethany was in her car that she realized her baby would be a few months old on Valentine's and that she'd want to celebrate the coming new year as a mother with her baby. She'd be going back to work early.

Bethany was used to a life of compromise and making things work. The money would be worth it.

She tapped her phone icon for recent calls. There was Theo's name. He'd left a voice mail.

She hit Play.

Hi, Bethany, it's Theo. First of all, I don't want you think I'm bad at listening. I heard what you said about taking a break from dating, but... The thing is, we had a connection and that's unusual for me, so... Okay, how about this. Call me back if you don't think it's a really bad idea.

Bethany had to smile. It *was* a bad idea, and they both knew it.

But he was feeling the same way she was.

Because of that connection he'd mentioned. And how rare was that? For Bethany, *very*. She thought of all the dates she'd had in the six months before she'd decided to look into single motherhood. She'd gone out with all kinds of men. From fix ups to a dating app to a few guys she'd happened to meet while simply being out and about in town. She'd start out excited about possibilities and end up just feeling lonely.

All right, here's what you do, she thought. *You go out with Theo Abernathy. Since it's a date, you'll both see really fast that of course it can't go anywhere. You'll both have gotten the what-if out of your systems. Then maybe you can be friends.*

She called him back.

The moment she heard his voice, she felt happy butterflies flutter in her belly.

"I called back to tell you we *should* go out so that we'd

see for ourselves it's a bad idea. We'll both run for the hills after a half hour."

He laughed. "I'll wear my sneakers, then. How about tonight?"

Tonight? That was coming right up. She suddenly felt nervous, those butterflies flapping hard. "Hmm, tonight's not good for me." Going out with him at all was asking for trouble. This man had her all turned around.

"Tomorrow night?" he asked.

She bit her lip. "Tomorrow's not good either."

"Any day next week, then," he said.

I'm busy for the next eighteen years, she wanted to say.

"My life is actually pretty complicated right now," she said. "In fact, we should just forget going out." Yes, they should. Spending a few hours in his company would only make her crave him *more*. Not less.

"I can't," he said. "To be very honest. I'd like to get to know you better. That's what I know for absolute sure. Tell you what—how about if we just get together, a walk on the Bonnie B? I'll show you my favorite spot to watch the sunset. My favorite goat. My favorite of the spring calves."

"Monday," she blurted out before she could not say it. "I don't have a wedding on Monday, so I'm free."

"Monday, July first," Theo said. "I'm penning it in."

She laughed. "It's a date." Her smile faded very fast. "I mean, it's… We're getting together."

Now he laughed. "It's okay, Bethany. It's a *walk*."

But it wasn't just *a walk*. It was the start of something. And she knew it.

CHAPTER FOUR

"AND THAT'S BUSTER, our new rooster," Theo said late Monday afternoon, pointing at the golden comet strutting around the chicken barn on his family's ranch.

Bethany wasn't surprised that the chickens—and Buster—had more than just a coop. The Bonnie B had many beautiful outbuildings, from ornate stables for the horses to stately red barns of various sizes for the cattle and equipment. What Theo referred to as bunkhouses for the employees who lived on the ranch were more like luxe cabins, and what he called cabins, like what he and his siblings lived in on the huge, majestic property, were log *mansions*.

"Love the name Buster," she said. "Did you name him?"

"My teenaged nephew got naming rights for the newest rooster, and we were all a little nervous at what he'd come up with. We can barely understand half his slang these days. But he declared him Buster, and we all love it too."

She liked that Theo talked a lot about his family, and not just his parents and siblings and their significant others but his aunts and uncles and cousins. It was clear the Abernathys were a tight-knit group, just like the McCreerys, and there were *a lot* of Abernathys in town.

She liked him, period, she thought as she bent down to pet a fluffy reddish-brown chicken pecking the ground near her feet. Theo was such a gentleman. He'd picked her up exactly on time for their "just a walk," had come upstairs to her second-floor landing when she'd buzzed him in, then held open the passenger door of his shiny pickup for her and closed it when she was settled inside. She wasn't used to that.

And maybe it was the wealth, but for a man in jeans and a Western shirt and cowboy boots, he managed to look *dressed*. She'd poked around her closet for just the right flowy sundress, then realized she shouldn't try to hide her baby bump anymore. Especially now that she'd told her parents. This might not be a *date* date, but it sure felt like one, and she'd have to tell Theo she was expecting at some point during this get-together. Maybe even early on.

Like now.

Blurting it out here, out of the clear blue, didn't seem like the time or the place, though. It would sound as though she'd been holding it in, holding it back, which was exactly what she was doing. Would he say, *Why the heck did you agree to go out with me, then?*

Probably. She hadn't told him at the wedding because she'd wanted to tell her mom first. And she hadn't told him when they'd spoken on the phone because...

She didn't have a good answer for that.

She'd had the past hour to tell him. And there'd been a time or two when she could have brought it up as they'd walked around the Bonnie B. Their conversation had centered mostly on their families, the two of them swapping sweet, funny stories about their nieces and nephews. But just as she'd been about to bring up the subject of her own child-to-be, he'd pointed out something on the ranch— the spot where he liked to watch the sunset and how if he needed to clear his head, he'd just walk the land, keeping his gaze focused on the cattle on the ridges in the distance, the green pastures as far as she could see, the mountains.

They'd talked easily, an hour passing in a snap. And

the entire time she'd rationalized her interest in him to how nice it would be to have Theo Abernathy as a *friend*.

A friend who happened to be very good-looking and deliciously built. She was well aware that she didn't notice every little detail about her male friends—like the mesmerizing green of Theo's eyes or the way the sunlight spun gold into his brown hair. He had a habit of running a hand through that hair when he was thinking about an answer to something she'd asked.

She wasn't going to kid herself about Theo. She was very attracted to him—the man who didn't want children anytime soon.

But she wasn't ready to say goodbye.

And not because she hadn't told him her big news. She gave the chicken one last pat, then stood. Maybe she would just blurt it out right now.

"I like a woman who isn't afraid to get close to a chicken," he said. "Not too long ago, one of my sisters set me up on a blind date with a friend of hers who grew up on a ranch but hated it her whole life. You'd think Stacy would have figured that would never work."

Bethany laughed. "My last blind date told me he couldn't stand live music—'it's so loud and all those annoying people singing along'—and that he hated that his dates were always suggesting going to concerts and music festivals. I said, 'Um, you know I'm a wedding singer, right? Live music is what I do.'" She shook her head. "That pretty much sums up how my dates went before—"

She clammed up. She'd been about to say: before she gave up on men and decided on in vitro fertilization, only to discover—surprise!—that she'd gotten pregnant the old-fashioned way.

That was a story in itself. And one she couldn't imagine telling Theo just like that.

"Before?" he prompted, glancing at her.

She bit her lip. He'd been doing this since he'd picked her up. Listening. Asking questions.

Making her like him. Dangerous when she was already so attracted. And had raging hormones.

"Before I took a break from dating," she said fast.

"Miss it?" he asked.

She laughed again. "Miss dating? Are you kidding?"

"Yeah, really dumb question," he said with a smile that sent goose bumps along the nape of her neck. "Except this kind of redeems the whole dating process," he added, wagging a finger between them.

Her heart lifted at the sweetness of what he'd just said, then crashed. Sigh. Wasn't it always like this? Right man, wrong time. Right time, wrong man. "This isn't really a date, though," she reminded him. "It's a *walk*."

He laughed, and she wanted to reach for his hand and just hold it. Why did she have to feel so close to this man?

"I suddenly have a mad craving for pasta," Theo said as they watched the rooster strut around. "Linguine carbonara with garlic bread. Hungry?"

Uh-oh. That would make this more than a walk. Dinner meant *date*. But now that he'd mentioned pasta and garlic bread, she had a major craving for both herself. And once a craving hit, there was no ignoring it. "Ooh, me too. But for penne primavera in a pink cream sauce. And definitely the garlic bread."

"Pastabilities?" he asked.

The casual Italian restaurant in Bronco Heights was perfect for tonight—not too romantic, not too date-like. Just right.

"I love that place," she said, her craving for garlic bread so strong now she just might order it as an appetizer.

He smiled. "Great. Off we go."

If he'd suggested riding there together on a white horse, she wouldn't have been surprised. He'd been having a knight-in-shining-armor effect on her this whole time. Which made absolutely no sense. Once she told Theo Abernathy she was pregnant—and she would before the night was over—he'd run for those hills. She'd never see him again.

They got back into the shiny pickup that probably cost the equivalent of three years' rent on her apartment. Twenty minutes later, they were seated at a table for two in Pastabilities by a window facing the main street and handed menus, the waiter asking about their drink orders. Theo opted for a hard lemonade. She said she'd have the soft version.

She waited for a light bulb to magically go off over his head like in cartoons. *Oh, you're not drinking, therefore you must be pregnant!*

No such luck.

When he mentioned that he might start with a Caesar salad, she could have said she loved rich, creamy Caesar dressing—and she actually had a serious craving for croutons and shaved Parmesan now—but raw egg yolk was a no-no on the pregnancy diet.

Instead she said she wanted to save her appetite for the main course.

"Hey, look," Theo said, upping his chin toward the window. "There goes your new sister-in-law's family."

Bethany looked where he was gesturing and smiled. It was no surprise he knew who they were. Three of Elizabeth's sisters, very popular rodeo stars who performed together as the Hawkins Sisters, were deep in conversation as they walked across the street.

Bethany turned her attention back to Theo, who was sipping his drink. "Jake and Elizabeth and the kids are on their familymoon. They're spending the week together right here in Bronco."

"I like that. Big blended family, right?"

She chuckled and nodded. "Five kids—Elizabeth's twin five-year-olds, Lucy and Gianna, and Jake's three—ten-year-old Molly, eight-year-old Peter, and six-year-old Ben."

"Wow, that's *a lot* of young children," Theo said. "I can't imagine coordinating that. My brother Billy has three teenagers, and just getting them to their summer activities takes incredible feats of timing between him and Charlotte. Plus, they just announced to the family that they're expecting a baby in January."

She felt her eyes widen. There was her in. *Me too—but in November!* she could say. But that wasn't what came out of her mouth. "Ah yes, that unmagical time of constant plans and no driver's licenses yet. I remember that from when Jake and I were teens." She smiled and sipped her lemonade. She just wasn't ready to tell him. For everything to change between them. "Jake and Elizabeth will make it work, though."

"I guess their lives will revolve around the kids," Theo said. He let out a low whistle to clearly highlight that it sounded like a lot.

Bethany shook her head. "I wouldn't say that. Next week, Elizabeth is performing in the rodeo here in town with the Hawkins Sisters. She doesn't have to give that up. And Jake has his ranch and volunteers at the Pony Club that Elizabeth is heading up—a riding academy for kids. But yes, to a point, they're now accommodating five kids' schedules—but in *addition* to their own."

The waiter came with a tray bearing their orders. The garlic bread smelled heavenly.

"Bon appétit," Bethany said, putting a piece of the bread on her plate.

"Bon appétit," he seconded, twirling his fork in his linguine carbonara.

They dug in for a few minutes, each pronouncing their dishes delicious.

"Try some?" he asked, pushing his bowl toward her.

Of course he was a sharer. Last year she'd gone on a blind date with a cowboy who'd hoarded his truffle fries and not only didn't share but had actually said no when she asked to try one. Deal-breaker right there.

"Mmm, definitely," she said, slipping her fork in. "Ahh. So good." She did the same with her bowl, and he took a forkful of her penne primavera.

"Excellent," he said. "I've loved everything I'd tried here."

"Me too." She picked up her garlic bread and took a very satisfying bite. Ahh, scrumptious.

"Beat you to the table!" came a loud voice.

"No, you won't!" came a louder voice.

Bethany glanced over—identical twins, seven or eight years old, were racing to a nearby table, their parents, whom she recognized from around town, hurrying over to them.

"We use inside voices in a restaurant," the mom said.

"And we don't run," the dad added.

They sounded more weary than stern. It had likely been a *long* day.

The kids declared that whoever sat down last was a rotten egg. Both boys practically flew to their seats.

The parents sighed and looked around with embarrassed, apologetic expressions.

I can't wait to be you, Bethany thought, smiling at the family. That was life. Busy, harried, beautiful life.

She suddenly wondered if her baby would have a sibling—someday, of course. She knew she wasn't having twins. But maybe in a couple of years...

Getting a little ahead of yourself, Bethany, she thought happily.

"Where are my earplugs?" Theo asked on a laugh. He sent a smile toward the family.

But he probably wasn't kidding.

"Speaking of kids," he said on a chuckle, "I guess I'm used to living life on my own terms. If I had kids, the time and attention I give to the ranch would have to change. I take my responsibilities very seriously, and as a Dad, my kids would come first. Besides, I'd be up at the crack of dawn making a lot of pancakes and probably burning them because I'd be distracted by sibling arguments. And that's after a few years of waking up all night with a crying baby." He gave a mock shiver.

His tone was light, his green eyes twinkling, but Bethany could see he'd *meant* that shiver.

She swallowed. She had to tell him *now*. He was certainly entitled to his point of view. But if he knew she was pregnant, he wouldn't be saying any of this. And that was unfair to him—putting him in a position to feel funny once he did know.

But of course, they wouldn't *be* here at all. Shouldn't be.

She sighed inwardly and glanced out the window. Bethany noticed Bronco's mayor, Rafferty Smith, and his wife, Penny, heading down the street, hand in hand. They'd celebrated their thirtieth anniversary a few months ago. As the couple passed by, Bethany could see Penny was wearing the beautiful antique pearl necklace Rafferty had given her for the occasion.

Thirty years. Back when Bethany used to assume she'd get married "someday," she'd imagined herself growing old with her beloved, sitting on her porch swing, her head on her husband's shoulder, grandchildren playing in the leaves. But here she was, pregnant and on a nondate at age thirty-five—with a man who liked it quiet at 3:00 a.m. because he'd have to wake up with the roosters to start his work day on the ranch.

Hey, just because Theo won't be sitting with you on that porch swing doesn't mean you'll be sitting there alone. You can still find love. Who says you won't be married and celebrating your thirtieth anniversary when you're in your late sixties?

Your brother found love again with three kids.

Elizabeth with two. And twins at that.

She perked up a bit at the thought.

But as she looked at her handsome date, the first man she'd felt a spark within a long time, she wished it *could* be him beside her on the swing.

"But I guess you're ready for your life to dramatically change," Theo said with a warm smile. "I didn't mean to knock family life. I know you said you're looking forward to that in your near future. It's just not for me right now."

"Well, my future has actually arrived," she said. "I have something to tell you before another second passes. Something I should have told you on the phone when we were making plans."

He was staring at her, head slightly tilted.

Bethany took in a breath. "I'm four months pregnant."

THEO WAITED A bit just in case she was about to say, *Kidding!*

And waited.

But she didn't say anything else. And she didn't look like she was joking.

"Congratulations," he said somewhat tentatively. He had no idea what her situation was.

Clearly, she wasn't involved with her baby's father if she was here with him, "just a walk" or not.

"I should have told you before tonight that I was pregnant. But when we were talking at my brother's wedding, I hadn't even told my parents. Not to mention the baby's father."

Interesting. There was definitely a story here. "I completely understand," Theo said. "I'm the one who kept trying to talk to you, trying to get your number, trying to make tonight happen. And that's after you told me you wanted a child in the near future."

All true. And he knew why. It had started with her voice; she'd captivated him. And then they'd talked so easily, something very clearly there between them.

If a woman told Theo Abernathy that she wanted a baby now and he'd actually pursued her...

What did that mean?

He didn't have an answer for that one. He hadn't changed his mind about how he felt about being a father now.

They'd both been honest about what they wanted. And they were here because they'd *both* felt that spark.

A little too powerful to ignore.

"And *I'll* completely understand when you get up and leave," she said.

"I'd never do that." He paused, then asked the burning question. The immediate one, anyway. "The father— he's not..."

"In the picture?" she finished for him. "No."

He waited for her to elaborate, but she didn't.

"What are your plans?" he asked. "For when the baby comes?"

She took a long sip of her lemonade. "I'm working as much as I can now to allow me to take maternity leave starting in November. My parents both work, so I'll need to find a nanny or day care. But my plan is to be a great mom."

"I'm sure you will be, Bethany," he said, and he believed she would be despite barely knowing her.

He wanted to know the story. Who the father was. What had happened between them. But he didn't feel he had the right to ask such personal questions.

Besides, after dinner, that would be that for him and Bethany. Right? They didn't know each other. Now was the time to walk away. When they were just two people who'd met at the wrong time.

She'd have a baby in five months.

He couldn't even *imagine* a baby in his life. If he wanted to record his intro to *This Ranching Life* and edit an episode at 3:00 a.m.—and sometimes he did—he couldn't if he had a diaper to change or a newborn to feed. He'd be too bleary-eyed and exhausted and busy to work his side gig, wouldn't he? And he'd never be able to get through a full day on the ranch.

No responsibilities except to the Bonnie B and his family—his two great loves.

Plus, traveling on a moment's notice.

Going out every night—not that he did much of that anymore. Last Saturday night he'd gone to a family birthday party and was on the couch watching a Marvel movie at 9:00 p.m. Asleep by midnight. But he *could* be at a late-night party at the Association or wining and dining a lovely woman in Vegas for the weekend if he chose to. In a couple of weeks, he'd be attending eightysomething-year-old Stanley Sanchez's bachelor party. If he had a baby, he'd *want* to be home. His life would be so different, and he liked it just the way it was.

"I can see the montage happening in your head," she

said with a smile. "A screaming newborn, a pile of diapers and burp cloths, baby bottles to wash."

Bachelor parties to leave early.

Huh. Maybe she *did* know him.

Theo Abernathy was rarely speechless. But right now, he didn't want to say anything.

Anything *final*, he realized, which confused the heck out of him.

He looked at Bethany, the beautiful singer with the voice of an angel. The woman he felt this inexplicable connection to. When was the last time he'd talked so easily to someone he'd just met? Thinking back to her brother and Elizabeth's wedding, Theo couldn't stop recalling the way he couldn't take his eyes off her, how he didn't want to stop talking to her, how he wanted to get to know her better.

Yeah, he had it bad for this woman. He could hear Billy and Jace insisting that, one day, he too would meet someone and life as he knew it would change. He'd thought they were being dramatic, but here he sat, when the former Theo Abernathy would never have pursued a woman who'd said she wanted a baby soon.

That meant something in itself—and he didn't want to think about it.

"Theo, since you look kind of...ill," she said gently, "let's just call it a night, okay?"

He should be jumping up and running out the door. But he couldn't move. He didn't want to move.

She was studying him, he realized. Trying to figure out why he wasn't getting up.

"Friends?" she said—but then she bit her lip. As if she thought that was a bad idea.

Because of the chemistry. The attraction.

The waiter came over then to ask if they wanted dessert. Bethany said she'd love to have her leftovers wrapped up, including all the garlic bread.

"Pregnancy craving," she added with a sweet smile when the server left.

Oh, God, he thought. He wasn't ready for pregnancy cravings. For something, *anything* taking over. Right now it was cravings and soon it would be exhaustion and then it would be the baby. He couldn't date this woman.

"It's all yours," he said, gesturing to the garlic bread and trying to force a pleasant expression on his face.

But he knew he must look as ill as she'd said.

The waiter returned with her takeout box and the bill. She offered to pay for dinner, but he handed over his credit card and insisted it was his treat.

She thanked him and stood, so he did too.

Just like that, their nondate was over. Before it had ever really had a chance to begin.

They went outside, and it was such a beautiful summer night that, for a moment, he wanted to suggest extending their evening for a stroll around town.

He was in shock. That had to be it.

This never was a date. And they needed to go their separate ways.

Except she'd put friendship on the table.

He drove her home to Bronco Valley in silence, neither of them saying a word until he walked her to her apartment building door.

"Thanks for dinner, Theo. I'll be having the garlic bread for dessert." She smiled, and he knew she was trying to lighten the tension in the air.

He felt like such a heel. He had to say something. But what? What was there to say?

"You're very welcome" was what came out of his mouth.

She gave him another brief smile and quickly unlocked the door and hurried inside.

Leaving him alone with thoughts he didn't know how to process.

CHAPTER FIVE

THEO HAD SPENT the morning riding fence far out on the ranch, taking photos and notes about repairs that needed to be made. It was someone else's job, a new hire, so Theo rationalized that he was just checking up so he could give the guy feedback. He'd spent most of the afternoon reorganizing the equipment barn, also not his job, and was now in the cattle barn, examining the muck rakes in the locker.

He'd been antsy and unable to focus since he'd woken up that morning, pouring salt instead of sugar into his coffee, looping his belt in his jeans in the wrong direction, Jace had raised an eyebrow and asked him if he'd had enough coffee yet.

Try two refills of his thermos. The caffeine boost hadn't helped.

It was now almost 3:00 p.m., and he still couldn't concentrate, couldn't think straight. Probably because he'd been trying so hard to get Bethany McCreery out of his head. Her face, her voice, her blue eyes, snippets of conversations they'd had—including the major revelation—kept sneaking into his thoughts.

He'd been unsettled since he'd driven Bethany home last night. He hadn't been able to shake it. Not through driving around Bronco Valley or Bronco Heights or walking the ranch in the moonlight.

Why couldn't he just say goodbye? They were wrong for each other. In a life-changing way. And Theo couldn't change his life. He wasn't ready to be a father. And Bethany would have a baby in five months.

What the hell was he going to do? He couldn't imagine just walking away. But how could he not?

Theo sighed hard and tried to focus on the muck rakes hanging in the locker at the end of the line of stalls, checking the wood handles for signs of splintering. Two could use replacing. He jotted that down in his phone's Notes app.

"You gonna start cooking in the caf next?"

Theo turned around to find Jace staring at him from the doorway with a quizzical expression. Billy was beside him, on one knee to pet the family dog and mascot, Bandit. Theo had been so lost in thought he hadn't heard any of them coming. And Bandit usually liked to announce his arrival with a *woof*. That was how far gone Theo was.

Billy grinned. "Please say no, Theo. Whatever has you doing every job on the Bonnie B but your own, please keep out of the caf's kitchen. You can barely flip a burger before it burns on one side. The cowboys and cowgirls and hands will revolt."

Both his brothers chuckled at how true that was, then they sobered up, continuing their deep study of him.

"Okay, what's going on with you?" Billy asked.

"Something is definitely up," Jace added.

Theo was about to say he was fine. That nothing was up at all. But just then, a memory overtook him—of beautiful Bethany in her flowered sundress telling him that not only was she four months pregnant but that the father wasn't in the picture.

He sucked in a breath and told his brothers everything—swearing them to secrecy since this was Bethany's private business. He needed their take on the situation. They were both engaged, they were both dads, and both had worked very hard to get where they were today: happy family men. Plus, they knew him very well.

"Here's what I think," Jace said. "Being friends with Bethany means dating without the sex for maybe the first week. You'll call yourselves friends, but mutual attraction won't go away. Trust me, you'll be in a romantic relationship by week's end."

Billy shook his head. "I don't know about that. I think the two of you will *repel* each other. Theo, you're not gonna be attracted to a woman who'll have a baby in five months, because a baby is not what you want. And she won't be attracted to a man who isn't interested in parenthood right now. So the attraction *will* disappear and you can be friends."

"If that were the case," Jace said, "he wouldn't be in this quandary. She told him flat out she wanted a baby soon, but he pursued her, anyway. And he told her flat out that he doesn't want to be a dad for, like, five years, but she said yes to the date. Oh, excuse me—a *walk*." He smiled and shook his head. "The two of you are a lost cause, sorry."

"Hmm," Billy said, considering that. "Kid brother might be right here, Theo. Sorry. You two will shake on friendship, but in a week or two, you'll be seriously dating a pregnant woman. Just know that from the outset."

Jace laughed. "Yup. I mean, look at *us*. Not quite the same situation, but…"

Theo did look at his two brothers, and his head almost exploded. The idea of being a father hadn't been a thought in Jace's head when he'd found himself taking in the orphaned newborn he'd delivered. But his brother had been unable to walk away from Frankie. And despite not looking for love herself, the ER nurse who'd examined the baby was now his fiancée.

Then there was Billy. Engaged to the very woman who'd

stood him up at his own wedding twenty years earlier. The recently divorced dad of three teenagers had been dealing with betrayal and custody questions—and was now actually excited about planning his wedding to Charlotte Taylor. They were expecting a baby in January, and Theo knew how excited his brother was about the new addition to the family. *Four* kids!

He swallowed. Surely Theo had a say in all this. It was, after all, his life. "Maybe I'd better keep my distance from her."

"Until the baby's born, anyway," Jace said. "Once you see her with a squawking baby crying his little heart out in Bronco Java and Juice when you just want a strawberry-banana smoothie, you'll be fine. You can be friends then."

Theo caught the sly smile that passed between his older and younger brothers.

"Ha, just kidding," Jace added. "The problem with someone getting under your skin is that you won't be able to stay away. You'll be bringing her dinner tonight, no doubt. All the foods she's craving, like pickled herring and pickled eggs."

Billy grimaced. "I think you're confusing *pickled* with *pickles*. Pickles are the standard craving for pregnant women."

Theo had no idea what pickled herring was—or pickled eggs, for that matter. "So what you're both saying loud and clear is that I shouldn't even bother thinking about this life crisis because it's out of my hands."

"Pretty much," Jace said. "This thing," he added, slapping a hand over his heart, "will be directing you from now."

"But, very seriously, Theo," Billy said. "You can't casually date a pregnant woman. You're either in it or you're not."

Theo let out a hard sigh.

What Billy had just said was exactly the problem. There was no casual when it came to pregnancy. To a baby coming in five months. To a woman who was a package deal.

Theo *couldn't* be in it. "I know I'm not ready to be a dad," he said. "I'm meant to be fun Uncle Theo. Giving kids *back* after two hours of babysitting."

"Then you'll have to become a Bonnie B hermit," Jace said. "And never leave the ranch to avoid running into Bethany. So that means no rodeo next week, since she'll definitely be there to see her new sister-in-law perform. Oh, and you'll have to bury your phone so that you can't text Bethany under some pretext."

"But just till the baby comes," Billy said on a chuckle. "Since a baby is the last thing you want."

Again Theo caught his brothers sharing a glance. And he knew what that look meant too. That they didn't think Theo stood a chance. That he was too interested in Bethany McCreery to walk away.

Theo scowled. Why had he thought his brothers would be of help? He was actually more confused now.

Bandit let out a *woof*, his tail wagging excitedly. Was the pooch offering an opinion on the situation?

Billy glanced at his watch. "Good boy, Bandit," he said, bending down to give the dog a pat. "Who needs a watch when we have Bandit to tell us that the day camp bus should be pulling up to the stop right about now?"

Theo put back the muck rake he'd been holding—gripping like some kind of a lifeline—and the three of them left the barn, Bandit hurrying ahead to the ranch's long drive, tail wagging away in excitement. If only Theo had a dog's mysterious way of knowing what was coming.

"Time to put on my dad hat," Billy said, tipping up his Stetson. "Three teenagers are about to come barreling up the drive to raid the fridge for a snack before I have to drop them all off in three different places. *That* is the life of a dad."

"Unless you're me and it's still about changing diapers," Jace added with a grin.

"I wouldn't trade my life for anything," Billy added. "I might sound corny but being a dad is the best thing that has ever happened to me. Watching my kids grow up and become teenagers has given me a few gray hairs, but it is amazing watching these little babies become independent." He laughed. "And if the learner's permits don't give me gray hair, the dating definitely will. And with a fourth on the way, I couldn't be happier."

"Yup," Jace said with a nod. "Fatherhood changed me in the best in of ways. That a tiny little human who can't even talk yet can teach you so much about life and love—that's amazing. And hey, Frankie brought Tamara into my life, so I have to give him extra props."

Huh, Theo thought, taking all that in. He was about to ask his brothers if they missed being able to focus solely on the ranch, but he just heard the bus pulling to a stop and the door opening and closing. The sounds of chatter and laughter were heading in their direction. And then Billy's kids came up the path, talking a mile a minute, interrupting each other, laughing, teasing.

Theo adored his niece and nephews. Branson, the oldest at seventeen, still didn't have his license because he'd flunked his driver's test. According to Billy, Branson had been doing great on the road test, then noticed a girl he had a crush on going into the Gemstone Diner and took his eyes off the road long enough to almost swerve into an oncoming car. He'd try again in a few weeks.

Fifteen-year-old Nicky had recently gotten his learner's

permit, and Billy and Charlotte had gone to bed each night since with their nerves stretched to the limit.

Then there was Jill, soon to turn fourteen and starting high school in the fall, begging to be allowed to wear makeup this summer so she could be a pro at it for the first day late next month. All three teens had the Abernathy green eyes, but they couldn't be more different from one another.

"You're dropping me at Kara's, right?" Branson asked his dad. Kara was the girl he'd failed his road test over.

"If a parent will be home—as we talked about," Billy countered.

Nicky and Jill snickered.

"Fine, yes, her mom will be home," Branson said.

It took Theo a minute to figure out why Billy cared if a parent would be home. Hormone-raging teenagers with huge crushes on each other home alone? Got it.

"Dad," Nicky said, "I have to be at Bronco Brick Oven Pizza at three forty-five for the lacrosse team's fundraiser. Oh, and you're supposed to Venmo the payment to the assistant coach for the end-of-summer barbecue in August."

"Got it," Billy told his son.

"Dad, you can drop me off at Heather's before that, right?" Jill asked. "You know you always end up chatting away with other parents during drop-off. And can I adopt two kittens?" She gave her dad serious puppy-dog eyes. "A girl at camp has four left to find homes for. We'd be doing a good deed! Pleeeeeze, Daddy?"

"Listen, Jilly Bean. We have two cats already. And a dog. And three fish tanks. So that's gonna have to be a hard no."

"Can I get a bearded dragon for my birthday, then?" Jill asked. "Charlotte *loves* lizards."

Billy raised an eyebrow as his brothers swallowed their

laughter. His fiancée was a marine biologist who loved sea creatures. Theo had never heard her mention lizards. "We'll talk about that."

"Yes!" Jill said. "That's not a no!"

"Dad, don't forget I need to get to camp an hour early tomorrow," Branson said. "The CITs are having a meeting."

"That means you two will need to get there an hour early too," Billy said to Nicky and Jill. "Unless Uncle Theo wants to take you before he goes to the first of many cattle auctions." Ah, the pleading look in his brother's eyes.

"Uncle Theo would love to," Theo told Nicky and Jill.

"Awesome!" Jill said, holding up her hand for a high five to Nicky, who was busy digging deep in his backpack for who knew what. Probably the source of the strange odor wafting out. Like a three-day-old half-eaten fast-food burger.

Jace leaned close to Theo. "At least you'll have a good twelve years before you hit the teen stage. That's if you survive the terrible twos." He laughed. "Not that I'm looking forward to that. I've heard horror stories."

Theo swallowed. Terrible twos? If he did get involved with Bethany McCreery, the terrible twos were right around the corner.

He knew he was ready for a serious relationship. Marriage, even. But this? Babies and toddlers and teenagers depending on him? Needing him? For everything?

He loved his nephews and niece to pieces. But he just couldn't see himself in Jace's and Billy's roles. Not yet.

"I definitely shouldn't start something I can't finish," he whispered to Jace as the kids ran down the path to their house to grab drinks and snacks and very likely mess up the kitchen.

"Except when love gets you, you're gotten," Jace said, enjoying this a little too much.

Theo shook his head. "Who said anything about love? I had *one* date. And it wasn't even a date. It was a *walk*."

"A walk into Pastabilities for dinner," Billy reminded him. "That's a date." He gave his brothers a wave and started after his kids. "See ya later."

Theo wasn't *gotten*. But he had to admit that Bethany had been on his mind throughout this entire conversation. And not because they were talking about her. And her baby.

Because he couldn't stop thinking about her. Seeing her face and silky brown hair. Her big blue eyes. Her beautiful voice.

I'm not gotten, he told himself. *I'm just...*

Something.

Something he couldn't think about anymore or he'd drive himself crazy.

ALMOST A FULL day had passed since Bethany had told Theo that she was pregnant. Not a word from him.

As it would be tomorrow and the next day and...forever.

Right guy, wrong time, she reminded herself.

Actually, he wasn't the right guy. The right guy would want a baby now. Particularly in five months. He'd be ready for fatherhood. Ready to share his life with his family.

You have to forget him, she told herself.

She'd had a group video chat with her two besties, Suzanna and Dana, last night when she had got home. They were both away, Suzanna visiting her sister who'd just had a baby, and Dana on vacation with her husband to celebrate their fifth wedding anniversary. Bethany had finally told them her big news, and the surprise and happiness on her friends' faces buoyed her. They made sure she knew that no matter what, they'd always be there for her and would throw her one heck of a baby shower.

She'd told them all about Theo too. Both had counseled her *not* to forget him, to give it a little time, to give *him* a little time. People, relationships evolved, they'd both said. She'd gone back and forth during a restless night in bed. *Forget him. Forget him not.*

All she knew was that sitting in the waiting room of her ob-gyn's office, her brother beside her, had her wistful. On one hand, she was grateful she wasn't here alone for her monthly checkup. She'd called Jake this morning to ask if he had some time to meet today, that she had something big to tell him. He'd appeared at her apartment door ten minutes later with bagels and veggie cream cheese. Elizabeth and her sisters had taken all five kids to the Bronco Convention Center to watch them set up for the rodeo that would open this week. The Hawkins Sisters were performing, but they weren't practicing until later in the afternoon, so Jake had a couple of hours to himself.

His mouth had dropped open at the big news that he was going to be an uncle. She could see how truly happy he was for her, despite the less-than-ideal details.

"Are you going to tell Rexx?" he'd asked.

"I want to. But given the way he hung up on me when I called... The last thing he and his fiancée are going to want to hear is that his former bandmate is pregnant with his baby."

"No doubt," Jake had said. "But you should call him again. He is the father and he should know, period."

She'd nodded, in full agreement. It was one thing when no one knew. But now that she'd told her family, her bandmates were next. Rexx had cut Harry, Cord, and Petey from his life too—apparently the fiancée didn't think he should have any connection with his old life. Bethany and the Belters were meeting up in a few days to practice a few new songs that an upcoming bride and groom had put on their list; she'd tell them then. And call Rexx that night.

Right now, she just wanted to get through this appointment, to hear that all was well with her baby.

Earlier today, when she'd mentioned that she was going to her ob-gyn checkup alone, Jake had insisted on accompanying her. He'd shown up at her apartment to pick her up for the appointment bearing gifts: a book called *Your Pregnancy Month by Month*—which she already had—and a pink highlighter, soft orange pj's with little horses down the zipper, matching orange socks, and a furry stuffed sheep. He'd also gotten himself a T-shirt that read, Montana's Newest Uncle.

Bethany had burst into tears at how thoughtful her brother was, how supported she felt.

"Thanks for coming with me, Jake," she said. Here he was, a newlywed, father of five now, and he'd made time for his sister.

He squeezed her hand. "Of course. Anything, anytime. You just call me or text me, okay?"

"I really appreciate that," she said, tears misting her eyes. She tried to blink the tears away.

There were three other expectant moms in the room, all at least six months pregnant. And all with husbands. She knew because they were wearing wedding rings. And sitting with their arms or hands entwined.

She was with her brother.

At least she was here with someone who cared about her. Thank God for her family.

The nurse called her in for her checkup, and Bethany stood, grateful Jake would be waiting here for her. These appointments were nerve-racking. She just wanted to hear that her baby was okay.

Fifteen minutes later, in her paper scrubs, Dr. Rangely assured her all was well. Bethany breathed a huge sigh of relief and touched her hands to her belly, which felt bigger.

Pow!

Bethany gasped. "The baby just kicked again! He or she did that a few days ago for the first time. And now again!"

The doctor laughed. "It's the best feeling—except when you're nine months along and trying to sleep in any position you can and get a foot in the side."

Bethany smiled. "I can't wait for it all. The kicks, being nine months pregnant. Meeting my child."

"Five months will be here in a snap," Dr. Rangely said. She went over some basic details of what Bethany could expect in the next couple months. "Bronco Valley Hospital offers a wonderful one-day seminar for expectant parents. There's a one scheduled in August. The receptionist can give you an information packet on your way out."

"Great," Bethany said. "I definitely want to take that class."

She'd take it alone…but that was okay. She was going to be a single mother and needed to get used to doing baby-oriented activities on her own.

You can do this, she reminded herself. *You have the love and support of your family.*

And you'll be a mom—your dream come true.

But as she headed out to let her brother know all was well with the baby, she thought of Theo Abernathy.

That *you can't do*, she told herself. *Let it go. Let your fantasies of him go.*

She had to admit that, since their walk and dinner and the big reveal, she had fantasized that he'd come rushing to her apartment with a pronouncement that there was something special between them and he just couldn't walk away.

But he had.

Still, Bethany had always been optimistic. Which might be her downfall when it came to Theo Abernathy.

CHAPTER SIX

THE NEXT MORNING, when Bethany was getting dressed for the Bronco Rodeo, she did a double take at her belly in the full-length mirror in the corner of her bedroom. She was definitely showing. The baby bump that was easily hidden by her flowy dresses and summer-weight cardigans now would be obvious no matter what.

She'd stood there for five minutes, marveling at the sight of her curved belly, turning left and right, trying on a bunch of different shirts and dresses to see how she looked.

Pregnant.

She settled on her favorite sundress and a meshy cardigan, since it could get cold in the Bronco Convention Center, where the rodeo would be held. Flat, comfy sandals, her lucky silver bangles on her wrist, and she was ready.

Last year her brother had picked her up, but this year he was carting five kids, and so she'd meet the McCreery-Hawkins crew and her parents at the rodeo. She was looking forward to spending the afternoon with her family. Tomorrow was the Fourth of July, a big deal in Bronco, with a barbecue that brought tons of people out, and the day after that was a fun event—the Favorite Pet Contest, which was cosponsored by Happy Hearts Animal Sanctuary, owned by her friend Daphne Taylor Cruise, and several other local businesses, including the company Daphne's husband, Evan, owned Bronco Ghost Tours, and his great-grandmother's very popular psychic shop, Wisdom by Winona.

Hmm. Bethany could use some psychic wisdom. Maybe she'd pay Winona Cobbs a visit if she had a booth set up at the rodeo. Her readings were free, and she often had pop-ups around town. The woman was in her nineties and engaged to be married to a wonderful man, an eightysome-thing charmer with a big smile, and surely she had some advice for Bethany. Or, at least, a prediction.

Bethany's burning question: Would she ever stop think-ing about Theo Abernathy?

Two days now and no contact. He clearly didn't want to be friends. He didn't want to be *anything* with her, a pregnant woman.

She pushed away thoughts of him and drove to the con-vention center, wondering if she'd have to move her seat back from the steering wheel soon to accommodate her belly. The parking lot was crowded, but Bethany found a spot not too far from the entrance. She was grateful, be-cause she was already tired and it wasn't even noon.

She found the big group of McCreerys and Hawkinses and settled into her seat. Suddenly she was hit with a pow-erful craving. "Who wants fried dough?" she asked. They were seated in the third row with a great view of the arena and the jumbotron, a huge video monitor to show close-ups and announcements. The rodeo would start in fifteen minutes—just enough time to get her treat.

"Meeeee!" came the chorus of all five McCreery-Hawkins kids.

Bethany's mom laughed. "Dad and I will split one. Sprinkle extra sugar on Dad's half," she added with a smile.

"Fried dough gives me a serious stomachache," Jake

said, "so none for me. The kids can split two among them or they'll all have bellyaches."

"Got it," Bethany said, glad her brother wouldn't be sharing hers. She could eat an entire paper plate–sized fried dough herself. With a generous sprinkling of powdered sugar. "Be back in a jiff."

She got up, wondering if the folks seated nearby had noticed her belly. Probably not. She felt so conspicuous, though. As she wove her way down to the food area, she did notice a few people she knew from around town giving her a belly a glance. Soon, gossipers would take the news all over town. Bethany McCreery was pregnant. And single. There would be phone calls and texts, acquaintances not wanting to ask outright who the father was but hoping she'd share the info.

The story, from the sperm bank to Rexx and the surprise pregnancy, was one she couldn't imagine telling people. She'd gotten it out to those closest to her, and that was enough.

The smell of burgers and fries and pizza and popcorn and fried dough took her attention as she entered the crowded area with the food booths. There was a longish line for the fried dough stand, since it was the only one.

And who was coming from the opposite direction to get in that line at the exact moment she was?

Theo Abernathy.

For a moment she was mesmerized by the sight of him. The ole long, tall drink of water. Muscles galore. An untucked Western shirt with pearl buttons, dark-wash jeans that hugged his hips in a way that had her swallowing. His thick brown hair sexily tousled as he took off his Stetson in a kind of Western greeting.

He looked flustered.

She *felt* flustered.

"Craving?" he asked, then looked even more flustered, as if he wasn't sure he should even bring up the subject of her pregnancy. His gaze dropped to her belly for a moment, and he tilted his head.

"I'm showing more today," she said.

"How are you feeling?" he asked. "I've been wondering. According to my brother Billy, his ex-wife had bad morning sickness with each pregnancy and she was tired a lot."

Hmm. That must mean he'd told his brother. *Brothers*, probably. And maybe his sisters too. Which meant he was talking about her. That was interesting—and made her happier than it should have. Was he getting their advice? She wondered what they'd said.

Stay far away!

Theo, you're thirty-five. It's time for a family, anyway.

She also wondered why he was asking. The man had practically turned green when she told him she was pregnant. She'd think he'd avoid the topic altogether.

Theo Abernathy was a nice guy, plain and simple. But asking how she was feeling told her loud and clear that he cared. That he was interested in the biggest thing in her life right now.

And that pulled her right back in.

"I got lucky with morning sickness," she said. "I'm rarely bothered by it at all. But I do get tired, particularly in the late afternoons. The last two weddings I performed at, I needed a stool on stage just in case and ended up using it quite a bit. Luckily, I sing a lot of ballads, and sitting and slow songs go together."

He seemed to be taking that in, as if picturing her on stage, sitting on a stool and belting out "Endless Love" and "Because You Loved Me."

"Well, you look beautiful," he said, then his eyes widened and she knew he hadn't meant to say that. "Glowing," he added fast.

She couldn't help but smile. The fact that she was expecting didn't seem to have cooled his attraction to her. *That* was interesting. And made her heart flutter. "A perk of pregnancy. My skin has never looked better. And thank you."

He nodded and was quiet for a moment. "I love fried dough," he said, upping his chin at the huge sign above the booth. "With a lot of powdered sugar."

It seemed so clear to her that he wanted to say more. And not about fried dough. But like him, she felt like she had to keep things to small talk.

"Me too. I'm getting a bunch for my family to split and an entire one for myself."

They inched up in line, standing beside each other. Like they were together.

It was their turn, so he gestured for her to go ahead. She placed her order, and once she had her fried dough on a cardboard tray, there was no reason to stick around. But walking away from Theo wasn't so easy. She could stand here and talk about her cravings all day.

Him included.

Sigh.

"Well, nice to see you," she said—awkwardly.

Guess you don't want to be friends, she added silently and felt herself frowning.

"I'll carry the tray to your seat," he rushed to say.

Oh, Theo, she thought. *We clearly feel the same way about each other, but not about the giant thing keeping us apart.*

Why prolong the agony?

"That's okay. It's light," she added, lifting the tray up for good measure.

"If you start craving cheese fries, I know where the best booth is for that," he said. "Crinkle-cut and extra crispy. Just shoot me a text and your seat number and I'll bring some over."

The man liked her—really liked her. That she was pregnant and he liked his life exactly as it was had to messing with him. In five months, he couldn't have her *and* life as he knew it. So avoiding her was the right thing.

"Sounds like something a friend would do," she said before she could shut her big trap. Why had she come out with that? That was goading him. And she didn't want to do that.

"Sorry," she said. "It slipped out. You have every right to keep your distance. It's the smart thing to do, actually."

The air-conditioning vent had blown a swath of her long hair in her face, and since she held the tray in both hands, he reached out to move the strand back, his gaze on hers.

"Smart, maybe," he said. "And just as hard as I knew it would be. It's been rough not calling to see how you are, how you're feeling. To just...talk."

She really, really, really liked how straightforward he was. That he just said it.

She wondered if he'd add something. That they should *at least* be friends. But he didn't.

A bit dejected, even though it was for the best, she offered a tight smile. "I'd better get back to the hungry crowd with their treats before the Hawkins Sisters are introduced."

She turned and hurried through the crowd, her heart finally slowing a bit when she was a good distance from the booth. From the man who'd kept her awake the past few nights.

She closed her eyes for a second to try to blink Theo Abernathy away and then lifted her chin and walked to her seat. Her nieces and nephews clapped at the sight of her, their sweet excitement giving her heart a lift. She sat down just as the announcer introduced rodeo superstar Ross Burris. He rode out on his horse, waving his Stetson at the crowd, which was cheering and wolf whistling, none louder than his champ brother Jack and Jack's wife, Stephanie. She couldn't help but notice that Ross's eyes were on one particular person in the first row—his new bride, Celeste, a sports broadcaster who was solely a spectator today so that she could concentrate on her husband and his family in the ring.

The love in his gaze was so touching that Bethany felt a little ache of longing in her chest.

She ripped off a piece of her fried dough, the powdered sugar sticking to her fingers, and took a bite. All she could think was that Theo was probably doing the exact same thing in his own seat. She glanced around, sure she wouldn't spot him in the crowded bleachers, but there he was, sitting a section over and up two rows with his family.

So close—and yet very far.

FOR THE PAST couple of hours, Theo had been half watching the rodeo riders and half trying to come up with excuses for going over to where Bethany was sitting. She was on the end of her row, which would make it easy to stand on the stairs and talk for a bit. He'd considered bringing her the cheese fries even though she hadn't texted. Given how awkward things had been on the fried dough line and her quick getaway, he hadn't been expecting to hear from her.

He could go say hi to a few of the Bonnie B ranch hands, who were sitting with a group in the row in front of hers. Then he'd just "happen to see her" and stop to say hello.

And then what? He had to stop this. It was bad enough that he was so drawn to a woman who was completely wrong for him. If they weren't friends and they weren't dating, he had no reason to stop and say hello.

He slid down in his seat, feeling sulky, and tried to focus on the arena, which had cleared for the next performance. A few workers were setting up, though Theo couldn't imagine what the little stage and podium were about. Or the red runner being rolled out to the stage. A worker carried a huge floor vase of white roses and set it beside the podium.

Suddenly, the wedding march blasted from the speakers. That sure got everyone's attention. What the heck was going on?

"Someone's getting married?" his mother asked, surprise lighting her face. "I love weddings!"

"Maybe it's an engagement announcement!" his sister Stacy said. "Remember how Dylan very publicly declared his love for Robin on the jumbotron back in February? How romantic was that?"

Theo had to agree that Dylan Sanchez had won the grand-gesture-of-the-year award. The new rancher hadn't been part of the rodeo; he'd been doing a live promotion for his car dealership when things took a very unexpected turn. The jumbotron had flashed, "Bronco Motors Car Deals for Cowboys" as Dylan had trotted around the arena on horseback, announcing the specials his dealership was offering that week. But then Dylan had suddenly veered from the live commercial. As the camera zoomed in on his face, he'd told the audience that he had an opportunity for one lucky recipient.

The cameras had then zoomed in on Robin, sitting in the stands, a close-up of her stunned face appearing on the jumbotron. Dylan raced into the stands and proposed, thousands at the rodeo cheering and clapping and wolf whistling.

All the Abernathys had been moved by that moment, no one more than Robin.

"Someone must have stolen Dylan's excellent grand-gesture idea," Jace said. He slid an arm around his beloved, Tamara, holding baby Frankie, giving his son a kiss on his cheek.

"What could possibly top what Dylan did?" Billy asked. "He'll go down in history."

Theo wished *he* could make some kind of grand gesture to Bethany. But again, to accomplish what? A grand apology for not being ready for a family of his own? For not staying far, far away when he should have? For pursuing her, anyway? Of course, at her brother's wedding, he hadn't known she was actually pregnant. In the back of his mind, he must have been thinking that if things worked out between them, he could convince her to wait a few years. He liked how that took him off the hook—a little, anyway.

The camera was now aimed right at an internal gate. Something was definitely about to happen. Had the wedding march music gotten louder? Sure seemed that way.

From where Theo was sitting, he could see the gate open, and it seemed like everyone was holding their breath, riveted, waiting for what was coming.

Suddenly, a man in a tux and black Stetson and a woman in a wedding gown entered the arena, both on horses. Theo's mom gasped. So did he and his entire family.

They all stood up to make sure they were seeing what they were plainly seeing.

When the jumbotron showed them close up, the Abernathys' mouths all dropped open.

Dylan Sanchez and Theo's sister Robin were on those horses.

"Okay, Dylan and Robin just outdid *themselves*," Stacy said, her eyes misty.

"Did you know about this?" Theo asked his parents.

Both Bonnie and Asa shook their heads. "News to us!" his mother said.

"How did they manage to keep this a surprise?" Billy asked.

"Right?" Jace said. "A pop-up wedding at the rodeo!"

"So romantic!" Tamara and Charlotte said in unison.

"And we're getting a new son-in-law!" Bonnie said to her husband, hand over her heart.

"Not to mention a family discount at Dylan's car dealership," Asa exclaimed on a chuckle.

The jumbotron flashed with "Something Old? Check. Something New? Check. Something Borrowed? Uh-oh! Something Blue? Check."

A whole bunch of people were rushing to the fence to offer the bride something borrowed—from hats to rodeo pennants and giant foam fingers. But Bronco's mayor's wife, Penny Smith, was already in the arena, handing over her pearl necklace, which Theo had heard her husband, Rafferty, had given her for their thirtieth anniversary. Theo had also heard people in town saying that the necklace was magical—that it brought those who came into contact with it forever love. Penny had temporarily lost the necklace, and as it had made its way around town, at least two couples—Shep Dalton and Rylee Parker, and Ross Burris and Celeste Montgomery—had fallen under its spell. Theo wasn't one to believe in legends and magic, but what did he know?

A close-up of the pearl necklace being clasped around Robin's neck by her groom-to-be appeared on the jumbotron.

The crowd went wild, cheering and clapping.

Theo glanced over at Bethany. She and her entire family were on their feet, all of them chatting excitedly and the kids pointing. She turned to look at him, and they locked eyes. She seemed to be mouthing something—he was pretty sure it was *Congratulations*.

He mouthed back a thank-you with a question in his expression and a shrug to indicate that this was a total surprise.

"Folks," the announcer said over the loudspeakers. "Surprise! You're all invited to a pop-up wedding right here at the Bronco Rodeo. This happy couple will say their I dos right now!"

The arena gate opened, and out came a minister on a white horse wearing a bow tie. That got the crowd going wild again.

And then, in front of thousands, Robin Abernathy and Dylan Sanchez vowed to love, honor, and cherish each other forever. Theo felt his eyes get a little misty. He glanced at his mom, who had tears streaming down her cheeks. His sister Stacy was full-out bawling.

When the minister pronounced Dylan and Robin husband and wife, the two gave each other a sweet, soulful kiss, and then the crowd roared again.

"Bethany McCreery, come on down!" the announcer called. "The bride and groom have requested that you sing their favorite song!"

Theo looked over at Bethany, who seemed surprised and touched. Given how mesmerized he'd been by her angelic voice at her brother's wedding, *he* was hardly surprised that the happy couple would want her to perform the first song.

He felt something shift in his chest, in the region of his heart, as she hurried down the stairs and was ushered through a gate into the arena. Just what was going on inside him? What did he feel for this woman who was supposed to be off-limits?

A lot, he was beginning to realize. He couldn't take his

eyes off Bethany as she was led to a mike set up in the center, the newlyweds facing each other, holding hands, their wedding bands glinting in the summer sunshine.

The minister whispered into Bethany's ear. She nodded and smiled, and then music began playing, a song Theo recognized. An oldie but goodie.

As Bethany began singing about letting someone into your heart and taking a chance, again the yearning and passion in her voice had the entire audience rapt. No one more so than Theo.

All the love in the air—and his own sister as the surprise bride—must be getting to him.

Because he couldn't imagine walking away from this woman. And he wasn't going to.

CHAPTER SEVEN

WHILE BETHANY WAS singing to the newlyweds and about three thousand guests at the pop-up wedding, she noticed Theo coming down the bleacher steps toward the arena floor as though he couldn't stay away from her another second. But then she realized that *all* the Abernathys, including his aunt and uncle and cousins and their spouses, were right there with him—to congratulate the happy couple.

They'd all stopped just inside the gate, since the bride and groom were slow dancing on the red aisle runner. Bethany noticed that Robin and Dylan hadn't taken their eyes off each other.

When she finished the song, she was stunned by the standing ovation, then realized it was more for the newlyweds. She shook her head at herself with a smile and gave a bow toward the couple, then to the crowd. As the Abernathys hurried to hug Robin and Dylan, she headed for the gate.

"Beautiful song," said a male voice from behind her.

She turned, hand on the gate, to find Theo standing just a few feet away.

"I'm amazed that you can just sing like that with no notice and in front of so many people," he added.

"I'm a little shy generally, but not when it comes to singing. I get lost in the music, in the lyrics, and I'm transported."

"I can tell," he said.

"Thanks, Theo. That's really nice of you to say." She bit her lip, so...schoolgirl around this man. "So was this a surprise for your family too?" she asked to get them on a neutral topic.

"Total surprise. We had no idea. But given Dylan's previous gesture at the rodeo, we should have figured." He smiled and shook his head. "Somehow, it managed to be really romantic."

Bethany laughed. "Right? I got all teary when they recited their vows."

"Okay, I might have too. My mother and sister were sobbing."

Bethany glanced over at the crowd hovering around the newlyweds. The Sanchez family was there too, and they were all talking and hugging and laughing.

A pang hit her in the chest. She'd likely never be that bride, basking in the love of two families joined together in happy celebration.

She felt a frown tugging her lips and sucked in a breath. Bethany always had to brace herself when she prepared to go on stage at weddings. The always-the-wedding-singer-never-the-bride feeling had been hitting her hard this past year—particularly the past four months. But at this surprise wedding, she'd been unable to prepare herself. The silver lining was her awareness of the passion in her voice as she'd sung the bride's favorite song.

She had to change the subject fast. "I actually have my own connection to the Sanchez family. I live in one of the apartments above the hair salon Denise Sanchez owns."

He smiled and nodded. "It's like *one* degree of separation in Bronco. Everyone knows everyone."

Okay, maybe that wasn't such a change of subject. Now she and Theo were connected by a Bronco Valley hair salon. Every time she pulled into her spot in the small lot of the building, she'd think of the Sanchez matriarch and her romantic son, Dylan, and his bride, Robin, Theo's sister. And that would make her think of him. She sighed.

She took off her cardigan and tied it around her waist. "Warm out. But a nice breeze." Now that was a change of subject. Nice and dull. Impersonal.

He studied her with concern. "Can I get you a cold drink? Iced tea? Water? Juice?"

That got a smile out of her—and made her feel equally wistful. "You know, for someone who doesn't want to be friends, you're doting on me a bit."

Sometimes she wished she had more of a filter. Was it the pregnancy that was making her more forthright? Saying what was on her mind? Probably.

He seemed flustered again, which tempered her confusion over what he did or didn't want where the two of them were concerned. "We're already friends, so I might as well dote."

Good comeback, she thought. They *did* feel like friends. *Oh, heck.*

"Well, I'm happy to be your friend," she said. "Because you sure seem nice, Theo Abernathy."

"My last few girlfriends wouldn't agree." His cheeks reddened a bit as though he hadn't meant to say that out loud. They were certainly a pair.

She could feel her eyes widen at that tidbit. "Because they'd figured at thirty-five, you'd be ready for marriage and family?"

He nodded. "They just couldn't understand. 'You're not twenty-five,' my last girlfriend would snap at me. 'Haven't you gotten doing whatever you want, whenever you want out of your system?'"

Well, honestly, Theo, haven't you?

"I feel how I feel, right?" he asked. "At least I know

I'm ready for marriage. That's a biggie too. I'm definitely ready to share my life with my soulmate. But not giving the ranch everything I've got because I have little ones who need all of me? That I'm not ready for."

Surely he understood that his brothers managed to do just that. Life was about balance. "Well, I do know what you mean about giving your work your all. It's a rare day like today when I have hours to myself to enjoy a rodeo. Usually if I'm not hustling for new wedding gigs, I'm performing."

"And even today you ended up working—for free, now that I think about it." He tilted his head. "As a representative of the bride's family, I'd like to make that up to you."

She put up her hand. "You don't have to. Really, I—"

"At least let me buy you lunch," he said. "I know which booth has the best corn dog. I'd take you somewhere much fancier than a rodeo stand—like the Association—but my family just made impromptu plans to get together with the Sanchezes at the ranch house to toast the newlyweds." He shrugged and leaned in closer. "To tell you the truth, I'd actually take a corn dog over a fancy restaurant any day."

She smiled. "Honestly, if I'm being treated, I'd take the fancy restaurant."

His warm smile went straight into her heart.

"Rain check, then," he said.

For a moment, they just stood there, gazing at each other like lovebirds without saying anything.

She had to put a stop to that pronto.

Bethany extended her hand. "To friendship," she said.

He slipped his warm, strong hand around hers. "To friendship."

Everything tingled. All her nerve endings.

She had to get away from this man and yet couldn't move. Couldn't drag her eyes off him.

"I'll be at the Favorite Pet Contest the day after tomorrow," she said fast. "I love seeing all the dogs. You going?" The contest was her favorite annual event of the town's July Fourth week festivities. It was being held in a large air-conditioned room in the Bronco Convention Center, since it could get very hot in July in Montana and the pets needed to be kept comfortable. There was an outdoor area where folks could walk their dog entrants too. A huge board of all the hopefuls with their photos and names was at the exit, and people would vote for their very favorite pet by marking an X under their photo. At the end of the day, Mayor Rafferty Smith would announce the winner, who'd receive a generous gift certificate to Bronco Pets Emporium.

"And miss the goofy rodents and occasional bearded dragon? I'll definitely be there."

"I'll see you there, then," she said.

He seemed about to say something but then clamped his mouth shut. She had the feeling he was going to offer to pick her up, that they could go together, but that probably seemed too date-like.

How exactly was this friendship thing supposed to work when he gave her butterflies and just the touch of his hand on hers made her toes tingle?

"Theo, we're heading out," a voice called.

They both turned. His brother Jace, holding the cutest baby, held up a hand in greeting.

She smiled back. "Well, I'll let you go."

And she really had to.

But having shaken on friendship, how exactly was she going to get this man out of her heart?

THE TWO FAMILIES had decided to celebrate the newlyweds with a quick toast in the parklike backyard of the Bonnie

B. The bride and groom were there, stealing a kiss behind a stately maple tree, and all Theo's siblings and their significant others and children, plus the Sanchezes—Dylan's parents, four siblings, their spouses, fiancées and his adorable niece. Plus Dylan's great-uncle Stanley and his bride-to-be, Winona Cobbs, the town's resident psychic.

When he'd been talking to Bethany in the arena, Theo had been thinking about inviting her along to the party, but that seemed a little beyond the scope of their new friendship. Not to mention that Theo could only imagine the grilling he'd get from his brothers—and his sisters—if she was his plus-one.

He glanced around, summer itself decorating the yard for the impromptu occasion with the brilliant green grass and beautiful gardens his mother loved tending to. Bronco, Montana, had gifted them with gorgeous weather for the rodeo and the party—sunny and breezy and a temperature in the low seventies now. Bandit was enjoying a patch of sunshine in his dog bed on the deck, two kids petting him and chatting him up, which he seemed to be enjoying, since he rolled onto his belly for a rub. The kids were delighted.

He looked around for his parents and found Asa and Bonnie chatting with Denise and Aaron Sanchez on the deck, each holding a glass of champagne. His mother was still misty-eyed, the softy. Theo heard the word *reception* a few times; he had no doubt they were planning a grand celebration. Stacy and his brothers were in a big circle on the grass with Dylan's siblings: Camilla and her husband, Jordan Taylor; Felix and his fiancée, Shari Lormand; Sofia and her husband, Boone Dalton, a fellow rancher; and Dante and his fiancée, Eloise Taylor, sister of Billy's fiancée and cousin-in-law of Camilla Sanchez-Taylor. Lots of kids were running around the backyard.

Theo watched parents being constantly interrupted by

their children, whether toddlers or big kids or teens. His nephew Branson apparently wanted to slip out to meet his friends and had gotten a no from his dad—*three* times in the past hour. Niece Jill asked why she couldn't have a teensy sip of champagne when everyone else had a glass, and other nephew Nicky had to be told twice to take off his headphones and engage with the guests.

Meanwhile, Jace's son, Frankie, had grabbed on to Camilla Sanchez-Taylor's hair as she'd been passing by—and still wouldn't let go. That was getting to be Frankie's trademark move. A small crowd had gathered, trying everything from tickling Frankie's tummy and neck to get him to release her hair to attempting to peel his fingers off without a hank being ripped out. At this moment, Camilla was still held prisoner by a twenty-two-pound cherub.

One of the kids had climbed that stately maple and now couldn't get down, requiring her dad to climb up after her.

No, thanks, Theo thought. He was one of the only ones at this pop-up get-together who was enjoying his champagne and chatting with the Sanchezes without constant interruption.

"She's free!" Jace called out.

Theo glanced over to see poor Camilla dart over to safety behind her husband her hair askew. She was smiling but rubbing her head.

"Theo, Theo, Theo," said a crackly voice from behind him.

Theo turned to find Winona Cobbs eyeing him. Winona was a marvel. She had her long white hair in a braid and wore a purple Stetson and a purple pantsuit with fringe along the hem of her jacket. And silver cowboy boots.

"Afternoon, Winona," he said, taking off his hat. "So I figure you knew about the wedding."

"In spirit, sure," she said cryptically. Which was her

way. He was still trying to figure out what she meant when she added, "You only think you know what you want."

He studied Winona, waiting for her to elaborate. Instead she simply walked away and joined Stanley by the patio table, where Theo's mother had set out a platter of treats that she and his father had paid a small fortune to a few town cafés and bakeries to deliver pronto—at least three dozen treats from Kendra's Cupcakes and an huge assortment of cookies and scones from Bronco Java and Juice. The kids had beelined for the table and were now sitting on the steps of the deck, frosting on several little noses.

Theo had to admit, when they were quiet and adorable like that, he could almost see having a child of his own. Someday down the line.

He felt eyes on him and turned to find Winona Cobbs staring at him—hard. No expression whatsoever.

You only think you know what you want.

What did that mean? Theo might not be the biggest believer in psychics—if at all—but he'd heard enough about Winona's spot-on comments and predictions that had come true to know that when she did say something, folks took her very seriously.

And Winona had been around a long, long time. Ninety-plus years. She'd lived a hard life and had gone through more before she was eighteen than a lot of people ever did. Like himself. He knew he had it easy.

He thought about Bethany, wondering if she was chasing after a gig as she'd mentioned earlier about either working or looking for work. Darn it. He'd been trying not to think about her, and now she was on his mind again.

They were now friends. Officially. He'd never wanted to kiss any of his female friends, though.

He'd also never wanted to attend the Bronco Favorite Pet Contest so badly. Bethany would be there. And therefore, so would he. Not that he'd lied when he said he liked seeing the residents' pets. He did. But spending time with Bethany while looking at gerbils and guinea pigs and a lot of dogs was the big draw.

He felt an arm sneak around his. He turned to find his sister Stacy beside him.

"Looks like we're the last two standing," Stacy said, pushing her brown hair behind her shoulders. "Who's gonna fall first, you or me?"

He laughed. "I'm on the market, so it's anyone's guess."

"Really?" she asked, her eyes lighting up. "Actively looking for your Ms. Right?"

"I've been for a while now," he said, sipping his champagne. "I *am* thirty-five," he added.

"Wow, Theo Abernathy, settled down with a wife and two-point-five kids. I can't see it, but I want to." She grinned.

"Well, at this point I'm more interested in the wife than in the children."

Bethany's beautiful face flashed into his mind. And her baby bump.

He quickly took another sip of champagne.

"Not ready?" Stacy repeated. "Why? You did say you were thirty-five. Marriage and kids are the next step, right?"

"But what about the ranch? And let's say I wanted to jet off to Rome for pasta?" he asked. "For chicken Milanese?" Where that had come from, he had no idea. But suddenly—no, lately—he felt like he needed to justify his feelings.

She raised an eyebrow. "Um, what? When have you ever flown to Italy for linguine?"

"But I *could*," he said. "Because I don't have responsibilities for children. I can take off at a moment's notice. I'm not ready to give that up."

She chuckled. "I see. You do realize women your age will likely want kids. I mean, if you date, say, a thirty-year-old single woman..."

He let out a sigh. "Yes, that's been made clear."

The issue there was that he enjoyed dating women his age or close to it. Same life experiences. Same wavelength. Same references.

Stacy looked pointedly at him. "You wouldn't let the right woman get away because she wants kids now and you don't, though. Right?"

"But wouldn't that make her the *wrong* woman?" he asked.

Stacy lifted her champagne glass. "Touché," she said. "Hey, if you're not ready, you're not ready. But maybe you just *think* you're not."

Winona's words came back to him, making him frown. *You think you know what you want...*

Eh. He knew what he wanted. And didn't want.

He definitely wanted Bethany.

And he *definitely* didn't want kids. Not yet.

The problem was that Bethany McCreery was a package deal: her and a baby.

Which was why they'd shaken on friendship.

But he also didn't want to be just friends with Bethany. He wanted more.

A big conundrum. He looked around for the purple cowboy hat and easily spotted Winona Cobbs dancing with her fiancé to Frank Sinatra via Bluetooth speaker. Maybe he should pay Winona's psychic shop a visit. Get her words of wisdom. Ask her outright what a man in his situation was supposed to do.

Yes, maybe he'd go see Winona Cobbs for a reading.

Jeez, was he really considering going to a psychic for her thoughts on his life? What was happening to him? Just how bad did he have it for Bethany McCreery?

CHAPTER EIGHT

BETHANY LOVED THE Fourth of July—the patriotism and fireworks and barbecue, which she'd attended yesterday with her family—but she'd been eager for today to arrive. She'd be meeting up with Theo at the Favorite Pet Contest in the convention center. As she walked among the tables with many cages containing everything from rabbits to hamsters to snakes and lizards, she tried not to look around for him.

But her gaze kept scanning the crowd. Theo didn't seem to be here yet. Her new nieces were exclaiming over two long-haired guinea pigs, clearly taken by their funny antics. Bethany was charmed by all the dogs being walked around, many still wearing red, white, and blue bandannas. She didn't have any pets since she traveled a lot and was gone for long stretches during the day or evening, but one day, when her baby was a few years old, maybe she'd finally adopt a dog of her own.

Bethany was eyeing a snake slithering up a branch in its tall cage when she noticed elderly lovebirds Winona and Stanley beside her, smiling at the long-haired guinea pig. Its name, according to the information sheet on the side of the cage, was Lovey.

"Morning, Winona, Stanley," Bethany said with a smile. "Enjoying the pets?"

Stanley grinned. "Yes, very much. I love all creatures—even mosquitoes."

Winona chuckled. "I wouldn't be surprised if one of the contest entrants was a bunch of mosquitoes with names. Spike, Buzzy, George."

"A mosquito named George," Stanley said, then gave his fiancée a kiss on the cheek. "Love it."

They laughed, and right there, in the middle of the room, Stanley took Winona's hand and twirled her around.

Bethany watched them in awe. Stanley, so tall and handsome in his vest and bolo tie, and Winona in her trademark purple, including her cowboy hat. They were clearly so in love—and there wasn't a bit of the tension that she'd noticed over the past couple of months. Bethany was friendly with Winona's great-granddaughter Vanessa Cruise John, and had heard little updates about the couple. Apparently over the winter, Winona had had cold feet about actually getting married. Stanley had wanted to set a date, but Winona insisted they wait until the time was right, saying, "Love cannot be rushed." But in March, they had set a date. Stanley was so excited and started planning a big wedding, even though Winona would have been fine with a justice of the peace at the Bronco Town Hall. But then for a while, there had seemed to be tension between them—something to do with Winona's harrowing past and whether Winona wanted to marry at all.

Bethany didn't know many of the details, but she'd heard that Winona had been an unwed teenaged mother who'd been told her baby had died—and had no idea until decades later that the child had really been placed for adoption. She and her daughter, Daisy, with whom she now lived, had only been reunited a few years ago—after a seventy-plus-year separation. There had to be a very heart-rending story there.

It was one of the reasons why Bethany had been so happy to hear last month that Winona had assured her fiancé she did want to marry him. The wedding was set for just a couple of weeks from now, and Bethany and her band had been hired to perform. She couldn't wait to serenade the wonderful couple.

If Winona could find love in her nineties and be a first-time bride…

Bethany had been very touched to be invited to Winona's bridal shower last month. There had been so many women there that she hadn't gotten to talk to Winona much, but the happiness on the dear woman's face was unmistakable. Winona's daughter, Beatrix, had given Bethany a song list for the wedding, and she'd been practicing some of the ones she didn't know by heart. Bethany wanted to make sure she got every song just right. She and her band would get together a couple of times over the next two weeks to rehearse.

Winona slipped her arm through Bethany's and pulled her aside. "A baby is a blessing, no matter the circumstances."

Bethany gasped. How did—

Ah, of course. Winona *was* psychic. But now that Bethany had an obvious baby bump—however small at just four months—her flowy sundresses weren't hiding it.

As Bethany looked at this beautiful, strong woman, she thought of Winona being told her baby had died when she was just seventeen. Suddenly, she wished she knew more of the story—not because it was any of her business, but because Winona meant so much to Bethany and to the whole town, really. She did know that the Abernathy family was involved. Maybe she could ask Theo.

Winona winked at her and squeezed Bethany's hand, then returned to Stanley, who was waving at a long-eared black-and-white rabbit in a large crate. Stanley turned and kissed her so tenderly on the cheek, gazing at her with such affection.

Bethany sighed. Everyone around her seemed to be finding love and getting married. Not that she didn't feel blessed—she was so excited to meet her little one.

But love did seem to have passed her by...

Of course, at that moment, whom did she see but Theo Abernathy in his black Stetson, Western shirt and hip-hugging dark jeans. Her entire body vibrated for a moment, and it had nothing to do with her pregnancy. Then again, she had serious hormones coursing through her.

Her reaction to Theo was more about her being a red-blooded woman.

The moment he saw her his face lit up, and right there, Bethany knew she was sunk, that she really did have feelings for this man. And unless he was just really happy about having her as a friend, that lit-up face, the twinkling green eyes, the way he wove through the crowd to get to her, told her he had strong feelings for her too.

She got another hand squeeze, this time from Theo.

"The Bonnie B already has a dog, but all these pups make me want to adopt five more. Maybe ten."

Bethany smiled. "I know what you mean. I saw one of those little sausage dogs and immediately wanted to scoop him up."

Theo nodded. "Small dogs, big dogs, I love them all. Through my brother Billy's fiancée, Charlotte, I'll be related, albeit distantly, to the woman who's cosponsoring the pet contest—Daphne Taylor Cruise. She owns Happy Hearts Animal Sanctuary."

"I love that place! I actually go whenever I'm feeling down or need to count my blessings. All those sweet horses and cows and pigs and dogs and cats who needed rescuing and a good home. Last time I was there, there was a family of ducks and a rabbit that just came in. But I think the rabbit got adopted because I saw one here—someone's favorite pet—who looked just like that bunny."

He smiled. "Daphne is a marvel. She comes from a huge family of cattle ranchers but is a vegetarian herself and an animal rights activist. Took her a long time to make her father accept that. Oh—and when I arrived, I saw you talking to Winona Cobbs. Daphne's husband, Evan Cruise, is Winona's great-grandson. Her psychic shop, Wisdom by Winona, is actually on the property of his ghost tours business."

"I adore Winona," she said. At some point, she'd ask if he knew what had happened between Winona and her first love, who was an Abernathy. But right now, she wanted to explore the pet contest with Theo.

"To be honest, that woman scares me a little," he said. "She *knows* stuff. I never believed in psychics or 'gifts' of that nature, but Winona sure has proven herself time and again."

Bethany nodded. "I'm so tempted to go to her for a reading. But she might blurt out whether I'm having a boy or girl, and I want it to be a surprise."

"I do like surprises," Theo said. "But yeah, I'm tempted too. Just to get some feedback on myself that's not from my very opinionated siblings."

She laughed. "Do they know you well?"

"Both fortunately and unfortunately—yes." He chuckled, then bent to look in the cage of a pet rat named Gizmo.

"Are rats *pets*?" he asked. "News to me."

She smiled. "I think my brother had a pet rat once."

"Um, what *is* that?" he asked, pointing at something in a cage across the aisle.

Bethany peered in. "I think it's a cat. A hairless cat!"

They both read the info sheet. It was indeed a hairless cat, named Lavinia.

They spent the next hour roaming around, admiring the dogs on leashes, the graceful cats and adorable kittens, the birds and rodents and all the rest.

"Craving anything?" he asked. "Tacos from the food truck? Corn dog?"

She smiled. "I actually would love a chicken taco with the works and a strawberry lemonade with ice."

"I'm on it. Why don't you sit and rest for a bit, and I'll be right back."

He escorted her to a bench in the outdoor area, and she was never so grateful to sit down. She set her sunhat beside her, but just then, a border collie on a long lead snatched her hat and ran off. It happened so fast she didn't think its owner, engaged in conversation, even noticed.

"I'd go chase that down for you," Theo said with a grin, "but I doubt you want a slobbered-on, chewed hat. But no worries. I'm on that too. Back in a jiff."

My hero, she thought before she could stop herself. He was back in ten minutes with a cardboard tray of four tacos, two lemonades, and a bag dangling off his arm.

"For you, m'lady," he said with a half bow.

For maybe the first time in her life, Bethany McCreery giggled.

He set down the tray beside her. "Okay, be on the lookout for any taco-stealing dogs. These are definitely more enticing than a straw hat," he said, gesturing toward the delicious-smelling tacos. Then he reached into the bag and pulled out a hat almost identical to the dognapped one and set it on her head. "Lovely."

Oh, Theo, she thought. *Why are you everything I want when I'm everything you* don't *want?*

"Thank you," she said. "Very much. You sure are a nice friend."

He smiled and sat beside the tray, then handed her a taco. He pointed out the choices of taco sauce, and for the next fifteen minutes they ate and sipped their lemonades and people-and-dog-watched, sharing funny thoughts and imagining what the dogs' names were. She could sit here with him forever.

But all the happy families passing by had her feeling so wistful. Lots of couples with baby strollers or babies in chest carriers. Many toddlers between parents with a hand holding each. Couples in love with arms around each other. All manner of people holding hands.

And then there was Bethany. Alone but with...a friend.

You aren't alone, she reminded herself and immediately brightened. A hand went to her belly.

As they finished the last of the tacos and drained the lemonades, he pointed out every dog and owner who looked alike, making her laugh.

But if she sat here for another minute, she might burst into tears, thanks to her raging hormones and her crush on this man. It was time to get off this bench and move along—literally and figuratively. At least if they were going to look at more pets, they'd be focused on more than themselves.

As she thanked Theo again—for lunch and the hat—she was dying to lean over and kiss him, even on his cheek.

She wanted more. So much more. To be held by him. To kiss him on his lips.

She wanted him. And couldn't have him.

She stood but then dropped right back down. She felt... not quite faint, but not quite right either. All that walking and bending and kneeling down to pet dogs and look in cages, plus the hot sun by late afternoon, had done a number on Bethany, despite their twenty-minute rest on the bench.

She moved both hands to the back of her waist to give the tender spots a rub. She couldn't reach where it really felt achy.

"Are you all right?" Theo asked, his eyes on her with concern. "Do you need to move to a shadier bench?"

"That and a back rub," she said, then immediately felt herself blush. She hoped he wouldn't take that as fishing for a massage. But the thought of Theo's strong hands rubbing her back—ooh, la-la.

He peered at her and took her frown—directed at herself and her big mouth—for pain. "Let me take you home. I'll have your car dropped off for you."

She tilted her head. "Dropped off? What do you mean?"

"I mean that you seem in need of the comfort of your own sofa—and that back rub, pronto. So I'll drive you home and help you in and give these puppies a workout." He rubbed his hands together with a sweet smile. "I'll arrange to have your car driven to your place."

Okay, she was still on the fact that he'd said he was all in for that massage. But the car thing? "I'm not following, Theo. Why would you have my car dropped off? I'll just get a ride to the convention center in the morning."

"No worries," he said. "The ranch has runners who do odd jobs as needed. A nice tip and your car will be parked at your doorstep in a half hour."

Wow. Must be nice. "You definitely live in a different world than I do, Theo Abernathy. My dad's a truck driver. And my mother is part-time secretary. As I was growing up, we clipped coupons, watched our water usage, drove cars past the two-hundred-thousand-mile mark, and went on lake vacations every other summer for a long weekend.

I've never left the country—heck, I've never been east of North Dakota."

He looked at her thoughtfully and nodded. "Well, now that we're friends and you're expecting a baby, I hope you'll let me spoil you a bit."

She bit her lip. She could use some spoiling. To a point, of course. Including that back rub.

"Well, I definitely don't think I can drive right now, so I'll take you up on that offer for a ride home. But I'll get my car myself tomorrow. Thank you, though. Old habits die hard, and I'm used to making arrangements for my own life."

"Gotcha," he said. He took her arm, the gallant gesture making her knees a little weak. "Your chariot awaits. My pickup truck, but it has very comfortable seats and a smooth ride, so that should help on the way home."

She inwardly sighed. Her eleven-year-old car made her feel every bump on the road.

As they made their way to the lot, his arm still entwined with hers, she caught a few folks noticing. She could only imagine the speculation. *Is Theo the father of Bethany's baby? Are they dating?* It would be all over town in an hour.

Just friends, she'd tell anyone who asked her directly. Like her family and girlfriends.

Which was unfortunately the truth.

CHAPTER NINE

AS THEY DROVE toward the apartment building in Bronco Valley, Bethany had to admit a gazillion-dollar pickup truck did have the smooth ride Theo had said it would. And excellent air-conditioning. He pulled into a spot in the small lot and hurried around to the passenger-side door to open it for her. As someone who traveled for wedding gigs in the band's guitarist's beat-up van with all their equipment, she wasn't used to anyone opening car doors for her—not that they should, of course. And she lugged equipment like everyone else. She tried to imagine Theo letting her lift a picnic cooler even if she wasn't pregnant. Ha—that would never happen.

Who wouldn't like a little doting? Especially when tired and hormonal. She smiled as he walked her to her door, feeling...cared for. Which helped her realize she really shouldn't let him upstairs for that back rub. That was just asking for trouble. He must know that.

But he had put himself at her service, anyway.

The man had a crush on the wedding singer with the voice he admired. She'd been there, experienced that. Men who liked that she was "artsy" and a free spirit—until she wanted more from them, like consistency, respect, and follow-through.

"I wonder who won the pet contest," Theo said as they stood on her doorstep, which was around the side of the hair salon.

"I hope that hairless cat, Lavinia," she said. "Anyone who'd adore that strange-looking creature deserves the win."

Theo laughed. "I think the chatty parrot named Goodie will win. He was my favorite. Especially when I said, 'Hi, Goodie,' and he said, 'Hi, Baddie.'"

Bethany grinned. "Clearly well trained by someone with a sense of humor." She bit her lip and avoided looking directly at Theo. She was afraid she'd grab his face and plant one on him. "I'll let you get going," she said. "Thanks for the ride."

"I promised you a back rub. And I've been told I give excellent massages," he added, holding up his hands.

Oh, by whom? she thought jealously.

That should have her making an excuse to get him to leave. Instead she unlocked the door and they went upstairs.

"My place isn't much, but it's cozy and serves its purpose," she said. "Depending on how far the wedding venue is that my band performs at and how late the reception goes, we often have comped rooms at a local hotel, so I'm really only here half the time."

As she huffed up the narrow, steep stairwell, she wondered how she'd navigate this at six months along, let alone nine months. And how she'd carry up a baby *and* a stroller. She hadn't really considered that when she'd first rented this place. Something to add to her long to-do list: check out affordable two-bedroom first-floor apartments.

Bethany opened the door to her apartment and immediately wondered what Theo would think. She liked the place a lot; whenever she came home, she always felt cheered by the bright, cozy space with her funky thrift-store treasures—the emerald green velvet sofa, the Persian rug, the gauzy curtains that warmed up the large windows. Her

bedroom was her sanctuary and also thrift store decorated—the wrought iron bed and big fluffy rug that had
cost more to have cleaned than to purchase.

She gave him a very quick tour, pointing out the gal-
ley kitchen, the tiny bathroom, her bedroom and the small
guest room that would serve as a nursery. Hopefully she'd
find a more suitable home before she started looking for
a secondhand crib in excellent condition and a changing
table.

"Nice place," Theo said, looking around. "I like your
eclectic taste." He picked up a photo of the band on the faux
fireplace mantel. "I recognize everyone, I think. I've been
to several weddings that you and your band performed at."

Little did he know that her baby's father was in that
photo. She'd almost replaced that picture with a newer one
that didn't include Rexx, since he hadn't been in the band
for a few months now. But something had always stopped
her. He, like herself and the other three guys, were the original members and had been together for years. Plus, it kept
Rexx in her life, even through just the sight of him in the
photo, and she felt that was meaningful for her baby. She
was going to try calling him again in the coming days to
let him know she was pregnant, but she had no idea how
that would go, what he'd say, what he'd want to do.

"I thought Bethany and the Belters were a foursome,"
Theo said, looking at the photo. "There are five here."

She swallowed. If only they'd hired a new bassist, he
wouldn't have noticed. For now, the band was using a syn-
thesizer until they found a replacement for Rexx.

She could feel herself about to blurt out a fact and went
back and forth about it. *Just say it.* "The curly-haired blond
on bass—that's Rexx. He's the baby's father."

His gaze darted to hers, then back to the photo. "Ah.
You said he wasn't in the picture—though he literally is."

He rolled his eyes at himself and held up a hand. "Forget I said that, since it almost sounded like a joke and I'm not making light of anything. He quit the band when you told him you were pregnant?"

She let out a breath. "Got time for a story?"

"I've got all night."

It was quite a story, though, and now she wasn't sure she wanted to tell him. It seemed so complicated. Theo would certainly find out how much being a mother meant to her, that she'd been about to get pregnant on purpose before she'd discovered a one-night stand had beat her to it. That was important for him to know, given how he felt about parenthood for himself.

She needed a little time to think and glanced at her phone, which she'd set on the coffee table. Just after 6:00 p.m. Dinnertime. "I could pop a frozen roasted-veggie pizza in the oven if you're getting hungry." It had been a few hours since they'd had those tacos, and now that she'd brought up the pizza, she was craving it.

"Sounds great," he said.

First lunch, now dinner. And making Theo dinner, even heating up a frozen pizza, seemed kind of…intimate.

Then again, it was just frozen pizza. Very casual. Something friends would share.

That made her feel better. Until she realized she'd also be sharing very personal details about herself and the pregnancy. Her friendship with Theo was only one day old. She'd feel even closer to him after telling him everything. That wasn't good.

She needed a little time to think. "Make yourself comfortable and I'll be right back," she told him, needing to flee into the kitchen.

"Better yet," he said, "*you* make yourself comfortable,

and *I'll* take care of the pizza. Really—go sit, relax, put your feet up. Pizza and a back rub on the way."

She sucked in a breath. She'd long stopped believing in Prince Charming and knights in shining armor. But here was Theo Abernathy, surprising the hell out of her.

Again, this wasn't good.

"You sure?" she asked, needing to sit down as much as she needed a little space from this man. "It's really no trouble. Opening and shutting the oven, setting the timer."

"Therefore, I can do it. Sit," he said again with a smile.

Yes, sir, she thought wistfully. She'd have her space to think—and a soft seat.

She sat.

He put the photo of the band back, then turned to head into the kitchen.

She glanced at the pictures of her family, instantly comforted. Her parents. Her brother. The McCreerys all together. Soon she'd have the prints she'd ordered of the photos she'd taken at Jake and Elizabeth's wedding, including a really special one of the five kids in their wedding finery making funny faces. All her relatives had asked for a copy of that one, and her mom had said she planned to have it blown up poster size.

Bethany heard Theo opening the freezer, then the oven door opening and closing. Theo Abernathy was in her kitchen. Making her dinner.

Now *that* seemed very romantic. Very intimate.

She heard drawers and cabinet doors opening and closing, the clink of plates on the counter. Was he humming a song? The one she'd sung at his sister's surprise wedding the other day? She strained to listen.

He definitely was. She smiled, her heart soaring.

The man liked her—*that way*—there was no doubt about that. He was pursuing her whether he knew it or not. Whether he called it friendship or not. Maybe she could just go with that, see what happened. She could get hurt and probably would, but she was willing to see where this thing with Theo went. Maybe that same mentality for him meant he was changing before her eyes. Before his own eyes. It was possible.

"What can I bring you to drink?" he called out. "I'm looking in your fridge, and you have a pitcher of what I think is iced tea, three bottles of ginger ale, orange juice, and a lot of water."

"I'd love a ginger ale," she said. He sure was comfortable in her home. In her kitchen.

In moments, he'd brought her ginger ale in a glass with a few ice cubes. The delicious aroma of the pizza was starting to fill the air.

"Just a few more minutes on the pizza," he said. "How's that back doing?"

"Actually, it's better," she said quickly. If he put one finger on her body, she would melt in a puddle on the floor. And besides, she was so hyperfocused on him that she wasn't paying attention to her aches and pains and fatigue. She was both tired *and* wide-awake.

He sat on the arm on the sofa. Was it her imagination, or was his gaze on her belly, which had a slight rise?

"Has the baby kicked again?" he asked.

She couldn't have been more surprised. "Just a few more times. I love every flutter."

"Does it hurt?" he asked, wincing a bit.

She smiled. "Not really. It's just super exciting. That's my baby in there. My future."

He nodded thoughtfully. And seemed relieved when the oven timer dinged, because he popped up very quickly. "Back in a sec."

A few minutes later, he reappeared with the pizza cut

into four slices on a round serving tray. He set that on the coffee table, then went back in the kitchen and returned with two plates and napkins, his own glass of ginger ale balanced on the plates. She could get used to this.

"We could move to the table if you prefer," he said, gesturing at the little round table by the window.

"I couldn't get up if I wanted," she said. And the table was way too romantic with its candlestick, even unlit, and view of the mountains in the distance.

"Sofa, it is, then," he said, sitting beside her. A few feet away but still close enough that she could smell the clean, masculine scent of him. Another sign she was hyperfocused on him, because the delicious aroma of the pizza had infused the air.

He set a slice on her plate and folded a napkin beside it. She had not expected a wealthy rancher who lived in a cabin-mansion and had "odd-job runners" at his disposal to be so domesticated.

"Bon appétit," he said, raising his glass to her.

She clinked her glass with his. "Bon appétit."

They ate and drank and talked about the day, the adorable pets they'd seen, his hilarious names for the dogs who'd walked by, and how he'd seen those lovebirds Winona and Stanley stealing a kiss by the cat section.

"I did too!" she said with a smile. "I'll be performing at their wedding. I can't wait to watch them say their I dos."

"Same here. They've both been through so much and deserve all the happiness in the world. When Robin invited Dylan to the Bonnie B for dinner to meet the family, he'd mentioned that his great-uncle had been widowed a few years ago after many decades of marriage. Stanley came to the US from Mexico soon after because he was so lonely. And then fell head over heels for an older woman." He smiled. "Winona's in her mid-*nineties*."

"I love their love story," Bethany said. "I know just a little about Winona's past. That she was reunited just a few years back with the daughter she'd had to give up for adoption as a teenager."

Theo took a sip of his ginger ale and nodded. "Such a sad story. At seventeen, Winona was madly in love with a boy her age named Josiah Abernathy—my great-grandfather. But when she got pregnant, her parents sent her away to a home for unwed mothers. Josiah was kept away from her by both sets of parents. He and Winona were told the baby died, but Josiah found out later that their baby was alive and had been adopted. By then, he'd been unable to find Winona. But he'd vowed to find their child."

Bethany felt her eyes widen. *My goodness.* What Winona and Josiah had gone through. "How did Winona and her daughter reunite? And what became of Josiah?"

Theo swallowed his bite of pizza. "A few years ago, Winona told her story to a new friend back in Rush Creek Falls. Melanie was determined to help Winona find her lost love. That led Melanie to Bronco and to the Flying A, where my aunt, uncle and cousins live. Melanie learned that Josiah was in a nursing home and suffering from Alzheimer's. But in a moment of lucidity, he'd told Melanie and his great-grandson Gabe Abernathy, my cousin, what he knew. That the baby was alive. Josiah soon passed away. Between Melanie and Gabe and a lot of help from people in Rust Creek Falls and Bronco, Winona was reunited with her long-lost daughter, Beatrix, now known as Daisy. They live together now."

"Such a happy ending for Winona. And a new love too."

Theo nodded. "Melanie and Gabe are married now. Winona ended up bringing a lot of couples together."

"Winona's been through so much that it's no wonder she got cold feet about marrying Stanley these past months,"

Bethany said. "But now, she's ready to say I do." She felt her eyes get misty and waved a hand. "I'm a softy. If we're going to be friends, you'll have to deal with that. I cry over emotional commercials too."

He smiled. "No problem. That's what tissues are for. And a strong shoulder," he added, raising his right one at her.

She laughed. "Watch out, I may take advantage."

"Go ahead," he said—very seriously. He added a warm smile, but it was too late. He'd already told her loud and clear that she could count on him.

Oh, boy. This really was getting dangerous. He was too wonderful.

"I was worried when it seemed like Winona and Stanley were headed for a breakup," Theo said. "But you can see how in love they are when they're together. Even *I'm* a softy when I see them around town."

"I've been through so many breakups myself," Bethany said, "but not once have I gotten back together with anyone. It's how I know none of my exes was the 'one who got away.'"

"Me either. Speaking of exes," he added, "have you and Rexx figured out how you're going to coparent?"

Bethany swallowed and put down her pizza, glad she'd eaten practically the whole slice already, because her appetite had now vanished. "He doesn't even know I'm pregnant."

The whole story poured out. That she'd never been particularly attracted to Rexx and they had little in common or chemistry, but they'd been at a hotel after a late-night wedding gig and had found themselves in the bar, drinking to how love had passed them both by. One drink too many, and they'd woken up at the crack of dawn in her room. Naked. That they'd both been embarrassed—and both had been grateful to see the empty condom wrapper on the floor. At least they'd been responsible.

Too bad the condom hadn't been. They hadn't known it at the time, of course, but it must have torn.

She told Theo how she and Rexx had decided for the sake of the band to forget that this had ever happened and go about their merry ways. "But in the following days, I thought, *maybe this is why I'm single. Because I keep moving away from potential love. Who's to say Rexx and I wouldn't work out? Maybe we have more in common than I think. I should give this a chance. I'm thirty-five, not twenty-five.*"

"I had that conversation with myself after some of my recent dates. But when you're forcing it, you're forcing it."

Bethany nodded. "Exactly. And thank the heavens that before I could share my epiphany with him, he announced that he was quitting the band, that he'd fallen for a bridesmaid at a wedding we'd performed at days later, and when you know, you know, sorry, bye."

"Ow," Theo said. "That still must have been hard on you."

"Well, it was really more a wake-up call. That I was willing to date someone I didn't have any chemistry with because love did seem to have passed me by and my biological clock was ticking and I wanted a child. So I realized enough was enough—that I was going to pursue in vitro fertilization and single motherhood. That I'd make my dream come true myself."

Theo's eyes narrowed. "Okay, now I'm confused."

Bethany smiled. "I had already been researching my options before I slept with Rexx. After that night, I realized I wanted to try to have a baby on my own, so I made my appointment at the fertility center, and after some testing, the doctor said, 'Congratulations—you're *already* pregnant.'"

"Ah," Theo said. "Wow."

"Yup." She told him the rest, how she'd called Rexx to tell him but he'd cut her off before she could share the news. "He's engaged to that bridesmaid and wants no contact with any exes. Not that I qualify as an ex. I'm planning to call him this week to tell him. It's wrong to keep it from him."

"Well, if you need that shoulder," he said, lifting it again, "I'm here for you, okay?"

She smiled shakily, because she could easily burst into tears. "Okay."

Despite what he'd just said, she still expected him to bolt out the door. Not only was she pregnant, but things were a bit complicated.

She gave him a minute to make an excuse to leave. He was done with his pizza and the ginger ale.

And he now knew just how far she'd been willing to go to have a baby.

But he didn't move. He just reached for her hand and held it.

And right there, Bethany felt herself falling hard for this man.

CHAPTER TEN

THEO WAS HAVING a hard time understanding himself at the moment. He was sitting here on Bethany's sofa, holding her hand. And desperately wanting to kiss her.

Not a sweet peck on the cheek.

Not a friendly lips to the forehead.

A long, slow, passionate kiss on the lips.

He'd wanted to kiss her all day. And now that she'd opened up to him, he was feeling even closer to her. But it wasn't their new friendship that had him feeling so warmly toward her.

It was red-hot attraction. Chemistry. An awareness that she was under his skin in a way no woman had ever been. And he'd had plenty of girlfriends.

He kept trying to remind himself that she was pregnant, that she was a package deal, that kissing her was out of the question.

But all he could think about at the moment was holding her. Touching her. Feeling her in his arms.

What the heck was wrong with him?

He didn't suddenly want to be a father in five months. He didn't suddenly feel ready to have a family.

Do. Not. Give. This. Woman. Mixed. Signals. He said it to himself three times so that it would get through his clearly befuddled head. It was one thing for him to be confused about what the hell was going on with him. It was another to confuse Bethany. She had enough on her plate. Enough to worry about.

No kiss. Period.

Instead, help her out, he told himself. *Be there for her in the ways you can be.* On the tour of her apartment, he'd noticed there were very few baby items—a big stuffed rabbit, a pair of pj's, but not any necessities, like a crib or even a bassinet. He could easily outfit her spare bedroom into a nursery with everything she'd need. Everything a baby would need. Jace could help him with that. So could Google.

He could also offer Bethany one of the spare guest cabins at the Bonnie B, two of which had two bedrooms. The furnished cabins were bigger than her apartment—and one story, no stairs for her to try to huff up when she was nine months pregnant.

Maybe he was getting ahead of himself. They'd just become friends. But the ranch *did* have the spare cabins, and she'd be much more comfortable. What were friends for if not to help out? Especially when it was easy-peasy.

He could just see his siblings' faces if he told them that Bethany would be moving into a guest cabin until she was ready to find a new place—probably not until the baby was six months old and she was more settled into motherhood. He could hear Jace now: *You sure do seem to care about this woman. This pregnant woman.*

He inwardly sighed. He had it right the first time— he was getting ahead of himself. In fact, he should get going. But again, he couldn't seem to stand up. Or leave this woman's side.

"What do you think Rexx will say when you tell him about the baby?" he said instead of walking out the door. Because he *did* care about Bethany. And what her immediate future held. Would she be on her own financially? On her own, period?

"Honestly, I don't know," she said. "I always thought of him as a decent guy, but he's about to get a bombshell dropped on him when he's engaged to be married. Will he suddenly say it's a bad connection and end the call? Will he say, 'Well, let's sit down and figure out how we can coparent'?" She bit her lip and seemed worried. "What a mess." She sat back against the sofa. "Everything is just so…unknown. Up in the air."

"Except for how happy you are that you're gonna be a mama," he said. Where *that* little burst of optimism had come from, he wasn't sure. He only knew he wanted to make Bethany McCreery feel better, smile.

She seemed so touched—to the point that she leaned forward as though to kiss him on the cheek. But in the same moment, he leaned forward. And his lips landed on her lips.

Once there, he couldn't make himself pull away.

She didn't either.

He inched closer, deepening the kiss. He reached up to cup her face with his hand. He felt her arms go around his neck. He moved even closer. Slipped his tongue inside her soft, warm mouth.

Mmm, he could do this forever, the sweet anticipation of more to come sending goose bumps up his spine.

Until she pulled away. He opened his eyes to see her not frowning, exactly, but hardly smiling.

"I think we both forgot for a second that we're not a love match," she said. She patted her belly.

"Actually, the fact that you're pregnant is always on my mind, Bethany."

She tilted her head. "Meaning?"

"Meaning…" What did he mean? He sighed again.

"To be honest, I don't know." He smiled and threw up his hands. "I'm usually very easy to figure out. Just ask my siblings."

"I think I know what you meant," she said. "You're interested in me as more than a friend, but I *am* pregnant and you can't forget that, so friends it is."

"Except we kissed. Definitely something friends don't do." He stood up and gathered their plates and glasses. "I guess I'd better get going." He paused and set the plates and glasses back down. "I almost forgot I promised you a back rub."

He really was out of his mind for bringing that up. But he had promised her. And Theo Abernathy kept his promises even when they were inconvenient.

Her eyes widened. "I guess back rubs are in the friend zone. I mean, my brother gave me a back rub the other day."

Still. Why the heck had he reminded her? He couldn't possibly touch her. Not after that kiss.

"Okay, sure," she said, as if settling something for herself. "There's just one spot that aches if I move wrong." She reached behind her to give the area a squeeze.

Just keep control, he told himself. He sucked in a quick breath. "Let me at it."

She laughed and turned slightly, giving a spot above her left hip a tap. "If you get rid of this knot, you'll be my hero."

I'd like to be your hero, he thought. *But that's the last thing I am where you're concerned.*

The moment his hand touched the fabric of her dress against her body, he felt electric pulses run along his nerve endings. He used both hands on her knot, careful not to rub or squeeze too hard. He wanted to take her in his arms and hold her—just hold her—so that everything in his jumbled head would make sense. Because when it was just the two of them, talking, sharing, opening up to each other, he felt as though he had everything he'd ever need.

This woman was starting to mean so much to him. No matter how hard he tried to step back, he couldn't. And touching her was taking him two steps forward.

He gently pressed into her soft skin, wanting to drop a kiss on the knot he was undoing. He loved her *aahs*, the little moans of pleasure making him wonder what she'd sound like if his hands roamed much lower...

"Oh, Theo, you're as good as you said. This feels amazing. You definitely made the knot much looser."

He was actually relieved to be able to remove his hands from her body. He wanted to touch every inch of her. Which meant he had to leave. Now.

He stood again, collected their dishware again.

"Thanks for everything today—and tonight," she said. "I had a great time."

He looked at her, beautiful Bethany. Pregnant Bethany.

"Me too," he said fast and practically ran into the kitchen. He placed the dishes and glasses in her dishwasher, adding the pizza cutter from the sink. He stared out the window to give himself a moment—to forget the kiss. To forget massaging her. To remember *himself*—that he was not ready for the life Bethany would have in five months.

Okay, time to go, he ordered himself. *You don't belong here. The two of you are* not *a match of* any *kind.*

With that clear in his jumbled brain, he went back to the living room. "See you," he said, taking his Stetson from the bottom tier of the coffee table and dropping it on his head. The *See you* was so stupid that he frowned and didn't move. *The door is that way*, he told himself. *So go already.*

He still didn't move.

Bethany stood. "It's okay, Theo. We are who we are, right? I want a baby—so much that I was going to make it happen through the wonders of science and test tubes. You want to live on your own terms—not via a baby's needs and schedule. No one's wrong here."

Except that I don't get to have you, then, he wanted to say.

But didn't.

"Maybe we can meet for coffee soon," he said—another inept goodbye.

Coffee. When he wanted to set her up in a guest cabin at the Bonnie B. Outfit the second bedroom as a deluxe nursery with everything she and her baby could possibly need. When he wanted to rub her back again. Kiss her again.

"I'd like that," she said with a warm smile. Which he knew hid how she really felt. That she likely wished he wasn't so…what? Stubborn. It wasn't so much living on his own terms that had put him off fatherhood; it was more his responsibilities to the ranch, to his family. To the podcast he so loved using so much of his spare time for. But his brothers cared about the Bonnie B just as much as he did, and they'd figured it out. Billy with his three teens and a pregnant fiancée, and Jace with a one-year-old and a fiancée of his own, weren't any less there for the ranch than he was.

So what was going on with him, *really*?

Theo gave her a tight smile and headed to the door. Pulling it open took just about everything out of him.

So did leaving.

THE NEXT MORNING, Bethany sat at her kitchen table and texted back her bandmate Harry, the guitarist, to confirm their rehearsal later this morning. She wanted to make sure all the songs they'd perform at Winona and Stanley's wedding were perfect, and they barely had two weeks. Plus the band needed to work on three additional songs for their two gigs this weekend. Just when Bethany thought she knew every love song out there, a bride or groom threw her a surprise ballad.

Between thinking about the band and the word *surprise*, Rexx came to mind. And her assurance to her mother and herself that she'd call him with the news.

She stared at her phone, which was beside her mug of steaming chamomile tea, whole wheat toast with strawberry jam, and the book she toted around everywhere these days—these months—*Your Pregnancy Month by Month*.

Call Rexx, she told herself. *Just do it.*

It wasn't yet nine o'clock, though. She'd wait till nine, which seemed a reasonable hour to call someone who wasn't family or a bestie.

How about the unwitting father of your child?

She wrapped her hands around the mug, breathing in the comforting aroma of the chamomile. She took a sip and turned to the bookmarked page in *Your Pregnancy Month by Month*. This week focused on digestive problems, breast changes, stretch marks, and vivid dreams.

Bethany was grateful she couldn't concentrate on what she was reading. She didn't want to think about heartburn and how she was going to need new bras in a bigger size—another expense. Not to mention that more stretch marks were coming her way, since she had a few already. But she didn't want to keep thinking about Theo either. The kiss. And his awkward exit, not just from her apartment but clearly from her life.

Maybe we can meet for coffee soon...

That was definitely a goodbye.

She'd barely gotten any sleep because of that goodbye. And the kiss. And the way he'd doted on her all day and evening.

Actually, the fact that you're pregnant is always on my mind...

A man who felt the way he did, who'd been up front about it, should have run when he found out she was pregnant. Instead, he was taking care of dinner and bringing her ginger ale. Rubbing her achy back.

Kissing her passionately on the lips.

Could he change his mind? Was that actually possible? Whenever Bethany used to tell her late grandmother about her bad dates, Gram would call up one of her favorite sayings: *When people show you who they are, believe them the first time.*

That was why Bethany hadn't written him off. He kept showing her that he was a kind, warm, caring person who'd make an excellent father.

Poor Theo. He said one thing, but his actions shouted something else.

She hadn't been surprised that she'd dreamed about him last night—as intensely and vividly as the pregnancy book told her to expect. She and Theo had been at his family ranch, but the Bonnie B had turned into a baby store that went on for acres. His sister Robin and her new groom, Dylan Sanchez, were riding together on a white horse up and down the aisles. Theo was holding a little green onesie with Big Sky Baby written across the chest. *We'll take a thousand of these*, he'd told the horse, who was for some reason doubling as the store clerk.

She'd woken up as he'd been putting onesie after onesie in the horse's saddlebag. Where the newlyweds had gone, she had no idea. Maybe if she hadn't woken up, she and Theo would have gotten on that horse and ridden off into the sunset together.

He *could* change his mind about being a father in the very near future.

But if he didn't, and she let herself fall for him…

She took a sip of her tea and glanced at her phone—9:01. Time to call Rexx.

Butterflies flew around her stomach, and she shoved aside the toast and took another few sips of her herbal tea. No caffeine boost there, unfortunately.

Just do it. Bethany picked up her phone and slid through her contacts until she got to Rexx. She was about to press the Call icon next to his name, but she needed a second. She sucked in a breath, bracing herself to hear his raspy voice saying, *Bethany, I told you—I don't want contact with my old life.*

Problem with that was that they'd created a *new* life.

Okay. Here goes. She pressed the little phone icon next to Rexx's name.

But instead of his annoyed voice, she heard an automated message: "The number you have reached, 406-555-2522, is no longer in service."

She gasped. He'd changed his number.

She hadn't expected that at all. But she probably should have.

Rexx really didn't want anything to do with her. She was the last woman he'd been with before he'd fallen hard for his fiancée, and the new lady in his life was clearly the jealous type and had insisted he cut off contact with anyone from his life before her. After all, he'd gone as far as to quit the band, which was a big deal given that they were reasonably successful and got along well.

Granted, she doubted it had entered his mind that the reason she'd call him was because she was pregnant. They *had* used a condom. It just hadn't done its job, and Rexx clearly hadn't noticed the tear.

Now what? Did she respect how he felt when she had something monumental to tell him? How could she? He deserved to know—no matter what. Just as her baby deserved for Bethany to make the effort.

Maybe one of the band members had Rexx's new number.

Then again, he'd been so quick to walk away from the band that he likely had cut them all out of his life. She'd find out at today's rehearsal.

She sighed for tenth time that morning and reached for her book. Reading about stretch marks and heartburn couldn't be worse than how up in the air she felt.

AFTER TWO CATTLE auctions this morning, Theo was on his way back to the ranch when he was about to pass Hey, Baby, where everyone in town, including himself, bought their little relatives birthday gifts. When his brother and soon-to-be sister-in-law Charlotte announced they were expecting, he'd popped into Hey, Baby for a gift, the saleswoman giving him five good ideas for what to buy. He could stop in and pick up a few things for Bethany's nursery since he was right here. He slowed down and turned into the parking lot.

Theo hadn't spoken to Bethany since he'd left her apartment last night. Three times he'd pulled out his phone to shoot off a quick text, just something casual and friendly to get them both away from the awkward way they'd left things.

See you, he'd told her as he'd left her apartment, as though she was an acquaintance he'd run into in the grocery store. And then he'd said something inane about meeting up for coffee sometime.

Last night, when he'd tried to sleep, he'd replayed their night together over and over. How much he liked her. How attracted he was to her. The way he'd fussed over her—making the pizza, serving it, rubbing her back.

Kissing her.

And if she hadn't put an end to that kiss? What if it had led them into her bedroom?

We are who we are, right? I want a baby—so much that I was going to make it happen through the wonders of science and test tubes. You want to live on your own terms—not via a baby's needs and schedule. No one's wrong here.

Her words echoing in his head, he parked and went inside the store. He pulled out his phone to consult the "nursery essentials" lists he'd bookmarked just as a couple with a stroller entered the shop—arguing.

"No, you can't go to Ethan's bachelor party," the woman said. "Stop trying to get me to change my mind."

The man threw up his hands. "It's one night, Lizzie. Jeez."

Theo literally saw the woman's hands blanch on the handle of the stroller, her gold wedding ring glinting. She turned to the guy. "Well, we have a baby and a sick toddler at home, and neither of our families can help me tonight. How could you even *want* to go?"

"It's a few hours," the man whined.

Theo couldn't help but notice the guy was twisting his own gold wedding ring on his finger.

"More like seven or eight hours, and then you'll come home drunk," the woman said with more exasperation than anger in her voice. "Lot of help you'll be with Danny's 3:00 a.m. feeding. You'd probably drop him."

The man sighed. The woman shook her head. "Fine, I won't go. Happy?"

It was clear to Theo they'd had a version of this conversation a million times. "No, actually. I'm not. I want you to *care*."

The man put his arms around his wife and tilted up her chin. "I do care. Of course I care."

Theo had heard enough. He did a literal 180 and headed for the door. He suddenly had little interest in shopping for cribs or bouncy seats or any of the other baby essentials he'd researched during his morning coffee. His search had led him to a bunch of baby shower registration lists, and there were countless items, from smart bassinets that you could set to rock or play a lullaby with a tap on your phone's app to a wipe warmer so that baby's tiny tush didn't get startled by a cold touch during a diaper change.

He'd learned quite a bit from the registry lists. He could create a top-of-the-line nursery for Bethany with a few clicks of his keyboard, but he'd wanted to see some of the big-ticket items for himself, make sure the quality was there.

It hadn't been lost on him that he had been researching all that stuff. But he'd figured he was doing it because Bethany was on her own and money was tight.

But he suddenly felt a little queasy.

He would never be like that dad, more concerned with a fun night out than with his responsibilities at home. His sick toddler needed him. His wife needed him. Theo's heart would have him at home, so he and his future wife would never have a conversation like that.

But, but, but... How could Theo be there for his wife and child—*children*—if he was on the range or the barn, giving one hundred percent to the Bonnie B? The ranch was his world. And maybe because his brothers *did* have responsibility to their own families, Theo felt it was *his* responsibility to step in when they were needed elsewhere— at home with a sick kid or at a parent-teacher conference, or cheering from the stands at a school game. He couldn't be pulled in different directions. Period. Maybe in a few years he'd feel the tug of fatherhood. But he wasn't any-where close to that.

The key was not to do something you weren't truly ready for.

Which meant keeping his friendship with Bethany squarely in the friend zone. No more kissing.

With that settled, he turned back around—ready to shop. Friends could definitely help out new-mother-to-be friends with a few necessities.

But as he studied the bassinets and consulted the regis-try lists he'd saved, he realized he was putting a lot more time and energy into Bethany's baby than he had for his nephew Frankie over the past year. He'd practically bought out the internet for Frankie once it was clear that Jace would adopt the baby. So had his siblings, and since they hadn't coordinated, Jace and Tamara had ended up with three bouncy seats, four baby bathtubs, four strollers, and so many huge stuffed animals that they didn't fit in the large nursery. Theo had just pointed and clicked then; he hadn't studied the reviews the way he was doing now, only considering a baby monitor with five stars and more than one hundred positive write-ups.

As he tried on a model of a top-of-the-line infant car-rier, spending a good twenty minutes figuring out how the contraption buckled onto his chest and testing its security, Theo was once again left wondering what was going on.

His phone pinged with a text.

Hey, bro. Up for babysitting Frankie tomorrow night? 6:30 to 9ish. Something came up last minute and you're my only hope.

Uh oh. Two and a half hours on his own with a baby? He loved his nephew and Frankie was an easy baby who'd be asleep most of that time, but hadn't Jace mentioned that Frankie was teething and woke up cranky a couple times a night? Theo had been planning on recording the introduction for next week's episode of *This Ranching Life* tomorrow night, and now he'd have to put it off. He had little free time as it was.

But given how he couldn't get Bethany off his mind and the fact that he was here in Hey, Baby with a carrier on his chest, babysitting Frankie was exactly what he needed to do.

Tomorrow night would reinforce that he wasn't ready to be anyone's dad. Theo instantly brightened. Yes. That was exactly what he needed. To have his truth brought home for him.

Plus, if Theo was his brother's last hope, that meant he'd asked everyone else and no one was available. He texted Jace a yes. It was a win-win for both of them.

CHAPTER ELEVEN

BETHANY HAD A lot on her mind when she finally pulled into her apartment building's parking lot after a long but good rehearsal with the band. Including the fact that none of the guys had Rexx's new number. The drummer and keyboardist had said they wouldn't care if they ever heard from that "jerk" again after the way he'd left them high and dry without a bassist, but the guitarist, who was also their backup vocalist, had never liked Rexx anyway and insisted they were fine without one. The way Bethany saw it, splitting the money by four instead of five made a huge difference.

When she explained to the band why she needed to talk to Rexx, they were all full of congratulations and hugs and they'd come up with a hand gesture Bethany could give during a gig if she was ever feeling sick or tired and needed to dash off suddenly for a bit. They'd all quickly cover for her. They were such great guys.

The drummer had suggested getting in touch with the bride at whose wedding Rexx had met his fiancée to get *her* contact info. Hmm, Bethany couldn't see doing that. *Um, hi, could you give me your fiancé's cell number even though he changed it to avoid hearing from me? I need to tell him I'm pregnant with his child.*

She sighed and got out of her car. She wasn't giving up on getting in touch with Rexx, but she was exhausted and done thinking for the day. What she wanted now was to make some popcorn, watch a rom-com, and then practice the two ballads that had a couple of tricky high notes. That should keep her mind occupied so she wouldn't think about Theo. She'd been failing at that all day. The good news was that she hadn't heard from him. *Good* because they really couldn't be friends. And the fact that she'd been disappointed by not getting a call or text from him made that very clear. Her heart was already involved, and she had to put the kibosh on that.

She opened the front door, surprised to see a stack of packages both big and small from Hey, Baby—her favorite shop to explore, if not buy from since it was on the pricey side—piled high on the side of the stairwell. Huh. There were only two apartments, hers and the young single cowboy who lived on the third floor. He was definitely home since she heard his loud country-western music from down here, but wouldn't he have brought up his deliveries already?

She eyed the name on the top package. Bethany McCreery. What was this? A mistake? She hadn't ordered anything in weeks. All the packages—five of them—had her name and address. She opened the top one and pulled out a pair of adorable silver baby booties embroidered with tiny stars. Someone had sent her a baby gift? Five baby gifts, including two that were very large? She slid out the packing label. The billing name and address were Theo Abernathy's.

What was going on?

She took out her phone and called him. He answered right away.

"Theo, there are five packages of varying sizes in my tiny lobby," she said. "I opened one and it's from you. Really cute baby booties."

"Oh, good," he said. "Everything arrived. I'll come

over and bring them up for you. I can put everything together too."

Um, the whole point of the popcorn and rom-com was to relax and busy herself so she wouldn't think about him. Now he was coming over? "Wait—put *what* together?"

"I wanted to surprise you with a few things for the baby's nursery. The store had a same-day delivery option and my truck was packed with some ranch equipment I bought today, so I opted for that."

She stared at the boxes. The bottom two were quite big. What the heck was in there? "Theo, you didn't need to buy me anything."

"I wanted to," he said. "I'm very handy with an Allen wrench too. See you in a few?"

"Okay," she said. She was confused. First he was doting on her. Now he was buying out Hey, Baby. What was he doing? They were new friends, and new friends didn't do this. Old friends didn't do this. Baby booties, sure. But there were *five* packages here.

They also didn't show up with Allen wrenches to put together a crib or a high chair.

And when had he bought all this stuff? Today at some point. Which meant he'd been thinking about her. And had spent quite a bit of time making choices and purchases. He had to be working out his feelings for her, for the pregnant woman he was unexpectedly interested in. But just as she'd thought earlier, as he worked it out by spending time with her, by buying silver baby booties, by making her feel special and desirable, she was being left to fall for him.

And when he decided that he'd been right to begin with, that he *wasn't* ready, that he didn't want this, she'd be left with a bruised heart.

With a baby to care for. She'd be exhausted and stressed

enough as a brand-new mother; she wasn't adding sad and confused to the mix. Her baby deserved better than that.

She stared at the packages and shook her head. Theo would have to take all this back. That was the end of it.

Bethany sat down on the third step, since that would be the easiest to get up from, and waited. She played a word game on her phone, trying to keep her irritation at bay. Theo clearly meant well. But working out his confusion at her expense, whether he knew what he was doing or not, was a big problem.

She saw him pulling in. Dammit. She should have told him to bring a truck because he was taking all this back.

He saw her through the glass on the door and smiled, then came inside. He held what looked like a toolbox.

She got herself up. "Theo, whatever all this is, I appreciate it. But I want you to take it back. I can't accept it."

His face fell. "I hope you can, Bethany. I noticed you didn't have anything set up for the baby's nursery yet. And you mentioned that money was tight, so…"

She frowned and lifted her chin. She had no doubt that he'd spent a small fortune without having to think twice or even look at price tags. "Theo Abernathy, I've always supported myself, and I'll support my baby just fine on my own."

He seemed at a loss for words. "I know, and I admire you, Bethany. To be honest, I was about to pass the store, but then I thought of you and went in. Between Frankie's nursery and my research, I knew what you needed, so I… bought a few things."

"But why?" she asked.

He stared at her, flustered.

Now she felt bad. But this was a bit beyond.

"I want you to have what you need," he said. "That's all there is to it."

"Because I'm on my own?"

"First and foremost because you're my friend. And yes, the baby's father isn't in the picture. Does he know now that you're pregnant? Is he planning to step up?"

She sighed and told him about the call to Rexx, about the automated message. And that none of the other band members had his new contact info either.

He shook his head. "So let me help, Bethany. Because I very easily *can*."

He looked so sincere, his green eyes warm—and friendly. But she had to call him out on his privilege.

"Theo, I appreciate that you care—and your generosity. But where I come from, which is Bronco Valley, I budget for what I can afford, buy only what I need—and I work for it. That's how I live, okay?"

He was looking at her intently, his head slightly tilting as if he hadn't expected that, hadn't even considered that what he'd said was…privileged. *Stick around*, she thought. *You'll be down to earth in no time.* "Bethany," he said, "I hear you. I absolutely do. I can't apologize for having money. But I also can't think of a better thing to do with it than help my friend create the best possible home-sweet-home for her baby. I just want to do something nice for you."

Swoon. He always knew what to say. "You're a nice guy, Theo Abernathy."

He smiled. "Money can't buy that. I was made this way."

She laughed. "I'll take the light packages."

That handsome face brightened.

She scooped up the three small boxes, including the one with the booties, still unsure about all this, where this was headed, where *they* were headed. She had more to say, but she didn't want to talk out here in the open, even though the upstairs cowboy's music would make it impossible for the guy to eavesdrop. Nor would he be remotely interested in the conversation.

Theo took one of the big boxes, his toolbox atop it, and followed her up the stairs, set it down, then went back for the other one.

She opened her apartment door and held it open wide for him. Once they were inside and he was putting down a box in the living room, she couldn't keep her thoughts inside anymore.

"There's something else too," she said.

He sat on the edge of the sofa. "I'm listening."

He was looking at her so intently. She'd gone out with men who gazed around even while she talked about something important. Especially lately, she wasn't used to having such undivided attention. She liked it.

"I've been thinking about that kiss. And then after. How you left in a hurry. And then suddenly you're buying out the baby section and here in my apartment with your toolbox. It all makes me think you're playing out your feelings about me being pregnant."

He seemed a little confused by that. "I don't think so, Bethany. I told you why I got all this for you."

He probably was doing it all unconsciously. Just going with the moment. But that would have the same end result.

Bethany with a busted-up heart. Expectations set up and squashed. Hopes dashed.

"In the end, you're not going to be my boyfriend, Theo. You're not going to be a father figure in the baby's life. Which is fine—you've been very up front about that. The problem is that…"

He was waiting. And she felt close to tears. As if everything she'd been hoping for over the past year was right in front of her but still unattainable.

Out with it, Bethany.

"I'm afraid that this knight-in-shining-armor stuff is going to affect me too much. Know what I'm saying?"

It was clear that he didn't. But then his brows kind of knitted and he seemed flustered again. She saw when the light bulb went off in his head and he understood.

"I can't afford to get hurt, Theo. Not when I need to be preparing for motherhood."

Now he was looking at her thoughtfully, as though he was taking in everything she'd just said. "Right, so no more kissing. But are you saying we can't be friends?"

Was she? She supposed she was. But that wasn't what she wanted either.

"I don't know what I'm saying, Theo. That's why this is so hard."

"Yeah, same here. I mean, I had an answer about why I bought all this stuff. Why I'm here at all. But it doesn't really make sense, does it?"

She shook her head. She would just have to focus on the word *friendship*. Friendship, friendship, friendship. There would be no more kissing. Theo Abernathy was like a new instant bestie. *Yeah, right*, she thought. This was just the beginning of a lot more to come and she knew it.

"Well, let me get everything put together," he said, opening the toolbox and holding up the Allen wrench. "I like assembling. It's easy when the directions come with labeled illustrations. Unlike…"

"Us," she finished for him.

He nodded and knelt down beside the box, getting out an X-Acto knife.

She sighed. "Theo. You're supposed to make yourself less desirable, not more. And the fact that I've got this baby bump, that these things are all baby stuff, should make *me* less desirable to you. Not more."

He smiled, and it went right inside her. "Like I said, we don't make sense. But here we are."

Yeah, and now what? But unless she told him to leave and take all the baby stuff with him, there would be a tomorrow and the next day and the next day. Before she knew it, he'd be coming to Lamaze class with her.

He patted the box. "This is probably the deluxe baby bouncer. It's a smart one. Tap a button on the app and it plays lullabies."

Oh, Theo, she thought for the millionth time since her brother's wedding.

What was she supposed to do about this man?

THEO PRESSED THE button marked Gentle Play, and the pastel-colored mobile with its tiny dangling stuffed animals began spinning. "And my work here is done," he said with a smile. It had taken almost two hours to put everything together, but now he wished he had something else to assemble so he wouldn't have to leave.

He stood with Bethany in her spare bedroom, which was looking a lot like a nursery now. There was the bassinet across from the window with the cute mobile atop it, the smart bouncy seat, the changing table with a terry cloth–covered pad and three drawers underneath, the baby booties, and ten pairs of birth-to three-month-sized pajamas.

"Oh, Theo," she said, looking around the room, her hand over her heart, which touched him. "I love everything. Thank you."

"You're welcome. And the reason I opted for a bassinet and not a crib is just in case we don't have the same taste. They had very fancy ones and plain ones and everything in between and in all different colors—white and gray and light and dark wood."

Bethany smiled. "I have no idea what style I'd like. I

guess I'd have to go to a baby store and look around to know my own taste. I'd think I'd like plain so I could stencil the baby's name on it, but who knows? Maybe I'd want some huge sleigh crib."

"Speaking of a huge sleigh crib," he said. "There are a couple of guest cabins at the Bonnie B with two bedrooms. You're welcome to move into one if you'd like. They're pretty roomy. A sleigh crib would fit with no problem."

He saw her bite her lip before she glanced away. Maybe he shouldn't have brought it up yet. Too much, too soon, probably. He was the king of that lately.

"That's some offer, Theo," she said.

"I just want you to be comfortable. I'm trying to imagine you getting up those steep stairs at nine months pregnant, and then carrying a newborn down with whatever else you might have to take with you. The guest cabins are one story. And they're a good distance from the main working areas of the ranch, so you won't be woken up by Buster crowing."

She laughed, but her smile faded some. "This apartment definitely isn't ideal. And yes, I'll probably need one of those chairlifts to get up here in a couple of months," she added on a half chuckle. "But... I don't know, Theo."

He nodded. "Just know the offer stands."

"I appreciate it."

He figured he'd better change the subject fast, because she looked uncomfortable. He was definitely going too far. Getting ahead of himself *and* going too far.

He showed her how to use the app on her phone to remotely operate the mobile. "According to the description, you could be in the kitchen making dinner and hear the baby fuss and just tap a button on your phone and voilà, the mobile will remotely spin and play a lullaby to keep Bethany Junior occupied, giving you a few minutes."

"Bethany Junior," she said, her beautiful face lighting up. "I like it."

"Have you thought about names?" he asked.

"Like everything else, no. I've barely bought anything for the baby either. Either it doesn't feel real that I'm going to be a mother in five months or I'm actually a little scared."

"Scared of what?"

She bit her lip again. "Well, I will be on my own. In the middle of the night, when it's time to feed a two-day-old baby, it'll be just me, you know? And I barely know anything. I was reading about how to care for the umbilical cord stump in the days after birth and got so nervous I had to close my pregnancy book." She let out a breath. "I had so much experience with babies when my niece and nephews were born, but the youngest is six now. I haven't picked up a baby in years."

His green eyes lit up. "If you're looking for a refresher course, I'm babysitting tomorrow night for my brother's son, Frankie. He's only twelve months old. And trust me when I say I could use your help."

She laughed. "Of course I'll help. Count me in. It's the least I can do after all this, Theo."

He held her gaze and couldn't drag his eyes off her if he wanted to. He was about to say something stupid like *that's what friends are for*, but he just sucked in a breath.

"Try out the mobile app," he said, needing to ruin the moment.

She pressed the button he'd pointed out, and looked almost astonished when the mobile began playing Brahms' lullaby. "Amazing, Theo. I love technology." She watched the little dangling animals spin around atop the bassinet, the lullaby playing softy.

She dabbed under her eyes. "I didn't think I'd get all

emotional, but aww. This is real, you know? The baby will be here in five months. And now I have a nursery." She gazed around and looked so moved that he wanted to take her in his arms and just hold her.

But he wanted so much more than that. He wanted to feel her against him—her body, her mouth. He wanted to tell her she'd never want for anything with him in her life, that he'd always be there for her.

But how could he when he couldn't be the one thing she needed? A father for her child.

He reached for her hand and gave it a quick squeeze. "I just want you and the baby to have everything you need."

She looked at him, then quickly glanced away.

"Really, Theo, thank you for all this. Especially after the big...nothing from Rexx, the extreme of too much from you turned out to be just what I needed."

He smiled, feeling much better about his decision to get her nursery going. "I just want you to know that no matter what, I'm here for you."

"Friends," she said, sticking out her hand. "I think we need to be clear on that. Because like I said, I really can't risk getting hurt by you."

He had so much to say, but nothing would come out of his mouth. He couldn't imagine hurting her. But she was right to back off. As much as he cared about her, *wanted* her, he wasn't what she needed.

Finally he just nodded. "Friends." He shook, the feel of her warm, soft hand sending tingles along his nerve endings.

At the least, he wanted to add.

Theo could feel himself on a course for trouble here.

CHAPTER TWELVE

THE NEXT AFTERNOON, after another rehearsal with the band, Bethany had plans to meet her new sister-in-law, Elizabeth, for an early dinner at the Gemstone Diner. For once, it would be just the two of them. Usually they were surrounded by Elizabeth's five-year-old twins and Jake and his three kids, but finally they'd be able to have some much-needed girl talk. Elizabeth only had an hour before she'd be meeting her sisters for their own practice for an upcoming rodeo out of town, and Bethany would be meeting Theo at his cabin at six for their night of babysitting.

When she pulled open the door, she immediately saw Elizabeth because there was a small crowd around her table. That was life for the Hawkins Sisters—they were superstars in the rodeo community, and since Elizabeth, some of her sisters and several of her cousins had married Bronco residents, they were now hometown celebrities.

As Bethany approached the table, the crowd dispersed. Elizabeth stood and gave Bethany a warm hug.

"How's married life?" Bethany asked as they sat down.

Elizabeth's face lit up. "I love it. I love your brother to pieces. And the kids are getting along beautifully." She sighed. "I never thought the girls and I would find another chance at family again. Or even want one. But meeting your brother changed everything."

"I'm so glad," Bethany said. Her sister-in-law's joy was so evident.

Elizabeth had been living in Australia with her sister Carly and their parents, performing on the rodeo circuit, when she met Arlo Freeman. Their marriage was a happy one until Arlo sadly died young of cardiac arrest. After feeling lost for two years, Elizabeth had brought her daughters to Montana to meet the rest of the Hawkins family—and when she met Jake McCreery, himself a widower with three children, both families got a fresh start, together.

The waitress came over and took their orders—a BLT for Bethany and a chicken Caesar wrap for Elizabeth. They were splitting a side of sweet potato fries, which Bethany had been craving all day.

"And how are *you* feeling?" Elizabeth asked. "I hope it's okay that Jake shared the big news with me. Pregnant! I'm so excited for you, Bethany."

"Of course it's okay. You're family!" She told Elizabeth the story about Rexx, including finally calling him the other day only to find out he'd changed his number. Then she found herself sharing everything that had happened with Theo.

Elizabeth's eyes widened a few times as Bethany relayed the story, from their conversation at the wedding to her unexpected delivery last night to Theo showing her how to use the mobile's app. "He ordered an entire nursery for you?" she asked as the waitress set down their food.

Bethany swiped a fry in ketchup. "This morning I almost wondered if I dreamed the whole thing. Pregnant women are supposed to have vivid, intense dreams, right? But when I went into the spare bedroom, there it all was. The stack of pj's almost made me burst into tears."

Except for her parents and her brother, who had ever done anything like this for Bethany? No one, she full well knew. Even when she'd had boyfriends over the years, a few that had lasted a year, none had ever doted on her the way Theo had. One guy had broken up with her after she told him she had the flu and asked if he'd drop off chicken soup. *Sorry, but I have a big meeting at work in a couple days and can't afford to catch anything.* Another had insisted she and her band perform at his cousin's destination wedding in Mexico for free and that she and the guys would have to pay for their flights and hotel rooms. He'd dumped her when she said they had a *paying* gig that night.

Yet here was a guy she wasn't even dating who'd spent hours assembling baby equipment he'd also spent hours buying—and researching—for her.

"To make matters worse—or more confusing," Bethany said, "he's ready for marriage. He wants to find his other half."

"Theo Abernathy is probably the most eligible bachelor in Bronco," Elizabeth agreed. "He could have his pick of twenty-two-year-olds who might be looking for rich husbands but aren't necessarily ready for motherhood. That he hasn't been dating a slew of young beauty pageant winners is telling. That he's fallen for you—even *more* telling."

Bethany shook her head. "I don't know about *fallen*. And I'm not so sure he'll change his mind about wanting to be a parent. Maybe in the abstract, he might. But I'm having a baby in a few months. That makes it very real."

"I see him coming around," Elizabeth said, biting into a fry. "You know that saying, he doesn't know what hit him? Theo doesn't know what's *hitting* him. He's right in the middle of it."

Bethany smiled. "Well, maybe. Oh, wait—then again, maybe not. We're babysitting his year-old nephew tonight, and he'll likely know by the end of the evening if he could see fatherhood for himself."

Elizabeth's eyes widened again, and she pointed another fry at Bethany. "He asked you to *babysit* with him?"

"Don't read too much into that," Bethany said. "I'd just told him how I was a little scared about impending motherhood, that the last time I held a baby was, like, five years ago. So that's why he invited me along tonight. For a little on-the-job training."

"He sure is looking out for you. And wants to spend time with you. In quite a domestic setting," Elizabeth added with a grin. "Mark my words, the man has it bad for you."

Bethany's heart lifted—then deflated a bit. "He's been so up front about his feelings, though. I mean, he told me straight out in our first conversation—which was at your wedding, by the way—that he won't be ready for fatherhood for five years."

"Well, that was then, hon. For a guy who doesn't want to be a dad, he sure is overly focused on a pregnant woman."

Bethany took a bite of her BLT. That was true. He was.

"So just how serious is this for you?" Elizabeth asked. "Are you falling in love?"

Bethany couldn't deny it to herself any longer. "He had me at the back rub. I'm definitely falling in love."

Elizabeth's dark eyes twinkled, and she reached over to take both of Bethany's hands for a squeeze. "I have faith in him. Trust me, if Jake and I managed to get married…"

Bethany knew about the obstacles that had stood in the couple's way. After being widowed, Jake and Elizabeth had been afraid to risk loving again, to risk their children getting attached to a parental figure. But the thought of going on without each other had been unbearable.

She wouldn't dare hope that Theo would feel that way about her.

Elizabeth picked up the final bite of her wrap. "Tonight you have a perfect opportunity to show that man what domestic bliss will look like for the two of you as a couple."

Huh. When put like that… Maybe. Unless cute little Frankie Abernathy was a horror show. Gassy, overtired, missing his parents…who knew what could have that baby screeching his head off for the entire time they'd be in charge of caring for him?

Or perhaps he'd be adorable and cooing and sleep most of the time—and show Theo Abernathy the sweet, easy side of parenthood.

This really could go either way.

WHEN BETHANY HAD arrived at Theo's cabin a half hour ago, he'd known immediately that friendship was out of the question. He was just too attracted to her. He had a few female friends and wasn't overcome with the urge to kiss them, touch them, make love with them.

None of them were pregnant either. And Bethany Mc-Creery, in her pale pink dress that very clearly showed her baby bump, *was*.

His only hope was that babysitting Frankie tonight would go terribly, that the baby would remind him that he was as uninterested in parenthood as he thought he was. That when his nephew would be screaming and crying and all red-faced, neither of them able to calm him down, Theo would see that this would be his future with Bethany and her baby.

And that when Jace and Tamara came to pick up Frankie at 9:00 p.m., he would walk away from both taking care of a baby and his unwanted feelings for Bethany. He'd let her go. She might be alone without the father of the child, but she had a wonderful family and friends who'd stand by her and support her throughout the rest of the pregnancy and after.

And Theo could stop living in a state of confusion. He

could go back to thinking only of the ranch and his family and his podcast and, yes, himself.

Holding his nephew as he and Bethany walked Jace and Tamara to the door of his cabin, he wondered why she had to be so beautiful. And sexy. Why she'd had to put her long, silky brown hair in a ponytail that exposed her creamy neck. He was even more attracted to her tonight than he had been at her brother's wedding, which was saying something. Back then, he hadn't known she would be a mother in five months.

"Frankie shouldn't give you any trouble," Tamara said, caressing her son's soft brown hair. "He's such a good baby."

"Unless he gets cranky because he's teething," Jace added with a grin. He dropped a kiss on his son's head.

"Any tips or tricks if he does?" Bethany asked.

"He has a few teething toys he liked chewing on. And he does like being tickled," Jace said, giving the baby's belly a rub.

"Oh, and he loves when you give his ears a little tug. I don't know why, but he does. It makes him hoot with laughter."

"And watch your ponytail," Tamara said to Bethany. "Frankie's a grabber. He loves noses, eyeglasses, ponytails, earrings, and scarves."

"Uh-oh," Bethany said on a chuckle. "I've got two of those, so there's that."

"And if you burp him, make sure you have a burp cloth somewhere in the vicinity of his mouth," Jace added. "Theo learned that lesson last week."

Theo laughed. "I'm still traumatized."

His brother and sister-in-law said their final goodbyes and were gone. They'd left behind their precious baby, his portable playpen, and his car seat. Plus a backpack containing a few necessities, like diapers and wipes. Theo had offered to babysit at their place with the well-stocked nursery, but Jace had said something about wanting Frankie to get used to other environments like his aunts' and uncles' homes.

"Can I hold him?" Bethany asked.

"Sure," he said, transferring Frankie into her arms. Luckily the baby went to her easily, his big eyes alert on her face. In fact, he wouldn't stop staring at her.

Bethany giggled. "He likes me!"

"Who wouldn't like you?" Theo asked, then felt his cheeks warm. He hadn't meant to say that aloud. Something that happened a lot when he was around her. Things just flew out of his mouth, straight from his head, straight from his heart.

"Hear that, Frankie?" Bethany said, her smile so warm he could tell she was touched.

He inwardly frowned. Wasn't this whole night supposed to go south? It was off to *too* good of a start. Frankie was being cute and easy. Bethany was drawing Theo in just by being herself.

Bethany glanced around. "Cabin, huh? My version of a cabin is the kind of place my family went to on summer vacations every other year. A one-room log structure with a loft for me and Jake and barely indoor plumbing. This is…a mansion."

He saw her taking in the luxe-rustic beams and big stone fireplace, the wall of windows with the view of the woods and mountains, the expensive leather sofas and soft rugs. "I think my parents went a little hog wild on the cabins for their children so that they'd keep us on the Bonnie B for all time. But hey, it worked. We all love our homes and living right on the ranch. And it's nice to be so close to one another."

"That *is* nice. Anytime I thought about leaving Bronco and moving someplace that seemed more exciting, I'd picture my family, and I knew I'd never live anywhere else."

He nodded. "Same."

"You'd miss this little guy too much," she said, giving Frankie a little bounce. "And your other nephews and niece."

"Exactly. But after babysitting or getting together, it's also nice to be able to say, 'See ya tomorrow,' and go home to a quiet house and do whatever I want."

"It's funny," she said. "I feel like I've been doing that for thirty-five years. I have a little *too* much free time."

Touché, he thought, considering they were the same age. "I guess there's never really free time when it comes to working on a ranch. Even with my siblings and dad and the employees, there's always work to be done, whether in the office or the range." That was true; despite being management, Theo often got out his toolbox to mend a broken fence or he'd groom a horse or ride out with the herd of cattle, but he also had to admit he'd also do those things when he was feeling particularly restless. When it would hit hard that he really did want a wife to share his life with. And that none of his recent relationships had worked out. And yes, because the past three, all women he liked and respected, kept bringing up wanting to start a family very soon. But it hadn't been just that. Theo had been aware that something bigger, less tangible, was just missing.

Like what he had, what he felt, when he was with Bethany.

"How about you give me and Frankie the grand tour of your 'cabin'?" she asked. "I'd love to see the place."

"We can start right here in the foyer. This is one of my favorite spots in the house, because when I walk in, my eye goes to the grand staircase and the fireplace beyond it. I always give a happy sigh when I walk in the door."

She grinned. "I like my place, but I definitely don't have that same reaction."

"Have you thought about my offer to move into a cabin? Say the word, and I can have your furniture brought over."

The grin faded fast. "Theo, I appreciate that. But I'm fine where I am for the time being. Even if the time being is, like, another month."

He nodded. Five minutes ago he was thinking how he needed to walk away from Bethany. Now he was almost pressuring her to move a quarter mile down the path into a guest cabin?

His feelings were all over the place. He had to get a handle on himself, how he *felt*.

To get his mind off her, he led the way to the kitchen.

"Wow, I hope you cook," she said, looking around the large room. "There's no way you could let the state-of-the-art everything in here go to waste."

"Actually, I'm not much of a cook. I'm fine with the basics—burgers, pasta, chili—but my siblings would disagree." He smiled and turned to her. "I can whip us up dinner when Frankie goes to bed."

"Sounds good. I had an early dinner at the diner with my sister-in-law, but to be honest, I'm craving spaghetti Bolognese. Is that in your repertoire?"

"Spaghetti and meat sauce are staples I always have, so your wish is my command. Tamara told me that we should put Frankie down at seven thirty, so I'll start cooking right after. Apparently, he loves the playpen and falls asleep in a snap. They say he's easy to transfer out too, like out of his car seat and into his crib. A good sleeper."

"God, I hope this little one will be too," she said, tapping her hand on her belly and then putting her arm back around Frankie. "I do love to sleep—especially after a late-night gig. I'm really looking forward to giving myself maternity leave for three months. The guys are going to hold auditions for a temporary replacement, so I'm glad about not leaving them high and dry." She frowned for a second. "I hope she's not so good that they want to permanently replace me."

He reached a hand to her shoulder. "No one could ever compare to you, Bethany."

Her warm smile went straight to his heart. "Aww, thank you. That means a lot."

Okay, he had to get away from that smile. He turned and headed to the living room.

"I spend most of my free time in here," he said. "I love the view of the woods and mountains. And even in summer, this fireplace makes me happy."

"It's easily the biggest fireplace I've ever seen. I love all the photos on the mantel." She brought Frankie over and peered at them. They were all of the family. "You definitely didn't have an awkward stage," she said, looking at a photo of him as a middle schooler holding a fish he'd just caught.

"Two minutes after my dad snapped that photo of me, my youngest sister, Stacy, caught her first fish, and it was five times the size of mine." He smiled at the picture, remembering that day.

Bethany laughed. "Don't tell Jake I said so, but I always catch a bigger fish than he does."

They moved to the deck, the warm, breezy air refreshing. He hadn't even realized how hot and bothered Bethany had him because of the central air-conditioning. But out here, he was aware of just how heated he was.

Frankie's gaze was on a white butterfly flapping its wings slowly as it landed on a flower lining the patio. The baby pointed, and when the butterfly flew up, Frankie laughed so loud that Theo could hardly believe such a sound could come out of tiny body.

"There is no better sound," she said. "I say that as a singer and a music lover."

"I have to agree. *I* say that as Uncle Theo, always happy to come home to this quiet house. But I could listen to that laughter all day."

Bethany smiled and gave Frankie a nuzzle with her nose on his cheek. "You are such a cutie-pie," she said to the baby.

Frankie immediately grabbed her ponytail—and hung on.

"Oops," Theo said. He stepped close to Bethany, so close he could smell her shampoo, and tried to gently extricate the baby's fist from her hair. No go.

Bethany smiled. "Well, thanks, but as long as he doesn't start pulling, I'm fine."

Frankie pulled.

"Owie," she said, laughing. "How are you all of what— twenty pounds?—and so strong?"

Theo gave the baby's neck a little tickle, and Frankie laughed and magically let go.

"Success!" Theo said. He held out his arms for the baby, and Bethany handed him over. He kissed Frankie's impossibly soft cheek as Bethany straightened her ponytail.

They went back inside for the rest of the tour. He led her upstairs and showed her his bedroom. He tried not to look at his king-size bed, because he'd immediately imagine Bethany lying naked on his sheets. He hurriedly showed her the two guest rooms.

"Wow, so there are three en suite bathrooms up here," she said, eyeing the marble floor, "and then a full and half bath downstairs. Good Lord."

He nodded. "Told you, my folks spared no expense for comfort. I'll live here forever, and one day my children will and my grandchildren and so on and so on."

She smiled thoughtfully. "That's the first time I've heard you say the words *my children*."

He felt a frown tugging at his mouth and tried to keep his expression neutral. "Well, in the future, I mean. The distant future. Far distant."

She bit her lip and nodded, then quickly turned. "Thanks for the tour. Your house is amazing. How it manages to be so welcoming and cozy, I can't understand."

He wouldn't tell her about the interior designer he'd hired with exactly those directives.

"I have my own set of Frankie's favorite toys in a chest in the living room," he said. "Up for building a very short tower of blocks?"

"Always," she said with a smile.

They sat down on the plush rug, Theo opening the toy chest and taking out the big pouch with the blocks inside. Bethany set Frankie down, and he immediately pulled up on the chest and looked inside.

"Ooh, is he walking yet?" Bethany asked, her arm protectively stretching out behind the baby.

"No," Theo said. "He's pulling up a lot but still hasn't taken his first steps. I sure hope he doesn't tonight while we're babysitting. Jace and Tamara will definitely want to see that big milestone themselves."

"Hear that, Frankie?" Bethany said. "Save your first steps for your parents!"

Frankie moved backward and plopped down to sit. Theo poured out the blocks, and for the next twenty minutes, they watched the baby pick up blocks and set them back down. He hasn't started stacking yet, but according to Jace, that should be coming soon.

After blocks, they watched Frankie crawl around the rug to look at the toys they'd set up. Frankie really loved a certain stuffed monkey and grabbed it, shaking it like crazy. A half hour later, after rounds of peekaboo and a made-up story by Uncle Theo about a calf named Bugz, Frankie started yawning.

"Right on time," Theo said. "Seven thirty and beddy-bye time."

"I guess you'll change him and then put him in the play-pen?" Bethany asked.

"Yup. You can have the honors, if you'd like."

Her beautiful face lit up. "I am actually dying to change a diaper. It's been a few years."

He laughed. "Be my guest—*please*." They headed into the bathroom, which had a diaper station for Frankie. He stood in the doorway while she laid Frankie down and gave his tummy a tickle, then made quick work of changing his diaper and zipping his pj's back up.

"All done," she said, scooping up the baby and cuddling him close. "You are so precious," she whispered.

She looked so beautiful, the expression on her face so moving that Theo took his phone from his pocket and quickly snapped a photo. Bethany looked at him in surprise.

No one was more surprised than *he* was.

"I'll send it to you," he said.

"Why'd you take it?" she asked, putting him on the spot. Not purposely, he could see. She was looking at him with genuine curiosity.

"Just the look on your face," he said honestly. "Like Frankie is the eighth wonder of the world."

She laughed. "I kind of feel that way. Babies are remarkable."

He held up the photo on his phone.

"Aww, I see now," she said. She put her hand over her heart.

He quickly texted her the photo, then put his phone away before he got in more trouble.

Back in the living room, Bethany laid Theo down in the playpen. He stretched out, his eyes drifting closed, then opening, then closing again. He let out a little whine and seemed to be fighting sleep, but then he closed his eyes for good, his bow lips quirking up a bit.

"Could it really be that easy?" she asked. "I definitely don't remember that from babysitting my niece and nephews."

"They did say Frankie was easy, and I guess it wasn't a lie to get me to babysit." He chuckled, gently caressing the baby's soft brown hair. "I've watched him a few times over the past year, and he hasn't always been so compliant."

Bethany laughed and looked down at the baby. "Well, Frankie, thank you for the great reintroduction to baby care. Good night."

Theo gave his little nephew one last sweet look. "Now to the kitchen so I can make dinner," he said, leading the way. But he quickly stopped. "Why don't you sit and relax in the living room. Are you tired?" he asked, peering at her. "I read on a pregnancy website that women get more fatigued as the months progress."

Bethany stopped in her tracks. "Pregnancy website? Were you doing some research?"

He bit his lip. "Just a little. To see what you'd be going through."

Bethany burst into tears. She covered her face with her hands.

Okay, this was unexpected. "What did I say? Bethany?"

She dropped her hands and wiped under her eyes. "You're everything I want, Theo Abernathy. A man who's reading up on month four of pregnancy? Rare. Trust me. It's just all too much. Everything."

Ah. Now he felt like a bigger heel than he had all along. Especially because they'd both shaken on friendship again. The big problem was that he couldn't be her friend. And he'd been unwittingly making her feel like he was the man of her dreams.

"Theo, I like you—a lot." She bit her lip, her beautiful eyes full of...disappointment. Sadness. *Oh, Bethany.* "And to protect myself, like I said yesterday I had to do, I'm gonna go. I can't do this. How can we be friends when there's so much more between us? That's not going to work."

He sucked in a breath. He wished he could say the right thing. But what was that? What could he say? He felt how he felt.

"I understand, Bethany. I wish I could just make you dinner first, though. I make a really good Bolognese sauce."

"You're making things worse, not better, Theo." She gave him a shaky smile. "I'm gonna go."

He should be grateful that she was making this so much easier for him. She was the one ending their friendship. She was letting him off the hook.

But the sharp ache in his chest told him that, once again, he didn't understand why he was feeling so torn up about it.

You're not willing to really think about how much you feel for Bethany.

She walked over to the playpen and bent down. "Good night, sweet Frankie." Then she straightened and headed for the door.

He followed, his stomach twisting when she opened the door. *Don't let her walk out of your life.*

He had to. For both their sakes.

He walked her to her car, and she got in without a word. She did look at him briefly before turning to reverse. And then she was gone.

CHAPTER THIRTEEN

HIS HEART HEAVY, Theo went back inside and paced in front of the wall of windows. What the hell he was supposed to do?

He paced and sat, paced and sat. He spent a good twenty minutes just watching his nephew sleep, the little chest rising and falling.

"I'm sorry, Frankie, but I'm not ready for you—my *own* you. That's just the truth."

With that clear in his head, he wheeled the playpen into his home office, which he'd turned into his podcast recording studio. He got everything set up to record the start of a new episode, an intro about the rancher he'd be interviewing in a few days.

As he hit Record and started speaking, he realized about twenty minutes later that he'd recorded the entire introduction and Frankie never made a peep.

"Well, my *own* baby won't be easy like you are," Theo said as he wheeled the playpen back into the living room and then set the diaper bag next to it. Jace and Tamara would be stopping by any minute to pick up their son. "And Bethany's baby will be a really difficult baby, probably," he said. "Murphy's law, right?" He tried to smile since it was just a joke, but he couldn't.

And suddenly, Theo himself could burst into tears. Something was just very wrong with him right now. His emotions were all over the place. He didn't even know this Theo Abernathy. It was as though *he* was the hormonal one.

His phone pinged with a text, which he hoped was from Bethany, but it was Jace. They were here and didn't want to ring the doorbell just in case it woke Frankie.

He opened the door as Tamara and Jace came up the steps.

"Was Frankie a good little guy for you and Bethany?" Tamara asked.

"Frankie was great. I, on the other hand..." Theo said with a frown.

"What's wrong?" Tamara asked, peering behind him and realizing that Bethany wasn't there.

"It's a long story," he said as they came inside. "No, it's a short story."

"What, Theo?" Tamara asked, looking at him with concern.

He sighed and dropped down on the edge of the sofa. "Bethany's pregnant and I'm crazy about her. But I'm not ready to be a dad. It's not what I want right now. So I need to let her go. Not that it's my choice—I upset her and she left."

"But you saw how easy taking care of Frankie is," Jace said. "To be very honest, it's why I asked you to babysit."

Theo narrowed his eyes at his brother. "I thought you asked because no one else was available."

Jace had the decency to look sheepish. "Okay, fine, Robin and Stacy were both free tonight. And Mom and Dad. But after our last conversation about Bethany, I wanted you to see what a total joy a baby is. And that they sleep a lot."

"I did get to see that," Theo admitted. "I even got the intro of this week's podcast done. Frankie napped like a champ. But I don't kid myself that that's what parenthood is like."

"You shouldn't," Tamara said. "Parenthood is no cakewalk. It's the most rewarding thing I've ever experienced, but it's also hard. You're right to take your time in figuring out how you feel."

Theo nodded. "Except Bethany left because we can't even be *friends*."

"Bro," Jace said. "Fix that."

"How? How can I be friends with a woman I'd marry in a heartbeat if she wasn't pregnant?"

Tamara stared at him. "God, Theo. Did you hear what you just said?"

"What?" he asked, looking from Jace to Tamara, who were staring at each other in a kind of disbelief.

"Theo, honey, think about it," Tamara said gently. "That's your job for tonight. Think long and hard about what you just said."

Theo dropped his head back and ran a hand through his hair. "I *can't* think. It's why I'm at this stalemate with myself."

"So you're gonna give up the woman you *would* marry because she's pregnant?" Jace asked. "Dude."

"If he doesn't want to be a father yet," Tamara said, "then he's doing the right thing."

I am, right? Theo wondered. *How could the right thing feel so wrong, though?*

But what else could he do? He wasn't ready for his entire life to change so drastically in five months.

"Maybe I'm just too set in my ways," Theo said.

Jace nodded. "Nothing wrong with knowing who you are and what you want. That's why you're pushing back against the idea of fatherhood. Because of how responsible you'd be if you had a child."

Exactly what he'd thought in Hey, Baby when he'd encountered the bickering parents.

But it just left him more confused than ever.

"Sometimes," Jace added, "when I'm really busy and Frankie is sick or cranky, and Tamara and I can't get a sitter, I envy your carefree life. But honestly, I don't right now. This is tough stuff."

Yeah, Theo thought, his heart aching. It was.

CHAPTER FOURTEEN

AT EIGHT THIRTY the next morning, Bethany sat at the kitchen table of her mother's house, drinking decaf and trying to concentrate on her mother's lists. Raye McCreery had four going, all on paper in her notebook—the old-fashioned way.

Thank heavens they'd had these early-morning plans. Because Bethany had woken up all puffy eyed from crying and needing a comforting place to go. And that was always her mother. It was hard to leave Theo's last night and go home to all those reminders of him in her spare bedroom. In the *nursery*. She'd tossed and turned and kept waking up.

"Okay," her mom said, tapping her pen against the page, "I have the necessity list, the wish list, the get-it-before-the-baby-comes list and the get-it-after list." She took a sip of her coffee. "Let's start with necessities. I can cross off or add, so this is just off the top of my head and from consulting lists online."

Bethany instantly thought of Theo googling away on his phone to find out what was happening in month four of pregnancy. *Don't think about him*, she ordered herself.

But how could she not? Especially when she and her mom were talking about things she needed for the baby.

"Okay," her mom said, taking a sip of her coffee, then grabbing her pen and reading from the list labeled *Necessities*. "Infant car seat. Stroller. Crib. Maybe a bassinet too that can be easily moved. A playpen—portable. Changing table and pad. Maybe a dresser combo, even though you have a dresser in the spare bedroom. Infant bathtub, baby wash, thermometer, infant OTC medications, pj's, onesies, socks, booties, diapers, ointments, and cornstarch." She tapped her pen at the end of the list. "My goodness—those are just the necessities! And I might be forgetting a few things."

Bethany started mentally adding up the costs of some of that—what she didn't already have. Goodness, people weren't kidding when they said children were expensive. "Well, you can cross a few things off the list," Bethany said. "In my spare bedroom—in the nursery, I should say—is now a beautiful bassinet with an adorable mobile that plays lullabies and spins little dangling stuffed animals, a top-of-the-line baby bouncer, a changing table, ten newborn-sized pj's and a pair of baby booties." Plus the pair of yellow pj's and a stuffed rabbit she'd bought the day she'd found out she was pregnant.

"You bought all that?" Raye asked, surprise on her face.

"Actually, they were gifts," Bethany said. "From Theo Abernathy."

Her mother tilted her head. "Theo Abernathy—one of Bonnie and Asa's sons, right?"

She nodded. Everyone knew the Abernathys in Bronco, whether you lived in the Heights or the Valley. They were a prominent, altruistic family and their names came up often, particularly around the holidays, since they did a lot of sponsoring.

"There has to be a story here," her mom said. Waiting.

Bethany inwardly sighed. Talking about it would just get her all upset again. But she needed to get it all out—and hear her mother's thoughts.

"Let me catch you up," Bethany said, and it all came

pouring out. Starting with Theo at the wedding, then the latest about Rexx, then more about Theo, ending with what happened last night.

"Oh, Bethany," her mother said, touching her arm. "That's a *lot*."

She nodded. "And now it's over. Before it even began. Wait, scratch that. It did begin."

"Yeah, I'd say quite a bit happened in your relationship. Do you really think he's just going to walk away? I can't see how."

Bethany wouldn't have thought so either. But last night, he'd sounded so resolute. Just as he always had.

"He knows how he feels about being a parent right now," Bethany said. "That's never changed. He just happened to fall in like with a woman who's pregnant."

Her mother sipped her coffee. "Sounds more like love to me."

I wish. If he did love her, he'd never be able to let her go. So of course he didn't love her.

"He's just a nice guy," Bethany said, feeling tears poke at her eyes.

"There's a difference between nice and inviting you on a walk around his family ranch. Ordering a bassinet and mobile and assembling both. Buying ten pairs of pj's in the correct size. Making you pizza. Inviting you to babysit with him. Offering to make you spaghetti Bolognese."

"Don't forget the baby booties," Bethany said—and then she did cry.

"Oh, honey." Her mom got up and stood behind Bethany's chair and wrapped her arms around her. "The man is going through big changes. He met you and didn't expect to have his feelings challenged."

Huh. She hadn't really thought about it that way.

"I have a good feeling about the two of you, honey," her mom added.

Bethany brightened a bit at that. "Elizabeth said she did too. But I'm afraid to hope. I thought leaving his house before he had a chance to make me that romantic-sounding dinner meant I was going to save myself from a world of hurt. But I'm hurting, anyway."

In fact, she was *physically* hurting. Her belly—low in her belly—was suddenly cramping. She put her hand where the sharp pain was coming from. "Ow," she said, frowning.

"Bethany?" her mom asked. "What's wrong?"

"Ow," she said again, doubling over.

"I'm taking you to the emergency clinic right now," her mom said, sounding panicked. "Can you stand?"

Bethany tried to move and winced.

"I'm going to call your OB. Honey, hang on, okay? I'll be right back." Her mother ran from the room to get her phone.

Bethany let out a bunch of short breaths, hoping it would ease the pain. But the sharp, stabbing sensations kept coming.

What was this? Something to worry about? Something serious? Or normal aches and pains? She couldn't remember reading about a stabbing pain in the lower belly.

Scared out of her mind, Bethany felt a little better when her mother rushed back into the kitchen, on the phone with the OB. "Dr. Rangely wants you to go the hospital right away. She's at the clinic, but she'll meet us there."

Bethany let her mother ease her up from the chair. *Please let everything be okay*, she prayed.

Suddenly, all she wanted besides good news about the pains was Theo by her side.

AFTER A ROUGH night of thinking about Bethany and all that had happened, how they'd left things last night, Theo finally got out of bed and took a hot shower.

He stared at himself in the mirror—he looked like hell, like a man who hadn't slept. Like a man who'd lost something precious to him.

He threw his towel at the mirror and got dressed, then sucked down a cup of coffee. He had to do something to fix things between him and Bethany—something to clear the air.

And then what? He didn't feel differently. He couldn't change anything. He just hated the way she'd left. The way he'd let her just leave.

He grabbed his car keys and headed out. He had a vague idea that he'd pick up something for Bethany in town—what, he didn't know. As he was about to pass Kendra's Cupcakes, he decided an array of cupcakes would be a nice gesture.

A gesture. Small. Impersonal. Nothing confusing about a box of cupcakes. It would just let her know he was sorry.

It wasn't good enough. But it was something.

He'd drop off the cupcakes at her apartment, she'd say thank you, and then he would leave and at least there wouldn't be the same awful energy between them.

Once he'd given his order to Kendra, he turned to find none other than Winona Cobbs in line behind him in her trademark purple outfit. He heard laughter and glanced over to see her fiancé, Stanley Sanchez, at the far end of the bakery, chatting with a group.

He looked back to Winona. She was staring at Theo. No expression at all. Just staring. Could she *know* what had happened between him and Bethany last night?

"Morning, Winona," he said, tipping his hat. "I was, uh, thinking of calling you to schedule an appointment." He leaned a bit closer and whispered, "I could use a little wisdom."

He was really doing it. Making an appointment with a psychic. That was how unsettled he was.

"I'll save you the trip," she said, lifting her chin. "What's meant to happen *will*," she added, then practically pushed past him to get to the counter.

He turned to stare at her back, hoping for a little elaboration once she'd ordered.

Her coffee drink in hand, she turned and eyed him. "Like I said, you think you know what you want. But you don't." With that, she simply walked away. He watched her approach Stanley's table, the gentleman pulling out a chair for her.

What he *wanted* was Bethany *and* his life to go on exactly as it always had. That was not going to change. It was also not going to happen.

He sighed and stopped at a chair by the door to call Bethany to make sure she was home; he couldn't exactly leave a box of cupcakes in her unairconditioned tiny lobby on a hot July day. He planned to say that he felt bad about how they'd left things last night and wanted to drop off some treats. He had no idea if she'd hit End Call or if she'd say okay. He never found out because the call went straight to voice mail.

Maybe she was at rehearsal with her band? No—because a black-haired guy in a leather vest at a table in the corner was easily recognizable from the band photo on Bethany's mantel.

Could be that she just wasn't answering, that she was avoiding him, planning to cut him out, ghost him, that she was done.

Not that he could blame her. But now that he was faced with the actual end of their relationship, he couldn't stand it. He cared too much about Bethany McCreery to never talk to her again. To not know how she was doing, feeling, if she needed anything, whether to satisfy a craving or for her baby.

He'd text her. If she didn't respond, he'd have to respect that she didn't want to hear from him.

He typed a simple sentence: Can I stop by for a few minutes?

And waited.

No response.

His heart clenched. For a minute, he could barely breathe.

He had to get through his thick skull that she was done with him.

Theo closed his eyes for a second and got ahold of himself, then headed out, determined to drop off the stupid cupcakes in the ranch office, then hit the range like he always did when he needed to clear his head.

He'd just gotten into his car when his phone pinged with a text. Bethany.

At the clinic's ER. Having bad pains. I'm so scared.

Theo's heart started racing. Bad pains? What could that mean?

On my way, he texted back, then dropped his phone and started the car.

She had to be okay. The baby had to be okay.

He was definitely *not* okay.

BETHANY SAT ON the cot in the recovery room, staring at the curtain pulled around her for privacy. Her OB and the ER doctor had assured her everything was fine—with her and the baby—but they both wanted her to rest in their care for a good half hour before she was discharged. Her mother had gone out to the backyard where there were some tables and chairs to call her father and brother with an update. Just normal bad cramping that might happen occasionally, but Bethany had done the right thing by calling her OB and coming in to be checked out.

Now that she knew the baby was okay, she wished she hadn't texted Theo. What had she been thinking? She knew, actually. Despite what had happened between them last night, when she'd been scared and worried, she'd immediately thought of *him*, wanted *him* by her side.

That was how much he'd come to mean to her. How much she trusted him. Despite everything.

And within seconds, he'd texted back that he was on his way. She'd thought about texting him again that it was a false alarm, no need to come, but she didn't want to do that while she knew he was driving.

She heard his voice from down the hall; he was asking the nurse at the reception desk where to find her. Next she heard footsteps coming her way. Then his voice. "Bethany?"

"Come on in," she called.

He was holding a large box from Kendra's Cupcakes. She hadn't been craving cupcakes, but now she suddenly had to have one.

"Are you okay?" he asked in a rush. "Is the baby okay? What did the doctor say?" His green eyes held so much concern.

She told him what both the ER doc and her OB had said, and she could visibly see him relax, his shoulders unbunching, the color coming back in his face.

That he cared about her had never been in question.

He put the cupcakes on the bedside table and sat in the chair at her side, then held out his arms and she leaned into them, let him hold her.

Tears streamed down her cheeks, and she knew she was

crying from the scare and because of how good it felt to be in the warm comfort of Theo Abernathy's arms.

"I'm so relieved," he said, stroking her hair. "I was so scared, Bethany."

"Me too. That was the first time I'd been hit with pains like that. I was at my mom's house when my belly started hurting out of the blue."

"I'm so glad you weren't alone," he said.

Alone. She'd gotten lucky that she'd been at her mom's. But what if the pains happened again and she was alone? She'd be nervous all over again, and Theo would be the one she'd want beside her.

This was crazy. They weren't even friends anymore.

"I'm sorry about the way I ran out last night," she said. "Self-preservation, particularly when pregnant, must be a thing."

She mentally shook her head. She definitely hadn't meant to say that.

"I totally understand, Bethany. I wish I—" He paused and but didn't have to finish the sentence. She knew.

This was a lost cause. She had to let him go. He wasn't going to magically change just because she was in love.

Oh, God. She closed her eyes at the monumental truth. She was in love with Theo Abernathy.

Now she knew why it felt so good *and* hurt so bad to be in his arms.

He held her for a few more seconds, then pulled back when footsteps could be heard coming their way. "Bethany, you decent?"

Her brother.

She gave Theo's hand a squeeze, and he stood up and moved to the side of the small room. "If you consider my flowered hospital gown decent, sure."

Jake, along with their parents and Elizabeth, came in, a

flurry of questions and hugs and kisses. They all seemed to freeze with surprise when they noticed Theo, then gathered themselves to nod or say hello.

"Well, I'll leave you to your family," Theo said. "There are enough cupcakes to go around," he added, pointing at the big box.

For the millionth time since her brother's wedding, all she could think was *Oh, Theo.*

CHAPTER FIFTEEN

"FOR GOD'S SAKE, Theo, just go see her," Billy said.

"Put us all out of our misery," Jace added. "Yourself included."

Theo glanced up at his brothers at their desks in the ranch office, the conversation registering but barely. It was almost 4:00 p.m. and he'd been distracted by thoughts of Bethany all day. He'd shaken salt in his coffee when he'd arrived this morning, despite the fact that the salt-shaker required twisting. He'd walked into the wall instead of through the bathroom door. And he'd been unable to make sense of anything he was looking at on his desktop monitor.

Billy took a sip of his coffee. "You've been staring at the same spreadsheet of figures for the past twenty minutes, Theo. Just go talk to Bethany, tell her you love her and are looking forward to fatherhood, and then everyone will be happy."

"I second that motion," Jace said.

From the moment Theo had arrived in the office—after leaving the clinic, he'd taken a ride out on the range to stare at the cattle and mountains—his brothers had been full of advice. None he could take. Jace had told Billy everything that had happened last night—right in front of Theo, so he knew every word was correct.

"You want to marry this woman but you're now not even friends?" Billy asked.

Theo sighed. "It's a moot point. You can stop bringing it up. I only used that word last night to drive home how hard this all is. Yeah, I could see myself getting very serious with Bethany if she wasn't pregnant. Other than that, she's everything I've been looking for. All the feelings I've been looking for."

His brothers were staring at him like he'd grown an extra head.

"Theo," Billy started to say in his I'm-the-older-brother voice.

He held up a hand. "Billy, we—Jace and Tamara and I—talked it out last night. If I'm not ready, I'm not ready. So why should I go see Bethany now? She's fine, just had a scare, and we can both move on with our lives now."

Jace laughed. "I don't recall us reaching any kind of conclusion last night. What I do know is that this morning, the woman informed you that she was having pains and you rushed to the clinic. Neither of you has moved on, Theo."

Theo sighed hard. He took a long slug of his coffee, which still had the faint taste of salt. "I ran into Winona Cobbs at Kendra's Cupcakes this morning. She told me, 'What's meant to happen will.' At first I didn't really get it—it sounded like what I'd pull out of a fortune cookie. But I've been thinking about it all morning, and now I understand the message. What's meant to happen is absolutely nothing."

Jace shook his head. "You're kidding, right? You're on a speeding train to fatherhood, bro. Go get some cigars now."

Billy laughed. "Sorry, Theo, but I agree. I happen to have a few cigars leftover from when Charlotte first told me she was pregnant."

Theo scowled, and his brothers cracked up even harder. Great. Like he needed this?

"In all seriousness, Theo," Jace said, "you should go check in on Bethany. Code of the West pretty much insists on it."

He narrowed his eyes at Jace. "I was thinking I should, anyway. I mean, I do care about the woman."

Billy nodded. "Go now. You'll have to stop to pick up something since you gave the cupcakes to her family." He and Jace shared a grin that Theo caught. "Whatever Bethany is having cravings for."

"Give me some good suggestions," Theo said.

"Charlotte's been craving sour cream and onion potato chips," Billy said. "But my ex only wanted sharp cheddar cheese with a certain kind of crumbly crackers I had to drive forty-five minutes to get."

Billy had gone through a rough divorce, but because he was so in love with fiancée Charlotte Taylor, he could talk about his marriage without the haunted look in his eyes. Now that they were expecting a baby, they liked the idea of getting married before the little one arrived and they were in the throes of wedding planning. Billy had even asked if Theo would check with Bethany about her band performing at the reception. He had no doubt Bethany would be touched about that.

And Theo had to admit that seeing his older brother so happy made Theo feel like anything was possible.

Except when it came to him and fatherhood.

But at the very least, he and Bethany McCreery *were* friends—no matter what either of them said.

"Fine," Theo said. "I'll stop by the diner and bring her an early dinner."

His brothers were chuckling as he left. But as Theo stood to the side of the porch to straighten his Stetson, he also heard Jace say, "The poor guy doesn't know what he's in for."

And Billy respond, "I think he actually does."

Theo scowled again. More doublespeak like Winona! The only thing that was going to happen was that he and Bethany would have to figure out how to be friends. They cared about each other too much to walk away.

He'd go pick up food for Bethany, then stop by for a half hour and bring up the idea of giving friendship another try. What else could they do, right?

He went to the Gemstone Diner, since he knew she liked the place, and texted her.

I'm at the diner and thought I'd stop by with dinner. Craving anything?

Perfect. Sounded like he just happened to be there. And happened to think of her.

Three dots appeared and then disappeared, then reappeared.

Okay, I finally narrowed it down. I'd love a Western omelet with home fries and an English muffin with strawberry jam. And thanks!

Actually, that sounded good to him too. But butter instead of jam.

With cheddar cheese, she added with a smiley face wearing a cowboy hat.

Coming right up, he texted back.

Fifteen minutes later, their orders in hand, he got back in his car and drove to her apartment. She buzzed him in, and when he neared the top step, he could see her standing in the doorway looking so beautiful.

He held up the bag. "I got the same thing as you."

Bethany smiled. "I'm dying for those home fries."

She stopped in the kitchen to grab two bottles of water, and then they sat at the little round table by the window, Theo taking out containers and packets of the strawberry jam for her.

"Did you get cheddar too?" she asked, eyeing the bite of omelet midway to this mouth.

"Actually, it's Swiss."

"Oooh, I'll trade you a bite," she said, her eyes lit up.

Theo laughed. "Deal."

They sure seemed like friends. This was going great.

"I guess we are friends, whether we like it or not," she said as though reading his mind. "And *good* friends, at that."

He smiled and nodded. "We just have to go with it, I guess." *What's meant to happen will*, he thought suddenly, Winona Cobbs's words echoing in his head.

Maybe he'd been wrong about what he thought she'd meant. That *nothing* would happen. Now he was pretty sure Winona had meant that he and Bethany were meant to be friends.

With just crumbs on their plates, Bethany let out a big yawn. He got up and cleaned up the table.

"Thanks, Theo," she said, moving over to the sofa and stretching out. "How about a movie. Thriller?"

"Sounds great," he said. Friendly. And it was early too. He'd be home by eight and would work on his interview questions for the podcast episode.

Yes, this friendship thing was working out fine.

He took the bag and empty containers into the kitchen, and by the time he was back with a bowl of popcorn and more water, Bethany was out cold. He smiled as he watched her sleep, her long, silky hair falling across her face. He moved the strands behind her ear.

Before he could think too much about it, he scooped

her up, her arms slinging around his neck with a little sigh that almost undid him. He felt it right in the strain behind his zipper.

"My hero," she murmured as though she were half-asleep, half-awake.

I'm no one's hero, he wanted to say. But for the moment, he liked the sentiment.

He laid her down on her bed, glad she was wearing a T-shirt and yoga pants, which were pajama-like. He slid the blanket folded on the edge of her bed up and over her, and she snuggled in and turned with another sigh, her eyes closed.

He couldn't imagine leaving. As a precaution, he figured he'd stay the night on the couch, just in case she woke up at some point and was disoriented. Or had another scare.

Or just needed...a friend.

BETHANY WOKE TO the remnants of another of those vivid, intense pregnancy dreams. Theo had carried her to her bed from the sofa, kissing her all the way there, then laid her down on top of her quilt and peeled off her yoga pants, then her T-shirt. His hands and mouth had roamed everywhere, and finally he'd taken off her bra, feasting on her breasts, then inched down her underwear. He'd started taking off his own T-shirt, revealing rock-hard abs and a faint line of dark hair disappearing into the waistband of his jeans. Oh, how she'd wanted those off. But just as he'd been about to flick the button of his jeans, her eyes had opened.

She was alone in her bedroom. Fully dressed. A strand of hair across her cheek.

Theo was not in bed with her.

Eyes opened wide, she sat up, not sure what time it was. What day it was.

And she remembered—one-sixteenth of her dream had

actually been real. Theo had picked her up off the sofa, where she'd been dozing after dinner, and carried her to her bedroom. Not a single kiss. But he had laid her down on her bed.

And left the room.

Was he still here? Probably not. She eyed the alarm clock on the bedside table—1:22 a.m.

She got out of bed and walked lightly to the door, which was ajar, and then pushed it open with a finger, peering into the living room. The lights were all out. The table where they'd had dinner was clear and smelled faintly of the citrus wood cleaner she kept under the sink.

She smiled at how thoughtful the man was. As she stepped farther into the living room, she gasped—Theo Abernathy was stretched out on the sofa, her chenille throw half covering his legs and torso. The moonlight coming from the window softly illuminated him, his thick, tousled dark hair, the fringe of dark eyelashes against his cheeks. The way his shoulders filled out that Henley T-shirt.

Part of her, a big part, wanted to take off her clothes and wake him up with a kiss. Or more. In the dream, he'd been about to unbutton his jeans. She could simply finish that for him.

If she were more brazen.

If they were on the same page.

She tiptoed over to him and pulled the throw up a bit since the windows were open to bring in the summer night breeze. His eyes opened.

"Mmm," he whispered—as if he'd been having a hot dream of his own.

"Sorry I woke you," she said. "I just wanted to pull the blanket up a little."

He sat up, running a hand through his hair. "I didn't want to just leave while you were asleep. I thought I'd sit on the sofa till you woke up, but you never did and I guess I fell asleep too."

"You're a sweet guy, Theo," she said, unable to take her eyes off him as her dream replayed in her head. "I had a really sexy dream about you," she dared to add.

"Oh, yeah?" he asked, his voice a bit ragged.

She nodded. "You carried me to my bed, but instead of leaving the room, you undressed me. Touched me, kissed me everywhere. You were about to take off your jeans when I woke up."

She saw him swallow.

She wanted the dream to become reality. All of it.

Every inch of her body was tingling. With desire. Need.

Go for it, she told herself. *Put yourself out there. You want this man. Even if it's just for tonight, you'll always have the memories.*

"I think we can make that dream come true," she said before she chickened out.

He was looking at her, intently, desire in the green depths of his eyes. His expression was serious, as though he was restraining himself, controlling the urge to pull her onto him.

"And I'm not talking about friends with benefits," she said. "That never works. I'm talking about just tonight. One night only."

"Are you sure?" he whispered.

"One hundred percent."

He studied her for a moment, and she knew he was giving her time to back out and making a decision himself.

He took her hands and gently tugged her toward him so that there was nowhere to go but on him, to straddle him. Her softness met his hardness, and she wrapped her arms around his neck, pressing into him. He groaned and kissed her. A long, hot, passionate kiss.

Then he picked her up and carried her toward the bedroom. "Tell me everything I did in the dream," he said.

She smiled as her nerve endings lit up. "You kissed me the entire way to my bed."

He bent to kiss her, his tongue trailing along her lips, then down to her neck and collarbone. She moaned and scratched at his back. If he could get her this hot and bothered by kissing her...

He used his foot to push open her bedroom door, then resumed kissing her all the way to the bed.

As he laid her down and then covered her body with his own, but propped up on his strong forearms, he said, "It's safe?"

"Absolutely," she assured him. "Doc said so."

His hand was cupping her cheek, and he was looking at her suddenly with more tenderness than desire.

Noooo. Please do not get up. Please do not say this is a bad idea. For tonight, it's a great idea.

"I've wanted to rip your clothes off from the moment I saw you on stage at your brother's wedding," he said. "And every day since."

"Same here."

He was looking at her again, giving her time to tell him they couldn't do this, shouldn't do this. That it would only make her want him more. And who knew how it would affect him?

She bit her lip. She should put a stop to this.

But she looked at his face, his gorgeous face, and the muscles of his arms, his long, strong body, and she wanted him so badly that the fallout would be worth it. No matter what the future brought, they would have tonight.

"To tonight," she said. "I'm raising a pretend drink. A Shirley Temple."

He smiled. "To tonight."

And then her dream started to come true, bit by bit. Her T-shirt was peeled off, and she heard his sharp intake of breath as he gazed at her breasts barely contained by the bra that had recently become too small. A moment of insecurity hit her. Would the baby bump send him running?

It didn't. His hands didn't sweep over it, but then again, at the moment, they were headed north, caressing her breasts, his mouth following. She wasn't sure if he was purposely trying to be tender, but everything he did was just right.

The bra had a front closure, and she undid it, the serious anticipation on his face making her toes curl. His hands and mouth and tongue explored every bit of her bare breasts and her nipples, one moment tenderly, the next passionately, and both felt so damned good.

She reached to get his shirt off, and he lifted his arms. His chest, his shoulders, his stomach—all things of muscled beauty. His body was rock hard, rancher hard. He carefully flipped them so that she was on top of him. She dragged her lips down his neck, across his collarbone to his pecs. Then she kissed a trail lower to his stomach. Finally, they were up to the part of the dream where his jeans would be unbuttoned. She took care of that, his eyes never leaving her face, and as she pulled down the zipper he groaned and sat up, getting the jeans off and making quick work of taking off her yoga pants.

Now they were both in their underwear. His gaze traveled her body, and he groaned, his hands back on her breasts, one going into her hair as he lay back down. She moved against him and he groaned again, then reached to peel off her underwear. She shimmied it off.

Bethany straddled him, using her teeth to pull down his sexy black boxer briefs.

As he got them the rest the way off, she wrapped a hand

around his impressive erection, tightly, and he arched his back and almost grunted, delighting her. She moved her hand up and down, lying on top of him and kissing his chest and neck.

His mouth fused to hers, he flipped her over again. She could feel him reaching down to the floor as if looking for something. He had his jeans in his hands, then his wallet, then a foil-wrapped condom. Theo Abernathy, always prepared.

She did the honors, his groans and eyes closing in concentration to control himself making her feel like the sexiest woman alive.

And then he was inside her, thrusting gently at first, again obviously trying to keep in control, and then so passionately she screamed and dug her nails into his shoulders.

Waves of sensation released in such pleasure that she screamed his name and felt him thrusting hard, exploding at the same time. She pulled him into her embrace, spent and sated.

One night of that—this—would never be enough. How could she ever get enough of this man? Or let him go?

"That was amazing," he whispered, stroking her hair. "*You're* amazing."

"Takes two to tango," she said with a grin and kissed his cheek. It might be last time she got to do that. She'd take every moment of tonight. It had to last for the rest of her life. Because she couldn't imagine ever feeling this way about another man.

A lump formed in her throat, and she blinked back threatening tears.

She loved him. She loved Theo Abernathy.

"Bethany, in all honesty, there's no way this can be a onetime thing for me."

She could have cried. She squeezed her eyes shut, so

moved, so hopeful, and then propped up on an elbow. "What are you saying?"

"I'm saying I can't get enough of you. That's all I know."

She inwardly gasped. The very thought she'd had about him. Her heart soared. She could almost hear her friends whispering in her ear to be careful. As much as they were all for this romance and its possibilities, her besties had cautioned her to believe what he *said* even if his actions said something else—like that he loved her. "It's the same for me, Theo. Maybe we should just take this one day a time. No labels. No talking about the future."

He nodded. "Deal." He kissed her on the lips, nestled beside her and wrapped his arms around her. She rested her head on his chest, so in love she thought she might burst.

She had no idea what would happen in five months. Heck, she had no idea what would happen next week or even tomorrow.

But they were together right now, naked and breathing hard, neither willing to walk away from this beautiful encounter they'd had.

And she was going with it.

CHAPTER SIXTEEN

WITH EACH PASSING day since Theo had first slept with Bethany, he was more and more of a wreck. He couldn't sleep. He couldn't concentrate.

And despite his worries about dating a pregnant woman, he couldn't get enough of Bethany.

Just like he'd told her the night they'd slept together and had kept telling her in the three days that had passed since. He'd stayed over that night, so enthralled by her and how good they were in bed that he hadn't thought beyond the morning, when he'd gotten up early to make her breakfast. They'd spent the next two nights in his house, and when his brothers had seen him walking her out to her car in the mornings, they'd grinned and wolf whistled. In the office, he'd told him that he and Bethany were taking it day by day.

There'd been no talk about the future.

Jace had said he thought that was asking for trouble, because the future was right in front of his face in the form of Bethany's belly.

Billy had added that Theo might as well just accept now that his life was about to change with hers.

And Theo would smile and nod—while his stomach churned, his shoulders bunched, and his brain short-circuited. He'd never felt less like himself than the past few days.

That couldn't be good. Or right.

But he was trying. Trying to give this a chance, to be with Bethany, to think about exactly what this relationship would mean for him. The first morning he'd woken up with her, he'd thought that maybe he could do this. That maybe he had to stop being so stubborn, so selfish, if that was the right word. Was he being selfish by not wanting his great life to change so drastically—yet? He still wasn't sure about that.

But he was sure he wasn't ready.

This he kept from Bethany. He didn't want to play out his confusion with her. They'd agreed not to talk about the future—which was coming in under five months and then every day after that till forever. Maybe he had to give himself more time. To open himself up to change. To his life being turned upside down.

True to her word, she didn't bring up November, when she was due. She talked about the pregnancy but not about the delivery. And thereafter. Sometimes, he'd catch her deep in thought and knew she was worried, but he'd just take her hand or hold her in a sort of silent acknowledgment.

Maybe Jace was right—that he and Bethany were existing in a bubble where there was no baby to deal with. To take care of. And the rude awakening was coming fast.

Theo sighed hard and left the ranch office and walked the half mile to his cabin. In those fifteen minutes, he'd gone back and forth about it all. *Yes, I can do this. No, I can't.*

All he knew was that Bethany was worth all the soul-searching. He didn't have answers to the father question, but he knew *that.*

He pulled out his phone to check the time. In fifteen minutes, a new rancher was coming to be interviewed for Theo's *This Ranching Life* podcast. Theo admired the guy. Paul was in his early twenties, a new father to a three-month-old daughter, and had taken over his late grandfather's small, failing cattle ranch, determined to keep the family legacy going, to make his grandfather proud.

Theo was glad he'd made it a habit to arrange for the fees for the commercial spots to be paid into a fund to benefit ranchers in need. Like this young family. He hadn't missed the catch in the guy's voice when Theo had told him that he'd be turning over the revenue from the podcast episode to him. It was a good amount of money that would turn a corner for the ranch. Plus, *This Ranching Life* was popular in town and the county, and the new rancher would find himself getting emails and calls for freebies. Bronco was that kind of place.

Theo headed into his home office, where he'd just gotten the equipment set up when he heard a truck pulling up outside and went out to welcome his guest.

Theo couldn't have been more surprised to see Paul, a lanky blond in head-to-toe denim except for his brown leather cowboy boots, walking toward the porch holding a pink car seat—with a baby in it.

"Theo, I'm real sorry about this," Paul said, "but my wife is feeling really ill and I couldn't find a sitter. Maya here is a champion napper and she should fall asleep for a good hour and a half in about five minutes."

"Perfect," Theo said. "Beautiful baby," he added, bending a bit to play a round of peekaboo with Maya. Frankie loved peekaboo.

"Waaaah!" the baby girl screeched. Her face turned red.

"Sorry," Theo said to Paul. "Babies usually like me."

Paul smiled. "No worries. She's just cranky because she's tired. She'll be out like the ole light in a few."

Theo nodded. Frankie got fussy too when he was overtired.

He led the way inside the cabin and into his office.

Paul set the car seat on the floor next to his chair. When Paul removed his cowboy hat and set it on the table beside him, Theo could see the shadows under the man's eyes. He looked exhausted. He'd probably been up all night with the baby, just like Jace used to be when Frankie was under six months.

"Help yourself to coffee or juice," Theo said, gesturing at the refreshment credenza he always set up for these interviews along the back wall. There was a single-serving coffee maker and all the fixings and a small fridge with cold beverages. Theo used to have a basket of treats, like chips and pretzels and nuts, but after one rancher had crunched his way through the interview, Theo hadn't made that rookie mistake again.

Paul made himself a cup of coffee and sat down, checking on Maya, who wasn't asleep yet but was about to be. Her eyes kept fluttering closed.

Theo played the intro he'd recorded several days ago, the new rancher perking up with excitement as Theo discussed the Newton Ranch's history and how meaningful it was to Paul and his wife to continue the legacy. He'd worked at his grandfather's ranch from a young age and hoped to return the place to the successful, though small, cattle operation it had been when his grandfather was younger.

Theo got through one question before Maya began fussing. He stopped recording and let Paul try to settle his baby daughter. But she started crying.

"Sorry about this," Paul said, taking the baby from the car seat and holding her against him. He rocked her in his arms until her eyes got heavy again, then attempted to put her back in the car seat.

She screamed. Loudly.

"Oh, darn," Paul said. "This might not work today."

"It's no trouble. We can try again tomorrow if that's good for you."

Paul nodded and seemed disappointed. He bounced Maya in his arms. She screeched again, batting her fists. "I'd better get her home."

Theo watched the new dad take the moment to caress the baby's hair and coo at her a bit, telling her it was okay, that she was fine, that they were going back to see Mama. Paul seemed torn between loving his daughter and wishing he could do the podcast. Theo would make sure they got it done, if not for release this week, then for next week.

He assured Paul of that and watched the man leave, carefully holding the car seat. Theo could hear the baby crying even once Paul was at his truck, struggling to latch it into the back.

Theo watched out the window and sighed.

This was exactly what he didn't want for his own life. An opportunity ripped away because the baby had to come first, plain and simple.

He was supposed to go over to Bethany's tonight for dinner and to watch a movie. But he was afraid all his concerns and worries would manifest in him acting like a jerk—being quiet or distant.

And because she deserved much better than that, he'd tell her the truth, that he was very…uncomfortable with what he was facing in five months.

But the worst part was setting up Bethany to believe one thing and then blindsiding her.

And breaking her heart.

He couldn't bear that.

His phone pinged with a text. His dad.

Up for taking a shift with Thunderstorm tonight? He's got some stomach issues and the vet said I need to watch him overnight.

Of course, he texted back. The quarter horse was one of his dad's favorites.

He'd miss his night with Bethany, but this was for the best. He needed a little time to think. A lot of time. And since tomorrow night was Stanley Sanchez's bachelor party, he'd have tomorrow night too to figure out how he felt.

What he wanted.

You think you know what you want...

Stanley's psychic fiancée's words came back to him. At least he understood more now that he didn't seem to know what he wanted anymore. He couldn't imagine saying goodbye to Bethany, but she was a package deal. So...

What is meant to happen will...

The problem was that his understanding of how that applied to him kept changing.

DARN IT, BETHANY THOUGHT, flopping down on her sofa and putting her phone on the coffee table.

Theo had been quiet all day. Usually he texted a couple of times, just cute little things—to ask if she had any cravings he could fulfill, adding a winking emoji and then a string of foods, like pie or a burger or a taco. But today, not a single text.

And just a second ago, he'd called to say he wouldn't be able to come over tonight, after all, that his dad had asked for his help in watching over a sick horse in the stables.

Theo hadn't asked her to join him. Not that taking an overnight shift in a barn sounded like fun for a pregnant woman who got backaches even from her extremely comfortable bed, but still...

Maybe he was having second thoughts about their dating.

After a few nights spent together, having a great time,

having great sex, he probably had started thinking about what was coming.

A baby.

A night off to get his head together was probably a good thing.

But tomorrow night he'd be busy for hours at Stanley's bachelor party, so she wouldn't see him until the day after.

That might be a little too much time to think. She was only half joking about that, she realized.

She sighed and took a sip of her iced tea. She'd go over her song list for the Cobbs-Sanchez wedding, do a final practice of the song for their first dance, a '50s ballad that gave her goose bumps every time she heard the original.

For the next hour, she worked on the song, ate cereal with a handful of blueberries tossed in for dinner since that was what she was craving, and then took a shower. She'd just dressed in her at-home uniform of maternity yoga pants and a T-shirt when her doorbell rang.

Her heart soared. Theo?

She ran to the intercom and pressed it. "Hello?"

She was so excited to see him. Maybe he was stopping by for a kiss before his night away from her.

Aww.

"Bethany?" came a familiar voice that was *not* Theo Abernathy's. "It's Rexx."

She gasped. Rexx? *What?*

She sucked in a breath. And buzzed him up.

What the heck was he doing here? Wasn't he living in Colorado now? With his fiancée? Maybe he'd somehow heard through the grapevine that she was pregnant and had done the math and realized it might be his baby.

She pulled open the door. When she saw Rexx Winters standing there, she honestly wondered how she'd ever spent a night with him. She felt absolutely nothing for him—not even the connection of being parents. He looked different too—he'd cut his wild, rocker-like mane and now kind of looked like a bank teller with his short, neatly brushed blond hair and button-down shirt tucked into khaki pants. The Rexx she'd known had worn silver rings on all his fingers and thrift-store velvet shirts.

"It's good to see you," he said.

She nodded—feeling so awkward. She'd wanted to get in touch with him, and now here he magically was. But suddenly, sharing her joyous news with someone who seemed like a stranger and yet was her child's father... well, it just seemed odd.

"Come on in," she said. "Can I get you something to drink?"

"If you have a beer, that would be great."

"Actually, I'm plumb out of all alcoholic beverages," she said. "Because of this," she added, pointing with both hands at her baby bump.

He looked at her belly. Understanding did not dawn.

Rexx was a smart guy—immature but smart. And clearly he had things on his mind. Maybe he thought she'd just gained a little weight and wasn't drinking to save calories.

She inwardly sighed. "I'm *pregnant*."

His brown eyes widened. "Pregnant? Wow. You don't look too far along."

"Almost five months," she said. And waited.

Nothing. No math computing.

"I called you a couple of months ago," she said. "But you barely let me get a word in and then ended the call before I could tell you my news. *Our* news," she added.

Now his eyes bugged out. "Wait. Are you saying I'm the father?" he asked.

"Yes." She launched into the story, how she assumed

there was a tear in the condom that he hadn't noticed. That she'd gone to a fertility clinic only to find out she was already pregnant. She told him she'd tried to call him last week but had discovered he'd changed his number.

He had the decency to look sheepish. "Well, Bethany, I've come at exactly the right time. We have five months to get ready. To work on being a couple. That's awesome."

Huh? "What do you mean—a couple? You're *engaged*. You live in Colorado."

He sighed and moved to the sofa and sat down. "She dumped me. She said I wasn't acting the way I did when we first met. All gaga, I guess. She wanted me to give up being a musician, so I got a full-time job doing data entry for a bank, but she said it wasn't bringing in enough money." He frowned. "I really thought we were gonna be forever, you know? I tried so hard to change for her."

"That explains the hair and clothes," she said with a gentle smile.

"Yeah. She liked my old look, but then once things got serious between us, she wanted me to look more professional." He sighed. "But now that you're pregnant, I mean, now that I *know*...let's give this a go."

She appreciated the sentiment. But...and there were a lot of buts where they were concerned, she and Rexx had never been a match. They both had known that when they'd had that unexpected one-night stand. No chemistry. No real attraction even. They'd been two lonely people who'd had a little too much to drink and had been away on a gig. And afterward, when she'd been ready to write him off as anything other than a one-night stand, her bandmate who'd she'd not been close to, she'd beaten herself up about it. That maybe her quickness to say no, to walk away, was something she had to work on. She'd been willing to give him a chance. But then he'd turned the tables on her.

"Rexx, I'm glad I was finally able to tell you about the baby. But the truth is that I'm in love with someone else. I hope you'll be in the baby's life, but we can't be a couple."

He leaned his head back against the sofa. "Yeah, I know we're not really a match. Jeez, me a father? I never really saw that for myself, but if I'm gonna be a dad, then I want to be there as much as I can."

"As much as you can?" she repeated.

"Well, you know, birthdays. Christmas."

Gotcha. She mentally shook her head. "Look, Rexx, you just found out some startling news. Why don't you sleep on it and we can talk tomorrow? You can figure out how you want to coparent." She was so relieved that her baby would grow up knowing his father, that even if Rexx was going to be more absentee and there for just birthdays and holidays than truly involved in his child's life, at least he wouldn't be a big question mark.

He nodded and stood. "I appreciate that."

She walked him to the door.

"I'll text you tomorrow. You'll have my new number. Maybe we can have dinner tomorrow night and talk things out? Here, so we have privacy to really be open with each other, if that's okay. I remember you always liked Pasta-bilities. You can text me your order and I'll pick it up on the way over."

"Sounds good," she said. "See you tomorrow."

The moment she closed the door behind him, she let out a breath. *Whoa. Talk about unexpected.*

The whole thing almost made her think that anything was possible. Did that mean that even Theo Abernathy could be ready by the time she had her baby?

The truth is that I'm in love with someone else...

She absolutely was. And hoped with all her heart, everything inside her, that Theo would want to be a part of her life—and her future.

CHAPTER SEVENTEEN

THE GOOD NEWS was that Thunderstorm had pulled through just fine *and* that Theo had gotten to spend some quality time with his dad. The two of them had spent the night in the stables with the horse, in the large sick-bay stall, and they'd talked about so much—from the ranch to how Jace and Billy and now Robin had all found love. Asa Abernathy had shared that he and Bonnie were sure that Theo and Stacy, the last two holdouts of their five children, were soon to find their own loves and settle down.

And though Theo hadn't planned on opening up to his dad about his love life, he'd found himself pouring out what was going on with him and Bethany McCreery. How it made no sense that he could be so attracted—on every level—to a pregnant woman when he wasn't ready to be a father and couldn't see that for himself for years yet.

Instead of lecturing Theo about it being time to grow up, that he'd sowed his oats and all that, his father had counseled him with one line of advice: "Just follow your heart."

There was still a big but there, though. Where Bethany was concerned, he could only follow his heart to a certain point. And that point was the day before she gave birth and became a mother. Maybe as the months went on, he'd get more and more used to the idea of fatherhood. That was possible. He just couldn't see it.

But he missed her. So much.

This morning, he'd sent her a text to ask how she was doing, if he could bring anything by before he got busy in the ranch office. She'd texted back that she was fine, just a little backachy, and her mom was stopping by with not only breakfast and her favorite home fries from the diner, but a massage gun specifically for pregnant women.

Theo had missed her terribly all day. He wished he could see her tonight, but he had special plans. He wouldn't miss Stanley Sanchez's bachelor party for the world. All the Abernathy men would be there, including his uncle and cousins, which added to the fun; they were extended family now because of Robin's marriage to Dylan Sanchez.

When Theo arrived right on time at the Library, the restaurant in Bronco Valley owned by Dylan's sister Camilla, the bachelor party was just getting underway in a large private room behind the main dining room. He saw Stanley, in his trademark leather vest and bolo tie, and tonight a sombrero, surrounded by a small group, including Theo's brothers. Theo liked this restaurant. He'd heard that Camilla had offered to hold the wedding reception here, but apparently the happy couple had opted for the park, especially because the guest list was huge.

He extended his hand to congratulate Stanley, and the warm, kind man pulled him into a hug, careful not to spill his glass of sangria.

Theo was surprised when his father raised his own glass of sangria and tapped against it with a spoon to get everyone's attention. Asa then gave a brief speech about how Stanley and Winona had inspired the entire town, that their love was legendary.

Theo was moved by his father's words, and a look around the room told him everyone else was too.

Stanley then raised his glass. "I'm getting married! To love!"

A cheer went up, and there was much clapping and many wolf whistles. His guests joined him in the toast.

"I love my Winona so much," Stanley said, tears brimming in his eyes. "How could I have gotten so lucky to have a second chance at love?"

"Because you're the best, *Tío*," Dylan said. "You deserve all the happiness in the universe."

"I never thought you'd beat me to the altar!" Stanley said, making everyone laugh. "One surprise after another in this family."

Theo's uncle and Dylan's father tapped their glasses to give a speech, and a few others did as well, including Winona's great-grandson, Evan Cruise. Stanley had his hand over his heart, clearly moved by all the warm wishes and everyone's love and respect.

Once the toasts were over, Stanley sidled up to Theo and suddenly slung an arm around his shoulder. "I guess you'll be next. You and that lovely wedding singer, Bethany. Such a voice!"

"I could listen to her sing forever," Theo said.

Stanley nodded. "Marry that woman before someone beats you to it."

Theo swallowed. "It's not that simple."

Stanley lifted his chin and pointed a finger at him. "Oh, it is. Do you love her?"

Theo hadn't been expecting that question. This was all too much. He didn't respond, taking a long drink of his sangria instead.

Stanley shook his head with a mock frown. He waved his hand dismissively in the air. "Love is wasted on the young."

Theo's dad, in earshot, grinned at Stanley. "Yeah, sometimes I think it is," he said, patting Stanley on the back.

"Hey, don't include me and Jace in that," Billy said with a smile. "We're both engaged."

Stanley laughed. "*Some* young people spend too much time overanalyzing things instead of *feeling*, instead of following their hearts." He pointedly looked at Theo.

Asa's eyes lit up. "Exactly what I told my son last night."

Theo quickly downed the rest of his sangria.

"Hey, let's face facts," Jace said. "Theo isn't all that young."

That got a big laugh out of the group.

Theo looked at his brothers, both family men, both so happy.

Both so in love, like Stanley.

And me, he thought with a clarity that hit him right in the chest.

Whoa. Wow.

I love Bethany McCreery.

A lot.

He could actually feel his heart shifting in his chest. Could feel it cracking open. He swallowed against the lump in his throat. He loved Bethany. He loved her so much.

And he understood now that he always had. From the moment he'd been mesmerized by her voice and her face and her body as she sang on stage at her brother's wedding.

She'd had him at the first note.

He'd been so focused on what he'd be giving up that he hadn't spent enough time thinking about what he had. Why would he ever want to be free to jet off to Rome for the best pasta in the world when he'd be more content to pick up dinner for two from Pastabilities and eat in the living room while watching a rom-com with the woman he loved? Bethany.

Who was pregnant.

Bethany was a package deal, and because he loved her,

he wanted everything she was. That included the baby-to-be.

Goose bumps ran up his arms and across the nape of his neck.

He *would* have almost five months to get used to the idea that he'd be a father to her baby. But with Bethany at his side, he'd be happy to give up everything. Actually, there was nothing to give up. If he had Bethany, he had it all.

He'd be ready for fatherhood because she was going to be a mother. It really *was* that simple.

Because he loved her with all his heart.

He'd always been aware that his brothers had made it work—balancing family life with their responsibilities to the Bonnie B. He'd talk to them about how they handled it, how they managed to give all of themselves to both. If they could do it, he could.

They were Abernathys.

When the party wound down, he pulled Stanley aside.

"I owe you a big thanks," he told the man of honor. "Because I have an answer to your earlier question. I *do* love the wedding singer." He laughed and shook his head. "Turns out I knew it all along."

"So why are you still here?" Stanley asked with a wink.

Theo hugged the wise man and raced out.

Theo couldn't wait to get to Bethany. To tell her that he was ready for anything life with her brought him, including a baby. Fatherhood. For the next eighteen years and the rest of their lives.

He got in his car and drove over to Bethany's apartment, so excited to share his epiphany. To share his *life* with Bethany and the baby.

He pressed the buzzer, and when he heard her say, "Hello?" he felt butterflies in his stomach.

"It's me, Theo. I have something to tell you."

She didn't respond for a moment. Then the buzzer sounded, and he rushed in, taking the stairs two at a time, needing to get to her as soon as he could.

She opened the door and he was bursting with his *I love you*. But her expression stopped him cold. Something was wrong.

Bethany looked...uncomfortable.

She opened the door wider, and Theo saw there was a man sitting on the sofa, who suddenly stood. It took Theo a moment to realize the guy was the same one from the photo of the band on Bethany's mantel. With much shorter hair.

Rexx.

The baby's father.

What was going on here?

He noticed that on the coffee table was a takeout bag from Pastabilities—the restaurant where he and Bethany had had their first date. Not that he had called it that. But that was exactly what it had been.

And now she was having Pastabilities takeout with Rexx. Her child's father.

He saw Bethany lean over to Rexx and whisper something to him. What, he had no idea.

His blood ran cold. What the hell was going on?

Theo froze. Were they getting back together?

No. No, no, no. This couldn't be happening. He'd finally realized that he was ready for fatherhood, that he could be the man Bethany needed.

His chest ached and his gut burned.

Rexx came over, his hand extended. Theo didn't shake it. Couldn't.

The guy dropped his hand. "I'm Rexx Winters. I'll say my piece, since Bethany just told me that you two were involved and there were some unresolved issues. I found out last night that Bethany is pregnant—with my child. And with some time to think, I realize that I *do* want a second chance, despite our differences. I want us to be a family."

Bethany's mouth dropped open. She stared at Rexx, then turned to Theo, about to say something.

But Theo didn't wait to hear what it was—likely that no one was more surprised than she was to hear Rexx say those words, and that for the baby's sake, she and Rexx should be together.

That was true, wasn't it? Family was everything. If her baby could have his parents together, an intact family, wasn't that worth fighting for?

He'd lost her. He'd just discovered that she was his everything, that he wanted to be part of her family. And he had to let her go. For her sake. For the baby's sake.

His heart cracking in two, Theo rushed down the stairs and into his car and got the hell out of there.

BETHANY WAS STILL in a state of shock. That Theo had unexpectedly come over, that he'd said he had something to tell her.

And that Rexx had so outrageously interfered. What the hell had he been thinking?

What was Theo going to say? She really wanted to know. That he couldn't keep seeing her? That he knew in his heart he didn't want to be a dad in five months, that nothing had changed? That he was sorry?

The apartment door was still open, the downstairs door softly clicking into its locked position behind Theo.

She closed her eyes for a moment, trying to make sense of what had just happened. Rexx had arrived just ten minutes ago with takeout from Pastabilities and had told her he'd thought long and hard about the big news that he was going to be a father. But then the buzzer had rung before she'd had a chance to say anything.

"Sorry not sorry that I messed that up for you," Rexx said—selfishly. "We can work on our relationship for the baby's sake."

Bethany shook her head. "Rexx, first of all, you *should* be sorry. Very sorry. I care about that man. And you had no right to say one word to him." She was fuming. And wondering what Theo was thinking right now.

Rexx winced and peered at her. "Huh. I guess I am sorry." His shoulders sunk. "No, forget the guessing. I *am* sorry, truly. I know I have to learn to think first, talk second. But I was just hoping—"

"Its a nice thought," she interrupted. "And of course you can be in the baby's life. That's very important to me. But like you said last night, we're not a match. We never were. And there's nothing to work toward. We don't belong together."

He sighed hard and sat back down on the sofa. "Yeah, I know. I'm just really broken up about losing Veronica. I guess I'm rebounding."

Bethany forced herself to stay calm and not lose her temper. Rexx was immature. He didn't have feelings for her. He'd gotten dumped and seen an immediate in for a relationship with her. He'd be gone in a few weeks when he met someone new, child or no child.

"Look, Rexx. You're this baby's father, and you're always welcome in our lives. I do hope you'll take your responsibilities seriously. This little person in here," she added, patting her belly, "is counting on you to be their dad, you know?"

He sucked in a breath. "When you put it like that…" He frowned and looked kind of scared.

She had a feeling that Rexx would fall in love with

someone else pretty soon, and maybe that person, along with impending fatherhood, would end up directing Rexx to take life and his responsibilities seriously. She sure hoped so.

Rexx got up. "Thanks for being you, Bethany. You're all right."

Bethany forced herself not to roll her eyes. He was being nice and sincere, but boy, did he have a ways to go in life—and he was in his early thirties.

He reached into the Pastabilities bag and took out a container and a wrapped set of plastic flatware. "My chicken parm and linguine," he said. "Your pasta primavera and garlic bread are in there with the extra side of grated Parmesan cheese you asked for."

"Thanks, Rexx." She didn't have an appetite anymore, not even for the garlic bread.

"I hope I didn't mess anything up with Theo. Go get your guy," he said.

Huh. That was kind. Maybe there was hope for Rexx yet.

They said their goodbyes, and she felt good about Rexx growing up. She wouldn't hold her breath, but she had a feeling he'd try.

Once he left, she dropped down on the sofa—all this was way too much to process. She sat for a few minutes, then got up and put the bag with her dinner into the fridge.

She found herself drawn to the nursery and went inside. The bassinet Theo had bought and assembled waited in a corner for her baby, the mobile so sweet above it.

I love you, Theo Abernathy, she thought, her gaze going to the pair of baby booties on the dresser.

I want to raise my child with you at my side.

Maybe he'd come tonight to tell her he couldn't do that. But until she heard it from him, there was still hope.

The past few days they'd been a couple—not talking about the future at all. The subject of her impending parenthood hadn't come up.

Maybe these past few days he'd had that change of heart.

She hurried downstairs and into her car and drove over to the Bonnie B, hoping Theo was home. When she pulled up at his cabin-mansion, lights were on inside, and relief flooded her.

She knocked, and the sound of his footsteps approaching had her so nervous. *Please, please, please*, she whispered to the fates of the universe.

Theo opened the door and looked surprised to see her. "I thought you'd be deciding on names or something with Rexx."

He looked so hurt, so…heartbroken that Bethany realized they really *might* have a chance.

"Theo, I'm not going to be with Rexx. Surely you know that."

He stared at her. "But he said he wanted to be a family."

"And I want to be a family—with *you*. You're the man I love."

He looked away for a moment. "The connection between the two of you has to be powerful, Bethany. In a week, a month, with the two of you spending time together as parents-to-be, you'll probably realize that having such a monumental thing in common is enough. And you'll get back together."

What was he talking about? "Theo, that's not going to happen. I don't have feelings for Rexx. Yes, I hope he'll step up and be an active parent to his child, but that's as far as it goes."

"You could change your mind, Bethany. And I don't want to stand in your way."

She stared at him, trying to understand. "Is this an excuse? To make it easier on you to walk away from me?" Tears pricked her eyes. "Theo, when you came over tonight, you said you had something to tell me. What was it?"

"It doesn't matter now," he said. "We need to say good-bye, Bethany. I need to let you go."

No. No, no, no. This couldn't be happening.

Her heart was breaking. The ache in her chest hurt so badly that she touched her hand to the spot as tears pooled in her eyes.

Something was happening inside Theo that she didn't know how to reach.

"Theo," she began, but she could tell by the look on his face that he'd shut down. He was done talking, and there was no getting through to him.

Not tonight, anyway.

She didn't want to give up on this man, but she couldn't keep fighting for him when there was no getting through to him.

She couldn't keep giving him more time when she had so little left to give.

Even if it meant she'd lose him for good.

CHAPTER EIGHTEEN

A WEEK LATER, Bethany hadn't heard from Theo. Some-how, she'd managed to get through three weddings, each so different—a backyard, a campsite, and the private room of the Library, where she knew Stanley Sanchez had had his bachelor party the night she'd seen Theo last. Bethany had sung her heart out with her band, her own heartache adding a new dimension of yearning and authenticity to her voice that had actually earned her a couple of stand-ing ovations. She'd had many folks come up to her and ask if she and her band were available to perform on cer-tain dates. Her job this past week had been bittersweet, to say the least.

Today was yet another wedding, one she'd been wait-ing for, one the entire town of Bronco was so excited for: Winona Cobbs would say I do to her handsome groom, Stanley Sanchez. The ceremony was taking place in the Bronco Valley Church. A huge reception, to which hun-dreds had been invited, would follow in the park, and ev-erything from the necessary permit to the bride's gown to the tents and food and flowers had all been comped by various businesses and townspeople who adored the elderly couple. Had anyone in Bronco not been inspired by Winona and Stanley, moved by their stories, their ro-mance, their love?

Bethany sure had. And today, she'd put aside her hurt,

her tears, and the surety that Theo Abernathy was out of her life for good to share in that love between the couple.

Just a couple of days ago she'd listened to his latest podcast just so she could hear his voice, feel connected to him. Tears in her eyes, she'd been riveted by the story of a young ranching family, the Newtons, with a three-month-old baby. In Theo's introduction, which he'd said he'd revised and rerecorded three times until he got it right, he'd discussed how the young couple's ranching life wasn't easy, that they were trying to get a failing farm out of the red, and that their sweet baby girl, who was colicky, gave them all the extra motivation they needed when they were exhausted and worried that they wouldn't succeed.

"Our child stands for possibilities, for love, for hope," Paul Newton had said. "And to secure our baby's legacy and lineage, my wife and I will never give up, even when we've both been awake all night with nighttime feedings. Even when we're trying to soothe a colicky baby when we have a small herd to care for, the work of the ranch never finished."

"Because we love each other. We love our little family. our little ranch," his wife had said.

"I have no doubt these young ranchers—little family, little ranch, but with the biggest *hearts* will not only survive, but succeed," Theo had commented.

Bethany had been moved to tears by their story.

She'd been so surprised when the baby, Maya, had made her podcast debut with quite a screechy cry, Theo adding that this was life in all its messy glory.

"Its beautiful and blessed messy glory," he'd said.

When Theo had signed off for the week, she'd gone straight to Hey, Baby and bought Maya a stuffed animal and dropped it in the couple's mailbox with a note about how she admired them so much and how their story helped her know she'd always be okay because her love for her baby would guide her. She wished she'd been able to give more to the young couple, but Bethany had no doubt donations and toys and ranch equipment would come pouring in for the Newtons.

Now, Bethany stood with her mike beside the organist, doing a quick rehearsal of the song the couple had chosen for Winona to walk down the aisle. The wedding would begin in a half hour, and already so many people were milling about outside. Bethany had seen the Sanchez family, including Stanley, who looked so handsome and proud and happy in his tux and his elegant sombrero and bolo tie. Winona's relatives were here, corralled by her proud daughter Beatrix. Others began streaming in—there were newlyweds Dylan and Robin holding hands as they kissed and then joined a group of Dylan's relatives back out on the church's large porch. Ryan Taylor and Gabrielle Hammond came in and admired the beautiful stained glass windows as they chatted with Shep Dalton and Rylee Parker. A few other Daltons were with them, but Bethany could never remember all their names. On the porch, she could see the Burris family had gathered, including Ross and his bride, Celeste.

"Hi, Aunt Bethany!" a chorus of little voices said, and she glanced out the door to see her treasure trove of nieces and nephews waving, the adorable brood all dressed up. Her brother was in his suit and Stetson, and Elizabeth looked so pretty in her Western-style fancy dress.

Bethany waved back with a big smile. Twenty minutes until the music would start and the wedding would begin. That she'd cry her eyes out wasn't in doubt. That was what waterproof mascara and strong tissues were for. She only hoped she could get through the emotional song the couple had chosen to accompany the bride down the aisle without sobbing.

As Dylan and Robin went back out onto the porch, she got a glimpse of Theo in his own suit and Stetson talking with a group of Abernathys, his siblings and cousins.

Her heart squeezed, and she winced from the ache, tears already forming.

Suddenly she felt a hand on her shoulder and turned to find Penny Smith, the mayor's wife, looking at her with compassion. There was no hiding the heartbreak on her face, Bethany knew.

"Bethany, honey, will you turn around for a moment?" Penny asked.

Bethany looked at her, not understanding. Then she saw Penny reaching up to her neck to take off her pearl necklace.

Bethany gasped softly. Everyone in town knew the pearl necklace was rumored to have magical properties. It brought love to anyone who wore it.

She turned and felt the beautiful necklace drape around her neck, Penny's hands patting both shoulders.

"There," Penny said. "Wear it for the ceremony. It goes so beautifully with your pale blue dress."

Bethany took Penny's hand and gave it a squeeze. "Thank you," she barely managed to say.

Penny squeezed her hand back and then joined her husband, who was talking to a group of the Taylor clan. Daphne and her husband, Evan, Winona's great-grandson, suddenly moved up near where Bethany stood beside the organ, whispering to each other and both checking their phones.

Bethany's heart lurched when Evan looked up from his phone and whispered, "Cold feet?" She then heard Daphne say that Winona wasn't even here yet when she was supposed to be getting ready in the anteroom.

Stanley came in then with Beatrix and they rushed over to Daphne and Evan, everyone looking concerned but Stanley. Apparently, Beatrix had planned to drive her mother to the church a half hour before the ceremony so that Winona could put on the finishing touches in the anteroom, but Winona, who'd still been in her robe, had told her she'd walk over since the church was close to their house.

She hadn't.

"My bride will be here," Stanley insisted, straightening his bolo tie. He lifted his chin. "Winona is a free spirt, but we've been through so much together, especially these past six months. She'll be here soon, I'm very sure. She'd never leave me standing at altar."

That seem to brighten the group's expressions. But a look at Beatrix told Bethany that she was worried.

And ten minutes later, there was still no sign of the bride.

Winona wasn't responding to calls or texts. Evan had gone to check Winona's psychic shop at his Bronco Ghost Tours business, but he'd texted his wife that Winona wasn't there or anywhere on the property.

Where was the bride-to-be?

Bethany's heart lurched as she looked over at Stanley, nervously pacing by the stage now, several members of the Sanchez family trying to comfort him.

Was Winona not going to show up? Bethany couldn't believe it. The dear woman had to just be running late. Perhaps she'd had a psychic prediction about her own wedding and knew she had to arrive twenty minutes late or something bad would happen. Bethany was clearly grasping at straws here.

If Winona would stay away from her own wedding to

the man she loved, it reinforced for Bethany that Theo Abernathy wasn't ever coming for her.

THE WEDDING GUESTS were all outside now, since the ceremony was supposed to start a half hour ago and there seemed no point for everyone to sit in the pews, particularly the many children, who were getting antsy. The moment Theo had arrived at the church with his family, he'd seen Bethany standing at the front with the organist and for just a second he'd imagined she was his bride-to-be, that this was their wedding day. But no matter how much he loved her, no matter how much he'd changed and could now welcome her baby into his life, he wouldn't stand in her and Rexx's way.

As he stood with his brothers on the side yard, he wondered if Rexx was here, if he was Bethany's plus-one for the event. If, that was, there was going to *be* a wedding.

Theo, Billy, and Jace were all eyeing their sisters, Robin and Stacy, who were across the lawn with Dylan and his siblings, talking in low voices, all of them looking very worried.

"Dang," Billy said. "I did hear that Winona had cold feet a couple months back, but at Stanley's bachelor party, there was no indication from him that there was any trouble between them."

"The trouble may be one-sided," Jace pointed out. "Winona's a first-time bride, even at her age. Maybe she's still just not ready, given all she's been through in her life."

Not ready. That was Theo's line for his entire relationship with Bethany McCreery. But when love hit him over the head so hard even he couldn't ignore it, he'd believed he was ready for the package deal he'd be blessed with. But then Rexx came back, and how could Theo interfere in that?

Ever since he'd interviewed Paul Newton, who'd again been on baby duty because his wife had had a bad cold, Theo had been so focused on the word *family*. His own. Bethany's. And now the sweet idea that Bethany, Rexx, and their baby could be a family too. Paul had rocked little Maya in his arms during the entire interview, which had been one of Theo's favorites. He often learned a lot while putting together an episode of *This Ranching Life*, but the life experiences and wisdom coming out of twenty-three-year-old Paul Newton's mouth had bowled him over. All Theo's listeners too, apparently, because the family had received so many donations and offers of help with the ranch that Theo had felt his eyes mist.

"I'm doing this for the baby," Paul had said. "Everything my wife and I do is for her and her present and future. For today and tomorrow. I care about the Newton Ranch, but it's Maya who gives my life a meaning and purpose."

Theo had gotten that knocked into his skull along the way, but now it was too late.

Across the lawn, he saw the Newton family, Paul holding Maya and standing beside his wife, with a big group of people. Paul smiled and waved at Theo, and he waved back, moved by how his podcast had touched not only the young family but affected so many others. And one day, maybe Theo would be holding a baby and recording at 3:00 a.m. He understood now that life was full of the unexpected and challenges and you had to make them work, but your heart would always guide you. If you let it.

He got now that that was what Stanley had been trying to say at his bachelor party.

But it was too late now.

"Winona will show up," Billy said now, looking around like they all were and hoping that a purple pickup truck would suddenly pull up to the church, Winona stepping out.

But no sound of a truck or car or limo could be heard.

"I don't get it," Jace said. "Winona and Stanley have both lost so much in their lives. And here they are, so in love, so happy. Why would she be afraid of that?"

"Because of how damned scary it is to risk loving anything or anyone to the point that you vow to honor it forever," Theo said, then froze for a moment as he realized that was how *he* felt. His chest ached and his stomach churned as the stark truth hit him.

He'd come around, only to walk away from Bethany so that she could be with a man she'd said flat out she didn't have feelings for. What the hell had he done?

"Kind of like how you broke up with Bethany because you're afraid," Jace said as though he could read Theo's mind. "Not of giving up your carefree life. Of getting your heart ripped out of your chest."

Billy nodded. "You're scared out of your mind that Bethany and her baby will be taken from you. So you're not even trying."

He inwardly gasped. His brothers were right.

What had he done?

A better question was: Could he fix it before it was too late?

WINONA COBBS WAS now thirty-five minutes late to her own wedding. Bethany had no idea if the bride would show up. No one had heard from her. Not even Stanley.

Most of the families with children had walked over to the park just across the road because it had a playground and they could come back at a moment's notice. Sure, the kids' Sunday best outfits would be rumpled and maybe even dirty, but it was the ceremony and reception that counted, not a grass stain on a hem.

Bethany stood by the stained glass window at the front of the church, too afraid to go outside and see Theo. She couldn't bear it. To be that close and yet light-years away.

She touched the pearl necklace at her throat and felt her eyes mist up. The anniversary gift to mark thirty wonderful years of Rafferty and Penny Smith's marriage had brought together quite a few couples. But love always seemed to pass right by Bethany.

She'd been blessed with a baby who'd be here in just four and a half months, and Bethany was counting down the days. She would focus on taking good care of herself, eating well and taking her prenatal vitamins and signing up for Lamaze class—with her sister-in-law as her coach. Bethany had been so touched when Elizabeth had called the other day to make that offer.

Bethany might not be lucky in love, but she was rich in family.

"Bethany," called a familiar deep voice, and she whirled around.

Theo, looking so handsome in his suit and gray Stetson, stood at the church entrance. He took off his hat and held it against his chest.

She waited—for him to come closer, for him to say something. But for the moment, he just stood there looking at her.

Maybe to say his final goodbye.

He started walking toward her. His expression gave her pause; he didn't look particularly pained, like a man who was about to tear her heart out—again.

He stopped in front of her and reached for her hand. "I don't know where Winona is or why she isn't here, but I do know she is psychic. She told me that what's meant to happen will, and she was right. I was meant to go through all this—not thinking I wanted a family yet, losing you to the father of your baby—for me to realize I was making excuses."

Bethany gasped, hope suddenly soaring in her heart. What was he saying?

Theo took her other hand and looked right in her eyes. "My brothers helped knock into my head that I'm scared spitless of how I feel."

"And how *do* you feel?" she asked, hope blossoming in her chest.

"I love you, Bethany McCreery. So much. And I love this little one-to-be," he added, moving a hand to her belly.

"Oh, Theo," she said, smiling at how many times she'd yearned to hear those words. "I love you too."

"You told me you didn't have feelings for Rexx, that the two of you wouldn't be a couple, but I refused to listen. Once I opened up to the fact that I am ready to be a father, fear got a hold of me, and I used Rexx as an excuse to run. But I'm done with that. I'm here to stand by your side forever. To be a father figure to your child."

Bethany felt tears mist her eyes. "This may be someone else's wedding day, but it's become the happiest day of my life."

Theo kissed her, sweetly and tenderly, looking into her eyes with such love.

He glanced at the pearl necklace. "Why does that look so familiar?"

She smiled. "It's just something borrowed," she said.

"Well, it looks beautiful on you. *You* look beautiful."

She kissed him again and then touched the necklace,

wondering if the pearls really did have magical powers or if the magic came from those, like her, who believed.

Love was everything. And it hadn't passed her by. She'd just had to wait for it.

One minute Theo was right in front of her, and the next, he was gone.

Because he'd gotten down on one knee. He pulled something out of his pocket—something very big and very twinkly.

Her hand flew to her mouth.

"Bethany McCreery, with the voice of an angel and the most beautiful heart, will you make me the happiest man alive by marrying me?"

Bethany was speechless for a moment. She could only nod, tears pooling in her eyes. Finally she found her voice. "Yes, yes, yes. I'll marry you."

Theo stood and slid the huge, twinkling ring on her finger. "Okay, this is not your real engagement ring. It's a placeholder, which I borrowed from my twin niece's dress-up box. It's a beauty but your ring will be real, like my love for you."

Bethany was so touched she couldn't speak.

"In fact, it was at Stanley's bachelor party that I realized that I'd always loved you. I'm ready for you and the baby. Ready for anything that comes our way."

Bethany smiled and looked at her toy ring, then at her handsome fiancé. She really hoped she wouldn't have to give this back because she treasured it. Her heart felt like it might burst with happiness. She hugged Theo, and for a few moments, they stood there by the stained glass window and the organ, embracing, knowing that they'd be together forever.

They both looked toward the door, and Bethany hoped

she'd see Winona come walking through in a purple wedding gown, but there was no sign of her.

She had no idea what was going to happen with one of Bronco's great love stories. But she did know that her own was one for the storybooks.

* * * * *

The Rancher's Reunion
Lisa Childs

MILLS & BOON

New York Times and *USA TODAY* bestselling, award-winning author **Lisa Childs** has written more than eighty-five novels. Published in twenty countries, she's also appeared on the *Publishers Weekly*, Barnes & Noble and Nielsen Top 100 bestseller lists. Lisa writes contemporary romance, romantic suspense, paranormal and women's fiction. She's a wife, mum, bonus mum, avid reader and less avid runner. Readers can reach her through Facebook or her website, lisachilds.com.

Visit the Author Profile page
at millsandboon.com.au for more titles.

Dear Reader,

Welcome back to Willow Creek, Wyoming, where Sadie March Haven Lemmon has been so very busy! Not only has she matched up several of her grandsons but she's found the perfect match for herself! And if you were at her wedding in *The Doc's Instant Family*, you know she had a surprise guest show up at her nuptials! In *The Rancher's Reunion*, you'll find out how that happened and so much more about the Haven and Cassidy connections. But if you haven't read the previous books, you'll be fine, as there is so much else happening in Willow Creek...and especially between best friends since childhood Cash Cassidy and Becca Calder. Becca isn't a Cassidy or a Haven, but she's a lot like them because she's been keeping some big secrets of her own!

The Havens/Cassidys and everyone else in Willow Creek—even Feisty the dog and Midnight, that mercurial bronco—have become so real to me. They are like a branch of my family that I'm always thrilled to visit. I've heard from some readers and some of my real family and friends that they feel the same way. Please reach out and let me know what you like most about Willow Creek! I'd love to hear from you.

Happy reading!

Lisa

DEDICATION

I am dedicating this book once again to the strongest woman I know—Sharon Ahearne—and to the daughters and daughters-in-law who are lucky enough to have her as our role model for life: Maureen Ahearne Brown, Sue Brown Mullins, Wendy Ahearne, Becky Ahearne and Jenn Brown.

PROLOGUE

Three months ago...

IT HAD BEEN seventeen years since Cash had stood right where he did now, on the gravel driveway between the barns and the two-story farmhouse. Despite all the time that had passed, he could almost hear the echo of his shouts from so long ago. "You lied to me! You've been lying to me my whole life!"

After all the fear and grief and anxiousness he'd grown up feeling, the lie had been unforgivable to him. And so he'd said unforgivable things, too. "You're not my dad! I hate you! I'm never coming back!"

Even now, he flinched at the guilt and regret over what his eighteen-year-old self had said in the heat of the moment. He'd regretted his words almost immediately, but he'd been too stupid and too proud to take them back.

The summer he'd spent between high school and college, without his family, had seemed interminable. And so he'd returned to the ranch before his classes were supposed to start, but then *she* had been here.

Now, she opened the door, just as she had then, and stepped out onto the sagging porch. He waited for the flash of anger he'd felt seventeen years ago, for the resentment that she'd taken his mother's place way too soon. He waited for the anger that the man he'd thought was his father for most of his life had replaced Cash's mother so quickly, as if she hadn't mattered to him at all.

At the time, Cash had assumed that it meant he hadn't mattered at all, either, that coming back had been a mistake. Clearly, he'd thought, he wasn't missed.

She'd asked him then, "Are you a friend of one of the boys? They're at school now for orientation. They're just picking up their schedules and getting their pictures taken, so they should be back soon if you want to wait."

How hadn't she recognized him? Were the pictures of him, the few he'd consented to having taken, gone already?

She'd glanced at the house, and her hazel eyes had filled with such concern. "Maybe you should wait out here, though. JJ's resting…"

Cash had turned and walked away from her, believing that there was nothing at the ranch for him anymore. His mother was gone and nobody else had really needed him.

But now it was seventeen years later and he was older and wiser, though probably just as stubborn as he'd always been. Still, he had returned when she'd called him.

"Doc CC?" she asked as she walked down the porch steps toward him. Her eyes narrowed as she studied his face.

Since she hadn't recognized him seventeen years ago, she wouldn't recognize him now. He wasn't the skinny teenager he'd been then. Plus, he was blond and blue-eyed instead of dark haired and dark-eyed like his brothers. Seventeen years ago, he had discovered why.

But now he just nodded at her in acknowledgment and acceptance of the nickname he'd been given when he'd toured with the rodeo as a veterinarian. His partner in their veterinarian practice in Willow Creek, Wyoming, called him by the nickname, too, so much so that all of their clients only referred to Cash that way. Between the nickname and how much he'd changed, nobody had recognized him as a Cassidy from the Cassidy Ranch in Moss Valley, an hour's drive from Willow Creek.

"Yes, you called me about a mare," he said.

Darlene from Cassidy Ranch. Was she a Cassidy now? Had JJ married her?

He had no idea, but she'd been with JJ nearly as long as Cash's mother had been. A pang struck his heart over how easily a person could be replaced.

"Thanks for coming out on such short notice," she said as she walked up and extended her hand toward him.

Out of a sense of loyalty to his mother and with the suspicion that he was the only one who still felt loyalty to her, he hesitated for a moment before he shook Darlene's small hand. It was heavily calloused, and there were dark circles around her eyes. Despite how run-down the ranch looked, she must have worked hard to keep it going. But when he followed her into the barn, all the stalls but one were empty. And the hay in the loft was just a few short stacks of bales that looked moldy with age.

Where were his brothers now? Marsh was only a couple of years younger than him, and the twins only two years younger than Marsh, which meant they were all in their thirties now. Why weren't they helping at the ranch?

He felt that pang in his heart again, but this time it was of longing, of wanting to know them. Maybe Becca was right. Maybe it was time to come home for real, not just for a furtive visit like he had when she'd listed this property for sale. In stealth. At night. He hadn't been able to see then what he did now: how run-down it was.

"What's going on with the mare?" he asked. "Do you have any concerns about her health?"

The woman reached over the stall door and lovingly stroked the nose of the brown thoroughbred horse. "No."

She sighed. "I'm selling her, and I'd like to give the new owner a veterinarian's report of her health."

While he did as she'd requested and stepped inside the stall to examine the mare, Cash yearned to ask for a health report, too, though he was interested in JJ, not a horse. With the way that the ranch looked, he could guess JJ wasn't doing well. Seeing Cash now probably wouldn't be good for him...

Or for Cash.

So he limited his questions to asking Darlene only about the horse and nothing else. He'd been gone too long and had lost his right to ask the questions he wanted to. He'd lost his family, although he wondered if he'd ever really been a part of it. And now the ranch was for sale.

After he checked over the mare and got back in his truck, he reached in his pocket for his lighter but it wasn't there. He must have lost it. Even though he had never smoked, he always carried it with him, in his pocket, like someone might carry a rabbit's foot for luck. The family heirloom was pewter, engraved with the initials CC in the shape of horseshoes. Cash wasn't sure if it had ever brought him luck or even the clarity and solace he'd sought for so long.

Now that it was gone, he'd decided not to miss it...like he tried not to miss his family or his home.

CHAPTER ONE

Now...

"WHOA, EASY BOY," Cash murmured softly to the bronco. He ran his hand over the horse's velvety black coat. Midnight shifted away but didn't rise up and kick out at him like he had the first few times Cash had stepped into the stall with him.

And he didn't let out that horrifying cry that sounded more like a screaming banshee than a horse.

"Yes, see there, we're making progress."

But as if to call him a liar, the horse pawed at the ground of the stall, kicking some of the fresh wood chips up at Cash. Then he let out a sound, but it was more of a whinny, or maybe a mocking snicker, than a scream.

"What are you doing to my horse?" a soft voice asked.

Cash glanced up at the little face peering over the top of the stall. Eyes as blue as his own stared in at him. The little boy had blond hair, too.

"You're Dusty Chaps?" Cash asked, infusing his voice with awe. "The famous bronc rider?"

The little boy giggled. "No, silly. That's Uncle Dusty."

"I thought Midnight was Dusty's horse," Cash said. "Or did you win it off him?" Like Dusty had won the bronco because the horse's original owner had bet the rodeo champion that he couldn't stay on him.

He had.

Rumor had it that that was the only time Midnight had ever been ridden. And even though Cash hadn't worked with the rodeo for a few years, his old friends kept him apprised of all the gossip. And in Willow Creek there was a lot more gossip than there was in the rodeo, and most of it was about the Havens.

The little boy giggled again. "I can't ride him…yet…"

But he clearly had the ambition to try.

"Not for a good long while, young man," a deep voice scolded him.

Cash looked up from the little boy. He'd expected to see one of the Haven men. And while this was a Haven, it was Sadie March Haven, the matriarch, not one of her grandsons. She had to be eightysomething, but she stood straight and well over six feet tall. She had wide shoulders and long white hair. He'd met Sadie a few times when he'd come out to the ranch to treat the livestock. And he realized now, hearing her voice again, that she was the one who'd requested this appointment in the barn this morning.

"Ma'am," he said in greeting.

She nodded, then said to the boy, who must be one of her great-grandsons, "And nobody will try to ride Midnight until the horse whisperer here can get him to behave less erratically."

The little boy's forehead scrunched up beneath his wispy blond bangs. "Behaving less what?" But before Sadie could answer him, he focused on Cash again. "And you're what? You whisper to horses?"

Cash grinned. "That's not exactly how I—"

"But you were whispering to Midnight when I walked up!" he interjected in an almost accusatory tone.

"You ran up," Sadie said, and Cash noticed she was a bit flushed, as if she'd been running to catch up.

"Midnight needs to get his carrots," the boy said, and he

brandished a bunch of them over the stall door. The horse took them carefully, his lips just brushing the kid's skin. The little boy giggled again.

"Okay, Caleb. Midnight got his carrots," Sadie said. "Now you have to get back up to the kitchen and wash up for breakfast. We have a busy day ahead of us." And her face flushed a deeper shade of red.

Cash waited until Caleb hopped off the bucket he'd been standing on and ran out of the barn. Then he stepped out of the stall to talk with Sadie.

"Is Midnight the reason you requested this appointment?" he asked, glancing back at the bronco. While temperamental, the horse was perfect. Maybe that was why he was so temperamental, because he could get away with his bad behavior.

Sadie had turned away, staring after the child. Cash wondered if he was one of the boys who'd been in the crash.

Everybody in town talked about the Havens and the horrific accident that had happened that spring during a freak ice storm. The accident had claimed the lives of Sadie's grandson and his wife while sparing their children.

And he'd heard the rest of it, too. The other secret that JJ had kept from him and his brothers. That JJ Cassidy was actually Jessup Haven. But while Cash had the same mother as his brothers, he wasn't JJ's son. Which meant he wasn't related to Sadie, JJ's mother. He wasn't a Haven.

"Everything okay?" he asked, bringing them both back to the present.

She let out a shaky little breath and smiled. "Yes, everything is okay. Or mostly. But today is more than okay. It's extra special."

He realized now that her face was flushed with excitement, not exertion. His curiosity compelled him to ask, "What's so special about today?"

"I'm getting married."

"Congratulations," he said.

She made a noise that sounded almost like her great-grandson's giggle, then blushed a deeper red.

And Cash found himself wishing...

That she was *his* grandmother and not just his brothers'. But he'd learned long ago that his wishes didn't get granted, so he'd tried to stop making them and just live his life alone. Well, mostly alone.

At least, he would always have Becca, his best friend. He only wished he could be as good a friend to her as she was to him. He felt terrible about putting her in an awkward situation between him and his estranged family.

"Thank you," Sadie said. She was staring at him intently now, her dark eyes narrowed.

"You must have a lot to do today, so I don't want to take up too much of your time," he said. "Why did you want to see me this morning?"

"To invite you to my wedding," she said.

A chuckle slipped out. "That's kind of you, ma'am, but you don't know me, and you're certainly not going to lack wedding guests."

They'd talked a few times when he'd been here on calls, but that was just about the livestock and horses. He was always careful to reveal very little about himself to anyone.

But the way she was looking at him...

"I know you," she said, and her voice seemed to deepen even more. "I know *who* you are."

Cash chuckled again but uneasily as his stomach did a little flip. "Oh?"

"Doc CC," she said. "It finally dawned on me what the CC stands for."

His mind shot to his missing lighter, and he almost shoved his hand in his pocket to reach for it, to run his fingertip over those initials engraved in it. But it was gone, just like his family ranch, just like the family he'd never really known.

Could she know the truth? No. He doubted JJ had told anyone. And that was why he shouldn't be around them, especially if all the rumors were true and JJ had recently had a heart transplant.

"I know who you are, and I want you at my wedding," Sadie insisted.

Even if she did know his true identity, she couldn't know *everything*. Or she wouldn't be looking at him like she was now, like he'd seen her look at Jake and Baker, like he was her grandson. "The last place I should be is at your wedding," he rasped out. He shouldn't even be here, at Ranch Haven. Every time he came, he risked running into one of his brothers.

And that need to hide, to run, had almost led to tragedy. Like the day Colton had come out to the barn with Ian… Cash had rushed off to avoid being seen. If he'd stayed like anyone else would have, he might have been there to stop the boy from getting hurt. Instead, Ian had opened Midnight's stall that day and fallen while trying to let the bronco out. The little boy had injured himself in the fall, but thankfully Midnight hadn't touched him.

Midnight was the reason Cash kept coming back, because Dusty had asked him to work with the animal, who had wounded a horse groomer some months back. While wanting to calm him down so that the bronco wouldn't hurt anyone else, there was also something special about that horse, an empathy, almost. When Cash looked into Sadie Haven's dark eyes, he saw that same empathy and understanding.

Could she know?

He shook his head. "No…"

"You need to be at my wedding," she insisted, "and bring a date."

He'd heard about that, too, her legendary matchmaking.

"My coming to your wedding would be a very bad move…" And Cash knew all too well about bad moves; he'd made more than his share of them and had to live with the consequences.

BECCA SCRAPED THE shovel across the floor of the stall, scooping out the last bit of soiled wood chips. She turned to drop them into the wheelbarrow outside the stall, but her hair had fallen into her eyes. She exhaled a big breath to blow the black strands out of her field of vision, but they were stuck to her sweaty forehead. Trying to hold the shovel with one hand, she reached up with her other and pushed them aside, but then she noticed the manure stuck on her glove and grimaced. So *that* was smeared in the sweat on her forehead now.

The shovel began to slip through her other glove, spilling the contents onto the ground near the wheelbarrow but not in it. She swallowed down the curse burning the back of her throat, in case Hope was up and had headed out to the barn like Becca always had first thing as a kid. Although at six, Hope had probably already heard some bad words, probably from her grandpa, Becca's dad. She smiled.

He was the reason she had rushed out here to clean the stalls. If she didn't do it, he would, and she'd noticed last night at dinner how hard it had been for him to get up from the table and how stiffly he'd moved once he had. He was working too hard, doing too much around the ranch. Her ranch.

It wasn't big, not like Ranch Haven. Or the Cassidy Ranch back in the day.

Back when Becca had spent more time out there with Cash than she had at her own house. But the Cassidy Ranch was gone now.

Ashes...

What was the cause of the fire? Colton Cassidy, who was a firefighter, hadn't said. If he knew more, she was pretty sure he'd have mentioned something to her. She'd seen a lot of him lately, after all. He'd first come around looking for Cash, making the smart assumption that Becca would know his older brother's whereabouts. Then Becca had befriended Genevieve Porter and found herself at a couple of Cassidy-Haven gatherings, acting as Genevieve's ally. It had been a rough few months for her friend. Genevieve's sister had been married to Dale Haven, and both died in a tragic accident, leaving their three young sons behind. Genevieve had come to Willow Creek as a potential foster mother for the boys and had been worried the Havens might hate her.

But it had all worked out. The boys were in the process of being adopted by one of Dale's brothers, and Genevieve herself was part of the family now that she'd married Collin Cassidy. Because the Cassidys were Havens, too.

Another secret that JJ had kept.

Irritation with the man who'd been like a second father when she was growing up churned her empty stomach, followed by a jab of remorse. JJ had been through so much, had spent so much of his life on the edge of dying, that she felt guilty getting angry at him. But had he intended to take all of those secrets to his grave with him?

She sighed and blew out another breath, trying to let it all go. As she'd told Colton and Collin, she was staying out of it.

She had to.

"You missed the wheelbarrow," a deep voice rumbled. "Better watch it or the boss lady might can you. I hear she's a real fire-breathing dragon."

"Then you better not get too close or you might get burned," she said, then flinched with regret. She couldn't stop thinking about the fire that had claimed Cassidy Ranch.

She had an uneasy feeling that Colton suspected Cash had set that fire. But then, Colton didn't know Cash like she did. Cash had left his family long ago and never looked back.

He had gone back a couple of times, though. She knew that because he told her everything. Or so she thought.

But did *anyone* really share *everything*, even with a trusted friend? There were certainly things she hadn't told Cash. Things she never wanted him to know.

Speaking of Cash…she looked up and found him grinning at her.

"That's a risk I'm going to have to take," he said.

And her stupid heart reacted with a little somersault. She thrust the shovel at him. "You want to help me clean out stalls?"

"Looks like you're done," he said. "My timing is perfect."

She could have argued that, but she swallowed down the argument like she had the curse word. "Your timing for what?"

"For my invitation."

She furrowed her brows, which made her very aware of the mess she'd made of herself. Not that Cash had ever cared what she looked like, and she didn't used to, until she'd wanted him to care.

Heat rushed to her face. "Invitation to what?"

"To be my plus-one for a wedding," he said.

"What wedding? And when?"

"Today," he said. "Sadie Haven's."

She gasped. "What?"

He nodded. "She invited me to her wedding. She's marrying the deputy mayor, and she invited me."

She tensed. "But you can't go. Your brothers will be there. Your…" She stopped herself from saying *dad*. He always got upset when she did, even though JJ Cassidy was the only father he'd ever known. Or maybe that he should have ever known.

He'd met his biological father, and that had only made him more bitter. More determined to leave his old life and his family behind him.

So why did he stay in her life?

She'd wanted to ask him, but she'd been afraid that if she did, he would drop her, too, like he had everyone else who'd loved him.

"I know," he said.

"So you know that you can't go," she said. "It would probably become a horrible scene, and Sadie wouldn't have invited you if she'd known that."

"Oh, she knows who I am and exactly what she's doing."

Despite how sweaty she was from mucking out the stalls, a sudden chill raised goose bumps on her skin. She'd had some run-ins with Sadie Haven over the past couple of weeks. "Oh, Cash, this isn't good. But she didn't know when she came by my office." She then hastened to add, "And I didn't tell her." But she couldn't be certain that her mother hadn't. Phyllis Calder was Becca's receptionist, and she was sometimes a little too open and friendly with potential clients.

"I know," Cash said. "I know I can trust you."

He probably shouldn't because of those things she

hadn't told him. But those were things that Becca didn't want anyone to know.

"So trust me when I tell you that this is a very bad idea," she said.

The right side of his mouth curved up in that lopsided grin that always quickened her pulse. "*I* know it's a bad idea," he readily agreed.

She sighed. "But you're doing it anyway."

He nodded. "Yes, and that's partly your fault. You're irritated that you're in the middle of me and my brothers. I'll go to this wedding and see them where nobody will make a scene. Then they'll stop bugging you about me. And because I'm doing that for you, I need you to come with me, Becca. Can you juggle some appointments to be my plus-one?"

She sighed again. She couldn't let him go alone, not with the way his brother Colton had been acting. She didn't want this reunion to go badly. She cared too much about many of the people involved.

Growing up, she'd spent so much of her free time out at the Cassidy Ranch, that all Cash's brothers and his dad felt like her family, too. Which was ironic, since Cash didn't feel like they were his family at all now.

Then there was Livvy Lemmon, who was seeing Colton and becoming a good friend to Becca. And Genevieve Porter-Cassidy, who was definitely already a friend.

And Sadie Haven…

As intimidating as the woman was, there was something about her that amused and charmed Becca. Sadie could either be a formidable adversary or a loyal and loving friend. Since Becca's business in Willow Creek was still pretty new, she needed Sadie as a friend, not an enemy.

But most of all Becca would go for Cash's sake. Because she could deny him nothing. Not even her heart.

"Please, Becca, will you do this for me?" he asked.

She nodded, then couldn't resist teasing him. Making a sweeping gesture with her dirty glove down her damp T-shirt, ragged jeans and manure-caked rubber boots, she asked, "Am I fine going how I am or do you think I should change?"

He stepped forward and reached out, touching the bangs that were stuck to her forehead. "I'm fine with the way you look, Becca."

Her pulse quickened even more from his closeness and from his comment. But she knew that by fine he meant that he didn't really care. She was just his friend. That was all she had ever been to him and all that she would ever be. She'd accepted that long ago.

SADIE STOOD BEFORE the mirror in the ladies' room at city hall, staring at her reflection. She'd had to get out of the room where the other women had been helping her get ready. They'd all been *oohing* and *aahing* over how beautiful she looked. She snorted in derision, but then she really focused on the woman staring back at her.

Her long white hair shimmered around her face, highlighting the makeup that her granddaughter-to-be Taye had swept across her cheekbones. And Emily, another granddaughter-to-be, had wound flowers into a wreath and placed it atop Sadie's head like a crown. And the dress...

They'd all helped her pick it out. Taye, Emily and her granddaughters-in-laws, Katie and Melanie. It wasn't white. She was not a traditional bride. But it was lacy and long and dyed a pale pink. Blush, Katie had called it. The only dress Sadie had owned until recently was the black one that she wore for funerals.

She preferred this one; it was pretty. *She* was pretty.

Sadie had never expected to be a blushing or a nervous

bride. When she'd married her first husband right out of high school, she hadn't been. But she had definitely been blushing that morning in the barn with Doc CC when she'd told him about her wedding. She felt that little flutter in her chest again at the thought of marrying Lem.

She was more excited than nervous to marry Lem, though. The nerves were about her last-minute guest. Had she made a mistake inviting Cash to her wedding? The person she needed to calm her nerves, to make sure that she hadn't made a big mistake, or to call her out on her mistake, was the one person she wasn't supposed to see today, or at least not until she walked down the aisle toward him.

Or she would have bad luck.

She chuckled over the old superstition. She and Lem had already had their share of bad luck. They'd both lost their first loves and so many other people they'd loved. Like Sadie's younger son, and for so long, her older one, too. He was back now.

But what if the shock of seeing his estranged son again upset him?

She drew in a shaky breath. She'd already done it. She'd already invited Cash. While she wanted to run cold water over her hot face, she resisted, not wanting to ruin Taye's makeup job. Funny how Taye, the one who wore the least makeup, had been the one to do Sadie's. Maybe she'd picked up that expertise from her stepmom and stepsisters. Or maybe she was just the only one of the young women currently married or engaged to Sadie's grandsons who wasn't at all intimidated by Sadie. Because they were so much alike...

She walked out of the bathroom, and as she stepped into the hall, she froze. Her husband-to-be was currently pushing open the door across from her to the men's room.

"Lem!"

He wore a crisply pressed, expertly tailored black suit, and his white hair and beard were neatly trimmed. He looked adorable. Though she would never admit that out loud.

His blue eyes were squeezed tightly shut. "Jeez, woman, we don't need any more bad luck in our lives. I can't see you now."

"So keep your eyes closed," she said as she shoved him into the men's room. "And just listen..."

He groaned. "You're not breaking it off, are you?"

"No way," she assured him. "If I was, you could have opened your eyes. But *you* might want to break it off..." It wasn't just her wedding; it was Lem's, too, and she should have considered that before the last-minute addition to the guest list.

He sighed, but he was also grinning. "What did you do, Sadie March Haven?"

She grinned, too. He always said her full name with such exasperation and affection. Her love for him swelled in her heart, warm like sunshine. "I invited someone to our wedding."

He chuckled. "And why would that make me want to call off the wedding?"

"It's Cash."

"What!" The shout came from farther inside the bathroom, not from Lem.

Lem said, "Of course you found him." And his grin widened, though his eyes stayed closed.

She hadn't seen her son Jessup at the sink at first. Now he staggered forward, staring at her with shock. His dark eyes were wide, and his face was so very pale, like all the blood had drained away.

Alarm slammed through her. "Are you all right?" This was why she'd been worried that she'd made a mistake,

because she hadn't wanted to upset her son. But she also
didn't know if Cash would actually show up and hadn't
wanted to build up Jessup's hopes if his oldest child was
a no-show.

"You found him?" he asked, his voice hoarse. "You really found him?"

She nodded.

And tears streaked down his face, dripping off his chin
onto the lapels of his dark suit.

"I'm so sorry to spring this on you. I should have handled it better." Just like she should have handled so many
other things better, like Jessup's illness. The lupus that had
compromised his immune system and made him so sick
for so much of his life. Instead of being loving and supporting, she'd been overbearing and overprotective. She'd
been so scared of losing him.

And then she'd lost him anyway…for so many years.

Jessup shook his head as if in disbelief. "This is your
wedding day," he said.

She glanced at Lem then. Had she messed up? His eyes
were still shut, but he was grinning yet, too.

"You're supposed to receive gifts, Mother," Jessup told
her. "Not give them." Then he sighed. "I'm not sure if
Cash's brothers will consider him a gift, though."

Sadie wasn't, either. Something about Colton's sudden
urgency to find his brother had concerned her, but when
she'd realized that the long-lost brother was none other
than Doc CC, she'd figured that concern wasn't necessary. But now…

Now it was too late to uninvite him. And at least Jessup was happy with her.

She hoped her grandsons would be, as well.

Jessup sighed. "I'm also not sure if he'll even show up."
He sucked in a breath then and squared his shoulders, as

if bracing himself for that outcome. For Cash to decline her invitation.

Or worse.

Maybe he would take off again. And this time he would make sure that nobody figured out where he was. Which was why she hadn't mentioned him to Jessup sooner, because she was worried Cash might run again.

CHAPTER TWO

CASH WANTED TO RUN. He'd known the minute he'd accepted the invitation that he'd made a mistake. No. He'd made the mistake nearly two decades ago when he'd run away from the ranch.

And that was one of the reasons he was here now, at the wedding of his brothers' grandmother. So he could see them again. He'd missed them more than he'd even admitted to himself, but he wasn't sure that they'd missed him. He knew Colton had been bugging Becca to find him, but he suspected his younger brother wanted to blast him for taking off. That was why meeting them here had seemed like a good idea, because they would be unlikely to make a scene at their grandmother's wedding.

He watched as each brother arrived from his seat next to Becca, near the back of the mayor's office. He'd planted himself at the end of the aisle closest to the wall. Becca tensed every time he did, sucking in a breath when one of his brothers walked into the room.

Becca...

Despite her teasing, she'd cleaned up for the wedding. Heck, she'd cleaned up years ago. The old Becca, the one he'd grown up with, wouldn't have minded going out with manure smeared across her forehead, stuck in her hair.

But the new Becca always wore either a business suit or a dress in public, like the pale blue one she wore now that left her long legs bare. He missed the old Becca sometimes, missed how uncomplicated everything had been back then.

When they were kids…

But they weren't kids anymore. So maybe Becca hadn't changed; maybe she'd just grown up. Becca was an adult with adult responsibilities now. Too many adult responsibilities. But if he told her that she'd taken on too many things on her own, her business, her ranch, her family, she would just get defensive.

Her pride was her downfall. His was the same. Maybe that was why they were such good friends, because they were so much alike.

Fortunately there were so many Havens and friends and neighbors of the couple crowded in the room that nobody seemed to notice him at all. It would probably be better if his brothers didn't see him in case they did react badly. Cash didn't want to disrupt Sadie's wedding, even though she'd been the one who insisted he come.

Becca might be as new in town as he was, but she'd clearly done more networking. A lot of people nodded and said hello to her as they passed by to take their seats. Thankfully the little Haven boys captured everyone's attention before questions could be asked about Becca's date. They'd been helping decorate the room with a profusion of balloons they'd released to the ceiling, and now they were jumping up and down, trying to reach the strings that dangled just above them. As they jumped, the little white cowboy hats they wore with their little suits slipped down over their faces.

People smiled at their antics, and the blonde woman who sat next to Becca chuckled. The woman's face glowed with affection for the boys and with happiness.

Becca leaned toward her, giving Cash a little distance and a chance to draw a deeper breath that didn't fill his lungs with her scent, which reminded him of spring rain. "They're adorable," Becca told the woman. Since the blonde was sitting with them on the bride's side, she must have been some relation to the Havens.

Probably more relation than he was. But since he was Sadie's guest, he'd sat on her side of the aisle.

As if she'd read his mind, the woman said to Becca, "I'm surprised to see you here. I didn't know you and Sadie were that close." Her tone wasn't suspicious, though. She looked at Becca with a hint of sympathy.

Obviously everyone was well aware of Sadie's penchant for matchmaking.

"We're not," Becca said. "I'm kind of a plus-one."

The woman leaned forward to peer around Becca, who had stiffened again, probably reluctant to make any formal introductions.

"Mommy!" A little girl ran down the aisle from the back. Dressed like a flower girl in a white dress with a small crown of flowers in her curly brown hair, she must have been eager to start the ceremony. She stopped at their row and flung her arms around the blonde woman.

The woman hugged her close, and a memory pulled at Cash, of his mother hugging him like that. She'd been blonde, like this woman, like him.

"Oh, I missed you so much," the woman said with such heartfelt emotion that tears stung Cash's eyes.

He knew, all too well, how much it hurt to miss someone like that, like he missed his mother despite all the years she'd been gone.

"I missed you, too, Mommy," the little girl said.

"I thought you were mad at me," the woman said.

And now Cash thought of the rest of his family...that even though he missed them, they were probably furious with him.

"No," the little girl said. "I know it's always the best to tell the truth and be open and honest."

Cash nearly gasped at the words, like Becca audibly did. Or maybe she gasped because he leaned around her to address the child. "Wow, you're one smart little girl," he said. "How'd you get so smart?"

"From my mom and dad," she replied, and she hugged the blonde woman again. "This is my mom. She's a lawyer, and my dad is a doctor. A heart doctor." She pulled away from her mom to touch her chest. "He fixed my heart." Her attention skipped to the aisle and she exclaimed, "There's my daddy!"

"You have to get back to Grandma, so they can get started," her dad said, his deep voice full of affection. "Can't start without the flower girl."

"Nope," the child agreed, and she rushed back down the aisle with the same energy she'd run toward her mother with, the same energy with which the little boys leaped in the air to reach the balloons.

Cash felt a bit like one of those balloons himself right now, like he was rising up, floating, out of reach for the moment but probably about ready to burst.

And then he locked eyes with the girl's father—his brother Collin. Collin stared at him, his face tense, his dark eyes full of shock.

"I'm sorry I didn't warn you," the blonde woman said to him. "I just wanted to surprise you."

"With Cash?" Collin asked, his voice just a rasp now.

"With Bailey Ann," she replied, sounding uncertain.

"But Cash is here, too," Collin said.

"Where?" she asked. So she obviously knew about him.

Collin's throat moved as if he was struggling to swallow. He reached out tentatively, as if he was about to point to his brother, and asked, "Where have you been?"

"I've been here," Cash admitted. "In Willow Creek."

With his outstretched hand, Collin started reaching. Cash didn't know if his younger brother was going to grab him or hit him or hug him.

But music started. And one of the Havens, who looked so much like Cash's brothers, cleared his throat and said, "Everybody take your seats please. The wedding is about to begin."

Collin dropped into his seat next to the blonde woman, but the look he shot to Cash...

It confirmed what Cash had already suspected. That extending this invitation had been a bad idea on Sadie's part, and accepting it a bad move on his.

Before the day was out, they would both have to deal with the consequences. For Cash, it wouldn't be just for his actions today but for his actions of the past seventeen years. Or maybe his inaction...

Because he hadn't done anything he should have.

BECCA TRIED TO concentrate on the ceremony, on the beautiful exchange of vows between the octogenarian couple. But she was distracted by Cash, as was so often the case. She wasn't the only one he distracted. Collin kept shooting him glances. And Colton, sitting a couple of rows in front of them, kept turning around to stare, as well.

There was suspicion in their dark eyes. And something else...

Resentment?

Anger?

And she remembered all those times growing up when she'd stepped between Cash and his younger but taller and broader brothers, when she'd defended him from his family over some silly argument or wounded male pride.

Not that Cash had needed her to defend him, then or

now. Even though he'd been shorter and thinner than the other Cassidy boys, he'd been strong. Since graduation, and his disappearance, he'd shot up and bulked up so that he was nearly as tall and muscular as they were.

She hoped they were all more mature now and that they would avoid a physical confrontation, especially at their grandmother's wedding and in front of the younger Havens, the little boys, and the little girl Genevieve and Collin were in the process of adopting. That was why she hadn't wanted Hope to come with them just in case there was an ugly confrontation. She hadn't wanted her daughter to see the man she adored get into a fight. But she fervently hoped they would avoid all confrontations.

Cash must have been thinking the same thing as he leaned closer and whispered in her ear, "Wanna sneak out?"

His breath stirred her hair and something else inside her. She resisted the urge to shiver and shook her head. She wasn't about to act like a kid cutting class. Not that they'd ever cut class themselves. They'd both been good students, focused on their grades, and they'd both been awarded scholarships for their efforts.

Those scholarships had taken them in different directions, to different colleges. But she'd lost Cash for a while even before they'd left for school, after he'd found out the truth. Or what he stubbornly called the truth. She didn't think he could see the reality that JJ was his father no matter that they shared no DNA.

Turned out that wasn't the only secret JJ had kept from his sons. He'd hidden this whole other family from them: the Havens. They'd only discovered their connection to Sadie and her family a few weeks ago.

Ignoring the tension between Collin and Cash, Becca

focused on the couple exchanging vows in front of Ben Haven, the mayor, who was officiating the wedding.

Sadie talked about how much Lem Lemmon had always challenged and infuriated her and made her better. Becca hadn't lived in Willow Creek, Wyoming, long, but she'd heard all about Sadie and Lem Lemmon since moving here. Sadie and the former long-term mayor, Old Man Lemmon as everyone called him, had constantly feuded because she kept outdoing him. According to Lem, as he was saying in his vows, that had started in elementary school, with her literally pushing him a time or two, and had continued throughout their lives with her pushing him to do more, to be better.

They had been rivals throughout so much of their lives and then they'd become friends and now they were deeply in love. Maybe they had always been soulmates. They just hadn't liked each other enough to give each other a chance.

Why had Cash never given Becca a chance? Not that she'd asked for one...

But if he'd given her any indication that his feelings had begun to change from friendship like hers had...

But she was destined to always be just his friend and never anything more. And so she'd made peace with that.

Or so she kept telling herself.

Still, hearing the vows of the octogenarian couple, seeing their love, had tears filling Becca's eyes until she couldn't see at all. She was touched and happy for them, but she was sadder for herself than she'd been in a long while. She tried to blink away the tears but they spilled out, trailing down her cheek.

Cash's shoulder bumped hers, then he handed over one of his handkerchiefs, monogrammed with the initials CC in the shape of horseshoes. Becca had given him those handkerchiefs when he'd graduated with his Doctor of

Veterinary Medicine. After he'd earned his combined undergrad and vet degree in Iowa, he had joined the rodeo as their vet, constantly traveling. After she finished school in Cheyenne, she'd settled in the big city and launched a career in commercial real estate.

She was touched that he always carried one of the handkerchiefs with him. She used it now to dab the tears from her face.

"Are you okay?" Cash asked, his voice a deep rumble in her ear.

He probably thought she'd lost her mind; he knew she wasn't close enough to Sadie or Mr. Lemmon to be so happy for them that she would cry tears of joy. She certainly didn't want him to know how sad she was for herself. *She* didn't want to know how sad she was; it was pathetic. And Becca hated being pathetic.

That was why she'd done what she had. Why she'd stopped waiting for someone else to make her happy and had made her own happiness...when she'd made her daughter without the help of a husband or even a significant other. She'd chosen Hope's father from a sperm bank.

But nobody else knew that.

Not even Cash.

Because she hadn't wanted to seem pathetic. But she had wanted a baby so very badly before she turned thirty.

She drew in a deep breath and blinked away the last of the tears. Next to her Genevieve sniffled, so Becca passed the hanky over to her. She dabbed at her tears, too, and then started to hand it back, but Collin plucked the material from his wife's fingers and ran his thumb over the monogrammed horseshoe CCs. Cash reached across Becca and tugged the handkerchief from his grasp. Then the two brothers exchanged a tense glance, almost a glare.

"I now you pronounce you husband and wife!" Ben

Haven said loudly. Then he chuckled. "Let's all congratulate my dear friend and new grandfather, Lem Lemmon,
and this beautiful meddler, my grandmother. Love you,
Grandma."

Sadie reached out and patted Ben's cheek, maybe not
all that lightly from the sound of it and the slight grimace
on Ben's face. But then she sniffled and said, "From one
meddler to another, thank you." She leaned forward and
kissed the cheek she'd patted, and then she turned back
toward her groom and kissed him.

Maybe Becca should have felt heartened and hopeful.
These two had finally acted on feelings they might have
had for each other for a long while. But obviously their
feelings for each other had been reciprocated.

Cash had never given her any indication that he saw
her as anything other than his best friend. Maybe he even
saw her as a pseudo-sister like his younger brothers always
had. With her dark hair and eyes, she looked more like his
siblings than he did.

Maybe that was why it had hit him so hard when he'd
discovered the truth, because a part of him had always
wondered...

Maybe even suspected.

Did he realize that Becca wasn't telling the truth about
Hope? And if he did...

She doubted he would even want to be her friend anymore since he had such a thing about honesty now. Not
that being honest was a bad thing.

But she hadn't wanted her daughter to grow up being
teased for being the child of an anonymous sperm donor,
or maybe they would call her a test-tube baby. She was
too young to understand how much Becca had wanted her.
And also, out of pride, Becca hadn't wanted anyone else to
know that she'd had to turn to a sperm bank to make her

dream of being a mother before she was thirty come true. So she'd made up a whole whirlwind relationship, with an elopement to Vegas and a marriage that hadn't lasted once they'd realized they had nothing in common. She claimed she hadn't realized she was pregnant until after their annulment, and then he had left for a job overseas and she'd had no way of getting ahold of him ever again.

Cash had offered to try. So had her parents. And she felt sick every time they felt sorry for her or angry on her behalf for having to be a single mom. She didn't have the guts to tell them this was what she wanted.

Because it really wasn't...

She wanted Cash, as a husband, and as a father to her children. At least he was Hope's godfather. But now, if he discovered the truth, it wasn't pity he was liable to feel for her but anger. Betrayal.

Then he would undoubtedly treat her the way he'd treated his dad and brothers, cutting off all contact with them. Despite what Cash believed, JJ was his dad in every way.

She saw that familial connection between them when the older man followed his mother and her new husband down the makeshift aisle and his gaze slid over Cash like a loving touch. A father's touch. And tears pooled in his dark eyes like they'd pooled in Becca's just a short time ago when emotion had overwhelmed her as it was overwhelming JJ now.

Next to her, Cash's breath audibly caught as his gaze met his father's. Then he choked as if emotions or tears were clogging his throat. She hoped it wasn't resentment anymore. She hoped it was love. Or even regret.

She knew, although he rarely admitted it, that he hated how he'd treated JJ that day that he'd learned the truth. He hated how he'd lashed out at him. But she knew that like her, Cash struggled with his pride and that he allowed it to make him stubborn.

Like she'd allowed hers to make her lie.

JUST A SHORT while ago, Jessup "JJ" Haven had told his mother that she'd given him a gift by inviting Cash to her wedding. But when his gaze met Cash's, this gift reminded him of some of the ones that the boys used to make in school and bring home to him.

Like the ashtray.

He'd never smoked, so he hadn't been sure what to do with the gift. Fortunately it had come in handy for spare change. Not that he'd ever had much of that with all of his medical bills and some that had been left from Colleen's unsuccessful cancer treatments. Because she'd been more focused on his health instead of her own, the cancer had been discovered too late for anything to help her.

If Jessup had had more money, he would have tried harder to find Cash. He would have hired a private investigator. Or at least traveled to find him.

That first summer Cash had probably followed the rodeo, trying to retrace his mother's steps, his mother's life, to find the man Cash had called his real father in those heated moments when he'd hurled such awful words at Jessup. He'd been so angry, and Jessup had been too weak to follow him.

He'd been so sick for so long that travel had been impossible. Spending any money on anything but his medical care had been so difficult. But he'd ached with missing Cash.

He'd wanted to bring him home so badly. But now that Cash was here…

He had no home anymore to take him to. Even before

the fire, Jessup had put the ranch up for sale, so Cash probably blamed and hated him for that in addition to all the other reasons he hated him.

CHAPTER THREE

THAT URGE WAS building inside Cash like it had built up over the course of the first eighteen years of his life. The urge to run away from it all.

From all the uncertainty. All the fear. All the pain.

And the unbearable pressure of all those emotions weighing so heavily on him that he hadn't been able to breathe. He could barely breathe now with his brothers gathered around him, staring so intently at him.

While JJ and the other Havens had followed the bride and groom down the aisle and out into the hall, Colton and Marsh had cut into the empty row of seats and stood in front of him while Collin leaned over from the end of their row.

Colton began, "What the—"

At the same time Marsh said, "Why are you—"

Becca stepped in front of him, backing him against the wall. "Stop," she said like she used to when they were kids fighting about something. Usually over the horse they'd all liked to ride. Or the lighter...

Grandpa Cassidy's lighter. The one he'd lost. They would probably really want to rough him up if they knew he'd lost it.

"This is not the place for this conversation," Becca said.

"Then why did you bring him here?" Collin asked her in an accusatory tone.

That tone had Cash wrapping his arm around her waist

to try to move around her in the narrow space between the chairs. He wanted her out of the line of fire. But the minute he touched her, he felt a strange sensation, almost a jolt. It was probably just nerves. "Don't talk to Becca like that," he chastised his younger brother.

"Don't tell me how to talk to anyone," Collin said, his voice even sharper now.

Cash couldn't remember Collin ever talking to anyone like that. He'd always been so studious and serious that he'd mostly stayed out of the skirmishes the other brothers had had. Unless his twin had dragged him into it.

Despite not seeing them up close for years, Cash could easily tell them apart. He'd spotted Colton, wearing the black cowboy hat he'd always worn, the minute he'd stepped into the mayor's office.

"Becca's right, Collin, this really isn't the time or place," the blonde woman said. The two women obviously knew each other.

Had Becca mentioned Collin's…wife?…to him? Maybe. Whenever she tried to bring up his family, he usually stopped her and refused to participate in the conversation about them. She probably figured that was because he was still bitter, but it was actually the reverse, which made him feel sick…with regret.

"It's been seventeen years since we've seen him," Colton chimed in.

Marsh said nothing. It hadn't been seventeen years for him, but it appeared their younger brothers didn't know that.

Colton continued, "And since we don't know if it'll be another seventeen years, this might have to be the time and place, or we won't get another chance."

"I'm not going anywhere," Cash said. "I live here."

"In Willow Creek?" Marsh asked, his voice nearly hoarse.

Cash nodded.

"Why are you *here*?" Colton asked that question.

"In Willow Creek or at this wedding?" Cash asked.

"Sadie invited him to the wedding," Becca answered for him, trying to defuse the tense situation like she used to. "He's her guest, and this is her wedding. We really should go congratulate the bride and groom."

"Yes, we should," the blonde woman agreed.

A woman with long, curly strawberry blond hair walked back into the room and right up to Colton, sliding beneath his arm. "What's going on?" she asked, and she peered up at him, her beautiful face soft with concern and love. "I thought you were right behind me." She glanced around then at the rest of them, her gaze resting on Cash...the stranger.

And he did feel like one, had somewhat always felt like one. Or at least strange in comparison to his brothers. And then he'd found out why...

Apparently his younger brothers had all found love but for Marsh, who was alone. But then Marsh knew the truth.

For some reason, Cash suspected he'd never shared that with the twins. Because, obviously, their brothers had fallen in love. They didn't have the same issue with trust that Cash did and maybe Marsh had, as well.

"Livvy, this is my brother Cash," Colton said.

She let out a soft gasp, and her green eyes widened as she stared at him. "Wow."

"Apparently he's Sadie's guest," Colton said with a slight grin.

She smiled and chuckled. "Of course he is. Sadie actually wants us all right now for family photos."

The pressure already weighing on Cash grew heavier, making it harder for him to breathe. He nearly reached for

Becca again, not to ease her aside, but to clutch her close to him, like Colton had his arm around Livvy.

But Livvy was clearly more than just Colton's friend.

"And we have to hurry because the tattoo artist will be here soon," Colton added with a glance at his wristwatch.

"Tattoo artist?" Becca asked.

Livvy grinned. "Yes, Grandpa and Sadie… Grandma Sadie now…are getting their rings tattooed on." She glanced up at Colton, and her grin widened. "It was his idea."

"Which meant I had to find one who was mobile and would come here to City Hall." He glanced at his watch again. "I better make sure she's here."

"After the pictures," Livvy said, but she was tugging Colton along with her toward the aisle. Then she gestured at the rest of them. "You all need to get moving. You don't want Sadie coming to get you."

Collin and his wife slipped out of the row and followed Colton and Livvy down the aisle. Marsh hesitated, staring hard at Cash. "You need to come, too," he said.

Cash shook his head. "You know why I shouldn't be in those photos."

Marsh had tracked him down at college that first year, demanding to know why he'd run off. So Cash had told him. As well as wanting to see them, which was partly why he'd come here today, he wanted to know if the twins knew, and if they didn't, it was time that they found out.

"Then why did you come here today?" Marsh asked. "And don't tell me it's just because Sadie invited you."

Cash shook his head in reply. He really didn't want to argue with Marsh right now. Maybe he should just tell him what he'd told Becca about wanting to get the twins to leave her alone. Despite his trying to shut down every conversation she started about his family, he'd heard enough to know that she was stuck in the middle between him and his brothers and that she was tired of it. And as a single mom running a business and a ranch on her own, she was already too tired.

He was her friend, and friends were supposed to help each other, not hinder them. So it was true that that was one of his reasons for coming today, to stop his brothers from pressuring her.

Marsh shook his head, too, then walked out of the room, leaving Becca and Cash standing alone in the mayor's office surrounded by empty chairs.

"You were right," Cash said. "Coming here was a mistake."

Becca let out a long, ragged breath, as if she'd been holding it for a while. "That actually went better than I thought it would," she admitted. "I was worried that they might try to hurt you."

He was the one who'd caused the pain; he'd known that for a while. And for the past several years he'd figured that staying away was the best way to avoid causing more pain. He should have remembered that today and stayed away from this wedding. But it was too late now.

"Is that why you agreed to be my plus-one, Becca?" he asked. "You intended to be my bodyguard like you were when we were kids?"

She shook her head. "No. I wanted a front-row seat to the action."

He laughed. That was why he'd asked her to come with him; no matter how miserable he was, she never failed to make him feel better. He stepped closer to her, to slip past her in the narrow space between the rows of empty chairs, and as he did, his body brushed against hers. He felt that strange but unfortunately familiar little zip of energy he felt whenever he touched Becca, but as usual, he chose to ignore it. Then he grabbed her hand and tugged her along with him. "Now, let's sneak out of here…"

FOR A MOMENT, with her hand in Cash's, Becca closed her eyes and imagined that she was the bride and he was the groom walking down the aisle after exchanging their vows, after pledging their love and loyalty to each other for the rest of their lives.

Becca banged into Cash's back as he stopped suddenly.

"Good, you're coming," a deep, feminine voice said. "The photographer is getting impatient, not to mention the kids…"

Cash's body tensed against Becca's, and she forced herself to open her eyes and step around him. He sighed and said, "I can't be in those photos, Mrs. Ha—"

"Sadie," she interjected. "Or Grandma, like your brothers call me."

"JJ didn't tell you?" he asked, his voice sounding choked with emotion. His grasp on Becca's hand tightened, as if he needed to hang on to her to stay grounded.

Becca entwined her fingers with his and squeezed while Sadie just stood there in her lacy pale pink gown and waited.

"I'm not your grandson," Cash said gruffly. "I am not JJ's son."

Sadie's dark eyes narrowed for a moment, as if she was visually inspecting him for Haven DNA. Then she shook her head, rejecting his claim. "Yes, you are—"

"I'm not," Cash insisted.

"In every way that truly matters, you are my son's child," she said. "And that makes you my grandson, so you're going to be in these family photos."

From what Becca knew of Sadie March Haven, she had already admired the matriarch. Now she idolized her.

Sadie had put so simply what Becca had been trying to tell Cash for years.

Sadie didn't wait for his compliance, instead reaching out and grabbing his arm to tug him out of the room.

While Cash had every reason to be in those family photos, Becca did not. So she dug in her heels and tried to free herself from Cash's hold, something she'd been attempting to do unsuccessfully for years. He was too much a part of her life that letting him go would feel like part of her was dying.

"You're coming, too," Sadie told her.

Becca shook her head but smiled. "I'm not family."

"My brothers have considered you more of a sibling over the years than they probably do me," Cash said with a slight grin. His blue eyes twinkled, and she could imagine he was thinking that if he had to be part of this spectacle, then so did she.

She suspected his brothers weren't the only ones who looked at her like a sister; Cash did, too.

"Come on," Sadie said impatiently. "The tattoo artist is here, and we need to get these pictures done so she can get started on our rings."

Becca was still uncomfortable with the situation and protested, "But I shouldn't—"

"Yes, you should be in these family photos," Sadie said, and she looked from one to the other of them with such a telling expression.

She knew.

Not just who Cash was.

But somehow she also knew how Becca felt about him. Heat rushed to her face. It was embarrassing enough that she felt this way, but it would be absolutely humiliating if anyone else realized how she felt. Especially Cash...

Sadie reached out, clasping her hand, too, and she

guided them both down the aisle and into the hall where an argument had broken out.

But this one wasn't between the Cassidy brothers; it was between the little Haven boys and one of the Haven men. The one with the dark hair but the lighter brown eyes. Baker Haven. He was shaking his head. "No. Absolutely not."

"I want a tattoo, too!" a little blond boy was saying. Caleb was Katie Haven's son, Jake Haven's stepson.

"Me, too!" a boy the same size as him with darker blond hair said. Ian Haven. His older brother, Miller, stood behind him while his younger brother the toddler Little Jake, was in Baker's arms.

"Me, too!" Bailey Ann chimed in with the boys.

Instead of arguing with her, Collin laughed and shook his head. Becca couldn't remember ever seeing him this happy.

The Cassidy brothers had all been so intense as kids, especially Collin. Colton had always managed to be positive, bright and funny. Marsh had had his moments, too. He had a wicked sense of humor.

And Cash…

She could always make him laugh.

But Collin finally didn't look as tense and troubled as he always did. Love had done that for him. Not just love for the little girl he'd adopted but also for Genevieve. His arm was around his wife.

"Nobody is getting tattoos today but the bride and groom," Baker Haven said. "It wouldn't be fair otherwise. It's their special day. It has to be all about them."

Sadie snorted derisively at her youngest grandson's claim. Then she released Becca's and Cash's hands and clapped hers together. "This special day is all about family," she said. "All of our great, big, combined family. Let's get these pictures taken."

"I'm surprised to see you here, Doc CC," a man addressed Cash.

Becca tried to place him. Maybe he was one of Lem's grandsons? But those guys were standing around their sister, Dr. Livvy Lemmon. This man must be a Haven, though he was shorter, and his hair was sandy, not dark like Cash's brothers. His eyes were hazel…like two of the little boys. It took Becca a minute, but then she recognized him from the rodeos she'd watched. He was the champion bronc and bull rider Dusty Chaps. Maybe he recognized Cash from when he'd worked for the rodeo.

"You're a doctor?" Collin asked.

Cash shrugged. "Not a cardiologist like you. I'm a vet." Just like he'd always wanted to be.

"He whispers to horses," the blondest little boy said. With his blue eyes, he could have been Cash's son. And the way he looked at him, with such awe, had Becca wishing things she had no business wishing…

For a younger brother for Hope, for one who looked like this little boy, who looked like Cash…

But Cash was just her friend. He and his brothers weren't really her family. Yet for some reason she let herself be swept along, caught up in the family photos, along with Cash. And she couldn't help but think that someday, someone would look back at these pictures and wonder who she was and what in the world she was doing in them.

Because she knew that eventually Cash would fall in love with someone, like Collin and Colton had, and he would have a family of his own. And his new wife might see what Sadie so clearly had, how Becca really felt about Cash, and then even their friendship wouldn't last.

So Cash falling for someone else was another worry for

Becca. On top of her fear that he'd find out all that she'd kept from him, just like his father had. If he ever found out she'd lied to him, their friendship would be over forever.

THE SCENE IN the large atrium area of City Hall was nearly enough to need crowd control. But instead of stepping in to help, Michael March Cassidy, interim sheriff of Willow Creek, stood off to the side watching the festivities of the wedding reception. Marsh was the nickname Cash had inadvertently given him because, as a toddler, he hadn't been able to pronounce his new baby brother's full name.

Marsh had gone into law enforcement for a few reasons. One was that, even though Cash was the oldest, Marsh had usually had to step in as the authority figure with his brothers. Because of how sick their dad had been, Marsh had had to do that a lot to keep the peace in his family. When the tension had gotten too much over worries about their dad, the brothers had tended to take it out on each other in stupid ways: petty arguments and pranks. And Marsh had had to de-escalate the tension.

While Cash had always handled the animals with ease, he had trouble dealing with people. Except for Becca, of course. Marsh, on the other hand, was good at dealing with people. That was another reason he'd chosen law enforcement. He could usually tell when someone was hiding something or when they were guilty of something. He had a certain intuition that usually led him to the perpetrator. He had never picked up on the secrets his dad had been keeping, though.

About Cash or about himself...

Marsh hadn't found out about Cash until he'd *found* Cash. At least the stubborn fool hadn't turned down his scholarship when he'd turned on his family. But he'd refused to come home, insisting that it wasn't his home anymore. That they weren't his family.

Anger quickened Marsh's pulse just as it had back then. That was the last time he'd tried to talk sense into his older brother. Not wanting to hurt his dad and his younger brothers, Marsh hadn't told them about his visit with Cash. He'd let them believe he'd just spent that weekend camping with friends like he'd told them. And he was glad he'd even hidden all the pictures of Cash around the house, so that his dad and his younger brothers weren't constantly reminded of him.

While Marsh could usually ferret out lies, he was a really good liar himself when he had reason to be. He'd used this talent to get suspects to turn on each other and confess. He'd perfected the technique with his younger brothers. And as he watched the two of them, how they looked at Cash and then at each other, he knew something else was going on here. Had probably been going on for a while.

Ever since the fire at the ranch, Colton had been acting strange. For instance, he'd gone and fallen in love...

That was strange behavior for all of them. But now Collin had succumbed, too.

And even Sadie...

As she and Lem cut their wedding cake in the atrium area of City Hall, Marsh half expected her to smash a piece in her groom's face. But instead she just put a speck of frosting on his nose before she kissed him. Then she got the frosting on her nose, too. And they both laughed.

The fierce old lady was definitely in love. Marsh shuddered at the thought of ever falling in love. While he was happy for Sadie and Lem, he couldn't imagine ever trusting anyone enough to love them. His inability to trust had more to do with his family, and the secrets they kept, than with his job. That was why he was focused more on the twins than even on Cash at the moment. And the minute Colton slipped away to the restroom, Marsh followed him inside.

Colton glanced over his shoulder as Marsh entered, then tensed. And Marsh knew his intuition had not failed him.

"Give it up," he ordered Colton. "It's no use."

"You know?"

Marsh sighed. "Of course I do," he bluffed. "You know you can't keep any secrets from me."

Colton sighed, too, and shook his head. "Collin told you. I thought he agreed to wait, that we shouldn't put you in this position…"

Dread curled in Marsh's stomach as he realized this secret was even bigger than he'd suspected. He'd thought they were grappling with losing the family home and even, to some extent, their family as they'd known it.

"He and Genevieve have this whole open and honest thing going on now," Colton said. "And she convinced him that there's probably an innocent explanation for me finding the lighter where I did…"

Marsh's heart was beating fast now. And he held out his hand, palm up. "Give it up," he said again.

Colton reached into his pocket and pulled out the lighter. Cash's lighter.

"Where did you find it?" he asked.

Colton's brows lowered as his eyes narrowed. "I thought you knew everything…"

"Tell me."

"In the ashes of the house…"

Clearly Colton suspected Cash of using that lighter to start the fire that had burned down their family home. The fire that could have ended in even more tragedy than it did. Dad had gone back into the burning house to find his nurse's son, and Marsh and Collin had gone in after him.

Dad could have died from smoke inhalation and Collin's hands had been burned just as he'd been about to start his new position as a cardiologist at Willow Creek Memorial Hospital.

And Marsh…

He'd had smoke inhalation and burns, too. But now he was burning with suspicions of his own and with anger.

CHAPTER FOUR

IN THE CRUSH of people and kids and chaos, Cash had lost contact with Becca. His palm still tingled from holding her hand. And he felt again like those balloons, like he was going to drift to the ceiling if he didn't grab something or someone to anchor him down.

This whole wedding was so surreal.

How had he gone from treating Ranch Haven's most difficult horse just that morning to attending the wedding of Sadie Haven to the deputy mayor that same afternoon?

Knowing that he probably needed to explain his presence, Cash approached Dusty. He'd met the man years ago but had known him only as Dusty Chaps, the up-and-coming rodeo rider. He'd only learned Dusty was a Haven during one of his calls to take care of the ranch's livestock. And he hadn't known about his own connection to the Havens at that point. Not that he had a real one…

Except…

As he approached Dusty, the man was helping settle his very pregnant wife onto a chair. The woman had long brown hair and warm brown eyes, and she looked a little pale. Given her petite build, it was probably hard for her to deal with the size of her belly.

Concerned for a number of reasons, Cash asked, "Is everything okay? Can I get you anything?"

The woman smiled. "I'm fine. And while I appreciate

your concern, please no fussing. My husband and family fuss too much already."

"Melanie," Dusty said, "Doc CC is actually family himself. He's Uncle Jessup's oldest son."

She'd already been glowing but now she flushed. "I'm sorry. I'm learning now what this pregnancy brain is all about… I can't remember anything."

"You didn't forget anything," Cash assured her. "Nobody knew…" The truth. That he wasn't really Jessup's son. But he wasn't going to get into that now at a wedding.

"Doc CC was holding out on us," Dusty said. "I had no idea what your real name was."

"Now you know how I felt when I showed up at Ranch Haven and ran into *Dusty Chaps*," Cash said, teasing the rodeo rider.

Melanie giggled. "He's got you there. And now you know how I felt, my darling husband."

"About what?" Cash asked. He was very curious about Melanie Shepherd-Haven and had been since he'd found out about her and what she really was to him…

Melanie smiled and flushed even more. "Let's just say that getting married on a first date might not be the best idea."

That made him think of Becca, who couldn't have been seeing her husband very long before she'd married him. She'd never even mentioned him to Cash. A pang struck his heart—not that he was jealous of a stranger. He was just hurt that while he shared everything with her, there were some things she hadn't shared with him. At least not right away.

Dusty chuckled. "It worked out well for us." He leaned down and kissed the top of her head, and as he did, his hand touched her belly. "We're having twins, Doc."

"So you tell me every time I see you," Cash said with

a grin. He focused on Melanie again. "I hope you're feeling well."

"Exhausted," she said. "Totally exhausted and like I've swallowed a watermelon with two badgers trapped inside it that are trying to kick their way out."

"But no more ambulance trips," Dusty murmured.

Cash tensed. "What happened?"

She sighed. "Just a little low blood sugar. It's happened before. Last time when I fell, I let Midnight out of his stall."

Cash sucked in a breath. "Oh, no!"

"He was a perfect gentleman," she said. "He must have stepped right over me. And then, as Caleb insists, he rushed out of the barn to get help for me."

"Midnight in the Lassie role?" Cash asked.

Dusty snorted. "Not exactly. But with your help, he seems to be calming down some."

"I'm not so sure about that—"

"No shoptalk here at Sadie's wedding," Melanie admonished them. Then she looked past Cash and smiled.

"Do you need anything, honey?" a woman asked her. She looked a lot like Melanie but there was more auburn in her hair than brown.

"I'm fine, Mom." Then her smile widened and she added, "And before you ask, I don't need anything."

Another woman had come up behind Melanie's mother, and Cash tensed as he recognized her from the Cassidy ranch. The woman who'd moved in so quickly after he'd left, the woman who had replaced his late mother in his family.

"This is my mom," Melanie said. "Juliet Shepherd."

"And have you met my mother?" Dusty asked. "Darlene Haven. This is—"

"Doc CC," she said. "The vet…" Her forehead furrowed beneath strands of sandy blond hair, as if wondering whether there was another reason that he was here. And he realized that there was another reason *she* was here, as well. She was Dusty's mom? Then wouldn't that make her JJ's sister-in-law?

"I'm Cash," he said.

And she sucked in a breath.

The pressure on Cash's chest grew heavier. He didn't need anyone to ground him anymore; he was too weighed down by all the emotions gripping him. Had he been wrong about Darlene's reason for being on the Cassidy Ranch all those years ago? Had he made even more mistakes than he'd realized?

Overwhelmed with regrets and confusion, he had that urge again to run. To escape…

But he couldn't leave without Becca. Where was she?

BECCA WISHED SHE'D been able to reject Cash's invitation to the wedding, but she'd never been able to refuse him anything.

Except for the truth…

Of course he hadn't actually asked for it, but it was painfully clear, at least to her, that he expected honesty of her, probably more so than anyone else he knew.

That was why she'd slipped away from him after those awkward family photos. She'd gone into the bathroom to wash her hands, as if she could somehow wash away the tingling she felt whenever he touched her. She'd run cold water and hot water over her hands, yet she could still feel his skin against her, his grasp so firm that it had seemed like he never intended to let her go.

But he had. When he'd taken off on his family, he'd left her, too. That summer they were supposed to have fun before they left for college, but Cash had been too devastated for fun, and he'd just wanted to be alone. Even from her. She'd felt so rejected and abandoned, maybe because she'd just realized how she'd really felt about him. That she loved him as more than a friend.

He'd called her, at least, and they'd texted. While it hadn't been enough for her, they had kept in contact over the years even before they'd both moved to Willow Creek. She'd been talking about it first, moving closer to where her parents had moved from Moss Valley to Willow Creek. But Cash had actually done it first, buying into a veterinarian practice in Willow Creek.

Speaking of Willow Creek, just about everyone in town had shown up for this wedding. So she was surprised to find herself alone in the restroom but also grateful that she was. She didn't want anyone else to ask her how she had convinced Cash to attend Sadie's wedding when all the credit for that belonged to the bride.

Becca had actually thought it was a bad idea, and still thought it was. The only reason Cash had held her hand like he had was because he'd been overwhelmed. And the last time he'd felt like that, he ran away. She was worried that he'd run again, and now it wouldn't be just her heart he broke when he took off but her daughter's, as well.

But as overwhelmed as she was feeling with her fear and her attraction, she understood his urge to run. She found herself studying the bathroom window and wondered if she could squeeze through the narrow opening, which was high on the brick wall. If she wasn't wearing one of her favorite dresses, she might have tried, but she didn't want to rip the silky blue material.

With a sigh, she opened the door and stepped out into the hall, startling Colton and herself as she nearly collided with him. Marsh was there, too, but he didn't look surprised to see her.

He rarely ever looked surprised. Even during the wedding, he hadn't appeared as shocked as the twins had been over Cash turning up as a guest.

"You weren't waiting for me, were you?" she asked uneasily. "I really didn't have anything to do with Cash coming to this wedding."

Colton chuckled. "No. That was all Sadie." He glanced at his older brother. "I'm going to go find the blushing bride now and check out her tattoo."

Marsh laughed, too, as his brother rushed away. Curious about the tattoo herself, Becca started to follow Colton. But Marsh reached out and caught her arm, holding her in the hallway with him. "Before you go, I have a couple of questions for you, Becca."

His grasp on her arm suddenly felt like a handcuff. Instead of showing how unnerved she was, Becca smiled. "Are you asking these questions in an official capacity, Sheriff Cassidy?"

She'd hoped Marsh would laugh. Or at least grin. But his face remained serious and unreadable. All the Cassidy men but for Cash had dark, unfathomable eyes. Cash's blue eyes were sometimes too expressive, because she couldn't just see the pain he felt over his family but she could almost feel it, too.

"What's going on?" she asked.

"I just have a few questions," Marsh said as if they were inconsequential.

But from his tone and his lack of expression, she seriously doubted that. "About?" she asked, although she had a pretty good idea. Cash.

He seemed to be all anyone wanted to ask her about lately. Even her own daughter...

Hope was always asking, "Is Cash coming over tonight?"

"Is he coming to dinner?"

"Will he go riding with us?"

Hope was as fascinated with Cash as Becca was.

"When you listed the ranch for sale, did you ever bring Cash out there with you?" Marsh asked.

"What?" she asked, genuinely perplexed that he would ask such a thing.

"Did you bring him along to either show him the place or maybe to help you with something?" he persisted.

She almost shuddered at the thought. "Of course not." She wouldn't have dared to even ask him to go back there. "And he wouldn't have gone if I'd asked."

"You're sure about that?" he asked. "What about the lock you put on the door? Did he have the code for that? Could he have let himself inside?"

And now she shivered. But she didn't answer his question, because while she hadn't specifically given Cash the key code for her lockbox, he could have figured it out. Hope's birthday. "Why are you asking about Cash and the ranch?"

Marsh let go of her arm and shoved his hand in his pocket. Then he pulled something out of his pocket.

Cash's lighter.

It looked dirty, the pewter dark like it had been stained or burned...

"Where did you find this?" she asked.

"I didn't," he said. "Colton did. In the ashes of the house."

She stiffened, defensive. "And you think *Cash* burned down your family home?"

"I don't know what to think," Marsh said, his voice gruffer than usual. "I'm trying to find out what happened, though. How it wound up inside with the ashes."

"Then ask him," she said.

Marsh snorted. "And you expect what? That I'll get a confession?"

"I expect you will get the truth," Becca said. "Cash is the most honest person I know. He won't lie to you." Not like she had lied...

And if he ever found out, their friendship would definitely be over. He would probably even run again like he had the last time he'd felt betrayed. But this time, she doubted he would maintain any contact with her. Not even the calls and texts.

JESSUP APPROACHED HIS oldest son with all the care he'd approached the stray tabby cat that had showed up at the ranch just a few weeks before the house had burned down. He hadn't wanted to scare it away, so he'd made a point of not getting too close to it, just as he hadn't gotten too close to Cash during the reception.

But as things were beginning to wind down, the cake nearly gone as well as the other food, he knew he needed to catch Cash before he ran away again like he had all those years ago.

Seventeen years.

He couldn't believe how much time had passed. But he could see it when he looked at his oldest son. He wasn't a skinny teenager anymore. While he wasn't as tall as Jessup or as his brothers, Cash must have grown a few more inches, and he'd filled out except for his face, which was defined by creases, sharp cheekbones and a cleft chin.

Cash looked so much like his mother that Jessup physically ached for missing her. Colleen had been gone even longer than Cash, but at least now Jessup didn't ache for missing them both.

But when he approached and his son looked at him with such a tense expression, he knew Cash was still missing.

At least the Cash that Jessup had known, the one who'd loved him and his family so very much he'd wanted to make a huge sacrifice for them.

He'd wanted to give Jessup his kidney, and at eighteen, he hadn't needed parental permission. So despite Jessup telling him not to, he'd gotten himself tested to see if he could be a donor. And that was how he'd found out the truth, from some doctor who hadn't just told Cash that he wasn't a match but also that there was no way they could be related.

The tension on Cash's face held a trace of panic, reminding him of that feral cat again. Then he took a literal step back and held up his hands. "Please, don't go," Jessup said softly. "I've missed you so much. I don't want you to leave before we've had a chance to talk."

Hopefully now that Cash was older, he would give him a chance to explain. And he wouldn't run away again.

That had probably been karma, though. After all, Jessup had run away from his family at the same age that Cash had, and he hadn't had as good a reason.

He'd felt suffocated, blaming his mother's worry and overprotectiveness, though he knew now that it had been the lupus. The disease that kept attacking his body had kept him from being able to do all things he'd wanted to do. Like live without fear.

He still lived with fear. Decades later, he was healthier than ever thanks to a heart transplant, and he was scared his body would reject it. And he was just as scared that Cash would reject his family again. He wanted to reach out and pull his oldest boy in for a tight hug. But again he thought of that skittish cat...

And he felt a sudden pang of remorse.

"What is it?" Cash asked with alarm, and he reached for him, grasping his shoulder. "Are you okay?"

Jessup nodded. "Yeah, I just realized I forgot about something."

Cash arched an eyebrow. "What?"

He shook his head. "Just a cat... It was coming around the ranch. But since the house burned down I haven't been back to check on it."

"You're thinking about a cat," Cash said. But it wasn't a question.

They shared a love of animals. That was why Jessup had joined the rodeo after he'd run away from Ranch Haven, why he'd wanted to help Colleen with the ranch she'd inherited from her father. He'd been only too happy to help with the baby she was carrying when they reconciled after their brief break up, as well.

"The cat reminds me of you," Jessup admitted with a smile.

"Ornery and stubborn?" Cash asked.

And Jessup chuckled. "If that was the case, she would remind me of me."

Cash's lips curved into a slight grin before he grimaced and shook his head. "I can't do this. Not here. Not now."

Jessup noticed that other people were watching them even though they were pretending not to, including Becca. And some of Jessup's nephews...

And his sons.

"I don't want you to leave again, though," Jessup said. "I don't want you to run off like you did."

"I'm not going anywhere. I have a life here in Willow Creek. I own half a veterinarian practice. I'm not going anywhere."

"Thank God," Jessup said, breathing a sigh of relief.

"But I'm not doing this anymore," Cash said, and he gestured around at the family standing close enough to see but not hear everything they were saying.

"What do you mean?" Jessup asked.

"I'm not keeping your secret. That's partially why I came here, to let you know that and give you the first chance to tell everyone the truth."

"You won't accept the truth," Jessup said. "You won't accept that you're still my son."

Cash shook his head, and that look came over him again, the same look that cat had had before it ran off to hide in the barn. The same look Cash had had before he'd run off to hide for seventeen years.

Jessup wasn't convinced that Cash was going to stay in Willow Creek, even for the life he'd apparently built here. But then he followed Cash's eye line and saw that he was watching Becca. Becca was beside Sadie, admiring her tattoo.

He wondered if it was the veterinarian practice that had brought him to Willow Creek or Becca...

Becca and Cash had been inseparable growing up, closer to each other than the twins had been. When Jessup and the boys had learned that Cash had stayed in contact with Becca, the boys had been annoyed. But Jessup had been relieved. He'd known his son would be fine as long as he had his best friend in his life.

Jessup had always wished that someday Becca and Cash's friendship would become something more.

But she'd married someone else and had a child. And Cash, well, he seemed determined to let no one into his heart. Probably because he'd been hurt too badly.

By Jessup...

CHAPTER FIVE

CASH HAD NEVER been more grateful for all his years of friendship with Becca. Somehow she'd sensed when he had needed rescuing at the reception and had excused them both graciously because she had to get home to her daughter.

Becca and Hope had such a special bond. Cash didn't know if that was because Becca, being a single mom, was both parents to her daughter, or if it was just because they were so much alike. He often teased Becca that she'd cloned herself when she'd had Hope.

As he pulled up to the farmhouse on Becca's small ranch, Hope jumped up from the porch steps where she'd been sitting, her grandmother watching her through the screen door, and rushed down to his truck.

Acting as if they'd been apart days instead of hours, Becca opened her door and rushed around the front of the truck. Then she picked up her daughter and twirled her around. The skirt of Becca's blue dress swirled around them both, and the sun, dropping lower in the sky, illuminated them like a spotlight on a pair of ballerinas.

If he ever said such a thing to Becca, she would think he'd lost his mind. If she didn't already think that after he'd accepted the invitation to Sadie's wedding. And he wasn't convinced that he hadn't. But the invite had given him the push he needed to see his brothers, and he'd wanted to so badly.

He stepped out of the truck onto the gravel drive where mother and daughter continued their little spin.

Hope laughed as they twirled. With her long dark hair and big dark eyes, she looked so much like her mother had at her age. But they were more alike than just physically. Hope had the same walk and smile and laugh and sense of humor.

Looking at Hope brought Cash back to his childhood, to when he'd met his best friend in elementary school so many years ago. She'd been taller than him then, and tougher. And while he'd since outgrown her, she was probably still tougher. He doubted he could handle everything she handled on her own.

When they'd first met, he'd been handling a lot. At home, as the oldest, he'd had to be tough for his brothers and for his parents, who'd been dealing with his dad's health issues. But with Becca he could be himself and she never judged him for it. She might not agree with him, but she was still always there for him.

Like today...

He wished he'd been there more for her after he'd left. But even though they'd kept in touch with texts and calls, they hadn't been in each other's daily lives until she'd moved to Willow Creek with her young daughter.

If he'd been around, maybe she wouldn't have acted so uncharacteristically impulsive and married a virtual stranger. While it had worked out for Dusty and Melanie, it hadn't worked out for Becca.

She'd been left alone to raise a child.

No. She wasn't alone. She had her parents, and she had him. He was trying to be as good a friend to her as she'd always been to him.

But it still felt uneven.

Like she gave more...

Or maybe Becca, being Becca, just had more to give.

They stopped spinning, and Becca stumbled back a bit on her heels, either because of the driveway or dizziness. And he reached out, wrapping his arm around them both. "Hey, steady there…"

But he didn't know if he was talking to them or himself because he suddenly felt a little lightheaded, too. And his heart beat harder and faster.

Maybe he was just overwhelmed from seeing everyone again. His brothers. His…

He didn't really know what to call JJ. His stepdad? And were the others his stepfamily? He wasn't sure he would ever be able to think of the Havens as family, though, not when they'd started as clients.

And clients were probably all they would ever be to him. Sadie might have invited him to her wedding, but once JJ told her the truth about how horrible Cash had been to him when he'd run away, he doubted she would actually want a relationship with him.

"Are you okay?" Becca asked with concern.

He realized he was still holding on to her and Hope, maybe a little too tightly. "Sorry," he said, and he loosened his arm a bit but didn't entirely release them. "I just zoned out for a second."

He'd been doing that more and more in Becca's presence, when he watched her with Hope or at her office when she was all dressed up in one of her suits and heels. Even in the barn when she had manure smeared on her forehead, she was so beautiful. How had he never noticed that before?

"That's understandable," she said. "You have a lot on your mind."

Her. He had her on his mind.

Had she noticed?

He sighed and shrugged off his mood. It was probably just guilt that he hadn't been there for her. He should have recognized the feeling; he'd carried it with him ever since he'd left the ranch.

Becca pulled away from his loosened embrace, but as she did, Hope scrambled from her arms onto Cash's shoulders. "Piggyback ride?" she asked.

Becca shook her head. "Hope—"

"Please, Cash," Hope said in her most wheedling voice.

Cash chuckled.

"Cash might be tired," Becca said. "We've had a long day."

He flinched with the realization that she might not want him to stay. It *had* been a long day, and instead of fixing things for her, he'd put her in a horrible, awkward position between him and his family again. "I'm sorry," he said again. "I shouldn't have asked you to be my plus-one."

"Plus what?" Hope asked.

Becca smiled at her daughter who hung yet from his shoulders. "His guest at a wedding."

"You been going to lots of them, Mommy," Hope said. "I wanna go to a wedding, too."

Becca smiled. "For the next one, you can be my plus-one," she said.

"I wanna be Cash's plus-one," Hope said.

"I probably won't be going to any more weddings," he said. His brothers hadn't seemed happy to see him at this one; they and the Havens weren't likely to invite him to another, especially if JJ followed through and told them the truth.

"Hold on tight," he told Hope. "I'm taking you on that piggyback ride."

She squealed and giggled as she clung to him, and he jumped up and down as he ran around the ranch. He kept his hands on the arms Hope had looped around his neck, making sure that he didn't lose her...just as he'd made sure throughout the years that he hadn't lost her mother.

Even when they hadn't lived in the same town or even the same state, she'd always been the one constant in his life, the person he could always count on.

And if he ever lost her, he had no idea how he would manage on his own. Because sometimes she felt like all he had.

BECCA'S HEAD POUNDED, but she forced herself to keep reading to Hope. One of her favorite childhood memories was of her mother and dad taking turns reading to her at night.

Becca usually didn't have someone to take a turn with, though, other than when her parents stayed later than usual. They had their own little house on the property, and since they both insisted on working with her, they often went to bed early so they could get up early.

Once she and Hope and Cash had come inside, her parents had bid them a good-night and slipped away. Her mother continued to hang on to her romantic notion that one day Cash would open his eyes and see that Becca was his soulmate. But Cash had only come inside because Hope had pleaded with him to stay longer. Otherwise he would have already been gone.

After their nearly thirty years of friendship and nothing but friendship, Becca snorted at the unlikely chance of Cash ever seeing her as anything more, let alone a soulmate. She was just his sidekick.

"Is the snort in the book?" Cash asked.

She glanced up to find him standing in the doorway, watching them. He probably would have read with them if Hope had had the chance to ask him, but he'd had to take a call earlier. And Becca had taken advantage of the moment to get Hope to take her bath and get ready for bed.

Despite her protestations that she wasn't tired, Hope's eyes were closed now, and drool trailed out of the corner of her rosebud lips. Becca set the book on the nightstand next to the mermaid lamp that Hope insisted had to be left on or the Little Mermaid would get scared. Then she leaned over the bed and brushed her lips across Hope's forehead.

"I shouldn't be surprised you snort when you read," Cash said, his lips curved into a grin, "since you always snort when you laugh. You must be spending too much time around your horses."

"Says the horse whisperer," she said, teasing him back with what the Haven kid had called him earlier. The boy wasn't the only one who referred to Cash by that nickname. He'd always had an uncanny ability to connect with animals, like Dr. Dolittle.

"My dad agrees with you," she admitted. He wasn't too happy that she'd mucked the stalls before he'd had the chance that morning. The kid she'd hired to help out over the summer had left for college already, and she needed to find some extra help so her dad wouldn't keep overdoing it.

"You're a bit of a horse whisperer yourself," he said. "Or you wouldn't have bought the ranch."

She glanced down at her sleeping daughter. "I bought it for her," she said. "I know how much I would have loved living on a ranch when I was her age."

"She is your mini-me," Cash said, his grin widening. "And you basically did live on a ranch growing up with all the time you spent at…" His grin slid away, and he didn't finish what he was going to say.

Maybe because he didn't know what to call it.

His ranch?

Or had he stopped thinking of it as his home? It was

still his dad's property because the sale hadn't closed yet due to the fire. Could Cash really have had something to do with that?

She glanced down at her daughter once more, and love flooded her heart. Hope was everything to her now, everything she'd wanted for so long.

No. She wasn't everything. Becca had wanted Cash, too. But she'd made herself accept reality a long time ago where he was concerned. And with Hope...

She'd made her child a reality and had fulfilled her need to become a mother. Hope was more than enough, but sometimes Becca found herself still yearning for more.

As she passed Cash in the doorway of her daughter's room, she drew in a deep, steadying breath, but she also drew in the scent of him, of soap and leather and horse. Despite being dressed up for the wedding, they'd gone into the barn during the piggyback tour of the ranch. Cash was as drawn to animals as he'd always been, as she had always been. It was one of the reasons the two of them had become fast friends in elementary school. And the reason now she could never keep any of her shoes clean.

She'd left the heels by the door, which made her shorter than Cash. She smiled almost wistfully as she looked up at him. "I miss the old days sometimes," she admitted as she stepped into the hall and closed the door to Hope's room.

He sighed, and it was definitely wistful. "Me, too."

She smiled. "Even when I used to tower over you?"

"I didn't mind *you* towering," he said. "It was my younger brothers towering over me that bothered me." His forehead creased with worry lines. "Then I found out why..."

"Dusty is shorter than his brothers," she pointed out. "He just takes after his mom instead of his dad."

"I do, too," he said. "If I took after my real dad, I'd really be short." Then he grimaced.

"Real dad?" she challenged him.

He shrugged. "Bio dad. Whatever..."

JJ *was* his real dad, the one who'd been there for him and loved him. But Cash was so angry over the lies that he couldn't appreciate him that way.

"Dusty's mom is the woman from the ranch," he said, and the creases in his forehead deepened again.

"Ranch Haven?"

He shook his head. "Cassidy Ranch," he said with a glance at Hope's closed bedroom door.

Concerned that they might wake her, Becca led the way down the hall into the kitchen. The room was warm and cozy, with cream-colored beadboard cabinets and butcher-block countertops, and in a bay window area was a built-in breakfast table with deeply padded bench seating. Becca sprawled onto the bench, regretful now of wearing her heels around the ranch and not just because they were probably coated in manure now. Her feet were sore, so she propped them up on the cushions and waited for Cash to settle into a seat. Instead, he paced the kitchen.

"What do you mean? She was at the ranch?"

"When I went back that summer before college, *she* was the one who answered the door," Cash explained. "And when I..."

She tensed. "When you what?"

"When I went back a few months ago..."

"I didn't even dare to ask if you wanted to see it with me one last time. I was certain you would refuse," she said. "You've been saying for years that you didn't ever want to go back there." She hadn't realized he'd gone back anyway, without her. That he'd never admitted it to her. And she couldn't help but remember her conversation with Marsh.

He flinched now. "I hope I didn't sound that childish when I said that," he remarked. "I just meant I had no need to go back there."

"But you did," she said. "A few months ago? So before the fire?"

He nodded. "Yeah, she called me to check out the mare she had."

"Who called you?"

"Darlene," he said. "She had a mare that she was selling, apparently to Dusty."

Now Becca could feel her forehead creasing. "I seem to remember some gossip about the Havens' mom taking off after their dad died."

Cash shrugged. "I don't know. I don't know the whole story between her and my...between her and JJ. When I saw her that summer, I thought she was his girlfriend. That he replaced my mom right after she died..."

Replaced his mom, and replaced him, too. She suspected that was how he'd felt. "But now you know that she's his sister-in-law," she said.

He nodded. "But that doesn't mean they couldn't be together. I heard that the Havens' dad died a long time ago."

"Like your mom," she said with sympathy. She knew how devastated he had been when she died, how devastated they had all been. Most of all JJ.

"But she wasn't dead long when I found Darlene at the ranch that first time," he said. "She was there that summer, and she was there just a few months ago."

"And so were you," she said. Then she swallowed hard, trying to suppress the doubts Marsh's questions had brought up for her. But this was Cash...

Cash who was still so bitter and angry about his family situation.

She cleared her throat and asked, "Did you figure out where you lost your lighter?"

He stopped pacing and stared at her. "My lighter?"

"You didn't have it the other night when we were going to do s'mores in the firepit in the backyard," she reminded him. "You didn't know where you lost it."

He shrugged. "I still don't."

"I do," she said, and her stomach flipped a bit. "Marsh told me that Colton found it at the ranch."

He nodded. "That makes sense. I probably lost it in the barn when I was checking out the mare."

"It wasn't found in the barn," she said. "It was found in the house, in the ashes…"

He sucked in a breath. Then his eyes widened. "Does Marsh… Do they *all* think I started the fire?"

"Marsh just had some questions," Becca said. "But I do think the lighter might be why Colton was so anxious to get ahold of you. I thought it was about the Havens, about Sadie and the rest of your family—"

"Their family," Cash interjected.

"Colton and Collin don't know that," she said.

He grimaced. "I told JJ that he needs to tell them."

"It won't make any difference to them," she said. "Just as it didn't make any difference to Sadie."

He shrugged. "It was nice of her to include us in family pictures and all, but I'm sure there were plenty taken without us in them."

"Why are you always so mistrustful of everyone?" she asked.

"You know why better than anyone," he said. "You were the first person I told when I found out my whole life was a lie. You're the only one I do trust, Becca."

She suppressed an urge to flinch as guilt jabbed her. She hadn't been completely honest with him about some very important things. Her feelings. And her daughter. In the beginning she'd been too embarrassed to tell him the truth, and now that the lie had gone so long, she knew he wouldn't forgive her. If he cut her out of his life because of it, it wouldn't be just her heart he broke; he would be breaking Hope's, too. Her little girl was so attached to him.

"I hope you trust me," he said. "And that you know that I didn't start that fire."

She smiled reassuringly at him even as her own guilt twisted her stomach into knots. "I know. I told Marsh to just ask you and that you'd tell him the truth."

He rolled his eyes. "He probably expects me to confess."

"I don't know what he expects," she said.

Cash sighed. "Probably the worst. I don't think Marsh trusts anyone easily, either." He dropped onto the bench next to her then and looped his arm around her shoulders. "I'm lucky. I have you, and I know I can trust you."

And that guilt nearly made her gag.

DARLENE HAVEN DROPPED into a chair on the back deck next to Jessup, who stared out into the yard. Except for the strands of twinkling lights strung across the arbor over the deck and the flashes of the fireflies flitting around the garden, it was dark.

But for the first time in a long while, Darlene actually felt like she wasn't in the dark anymore. For the first time in years she felt light…on her and inside her.

The light had come of revelations…so many revelations. She'd lost a lot, and she would always mourn her son and his wife, a young woman she'd never had the chance to meet. But in losing Dale and Jenny in the car crash, she'd gained, too. Grandsons…

And forgiveness.

From those she loved and from herself.

She wasn't sure Jessup had been able to do the same. "Are you okay?" she asked. "You've been out here for a while." He'd come right outside after the wedding, and they'd not had a chance to talk.

To share their experiences about the day.

And she had something to tell him…about Cash. But knowing how much his oldest son affected him, she'd wanted to wait until Jessup was ready, physically and emotionally.

When her husband had died all those years ago, Darlene had felt responsible for his death. If only she hadn't been on that tractor with him…

If only she hadn't distracted him…

She'd blamed herself and had been convinced that her sons and Sadie blamed her, too. So she'd gone looking for Sadie's missing son, as if that could somehow make up for losing Michael. It had taken Darlene a little more than a year to find Jessup.

And he'd been so close to death, all on his own and with three teenage boys at home…

She hadn't been able to leave him, or to bring him back to Sadie. She didn't want to inflict any more pain on one of the women she admired and loved the most in the world; she hadn't wanted to put Sadie through another loss. But Darlene realized now there was no way to save someone else from that pain. It was inevitable that a person was going to lose someone they loved. Some just lost them sooner and lost more…

Sadie certainly had. That was why today had been exceptionally special to Darlene. Tears filled her eyes now.

And Jessup reached across the table and patted her hand. "Are *you* okay?" he asked.

Of course he would notice her tears. She dashed one away with her free hand. "These are happy tears," she said.

"That was a beautiful ceremony today." Then she sucked in a breath. "I didn't realize that might have been hard for you, though. To see your mother marrying another man..."

Jessup laughed, but with glee not bitterness. "I wouldn't have believed it if I hadn't seen it for myself. My mother and Old Man Lemmon."

"They're soulmates."

"Yes, I think they are," he said, still chuckling.

"So if you're not upset about that, it must be Cash that has you sitting out in the dark," she mused.

He pulled his hand away and sighed.

"He came to the ranch a few months ago," she said.

Jessup sucked in a breath and leaned forward. "What?"

"I didn't know it was him," she said. "He's a vet, you know? He goes by Doc CC. I called him to check out Sasha." She drew in a breath as she drew a memory from the back of her mind, the one that had been teasing her since she'd officially met Cash at the wedding earlier today. "And I think he stopped by the ranch before..."

"When?"

"Not long after I showed up that first summer," she said. "I thought he was a friend of one of the boys. I remember the boys weren't home, and I told him he could wait but he just drove off. It always stuck in my memory for some reason. Do you think he thought that you and I were to-gether?" She would make it clear that wasn't the case if that was the misconception Cash had.

"If he did, I can set him straight," Jessup said, "but I really don't know what he thinks anymore. Just that he's incredibly hung up on honesty. I'm going to have to tell his brothers the truth."

"They will understand," she said. "They've been very understanding about everything else. They know that peo-ple make mistakes."

Jessup sighed. "Yes, if only Cash could understand that...people make mistakes, and if only he could forgive those that do..."

CHAPTER SIX

IN THE FEW days since Sadie's wedding, Cash hadn't been able to think of anything but his family. Over the years, he'd gotten good at pushing those thoughts aside, of making his mind blank of everything but his work and Becca and now Hope, as well.

He smiled just thinking of the sweet little girl.

And Becca…

She was his friend. That was how he forced himself to think of her when occasionally other thoughts crept into his mind, like how beautiful she was, how kind and smart and funny. And how he felt lately when he touched her…

Like he was suddenly more alive than he'd ever been. But maybe that was just because of everything else. Because his family was here…in Willow Creek.

Over the years he'd wanted to see his brothers. He'd even wanted to see… JJ. But the way he'd left, how he'd acted, he wasn't sure they would want to see him again. Or if they hated him for what he'd done…

How he'd acted.

Sure, in his eighteen-year-old mind he'd had every reason to leave. But had it simply been justification for him to escape when everything at home had been so stressful? Even though he'd initially come back a few months after running away, he'd used Darlene opening that door as an excuse to run away again. He had no idea now if she and JJ had been involved back then or if they were just in-laws and friends. But in that moment, he'd felt betrayed all over again, like he and his mother had not been missed, that even the pictures of him must have been gone since Darlene hadn't recognized him.

He'd figured then that they must have been so angry that they'd hidden or destroyed all memories of him. But as badly as they might think of him, how could they think he was so hateful that he'd burn down the ranch?

For a moment the other night, he'd wondered if Becca might suspect the same thing. But she'd believed him when he'd told her he hadn't; she'd accepted his word because she knew him.

Apparently his brothers really didn't know him. So he was on his way to find Marsh now, since he'd been the one asking Becca all those questions at the wedding. Like she'd been a suspect, too, or a witness.

Cash was more intent on making sure his brothers knew she had nothing to do with that fire than he was about his own involvement. He couldn't really blame them for thinking the worst of him, not after how he'd run away.

But as he walked into the sheriff's department, his stomach knotted, and all that guilt he'd carried for so long intensified, making him feel like a criminal.

A woman sitting behind the glassed-in reception area looked up and greeted him with a smile when he walked in.

"How can I help you?" she asked.

"I'm here to see Sheriff Cassidy," Cash said, and now a surge of pride tempered some of his guilt. His younger brother Marsh was the sheriff.

Collin was a doctor, a cardiologist.

Colton had become the firefighter and paramedic he'd always wanted to be.

They'd all achieved their dreams, so maybe he could

let some of his guilt go over leaving them behind. They'd all thrived—even JJ had survived.

"If you'd like to file a report, I can have a deputy take your statement," the woman said with a smile.

"So the sheriff isn't available?" he asked. Willow Creek was growing, but it wasn't a high crime town. How busy could Marsh be?

Maybe he was out investigating the fire in Moss Valley. If that was the case, though, he probably would have followed up on his lead and interviewed his chief suspect: Cash.

"Is there any reason you need to see the sheriff, specifically?" the woman asked, and her smile slipped a bit. Clearly she was gatekeeping for her boss.

"I think he, specifically, wants to see me," Cash said. He cleared his throat. "I'm his older brother."

Her smile brightened again. "Another Cassidy-Haven," she said. Before Cash could correct her, she added, "I'll let him know you're here."

"I heard him," a voice that sounded a lot like Cash's commented, and then Marsh appeared behind the woman's chair. Seconds later he stepped around her and opened a door. "Come on back, brother."

Cash flinched a bit at the irony in Marsh's voice. Did he not consider him a brother anymore? Or was he just pointing out the hypocrisy of Cash claiming the connection after ignoring them for so many years?

Regardless, Marsh had every right to feel either way.

After a brief hesitation, Cash stepped inside, and Marsh pulled the door shut behind him. The automatic lock clicked as it engaged. Cash felt another moment of discomfort.

But he followed Marsh down a hallway into what must have been his office. There was a desk with folders piled so high on it that they nearly blocked the computer monitor. Files sat atop a cabinet and on the floor behind the desk, but the two chairs in front of it were clear. Marsh gestured toward one of them before he stepped behind his desk and dropped into his high-backed chair.

"I half expected you to be leading me to a jail cell or at least an interrogation room," Cash remarked as he settled onto one of the guest chairs.

"Why?" Marsh asked. "Are you here to make a confession? Have you committed a crime?"

Cash shook his head. "No. But it sounds like you suspect me of one."

Marsh leaned back and sighed. "Some evidence is currently pointing to you."

"Evidence of what?" Cash asked. "Did someone actually burn down the house?"

Marsh shrugged. "You tell me."

"I'm not an arson investigator," Cash said. "And I didn't hear anything about it being an arson fire. Wasn't it just a mechanical or electrical issue?"

"That lighter being in the house, in the ashes," Marsh said, "suggests there might be another reason the fire started."

Cash shook his head again. "It wasn't me. I don't even know how it got into the house. I wasn't in there. I just checked out Darlene's horse in the barn."

"You didn't go in the house with her while she got you a check?"

He flinched. "No. I didn't want to go anywhere near the house." Not even that night he'd gone in the dark to check out the ranch.

"Near Dad…"

"He's not my dad," Cash reminded him.

"Who else is?" Marsh asked. "Who taught you to ride? Who taught you to take care of animals?"

"Mom—"

"Mom didn't give you the time and attention that Dad did," Marsh interjected.

"Yeah, because she was busy taking care of him," Cash said, his stomach churning with all those old, bitter feelings. The biggest one of them, as always, was guilt.

"What would you know about that?" Marsh asked. "You took off."

"He was sick a long time before I took off," Cash reminded him. If JJ hadn't been sick, Cash might not have learned the truth. "And Mom was gone."

"That's really why you left," Marsh said. "It was all too much."

Marsh's accusation mirrored his own thoughts from earlier that day. That guilt churned now, making Cash grateful that he hadn't eaten anything yet, or he might have gotten physically sick. "I guess I wasn't as strong as the rest of you," he said. "Probably because I'm not a Haven."

Marsh shook his head, and his white cowboy hat slipped a bit down over his forehead. Ever since they were kids, he had always worn a white one, while Colton always wore a black one. Cash had opted for brown like the color of his favorite horse growing up. A warm sable brown quarter horse.

"You're an idiot," Marsh said. "And every bit as much of this family as the rest of us are."

"If you really believed that, I don't think you'd have these doubts about me," Cash pointed out.

"I'd have doubts about anybody whose lighter showed up at the origination point of a fire," Marsh said.

Cash flinched. "I don't know how it got there," he maintained.

Marsh sighed. "And it's not just you. I have doubts about everyone anyway."

"I can relate to that," Cash murmured.

"At least you've always had Becca," Marsh said. "You knew you could always trust her. She didn't wait long before telling you what I talked to her about."

Cash grinned. "No. Becca and I have no secrets." But then he felt a little niggle of uneasiness again. He hadn't told her what he'd been thinking about her lately, or how much he'd been thinking about her lately.

He wasn't sure why. They'd been spending so much time together, since it was summer and Hope wasn't in school. And Becca wasn't as busy due to the low housing inventory. Once school started and Becca's business picked up, everything would go back to normal. And this summer fancy or whatever it was would just be a figment of his imagination like the other times he'd considered that he might feel more than friendship for Becca.

They'd known each other for so long and were so close that it was probably natural to have those thoughts from time to time. To wonder...

Marsh snapped his fingers, and Cash jumped, realizing that he'd zoned out. He'd been doing that a lot lately. Maybe he was just having these thoughts so that he didn't have to think about his family turning up here in Willow Creek.

Maybe it was just since Becca had mentioned Colton coming around her office and the others taking up residence in Willow Creek that he'd started to focus on her instead. So that he didn't have to think about them and his guilt...

"You sure you don't have something to confess?" Marsh prodded him. "Because something sure seems to be weighing heavy on you..."

"Guilt," Cash admitted freely. "I do feel bad about taking off like I did, leaving that all on your shoulders..."

Marsh shrugged those shoulders. They were broader

now than when they'd been teenagers and pulled at the seams of his light gray uniform shirt that had a star embroidered on the pocket. Sheriff of Willow Creek.

"We managed," Marsh said. "Thanks to Darlene."

Cash furrowed his brow. "I don't want to talk about her."

"Why not?"

"I just..." It felt like just one more betrayal of so many... and he wasn't sure if it was JJ's or his. If JJ had replaced Cash's mother within months, that was one kind of betrayal. If Cash had made a snap judgment that had shaped nearly two decades of his life, that was another. He shook his head. "I don't have time," Cash said, and he glanced at his wristwatch. "I have an appointment I need to get to..." He stood up then. "Are you going to let me out or lock me up?"

He wasn't sure if Marsh believed him. Apparently he wasn't the only one with trust issues from their childhood.

BECCA HAD RECOGNIZED the Willow Creek Veterinarian Services truck when she'd first passed it on the way to her office. What was Cash doing at the sheriff's department?

Had Marsh called him in for questioning?

She couldn't get the thought out of her mind, and that urge to mediate, like she used to when they were kids, came over her again. When she'd pulled into her usual spot at the curb by her office, she'd just run in to grab something from her desk before driving off again. For once she'd parked there well under the two-hour time limit, which was all that was allowed for businesses on this side of Main Street.

And from how many tickets she had in her hand, she knew how well it was enforced. She needed to park farther away, in a spot with unlimited time, but Becca hated to walk too far in the summer heat and especially in the suits and heels she usually wore. She probably could have worn jeans and boots to work here in Willow Creek, but when she'd first started in real estate in the big city, she'd been expected to dress professionally. She'd been taken seriously and had made good money, enough to buy her ranch and start her own real estate business. And so she'd just continued wearing her office clothes in Willow Creek, at least in town.

She parked her SUV and walked into the sheriff's office. Cash and his lawman brother stood inside the reception area next to an open door to the back. While Cash just met her gaze and smiled, Marsh let out a soft whistle and said, "I still can't get over how much little Becca Calder grew up."

She snorted. "I was never little." She'd felt like a giant in elementary school, towering over the other kids. But that had never made a difference to Cash or his brothers. His brothers had caught up and surpassed her quickly, and so had Cash, eventually.

"I just meant you cleaned up really well from your days of hanging out on the ranch," Marsh said with a grin.

Cash snorted now. "You should have seen her the other day with manure smeared on her forehead," he said. "She's still the same old Becca."

Becca grimaced.

"Never call a lady old," Marsh chastised him. "No wonder you're still single."

"You know why I'm still single," Cash said. "Probably same reason you are."

"That's just because your grandma Sadie hasn't set her sights on matching up either of you yet," Mrs. Little, the receptionist, remarked.

And Becca laughed as expressions of horror crossed the handsome faces of the Cassidy brothers.

Cash began, "She's not—"

"She's not set her sights on us," Marsh interrupted his brother. "Because she's a smart lady who knows it would be a waste of her time."

"Or you've just gotten a reprieve because she's on her honeymoon," Becca teased even as her stomach churned with the thought of Sadie matching Cash up with someone other than Becca.

But if that was Sadie's intention, why had she insisted on Becca being in her family photos? Had the matchmaking already started? If so, Sadie would no doubt learn quickly that Marsh was right. Trying to match up Cash with Becca would definitely be a waste of the older lady's time. He was never going to see her as anything other than a friend.

"Speaking of reprieves," Marsh said, "I hope you're not here looking for one."

She sighed. "I didn't expect you to fix my parking tickets," she said. And she held up the bunch in her hand. "I came here to pay them."

"Oh, I thought you came here to defend this guy like you always did when we were growing up," Marsh said.

"I don't need her to defend me," Cash said. "And why would she need a reprieve from you?"

"For interfering with an investigation when she tipped off my prime suspect," Marsh said, and his dark eyes narrowed in a hard stare that he turned on both of them.

Becca narrowed her eyes and stared back at him. "Like you didn't expect me to tell him…"

Marsh chuckled. "Fair enough. I was counting on it.

Figured nothing has changed with the two of you. That you keep no secrets from each other."

She flinched as if Marsh had struck her. Then she quickly glanced at Cash to see if he'd caught her reaction. But he was staring at his brother, shaking his head with amusement and not the fear that Becca was feeling.

She wasn't worried about the lawman's threats regarding her interference in his investigation; she wasn't even worried about her parking tickets.

But she was worried that Marsh had caught her reaction and that he might tip off Cash the way that she had.

"And if I'm your prime suspect," Cash said, "then maybe you should be out writing parking tickets instead of investigating crimes that aren't even in your jurisdiction."

Marsh chuckled again. "I don't even think it's a crime, so relax...unless you have a guilty conscience." But he glanced at Becca when he said that, and she knew that he knew...

She was keeping secrets.

MARSH STARED AFTER Becca and Cash as they walked out of the sheriff's office after the real estate agent settled her parking citations.

And he wondered what Becca hadn't told Cash...

Because there was definitely something. He hadn't missed her reaction. That was why he was good at his job, why he knew when someone was lying or trying to mislead him.

Despite all the years that had passed since he'd seen his older brother, Marsh was still able to read Cash fairly easily, and he was pretty sure that his older brother was telling him the truth.

But Becca…

Becca was holding something back. Some secret she hadn't told Cash. And Marsh couldn't help but wonder what it was and why things had changed between them.

CHAPTER SEVEN

CASH HADN'T LIED to the sheriff about the lighter or about having an appointment. So he hadn't been able to stick around and visit with Marsh and Becca. She hadn't stuck around, either, had just quickly paid her tickets and walked out with him, as if she hadn't trusted Marsh not to interrogate her again.

Becca didn't know any more about the fire at the ranch than anyone else did, though. Even Marsh didn't know for certain if it had been arson or just a horrible accident. Cash hoped it was an accident, that nobody had deliberately been trying to hurt... JJ.

Or Darlene...

As if just thinking about her had conjured her up, he glanced over his business partner's shoulder to the woman walking into the barn. The barn was actually the business office for Willow Creek Veterinarian Services. The meeting Cash had scheduled was their usual Monday morning one he had with his partner to discuss who was handling what of their upcoming appointments and other obligations.

Dr. Forrest Miner, the vet who'd started the practice and kept threatening to retire, turned his head to see what had drawn Cash's attention. "I thought all your appointments were outside calls," the older man murmured.

"They are," Cash said with a sigh. JJ must have sent her to talk to him. He probably didn't want to tell his other sons the truth. But Cash wasn't going to keep anyone's secrets anymore but one...for now. Just until he knew it was safe to share...

The gray-haired man flashed a grin. "Hello, miss," he greeted Darlene. "How can I help you?" Despite his constant threats to retire, Forrest was probably still in his fifties, like Darlene probably was.

Her face flushed, and she quickly looked away from him to point at Cash. "I'd like to talk to Doc CC," she said.

"He has some outside calls to make," Forrest began.

"It's fine," Cash said. "I have a few minutes." After what Marsh had told him just a short time ago, that they wouldn't have survived without Darlene, Cash knew he owed her a lot more than just a few minutes. He owed her his gratitude, but the thank-you stuck in his throat.

She waited until Forrest reluctantly walked away from them, and then she said what Cash wasn't able to yet. "Thank you," she said, "for giving me a chance to explain. I realize that I met you not just that day you checked out Sasha for me, but years earlier. And I hope that you didn't get the wrong impression then about why I was at the ranch. I came there earlier that summer because I was looking for Jessup, but not for the reasons that you might have thought when you came home and found me there. There has never been anything romantic between us. He's like my brother."

"That's on me, whatever I thought," Cash said. So it was true—his hotheaded teenage self, still hurting so much from what he'd learned just a couple of months earlier, had jumped to conclusions. He'd felt betrayed and outraged on his and his mother's behalves, based on a bad assumption. "You don't owe me any explanations," he assured her.

"I just want to make it clear that your dad—"

"He's not my dad," he interjected, almost by reflex now.

"He is," Darlene insisted. "You are his son in every way that counts with him. He loves you so much."

Tears stung Cash's eyes.

Darlene blinked back some of her own. "Oh, I understand why you're desperately clinging to that," she said.

"What?"

"You're hanging on to your anger and resentment so you don't get overwhelmed by the guilt."

As if she'd sucker punched him, Cash sucked in a breath, shocked at how well she understood.

Her lips curved into a slight and somehow sad smile. "I know all too well how badly guilt will mess you up," she said. "I let it keep me away from my sons and from Sadie for eighteen years. It was easier to think they hated me than to face them and to face my own guilt."

He hadn't wanted to talk to her, to get to know her, but he found himself asking, "What did you feel guilty about?"

"I blamed myself for my husband's death," she said. "I was married to your uncle Michael, Sadie's younger son. That's why I was looking for Jessup. I thought if I could bring him back to Sadie that I could somehow make up for taking Michael away. But Jessup was so sick and his sons...were so scared."

Because they'd lost their mom just earlier that year and then Cash had taken off. But...

"You stayed," he said.

She nodded, and those tears brimmed in her eyes. "I'm glad I was there for them, but I hate myself for not being there for my kids. I know they had Sadie and her late husband, but they should have had me, too. I was just so convinced that they all blamed me for Michael dying. And I let that guilt paralyze me."

"Paralysis..." he murmured. That was exactly how he'd

felt whenever he'd thought of going back, of reaching out to his family. The guilt had paralyzed him.

Nobody had ever understood him like this woman did. Not even Becca...

Or maybe Becca did understand; he'd just refused to let her talk about his family, shutting her and the conversation down any time she tried to bring them up. Cash owed his best friend an apology. And he owed one to this woman, too, along with his gratitude.

"I am so sorry, Darlene," he said as he blinked away the moisture filling his eyes.

"For what?"

"For making incorrect assumptions about you," he said.

"You made those about your father. He loved your mother so much, still does, and he always considered you his child. Jessup is a really good man."

A better man than the biological father Cash had found; that man hadn't wanted to take on the responsibility of the children he'd had, while JJ had willingly cared for a boy that wasn't his. He sighed. "He is. But he has to stop keeping secrets."

She cocked her head slightly, and her sandy hair, with silver threaded in it, brushed across her cheek. Her hazel eyes narrowed slightly as she studied him much like Marsh had earlier in the sheriff's office. "You've never kept a secret, Cash?"

He hadn't shared a lot of his personal history with people, but that was because it wasn't their business. "I haven't kept an important one," he said. Then he thought of Melanie...and heat rushed to his face and he stammered a bit before admitting, "And if I am keeping anything secret, it would be just so that I didn't hurt someone."

Darlene smiled at him, then she turned and walked away, out of the barn.

"Now I understand what a mic drop is," Forrest remarked.

And Cash jumped as he realized his partner was standing beside him again. "You were eavesdropping?"

"Always," Forrest unabashedly admitted. "I'm a lonely bachelor with no life of my own so I live vicariously through you."

Cash chuckled and shook his head. This was why he hoped Forrest never retired; he had too much fun working with the older veterinarian.

"She's some lady," Forrest remarked with an almost wistful glance in the direction she'd walked out of the barn.

She had certainly given Cash a lot to think about. He'd been wrong again about JJ, but that didn't make it okay that he'd kept so much from them. He still had to tell the truth about everything. But how could Cash convince him to do that?

As always, when he needed to figure something out, he wanted to talk to Becca. But first he had to take care of some of his appointments.

Becca would be there for him after that; she was always there for him.

BECCA HAD HAD a surprisingly busy morning. Once she'd left the sheriff's office, she'd been requested for a meeting with the mayor. Apparently before she'd left on her honeymoon, Sadie had told her grandson Ben Haven that she wanted to sell some of the properties he managed for her. And she'd wanted Becca to list those properties.

"Why's she selling?" Becca had asked.

"With her and Lem getting married, and my own wedding coming up, we're going to be too busy to worry about these buildings," he'd replied.

"And why me?" Becca had asked.

But Ben had never really given her much of an answer, just a grin. Then he'd given her the addresses of the properties.

Becca had spent the rest of the day checking out the buildings, and now she was back at her office, looking over the photographs she'd taken. Her mom had already left to help her dad get dinner ready. He watched Hope during the day when she and her mom were both working.

Her mom must not have locked the outer door when she'd left because it creaked open now, the bell on it ringing to announce a client. She glanced up from her desk to see Cash walking toward her. And, as always, her heart did that little flippy thing in her chest at just the sight of him.

"Want to buy a house?" she asked with a teasing smile, although he could use something bigger than the studio apartment attached to the barn that was his and Dr. Miner's business office.

"Are you selling yours?" he asked. "That's the place I'd want."

If only he wanted her and Hope with it...

"You missed your chance," she reminded him. "It's mine now. And I thought it was too big for you anyway."

"The house is," he agreed. "But the rest of the property is great."

The house was too big for her and Hope, too. Becca had always wanted a lot of kids. If she wanted to get pregnant the same way she had with Hope, she was going to have to tell the truth, though. She couldn't lie about another whirlwind wedding without her parents and Cash having questions about her judgment and her credibility.

And if Cash figured out she'd already lied...he was as unlikely to forgive her as he had his dad.

"But I'm not here to try to wrest the ranch away from you," he said.

She shrugged. "You can try," she challenged him. "I can probably still take you at arm wrestling." She was in a sleeveless blouse, her suit jacket over the back of her chair, and she flexed her biceps to show off her muscles.

"Impressive," he acknowledged. "Comes from shoveling all that manure, and I'm not necessarily talking about you mucking out the horse stalls."

Her mouth dropped open with a little gasp of alarm. Did he have some idea? Had Marsh said something after she'd left?

"I'm just kidding," Cash said. "I know you're an honest salesperson."

Oh. He'd been referring to her career in sales.

"I am here to talk about honesty, though," he said. "I heard some hard truths this morning."

"During your meeting with Marsh?" she asked when he trailed off. "He can't seriously believe you had anything to do with your childhood home burning down."

Cash shrugged. "I don't know. I hope not. But no, this was from Darlene."

She nodded as she remembered meeting the woman at the wedding, the one who'd helped out Cash's younger brothers and JJ. The one who'd been married to JJ's younger brother. "What did she want to talk to you about?" she asked.

"Misconceptions, guilt and secrets."

She felt that little flip in her chest again, but this was fear, not attraction. She cleared her throat of the guilt and fear and started, "What did—"

A phone buzzed, and Cash pulled his cell from his pocket and stared down at his screen. His mouth tightened into a frown. "I don't recognize the number…"

"Answer it," she suggested, grateful for the reprieve from this conversation about guilt and secrets and misconceptions.

"Doc CC," he greeted the caller. "Oh…" His lips parted slightly with a gasp of surprise.

Who could have surprised him? It was probably one of his family. But she considered the other possibility. A woman. Cash dated. Not often and not lately, but he'd dated. And he tended to tell her about the women because he told her everything. If only she could tell him how much that bothered her…

But *she* didn't tell him everything.

"I don't need to be there," Cash said into the phone. But then he sighed and nodded, as if the caller could see him. "Okay. I'll be there." He clicked off the cell and closed his eyes for a moment.

She jumped up from her desk and rushed around it to grab his shoulders. "What's wrong? Are you okay?"

He opened his eyes, which were such a deep, beautiful blue, and nodded. "Yeah. JJ's going to do it tonight. He's going to tell my brothers that he's not my father."

She flinched. "Did he use those words?" She couldn't imagine JJ ever saying such a thing, not with how much she knew the older man loved Cash.

Cash's face flushed. Obviously he had misquoted JJ. "He's called a family meeting to come clean about everything. No more secrets."

Becca yearned to come clean, too. But she couldn't imagine the damage that would do, and not just to her friendship with Cash, but to her relationship with her parents and with her daughter. Hope was too young to understand what artificial insemination was, and Becca didn't want her child to be confused or frightened or humiliated. And Becca would definitely be humiliated, as well.

She pushed aside thoughts of her own secrets and focused on Cash. "You told him that you'd be there." This was progress for him.

He heaved a sigh. "Yes, I did," he admitted. "Can you get your parents to watch Hope tonight? I need you to come with me."

She held up her hands and shook her head. "No. Absolutely not. This isn't like a wedding where you bring a plus-one," she said. "This is an intimate family meeting."

"You're family, Becca," he said with one of his wide grins that always charmed her. "Even Sadie thinks so..."

Sadie was a schemer, but Becca might not have been opposed to her matchmaking if she thought she actually had a chance with Cash.

She shook her head. "You need to do this with your brothers. You need to be there for them." And for JJ.

He flinched like she had earlier, and she suspected it was for the same reason. Guilt. He felt guilty about how he'd abandoned his brothers. But she knew how badly he'd been hurting over not just JJ's betrayal but over his mother's, as well.

If he found out about Becca's...

Their friendship would definitely be over.

THE HOUSE WAS eerily empty. Jessup had sent Sarah and Mikey to the movies with Darlene. Sarah had been reluctant to leave him alone. The private nurse was a sweet girl who worried so much about his health despite how well he'd been doing since the heart transplant.

He'd been doing amazingly well. His body hadn't tried at all to reject his heart...as if it knew it belonged to him now. He absolutely hated that someone had had to die for him to live, but that person still would have died even if Jessup hadn't needed the heart. Even if he would have traded his own life to save the person whose heart he believed he'd received.

Because of the timing, he believed it belonged to his

late nephew. Darlene's son Dale. No, he *knew*. He felt as if this heart was a part of him because it was a part of someone who'd meant so much to him: his brother's son. Tears sprang to his eyes, and he blinked them back.

The door creaked open and boots stomped across the slate flooring of the foyer. Then a white cowboy hat appeared. Marsh was home.

"Where is everybody?" he asked.

"Sarah and Mikey are at the movies with Darlene. The rest of them aren't here yet." But the twins had promised they would show. And someone else had promised, too.

Or maybe he hadn't promised, but he'd said he would come. Jessup would get to see him again.

But was it only because he'd agreed to tell the truth? He'd known he needed to do that before, but this truth had always felt more like Cash's to tell than Jessup's.

The door opened again, and a black cowboy hat appeared in the foyer. Colton.

"Don't slam the door in my face," Collin said, and it creaked open again. Then he and his twin gasped. "You're here…"

And then a brown cowboy hat appeared. Cash had come just as he'd said he would. Now Jessup had to do what he'd promised he would do. He had to tell the last secret he'd kept from his sons.

CHAPTER EIGHT

CASH HAD HAD to ask Becca where his dad lived. No. Not his dad. JJ.

And Marsh.

And Darlene…and a home health aide and her child.

They all lived together. He wondered why JJ needed a nurse if he was really doing well now.

He'd looked well at his mother's wedding. He'd actually looked healthier than Cash could ever remember him. But Cash knew, all too well, that not everything was as it seemed. Like his whole life…

So Cash had followed Becca's directions to Livvy Lemmon's childhood home, which JJ was renting from Livvy's father. Everyone's lives were so entwined in Willow Creek…with the Havens.

Even Cash's…

His brothers were Havens. And as they all turned to stare at him when he stepped into the foyer of that colonial home, they clearly had no idea why he was there. They were surprised, and if JJ followed through on his promise, all but one of them would be surprised when they learned the secret. The reason why he'd left all those years ago.

Or at least the reason he'd used to leave.

"First the wedding and now here," Collin remarked with an arched eyebrow. He was the only one of them who wore no cowboy hat. He wore a white coat instead, though.

And Cash's heart swelled with pride in his younger

brother. "I can't tell if you're happy to see me or not." Or was he angry and resentful that Cash had left? He and the others had every reason to be mad at him.

And it probably wouldn't make a difference to them when JJ told them the secret. But it had made a difference to Cash.

"You didn't leave under the best of terms," Colton said, his voice gruff with emotion.

Cash nodded and sighed. "No. I didn't..." Then he followed the others through the foyer into a family room where JJ stood, and their gazes met.

He looked a little pale. A little shaky...

Cash grabbed Collin's arm and whispered to him, "Is he really okay? Sadie said he was doing so good..." Or Cash wouldn't have shown up at the wedding like he had; he wouldn't have risked surprising him.

"He is," Collin said, and his voice was gruff now with emotion. Gratitude. "And the lupus is pretty much in remission. He's the healthiest he's probably ever been."

That heaviness on Cash's chest eased. The concern was lighter now, but not the guilt. Not yet...

Maybe not ever...

"So it's okay to do this?" Cash asked, making certain.

Collin's dark eyes narrowed. "To do what? This isn't just a friendly visit to catch up?" He glanced from Cash to his father. "Why did you want us all here and without Genevieve and Bailey Ann?"

"Bailey Ann is too young to understand," JJ said. "And I'm not sure what you'll want to share with them."

"Genevieve and I share everything," Collin said.

Colton nodded. "Livvy and I do, too."

Marsh chuckled and shook his head. "Everybody I talk to is right here."

Cash would have laughed if he wasn't in the same place

himself. Just like Marsh, he had a career that he loved but nothing else. Well, he had Becca and Hope. But Becca was just his friend…

Colton had a fiancée. Collin had a wife and a daughter. And JJ…

He had Darlene, who swore they were just like siblings. Like him and Becca…

But he'd never looked at Becca like a sibling, just as a friend. But Becca wasn't actually *just* anything. She was so much more, and he wished she'd come along with him to this meeting.

"And whatever this is about, I bet Becca already knows," Colton added as if reading his mind.

Of course she knew. She was the first person he'd told after the doctor had told him. He'd been so devastated. And he started to shake a little as he remembered how he'd felt then, how shocked. And he wished Becca had come with him.

He looked behind him, toward the foyer and the door that would lead him out of the house and to his truck that he'd parked at the curb. He wanted to go to Becca now… even before this *family* meeting started.

"You wanted to do this," JJ said softly. "Cash, you want the truth out."

Colton gasped. "You're going to confess?"

"Confess to what?" Cash asked, and then he remembered where the lighter had been found. Where Colton had found the lighter…

The firefighter clearly suspected Cash of starting that fire at the ranch.

And Cash's stomach churned at the thought. Then he answered his own question. "The only thing I've come here to confess is the reason I left all those years ago."

Colton snorted. "Like you had a real reason."

"He did." JJ was the one who spoke up. "He found out something I never wanted any of you to know."

"About the Havens?" Collin asked. "About Sadie?" He turned to Cash. "You found out all those years ago and didn't tell us?"

"Why would you take off over that?" Colton asked. "We found out just a little over a month ago, and we're all still here. None of us took off."

Heat rushed to Cash's face. He knew what his brother was implying: the truth. That he hadn't had a good enough reason to leave. But they didn't know…

"He had every reason to be upset," JJ defended him again. "And it had nothing to do with being a Haven."

"Because I'm not a Haven," Cash said.

"It takes some getting used to," Colton said, "but we're definitely Havens and Cassidys."

"*You* all are," Cash agreed. "But I'm not. JJ is not my father."

Collin sucked in a breath. "What are you talking about? Why would you say such a thing?"

"It's the truth," JJ said, his deep voice soft. "Your mother never thought there was any reason for you boys to know."

"But you told *him*?" Colton asked, and he sounded horrified now.

"A doctor told him when he tried to donate his kidney to me," JJ said, and his vice vibrated with anger now. "He shouldn't have…"

"I had a right to know," Cash said. But he doubted it would have been easy to hear the truth from anyone. Maybe his mother…

But she'd already been dead, and Cash had been so afraid of losing his father, too, that he'd been desperate to save him. And at eighteen, he would have been legally able to donate his kidney. But it hadn't been viable.

"You tried to give him your kidney?" Collin asked, his voice cracking a bit with emotion.

Cash shrugged as if that didn't matter. But it had mattered that he hadn't been able to help either his mother or the man he'd always believed was his father. And that helplessness had broken him so badly that he'd had to run.

"Yes, he wanted to help me," JJ said.

"Then he shouldn't have taken off," Colton said.

Colton was the only one who hadn't taken off. Because of Becca, Cash knew about his brothers' lives. Marsh and Collin had gone off to college. But Colton...

His training to be a firefighter and paramedic hadn't taken him far away or for very long. So Colton had seen the most and had endured the most with his father. But maybe that grit was an inherited trait of every Haven.

Resentment and envy settled onto the guilt that already weighed so heavily on Cash. "Aren't you all missing the fact that I was lied to my whole life? That you all were?" he asked. "And not just about me but about the Havens and who knows what else?"

JJ sighed and then staggered back to drop into a chair. Colton and Collin rushed to him, kneeling on either side of him. "Dad, are you all right?" Each of them had one of his arms, checking his pulse...taking care of him in a way that Cash never had been able to...

And the one thing he'd tried to do to help had hurt them all so much more. Tears stung his eyes, and he had the urge to run again, so overpowering that he began to back toward the door. He had to get out of here.

"Don't go," JJ said. "Please, Cash...let me explain."

Colton began, "Dad, you're—"

Collin said at the same time, "Dad, it's too much—"

"No," JJ said, and his voice was uncharacteristically sharp. "Health-wise I'm fine. I'm better than I've ever been. It's everything else that I've carried for so long that's gotten to me. I need to get rid of this guilt."

Cash gasped. He'd thought Darlene was the only person who'd actually understood him. But JJ…

If the story he'd heard was true about how Jessup Haven had become JJ Cassidy…

But that had just been gossip around Willow Creek, which he'd mostly heard from Becca. People usually told Becca things. He certainly had. She was the only person he really talked to about everything. But he didn't know if she'd ever really understood in the way that Darlene had.

And JJ…

"Dad, you had your reasons," Marsh said, but his voice and his assurance sounded hollow, like an echo in an empty room.

Colton added, "We all keep secrets." And he glanced over his shoulder to give Cash a pointed stare.

He shook his head. "That lighter—"

"That isn't what we're talking about here," Marsh said. "I'm not even sure what we're talking about."

JJ glanced at his second son. No. Marsh was his first son. Cash was just…

Cash wasn't sure what he was or what his place in the family was. He'd left because he thought he didn't belong. He'd spent so long thinking that, and now he didn't know how to return or where he fit in.

JJ's brow creased. "What lighter?"

He wasn't sure what to do. He felt the urge to flee.

JJ was watching, and he said, "Stay, Cash, please." He knew Cash so well. They had always been so close…until Cash had learned the truth. But before that…

JJ had paid him more attention than his mother had.

Cash had just always figured that was because she had to do more for the younger kids and for her husband than she'd had to do for him. He'd always been independent. Except for Becca…

"You were right about no more secrets," JJ said. "I've kept too many for too long." He swallowed hard. "I guess I should just start from the beginning, for Cash's sake, because you don't know Sadie that well yet."

Cash's lips twitched into a grin. "Ranch Haven is a client," he said. "And I've lived in Willow Creek long enough to have heard the stories about how formidable she is."

JJ sighed and nodded. "And imagine how she felt to learn that her oldest son had a debilitating illness. She wanted to get rid of it, and when she couldn't, she tried desperately to protect me. I don't know what was harder, having to live with the disease or having to watch *her* live with the disease." He sighed. "But I left for my own self-ish reasons, because I wanted to live my life on my terms, however long I was going to have. So I ran off and joined the rodeo. That's where I met your mother." He smiled, and his dark eyes glowed with love. "I didn't think I had anything to offer her, though, but stress and heartache." His smile slipped away. "And I was right."

"Mom loved you," Marsh said. "So very much…"

The twins nodded in unison and agreement.

But Cash…

He couldn't quite accept that fairy-tale romance story, not when he knew the truth. "Then what about me?" he asked. "Why did she have me with another man?"

"She had you with me," JJ said. "Even though we were split up for a while before you were conceived, we were back together after she found out she was pregnant. And I was in the delivery room with her. I was the person who cut your cord, who held you first..." Tears pooled now in his dark eyes.

And Cash's heart swelled with love...for this man. "Then why aren't you my father?" he asked, and he could hear the tears in his voice, the ones that were clawing up the back of his throat.

"I thought your mother deserved someone healthy," he said. "Someone with a future that didn't include the flare-ups that left me bedridden or in the hospital. I didn't want to put her through that uncertainty. So I broke up with her while we were dating."

Cash gasped now. But then he shook his head. "That's not what I heard."

JJ closed his eyes and groaned. "I can imagine who you heard it from."

"My biological father said that my mother was crazy about him. She didn't want to be saddled with a..." He couldn't say it. Not now...

"A sickie, a dead man walking," JJ finished for him. "I can imagine what he told you." He sighed but it was with pity, not the resentment and jealousy he should have been feeling.

If Shep had told Cash the truth...

"He said that she wanted to live a little," Cash continued. "And that she didn't care that he was married."

JJ jumped up from his chair then, and there was the anger. "She didn't know." He shook his head. "His wife wasn't traveling with him. She was back home, pregnant, but that baby she lost and..." He shook his head. "Your mother didn't know, and she felt terrible. She'd been so upset with me pushing her away and that man sweet-talked her while she was so vulnerable. It was all a mistake."

The sudden jab of pain was so intense that Cash gasped. "I was a mistake."

"God, no," JJ said. "You were a blessing, Cash. Your mother and I were both so happy."

"You were happy she got pregnant by another man?" Cash scoffed. "Yeah, right."

"I was happy she would have a healthy baby," he said. "That I wouldn't have to worry about passing my illness on to you." Then he glanced around at his other sons, the big, healthy guys that were biologically his. "I let your mother talk me into taking a chance with all of you. And given how healthy my brother and my mom and dad were, the doctor pointed out the risks of me passing along this illness were low. And your mother wanted more children. And all I wanted was to make her happy."

"You did, Dad," Colton assured him. "She was happy. She loved you very much."

"And I loved her," he said. "Even though I didn't deserve her."

No. Cash was the undeserving one. He'd known that even when he'd learned the truth. But it had been all too much to bear...the loss of his mother, the illness of his father and then the terrible secret.

"You deserved her. You took on raising a child that wasn't yours." Cash was the one who said what everyone else was probably thinking.

JJ walked forward then and reached out, cupping Cash's face in his hands. "You are my child in every way that matters."

Tears flooded Cash's eyes then. But he shook his head. He hadn't been JJ's son in the way that had mattered most...because he'd taken off when he'd needed him. When they had all needed him...

And while he could forgive JJ for keeping Cash's paternity a secret, he wasn't sure he could forgive himself for leaving. And he doubted his brothers could, either.

BECCA SHOULDN'T HAVE made him go alone to that meeting. It had seemed like the right choice not to get in the middle of it at the time, but she should have gone with him. Nobody would have cared that she was there.

But she cared that she hadn't been there. And Cash might, too.

She could have asked her parents to watch Hope, though she wouldn't have wanted to explain to them why. So she sat on her front porch, alone since Hope had gone to bed a while ago. And she worried about how Cash's meeting had gone.

That family was hurting so much and for so many reasons. It had always been like that for Cash and his brothers, though, so much so that Becca had sometimes felt guilty growing up as she had, with her perfectly healthy parents and her perfectly happy, stable home life. Maybe that guilt, as much as the animals, was why she'd spent so much time at the ranch as a kid. Even as a child, she'd wanted to help them.

And then, as she'd gotten older and had started noticing Cash as more than a friend, she'd wanted to help him as a woman. As a partner, not just a friend.

Yet she'd had an opportunity to be there for him tonight and had turned him down. Was it really because she hadn't wanted to intrude?

Or was it because of all that talk of secrets?

She sighed. She had so many of her own right now. Or was it just one that had snowballed out of her control? Her feelings for Cash had made it impossible for her to fall for anyone else, so determined to have a child before she turned thirty, she'd chosen to do it alone. But her pride had kept her from admitting any of this to anyone.

But now it wasn't just her pride keeping her quiet. If she shared her secret, it could hurt and humiliate more people than just herself. It could hurt her parents. And most importantly, it could hurt Hope.

And Becca couldn't do anything that might harm her daughter.

So she understood why JJ and Colleen Cassidy had kept their secret about Cash's paternity. They hadn't wanted to hurt him. But the truth had come out and had wound up hurting him even more because it had been a secret for so long.

Would the same thing happen with Hope? Would she one day learn the truth of her paternity and hate Becca for keeping it from her?

The fear of that jolted her like a nightmare. And it was her very worst one…

Even worse than having Cash hate her for keeping it secret. And he no doubt would. Not that he really hated JJ or his mom. But he was like a wounded animal, lashing out in anger. Or that was what he'd done all those years ago with JJ.

Was he doing that tonight?

She really should have gone with him, but she hadn't wanted to intrude. And she hadn't wanted to keep putting herself in the position that she had as his plus-one at the wedding, starting to think that they were closer than friends.

That they were…

She sighed and closed her eyes, letting the dark and the quiet wash over her. With her eyes closed, she heard more, though. The strange chirp of tree frogs. The soft hoot of a barn owl. A quiet whinny from one of the horses in the barn. Answered by another…

Some of the tension eased from her until she heard the rumble of an engine. She opened her eyes to twin beams of light heading down the drive toward the house.

She didn't have to see it closely to know that it was Cash's truck. It wasn't as if she recognized the sound of the engine or the lights, but she just knew that if someone was showing up after dark, it would be Cash.

She jumped up from her rocking chair so abruptly that it struck the wall of the house behind her and then the back of her legs. She stumbled forward toward the railing and gripped it.

The truck stopped and Cash opened the driver's door and stepped out onto the gravel drive. He stood entirely still for a long moment and drew in a breath before softly shutting the door. He was probably worried about waking up Hope.

Becca should have been, too, after her chair hit the wall. But right now she was worried the most about Cash. "Are you okay?" she asked.

He was moving so slowly toward the house. Like he was tired. And he probably was…emotionally more so than physically.

She let go of the railing and rushed down the steps to him. Then she closed her arms around him to offer comfort and support, even though being this close to him, touching him, unsettled her so much.

Especially when his arms wound around her, pulling her closer as he settled his cheek against her hair. "I'm okay now," he said.

She had no idea if he was referring to the meeting with his family. Or being here with her.

But she didn't question him; she just stood there, holding him as he held her. Gradually the tension she'd felt in his long body seemed to drain away. And he uttered a heavy sigh that stirred her hair, brushing it across her cheek along with his breath like a caress.

And she found herself wishing for things she had no

business wishing for…unless she did what Cash's family had done tonight…revealed all the secrets…

But if she did that, she risked losing even more than Cash's friendship. She risked hurting Hope. And that wasn't a risk she could take…

CASH WAS GONE. So were the twins, leaving Marsh alone with his father. Well, relatively alone. Darlene and Sarah and Mikey had returned from their movie a while ago.

But the kid usually made himself scarce when Marsh was home. So did the nurse…

And after checking on JJ, Darlene, as intuitive as ever, had slipped away to give them some time alone.

"You think he'll be okay?" JJ asked.

"Who?" He knew who his dad was talking about. "Cash has had more time to deal with this than Collin or Colton have." While Marsh had already known the truth nearly as long as his older brother had.

"But Collin and Colton weren't affected the way Cash was," JJ said. "The way he still is…"

"He needs to get over it," Marsh said.

"Maybe he will now that he knows the whole story," JJ said. "He didn't let me explain before."

"He was a hothead back then," Marsh said. But hopefully he'd gotten over that as he'd gotten older. Hopefully he really hadn't had anything to do with the fire at the ranch. Since Marsh was no longer a Moss Valley deputy and was the interim sheriff of Willow Creek, the fire at the Cassidy Ranch wasn't Marsh's jurisdiction, at least not professionally.

Personally it was always going to be his jurisdiction. His childhood home, no matter who owned it now. But that sale hadn't happened yet. Even though the Moss Valley Fire Department had ruled the cause of the fire as mechanical failure and poor maintenance of the house, the insurance company hadn't closed their investigation yet.

Was there more to the fire?

More to Cash?

"Cash is a lot like me," JJ said. "We act impulsively sometimes. Emotionally. And even though we regret what we've done, we don't know how to undo it."

Marsh turned toward his father, where he sat again in the easy chair in the family room. And he studied his face intently. Did he know more about the fire and the lighter? Marsh had changed the subject earlier, but...

"What?" JJ asked as he met Marsh's gaze. "Why are you looking at me like that?"

"Are you really sure there are no more secrets now?" he asked. That was what he'd promised Cash when he'd left. That there were no more secrets to disclose. "Anything else you haven't told us?"

JJ chuckled. "Like what? Don't you think I already had more than my share?"

Marsh shrugged. "I don't know. Did you win the lottery or inherit millions you haven't shared with us?"

JJ laughed loudly then glanced nervously toward the stairwell. He wouldn't want to wake up Mikey. His dad cared about the nurse and her kid. He'd risked his life going back into that burning house looking for Mikey. And he hadn't let Sarah go even though he probably no longer needed her help.

Marsh knew there was nothing romantic in his dad's affection for the young woman, though he suspected she reminded him of Colleen. A woman who'd made some mistakes...

Not that Cash or Mikey were mistakes.

But caring about someone was, at least in Marsh's opinion, because it never seemed to lead anywhere but to pain and loss. He hoped his brothers Collin and Colton would prove exceptions to that; that they would find enduring happiness.

But Marsh wasn't going to take that risk. And he suspected that Cash wasn't going to, either. They both knew how hard it was to trust anyone...because it was hard to find anyone worthy of trust.

CHAPTER NINE

THE MORNING AFTER the family meeting, Cash felt as awkward as he had as a teenager. He and Becca hadn't really talked last night, but the way he'd clung to her…

Had left him feeling as awkward as a boy with a crush on a girl. Not that he had a crush on Becca. He'd just been so emotional over that meeting, too emotional to really talk to her.

So they hadn't.

But that was the beauty of a long-term friendship. Sometimes they didn't need to talk. He hadn't stayed long. Because he had an appointment early in the morning…

Out at the Cassidy Ranch.

And he felt awkward about going back out there now that everyone knew who he really was. No. Not everyone.

Melanie didn't know that they had more of a connection than through the Havens. Would she be at this meeting? Or would it just be her husband?

Cash's truck bumped along the ruts of the gravel drive. It had gotten worse since he'd been there to check out Darlene's mare. Probably because of the fire trucks…

As he bumped along the last of the driveway, the house came into view. What was left of the house…

And there wasn't much. Just a skeleton of the few blackened studs and trusses that remained. The porch was hollowed out in the middle and the stairs were askew. It was a total loss. But arson?

Would someone have purposely burned it down?

He couldn't imagine why they would, but clearly his brothers thought that he might have for...

What reason would he have?

Revenge?

Resentment?

The only person he resented and was still angry with was himself. But they didn't understand that and probably wouldn't believe it.

He suspected JJ understood. Dad...

Could he call him that again?

For the past seventeen years he hadn't allowed himself to think about him that way. He'd clung to the fact that JJ wasn't his biological dad, probably so he could justify staying away.

But there was no justification for doing that...not really. And clearly his brothers didn't think there was, either.

He'd felt so guilty for how he'd lashed out as he'd left that he hadn't been certain how to return. And when he had and had found Darlene at the house, he'd used her as another excuse to stay away, to accept his scholarship and go to school. His family probably knew as well as he did that his reasons for staying away had been selfish. He knew he'd done too much damage to ever repair his relationship with any of them.

A shadow fell over him and fingers tapped against the glass of the driver's window. He jumped and turned toward Dusty, who stood outside his truck. He shut off the engine and jumped out. "Sorry..." he murmured.

"I'm sorry," Dusty said. "This was probably pretty insensitive to ask you to meet me here."

Cash shook his head. "No. No, it's probably not any easier for you than for me. You didn't buy a burned-out house."

Dusty shrugged. "I was more interested in the property

and the barns." A whinny called out from the barn. "And Darlene's mare."

"Sasha is a beautiful horse," Cash assured him. He figured that was why Dusty had asked him out here, to check up on the mare.

"She is," Dusty agreed. "But she's not the horse I asked you to meet me here to discuss."

Cash glanced toward the barn. The roof had been replaced, as well as most of the siding. Becca had said that the property was still in escrow, so Dusty didn't have ownership yet. It seemed he trusted his uncle to sign off the ranch once they were able to proceed to closing, but apparently the insurance investigation was holding that up. "Did you get another horse?"

"Midnight is my horse," Dusty said, as if he'd needed to remind anyone of that.

But Cash cocked his head and grinned. "I thought that was Caleb's horse," he said, remembering his conversation with the boy.

"Yeah, that's what Caleb thinks, and he is so determined to try to ride him that Jake wants him off the ranch as soon as possible."

Grinning yet, Cash teased, "Caleb?"

Dusty sucked in a breath. "No. Jake loves that little boy like he's his own, which he is now that Jake married Caleb's mom. And if something happened to that little boy, it would destroy Jake and Katie and the rest of us, too. That's one special little kid."

"He idolizes you," Cash said.

Dusty's mouth curved into a slight grin. "Yeah, that's another thing that Jake's not happy about, or Baker or Ben for that matter. My brothers don't have any love for rodeo. But Caleb does. Too much for Jake's peace of mind. Getting Midnight over here as soon as possible is the priority, especially since Ian got hurt."

Cash flinched at the memory. "I was there that day, working with Midnight. If I'd stuck around…"

"That wasn't your fault," Dusty said. "It was mine. I never should have sent Midnight to the ranch, but I didn't have anywhere else to send him." He gazed at the barn now, and a smile crossed his face.

Cash chuckled. "You remind me of Becca. She always looked at the ranch like that, too. Like she was infatuated with the place."

"She was infatuated with the *place*?" Dusty looked at him now, and he was arching an eyebrow nearly to the brim of his cowboy hat.

Cash shook his head. "Not me, if that's what you're implying. Becca and I have only ever been friends." But last night, with her arms around him and his around her, his face against her silky hair…

Last night he'd felt something more than friendship. That was why he hadn't stuck around, but he'd used this early morning meeting with Dusty as an excuse to get out of there without talking more. That and after the family meeting with his brothers and…his dad, he'd been all talked out.

But he'd actually just wanted to keep holding her, even long after he'd left. "It was really the ranch that she loved."

"I'm surprised she didn't buy it instead of listing it," Dusty said.

"She'd already bought a smaller place in town," he said.

"Makes sense. This place would be a lot to manage on her own," Dusty said. "It'll probably be a lot for me to manage on my own…" He was staring at Cash now with an odd expression in his hazel eyes. "I could use some help."

Cash held up his hands. "I'm a veterinarian, not a rancher. But I'll help you with the animals."

"That's what I want," Dusty said. "Especially Midnight. He's special."

Cash smiled now. "Yeah, there's something about that horse. I wonder if he needs a therapist or if he is one."

Dusty laughed. "Baker made the same comment. I think Midnight has listened to a lot of Haven problems. Have you shared yours with him?"

Heat rushed to his face. "Patient-doctor confidentiality keeps me from answering that."

Dusty slapped his shoulder. "I like you, Doc CC. I liked you even before I knew you were a Haven."

He opened his mouth to deny the connection. But he had another connection to Dusty, so he just closed his lips again.

"I do think you might be stealing Caleb a little bit from me, though," Dusty said. "He keeps talking about the horse whisperer."

"I think he could be one himself," Cash said. "He certainly has a special connection to Midnight."

Dusty sighed. "It's going to be hard on him when I bring Midnight here, but it'll be safer for all the kids if Midnight is out of there."

"You're child-proofing Ranch Haven," Cash remarked. "What about here? You have some kids of your own coming."

Dusty smiled, but he looked a bit nervous. "Yeah, but it'll be a while before they're old enough to walk out to the barn on their own."

"They grow up fast," Cash said. "Becca's daughter went from being a baby to running out to that barn just like Caleb does. She's obsessed with the animals."

"I will worry about the babies after they get here," Dusty said, and his smile slipped away.

And Cash's heart sank. "Everything okay?" he asked with concern. "Is Melanie doing okay?"

Dusty nodded. "She's just so exhausted. But she keeps trying to push herself. I had to pull a Caleb and rush out of the house this morning before she woke up or she would have wanted to drive out here with me."

"And a drive would be too much for her?" Until that moment, Cash had been wanting to talk to Melanie, to clear away one more secret. But if a drive was too much, then learning that she had a brother would definitely be too much, too. Cash would have to wait to share what he'd found out when he'd learned who his biological father was.

"I would hate to have her out here and something happens and there's nobody close to help."

Cash nodded with understanding. "It's an isolated spot. It was scary…with my dad. There were a lot of times he got really sick, and we had to hope we got him to the hospital in time." Colleen had looked after him until her death and then the boys had helped. It was good that Darlene had showed up after Cash left. The nurse whose boy had been in the house when the fire happened must have just been hired after the heart transplant. So there had been just Darlene with him most of the time.

Cash really owed her for stepping up like she had. Like he hadn't…

Dusty glanced around. "Maybe we should just use the barns and the pastures then and not rebuild a house here."

"You're really worried about Melanie and the kids being here." And because he was worried, Cash was, too.

"When you've lost as many people as we have, don't you worry about everything?" he asked. "I do."

"You have reason to worry right now," Cash said.

"You're about to become a father to two babies at once." And his wife hadn't had an easy pregnancy from what he'd heard.

"I think I always worried," Dusty said, "which is probably why I left for the rodeo after school instead of sticking around."

Maybe Cash was a Haven despite not sharing the DNA because he seemed to have the same urge to run that some of the Havens had. His dad. Dusty. Even Darlene, though she was only a Haven by marriage.

"But I'm sticking now," Dusty said. "I'm going to try to be as good of a dad as my twin was." Tears shimmered in his hazel eyes for a moment, but he blinked them back. "And I need to start by making sure Dale's kids and the rest of the ones at Ranch Haven stay safe. Can we move Midnight out here soon? Do you think he's up for a ride like that or will it set back your progress with him?"

Cash stared at the overgrown pastures and the long stretches of fencing. Like the barns, there were repairs on them, too. New posts. New cables. "I think he'll love it here," Cash said.

Dusty grinned. "I think he'll love Sasha, too."

The mare whinnied again from the barn, as if she knew they were talking about her.

Dusty chuckled. "Don't tell Sadie, but I think I have more of her in me than I thought. I'm playing matchmaker."

Cash laughed. "To horses."

"Safer than playing with people's lives," Dusty said with a shudder. "It's a lot easier for people to get hurt."

And Cash thought of Becca, who'd been married so briefly before it had been annulled and the guy disappeared into thin air. Maybe she could have used Sadie's help to find her a suitable husband, one who would have stuck around and taken care of her and Hope.

Instead Becca did everything on her own. She was strong. And smart and...

Her husband had been a fool to let her go. At the thought of the man he'd never even seen in pictures, Cash felt a little sick. And it wasn't just with disgust or anger, but with jealousy, too.

If the guy had stuck around, he would have had it all: a beautiful, hardworking wife and a smart, sweet daughter. But he must have had that urge to run, too.

No matter how fast and how far Cash had run once, he knew he would never run away from Becca, especially if she and Hope were his.

CASH HAD DISAPPEARED pretty quickly the night before, without telling her much of what had happened during his family meeting. But it must have been bad with the way he'd clung to her. She could only remember him holding her that tightly once before, the day he'd told her that he wasn't JJ's son.

That was the day everything had changed for her. Because when he'd held her like that, she'd suddenly seen him as more than a friend. But he'd only seen her as his anchor in a storm.

Unfortunately for him, Cash had had a lot of storms in his life. Unfortunately for her, too, because her feelings for him sometimes threatened to overwhelm her. Now a rush of guilt washed over her that she'd been thinking of her feelings and not his, not what he'd been going through with his family.

"Looks like you could use this," Genevieve Porter-Cassidy said as she slid a cup of coffee across the counter toward Becca.

At Sadie's wedding, they'd set up this playdate for their daughters to get to know each other before school started, so that Bailey Ann would have a friend already. But after seeing her with the Haven boys at the wedding, Becca suspected Bailey Ann had a lot of friends and would make plenty more. The minute Becca and her daughter had shown up, Bailey Ann had opened the door as if she'd been watching for them. Then she'd taken Hope's hand and tugged her down the hall to show her new best friend her bedroom.

"I think you are my new best friend, too," Becca said as she reached out and wrapped her hands around the mug. "Thank you."

"Thank you," Genevieve said. "I thought you already had a best friend."

She did. But she just wished...

No. She was going to stop wasting her energy wishing for something that was never going to happen. She was already too tired. Needing the caffeine boost, she took a big drink of the coffee. "This is so good."

Genevieve had taken the time to grind fresh beans and brew them in a special little pot. "Thank you," the lawyer said again. "I really perfected my coffee-making skills during my first marriage."

Becca glanced at the cup Genevieve held, which contained a thin amber liquid. "But you don't even drink it."

Genevieve smiled and shook her head. "Herbal tea for me or I'll be bouncing off the walls."

Giggles pealed out, drifting from down the hall.

"Speaking of bouncing..." Genevieve pressed her finger to her lips and began to tiptoe from the kitchen, gesturing back at Becca to follow her.

With her coffee cup in one hand, Becca trailed behind her friend. Then they leaned against the wall outside the partially open door to Bailey Ann's room and listened as the girls played. Becca could see them jumping up and down on the mattress of Bailey Ann's race car bed.

"Do you wanna be a race car driver when you grow up?" Hope asked.

"I never thought about growing up before," Bailey Ann said, and she plopped down on the mattress, breathing a little heavily.

Next to Becca, Genevieve tensed and pressed a hand over her heart. Bailey Ann had had a heart transplant four or five months ago, and her body had nearly rejected it once. It was no wonder the child had never thought about growing up; she hadn't known if she would.

But then the little girl, with her profusion of brown curls, smiled. "I can think about that now."

"About what?" Hope asked; she was still jumping, something her grandparents probably allowed her to do all the time.

"Growing up, silly."

Hope tucked up her legs and landed on the mattress like she was doing a cannonball into a swimming pool. She was small but the bed was, too, and her movement bounced Bailey Ann up.

The little girl laughed. "Are you going to be an acrobat?"

Hope shook her head. "Nope. A vet."

"A vet?"

"Yeah, you know, an animal doctor like Cash."

Becca touched her heart now. Hope had mentioned being a vet before, but Becca had thought it was just because she loved animals.

"Who's Cash?"

"My mommy's best friend."

Genevieve turned toward Becca, and her blue eyes were narrowed slightly, as if she suspected there was more between them than friendship. A lot of people assumed that a man and a woman couldn't just be friends. But Becca knew all too well that it was possible and had been for most of her life.

"Maybe I'll be a doctor, too, like my daddy, and fix people's hearts."

Genevieve mouthed an *Aw* and smiled.

"Or a lawyer like my mommy who fosters kids and helps get them adopted."

Becca mouthed *Aw* back at her friend, who now had tears in her eyes.

"My mommy buys and sells houses and owns a ranch."

"Your mommy does a lot," Bailey Ann remarked.

And Becca *Awed* again over how sweet the little girl was.

But then Bailey Ann followed up that comment with the innocent question, "What does your daddy do?"

And Becca sucked in a breath and peered through the partially open door to see Hope's reaction. Her daughter just shrugged and replied, "I never met him. He doesn't even know he's my daddy, but Mommy doesn't know how to find him to tell him."

Genevieve reached out to grasp her hand and squeeze it with sympathy. Sympathy that Becca didn't deserve. She wondered what it would feel like to tell Genevieve the truth, but she couldn't risk the other woman saying something to Collin, which might get back to Cash.

At least what Hope had shared was factual. Becca had no idea how to contact the sperm donor, and he had no idea his sperm had been used.

"I don't remember my first dad," Bailey Ann said, scrunching up her little face as if she was trying to. But then she shrugged, too. "It doesn't matter, though, because my second daddy is the best. He would never leave me. No matter what I do he always loves me."

"I wish I had a daddy like that," Hope said.

And a pang sliced through Becca's heart as sharp as the blade of a knife. She'd always made certain to tell Hope that her daddy didn't know about her, but if he did, that he would love her very much. She hadn't wanted her child to feel abandoned or rejected by the man who should have loved her most. Like poor Bailey Ann had been rejected by her parents and then other foster families because of her health issues, until Collin and Genevieve, who couldn't wait to officially adopt her.

"Pick one," Bailey Ann urged her new friend, "like I picked Dr. Cass to be my daddy."

Hope smiled. "Dr. Cass. That sounds like Cash. That's who I would want to be my daddy if I could pick."

That was who Becca would pick, too, if she thought she had any chance of getting him. But she didn't. She hadn't in the past and she certainly didn't have one now. She'd done the things he despised the most: she'd kept secrets and had lied to him. And now she had her confirmation of how much her daughter loved him and how devastated Hope would be if she lost him, as devastated as Becca would be.

SADIE STARTED ACROSS the porch to the front door, but a hand caught hers, pulling her to a stop. She glanced back over her shoulder at her husband.

Husband. Old Man Lemmon. Who would have figured she would fall in love with her old nemesis?

Apparently her grandson Ben. "Yes?" she asked.

"Did you change your mind about cutting our honeymoon short?"

They'd spent the weekend at a lakeside cabin, which had been beautiful and romantic. She nearly giggled at the memories. But Sadie March Haven Lemmon was not a silly, giggling teenager. She was a woman. A mother, grandmother and great-grandmother.

But she was also a brand-new bride, and despite being eighty years old, she felt like that giggling teenager she had never been. Was this what giddy felt like?

Now she knew, and she wasn't entirely sure she liked it. But she sure loved Lem. "I was having a wonderful time," she assured him. "And I would have loved to stay…"

"But you have meddling to do, woman," he remarked with a grin.

And she chuckled. "I would stop all my meddling for you," she assured him. "We can go back to the cabin. Or we can book a cruise if you'd like."

He arched his bushy white eyebrows above his sparkling blue eyes. "A cruise?" He sounded more dumbfounded than intrigued.

"Don't people our age go on cruises all the time?" she asked. "The woman who owns the diner is always going on about her cruises."

Lem snorted. "She can't go on any more of them since you poached Taye from her and she has to run her own business now."

She shrugged. "She should have appreciated what she had in Taye." Like Baker appreciated his fiancée and soon-to-be bride. "I appreciate what we have, and if you'd like to do that cruise…"

He shook his head. "Why? Neither of us are much for traveling, and everything and everyone we love is here in Willow Creek."

She breathed a sigh of relief. His grandchildren were in town, too, so he had his own reasons for wanting to stick around.

"So who's next on your hit list?" Lem asked. "Or do I have to ask?"

Lem understood her better than anyone, even Big Jake, ever had.

"You tell me..."

"Cash."

Yup, he understood her better than anyone ever had.

She turned to head back to the door again, but he held tightly to her hand. "What?" she asked. "I thought you were fine with being back."

"I am," he said. "But there's a certain tradition here, you know. I'm supposed to carry the bride over the threshold."

She laughed, and it was a deep belly laugh that brought tears to her eyes and Feisty scratching away at the other side of the door. Lem was strong, but he was also a foot shorter than she was and probably fifty pounds lighter.

"What's so funny?" he asked, as if he was offended, but she could hear the laughter in his voice, too.

"That would be like Santa Claus trying to lift King Kong." She laughed harder at that thought. "You could barely get up from the ground when you proposed."

"You helped me up," he reminded her.

"So maybe I should carry you over the threshold," she suggested. It would probably be easier.

He chuckled. "I'm heavier than I look." He patted his belly. "Thanks to all of Taye's cooking."

The door opened and Feisty ran out onto the porch, bouncing around their legs like she hadn't seen them for years when it had only been days. Tears sprang to Sadie's eyes, though. She'd missed her pup, but the cabin had had a no-pets rule. Another reason she hadn't wanted to stay.

And because, like Lem had said, everything and every-one they loved were here. Her great-grandsons bounded out like the dog, jumping around them, as excited as Feisty was that they were back.

"Are you going to pick up Grandma and carry her inside?" Ian asked. "That's what Uncle Ben did after Aunt Emily proposed to him."

"And they aren't even married yet," Caleb said. He had such a crush on the young teacher that he was probably still holding out hope that they wouldn't get married.

Ben and Emily were a lot like Sadie and Lem. They were meant to be together. While they hadn't been quite the enemies that Sadie and Lem had been, they hadn't been friends, either. Not like Cash and Becca were. Sadie definitely needed to focus on him next, her oldest grandson.

But now she looked at the youngest one, her great-grandson, who held up his arms for Lem to pick him up. "How about I carry Little Jake over it first?" he asked.

Sadie winked at him and nodded. "And we'll just walk over it together," she said as she intended to do everything with him from now on.

They didn't have to do anything traditional. Instead of rings they had matching tattoos. The infinity symbol wound around their ring fingers. Lem had wanted barbed wire, but when he'd seen hers, he'd chosen the same. He usually came around to her way of thinking.

Hopefully Cash would, too.

CHAPTER TEN

CASH KNEW THAT the longer he stayed away, the harder it would be to come back. He'd learned that the hard way when he'd run away from his family. He didn't want to run from Becca, even if he felt awkward about the way he'd held her so tightly a couple of nights ago. So tightly and for so long, like he had never intended to let her go.

And he didn't.

He wasn't a fool like her ex-husband. He knew that Becca was the best thing that had ever happened to him, as a friend. And he'd maintained that friendship because they'd never crossed a line.

Every romantic relationship he'd ever had had ended in disaster. A lot of them had ended over Becca, because his girlfriends had been jealous of his close relationship with her. Then they'd tried to make him jealous back, breaking whatever trust he'd had in them. And once his trust had been broken, there had been no chance of the relationship lasting. And then he'd just given up for a while and focused on his work instead of his personal life. Except for Becca and Hope.

He always tried to make time for them, so he felt as awkward about letting two days go without texting, calling or dropping by as he felt about that night. He'd also felt awkward quizzing Dusty about his wife and her health.

Now that JJ had come clean about the Cassidys' relation to the Havens and the circumstances of Cash's own parentage, there was one more secret Cash needed to address. But he didn't want the shock of this final secret to cause any problems with her pregnancy, especially since it sounded as if it was already high-risk. The last thing he wanted to do was cause Melanie any pain. He'd already caused enough people pain.

Since that family meeting, he hadn't talked to any of his brothers or JJ, either. As he'd feared, no matter what his reason was, they weren't going to forgive him for leaving like he had. And they probably still suspected that he might have set his childhood home on fire.

As if he hadn't already felt guilty enough for leaving...

That was why he didn't want to do anything else that he would feel guilty about, like keep a secret or cross a line with his best friend. He had to figure out how to make those right.

And so he'd picked up dinner for Becca and Hope. Instead of walking right in, like he usually did, he rang the bell. When Hope opened it, she stared up at him with a puzzled expression, her little nose wrinkled with her confusion.

"Did someone order pizza?" he asked as he balanced the box on the palm of one hand.

She giggled and called back over her shoulder. "Mommy, it's the pizza delivery guy."

"I didn't order pizza," Becca said as she appeared in the foyer behind her daughter. Her mouth slid into a slight smile. "It smells good, though."

"I even had them put olives on it."

"Ew," Hope said.

Cash leaned down and whispered, loudly, in the little girl's ear. "Just on half of it."

"I won't eat half of it," Becca protested.

"Yes, you will," Cash teased.

She shrugged. "Yes, I will." She'd always eaten as much as Cash and his brothers. But she never gained an ounce, probably because she worked so hard at her job and on her ranch.

He wondered, not for the first time, how she'd looked pregnant. She'd still been living in the city, and he'd been traveling with the rodeo, so they'd only communicated through text messages and phone calls then. He hadn't seen her belly swollen with a baby, with Hope.

He felt a pang that he'd missed that, that he'd missed so much of her life. Even though they'd kept in almost constant contact over the years, it hadn't been enough. For some reason, he couldn't seem to spend nearly enough time with Becca. No wonder so many of his prior girlfriends had been jealous of his friendship with her.

"You going to bring that into the kitchen?" Becca asked. "Or just tease us with the smell while the box drips grease on the hardwood floor?"

A grin tugged at his lips. "Delivery service stops at the door."

"I'll give you a big tip to deliver to the table," Becca said, and she gestured for him to come inside.

His mouth watering from the smell of oregano and garlic in the sauce, and pepperoni and sausage, he didn't argue with her. It had been torture driving it here without sneaking a slice. He stepped in and closed the door, then followed her and Hope through to the kitchen.

"What's a tip?" Hope asked.

"Money," Becca said. "Like when we give the waitress money at the diner. We're tipping her for taking care of us."

Hope's dark eyes got wide. "But I don't tip you."

Becca chuckled. "You don't need to tip me."

"But you take care of me all the time."

"Aw…" Becca murmured. "You are so sweet."

She really was. Warmth flooded Cash's heart with affection for the little girl.

"A tip can be something else," Cash said.

"Like what?" Hope asked.

"You can tip your mother with a hug or a kiss," he suggested.

Hope immediately rushed to hug her mother's long legs. Becca crouched down and hugged her back. "And there's my tip to you," she said.

"For what?" Hope asked.

"For making me so happy all the time," Becca said.

"Even when I don't clean my room like you told me?" Hope challenged her. "Or when I don't brush my teeth? Or go to bed on time?"

Becca chuckled. "Well, maybe not then." She straightened up and took the box from Cash, setting it on a cutting board on the butcher-block counter.

Once the box was out of his hands, Hope hugged him.

"I get a tip, too?" he asked.

"You are the pizza delivery man," Becca reminded him.

"You take care of me, too," Hope said. "You're like my daddy."

Shocked at the comment, Cash sucked in a breath, but his heart, already warm with affection for the little girl, swelled with love. He picked her up, holding her close as she naturally looped her arms around his neck.

"Mommy, you should hug Cash," Hope said. "He takes care of you, too."

"Your mother takes care of herself," Cash said. His best friend was the most independent person he knew. She never asked for anything.

She snorted. "My mom and dad might argue with you about that."

"Where are they?" he asked, and he glanced around the kitchen. "I got an extra large."

"You're lucky it's date night, so you don't have to share your half," she said. "They're in town for dinner and a movie."

"Of course they are." Her parents had the kind of marriage other people envied and most, like him, didn't believe was possible. His parents had loved each other, but there had been no time or money for them to have date nights. They'd struggled so much.

"I know. I know," Becca said as if he'd spoken aloud. "I had the perfect childhood."

He'd often teased her about that, about her uncomplicated life. Had her impulsive marriage been her act of rebellion?

"You're going to have to hug Grammy and Grandpa when they get home," Hope suggested to her mother as she tightened her arms around Cash's neck like she was hugging him again. She was extra affectionate tonight.

Becca smiled. "Yes, I will."

"You know there are other kinds of tips," Cash said. "And that's the real reason I brought this pizza here, so that I could get that kind of tip…"

Becca's brow creased. "What is that?"

"A kiss?" Hope asked him. And she leaned forward and kissed his cheek.

He grinned at her. "You are the sweetest girl."

"Mommy's sweet, too," Hope said.

He snorted in unison with Becca. He knew his best friend too well to think she would consider that a compliment. Becca preferred to be tough and independent.

"Cash doesn't want my kisses," Becca said, but she didn't sound particularly disappointed about it because she added, "any more than he wants my half of the pizza with the olives on it." She plopped a big slice, loaded with black olives, onto a plate.

"Why not?" Hope asked, and she sounded a little disappointed.

"I don't like olives," Cash told her.

"No, why don't you want Mommy's *kisses*?" the little girl specified, as if she was offended on her mother's behalf.

If she only knew...

He'd been very tempted the other night as he'd held Becca to do more than just hug her. That was why he'd left abruptly, so that he hadn't crossed a line he couldn't uncross.

"Because we are just friends," Becca said, almost pointedly to her daughter. "And we will only ever be just friends."

Something very much like disappointment washed over Cash, bowing his shoulders so much that he let Hope slide out of his arms to land on her feet on the hardwood floor. Her shoulders seemed to be slumped, too.

"If you don't want Mommy's kisses, what do you want as a tip?" the little girl asked, and there was a little bit of grumpiness in her voice and a slight scowl on her face.

He glanced at Becca, who shrugged as if she didn't know what was up with her daughter. But she also shot Hope a warning look.

"A tip can be advice," he explained. "I'm here for your mom's advice." He realized he wouldn't have minded that kiss, though.

And that the line he didn't want to cross was getting harder and harder to see...

BECCA WASN'T SURE why her daughter insisted on going to bed early and without a story being read to her. But

Hope shooed her to the door and pulled her blankets up over her head.

Was she grumpy with Becca? Making up for not always going to bed as willingly as she could? Or was the little girl trying her hand at matchmaking, leaving Becca and Cash alone together in the hopes that he might change his mind about not wanting her kisses?

Ever since her playdate with Bailey Ann, Hope had been pressing the Cash issue. She'd missed seeing him the last few nights, and tonight he may have dashed her wish for him to become her daddy.

Or maybe Becca had been the one to do that. She'd made it clear that they were just friends and that was all they would ever be, just as she'd done a few times since that playdate.

"Are you sure you feel okay?" she asked, hovering inside the doorway to her daughter's room. Maybe she'd had too much pizza.

The little girl's head moved beneath the blanket. "Just tired, Mommy. Let me go to sleep."

She did sound tired.

"Come and get me if you feel sick," Becca said.

"Go give Cash his advice," Hope said.

That was why he'd claimed that he'd stopped by with the pizza, and ever since that admission, Becca had been curious. Of course it had to be about his family.

Had he had any contact with them since that night? Why hadn't he had any contact with her since that night? It was unusual for them to go a couple of days without at least texting or calling.

But she'd felt awkward reaching out first since she had been the one who'd reached for him first that night. Just to console him, though.

Clearly he'd been upset, and she'd wanted to comfort him. But then she hadn't let go.

And neither had he...

But he'd been upset, so he'd had an excuse. She had none.

She needed to accept what she'd told her daughter. She and Cash would only ever be friends. And right now her friend needed her advice. She drew in a deep breath and stepped out of Hope's room, pulling the door shut behind her. The last of the sunshine from the setting sun streamed in through the window blinds, so the little girl didn't even need her night-light yet.

But it was good that she was getting in the habit of going to bed early again. School was going to start soon. While Becca welcomed the return to a regular routine, she also was a bit wistful at how quickly her little girl was growing up.

Too quickly.

And too alone, like Becca had been. While she'd had the perfect parents, she hadn't necessarily had the perfect childhood because she would have loved to have siblings, specifically brothers like Cash had. She'd envied him his younger brothers. Even though they'd often aggravated him, she knew he'd missed them over the years.

"Are you okay?" she asked when she joined him in the kitchen.

He was loading their glasses and plates into the dishwasher. "What?" he asked with a slight grin. "Something has to be wrong for me to clean up?"

He always helped clean up, a habit he'd gotten into as the oldest in a household with ailing parents.

"I was already going to give you a tip for bringing the pizza," she reminded him. "Now I have to give you one for cleaning the kitchen, too?"

He pulled his mouth into an over-the-top frown and grimly nodded. "Yes, I'm afraid so."

"And this tip you want is advice," she mused. "About what? Your family?"

Now the frown wasn't feigned, and he uttered a slightly shaky sigh along with it. "In a way…"

"How did your meeting go the other night?" she asked. "You never said…"

His face might have flushed a bit, or maybe that was just the shadow from the brim of his hat as he dipped his head down. "Sorry about that," he mumbled.

"About what?" she asked. But she knew…

That moment had been intense. But she suspected it had been intense for him for a different reason than it had been for her.

"I turned up like that and then didn't even tell you anything…"

"And you've been radio silent the past couple of days," she remarked. Had that been over that moment? Or… "Have you talked to your brothers again? Or your…" She always called JJ his dad because he was, but every time she'd done that in the past seventeen years he'd corrected her. And since she had no idea how that meeting had gone, she was hesitant to say anything now. "…JJ?"

He shook his head. "I'm not the only one who was radio silent the past couple of days."

"You've been radio silent with them a lot longer than you were with me," she pointed out. "Maybe they're waiting for you to reach out." She knew why he'd been reluctant to do that, though. Guilt.

She knew that feeling all too well. She felt so guilty about not being honest with him about Hope. She felt guilty about not being honest with her parents or with Hope, either.

Maybe Genevieve was right about the whole being open and honest thing. Maybe that was the better way to live, even though it sometimes made things difficult. If only Becca knew how difficult things might get with Cash and her family and for how long...

But she couldn't risk upsetting Hope or losing Cash.

Cash sighed. "Maybe you're right about them, but my brothers and JJ weren't the family I was talking about..."

She stepped closer to him. "Your bio dad?" She knew he'd found the man years ago and that their meeting hadn't gone well.

He shuddered and shook his head. "No. Not Shep. It's about his daughter. When I found out he's my bio dad, I found out I have a half sister."

"Do you know her?" she asked.

Now the color drained from his face, and he nodded. "Yes, and so do you. Dusty's wife, Melanie. She's my sister."

"Wow..." She blew out a soft whistle of surprise. "That's quite a coincidence."

He shrugged. "I don't know. My mom was a barrel racer. That's how she met both JJ and Shep. And Dusty's a rodeo riding champion like Shep was. They know each other well. I figure that's how he met Shep's daughter. She was a physical therapist with the rodeo before she took the job at Ranch Haven."

"So the rodeo's a small world is what you're saying," she mused with a smile.

"Willow Creek is even smaller," he said. "Because we're all here now."

"Does she know about you?"

"I don't know if she knows she has siblings."

"Siblings?"

"Shep doesn't have the greatest reputation," he reminded her. "Her mom is married to Shep, so she's his legitimate daughter. But she doesn't have any idea that I'm her brother."

"You're keeping a secret?" she asked, astounded that he would do such a thing.

He groaned and pushed back his hat and a lock of his golden hair. "I know. I'm a horrible hypocrite."

Since he was keeping a secret himself, would he judge her as harshly as he'd judged his parents for keeping his paternity a secret?

"Sometimes people have very good reasons for keeping secrets," she said. "Like so that other people don't get hurt..." Like Hope.

He sighed. "That's why I haven't told Melanie yet. I don't want to upset her right now, not with her being pregnant with twins. I guess she's had a difficult pregnancy."

"I can't imagine being pregnant with twins," Becca said with great sympathy for the woman. "Being pregnant with one was physically demanding enough."

"And you were alone..." he murmured. And then he reached out, gripping her shoulders. "I am so sorry you had to go through that alone."

"You don't need to apologize," she said. Because that had been her choice. But she wasn't sure she could tell him that, and even if she could, she could not tell anyone before she told Hope. Her daughter deserved to know the truth first.

And Becca just picked up the creak of a door and a floorboard, so she suspected Hope was listening.

"But seeing Melanie, what she's going through, and knowing that you had no one there to support you," he said, and his blue eyes were full of sympathy for her. "I just wish I had been..."

"You're not the father." No matter how much Hope

wished that he was. No matter how much Becca wished he would realize he felt about her the same way she felt about him, and that they would marry and have children, lots of children.

"I still could have been there for you," he said, "if you'd told me. You're always here for me, always supporting me no matter how much I screw up."

"You don't screw up, Cash," she said. Not like she had.

"The way I reacted when I found out about my paternity, the way I lashed out at the man who it turns out didn't have to be a father to me but did it anyway." His throat moved as he swallowed hard. "I hate myself for telling him that I hated him. I can understand why none of them have reached out to me since that night."

Hearing all that self-recrimination in his voice, that pain and guilt, had her reaching for him now. She closed her arms around him like she had the other night.

But instead of hugging her back right away, he hesitated, his long, lean body tense. Then he mused softly, "Is this my tip for the pizza or for loading the dishwasher?"

"What?" She stared up into his face.

"A hug," he reminded her of the tips Hope had been handing out earlier.

She smiled. "I guess I better give you the hug since I really haven't given you any advice." She was just as much of a hypocrite as he was about keeping secrets, so she couldn't help him without being even more of a hypocrite.

"You could give me something else," he suggested, and there was a mischievous glint in his blue eyes. This was the Cash who'd teased his younger brothers into trying to best each other, whether riding, roping or throwing bales of hay into the loft. This was the Cash who goaded and challenged.

Like he'd challenged her so many times to a horse race,

to an arm-wrestling match. He brought out the Becca who'd always accepted that challenge and had usually bested him.

"What's that?" she asked.

"A kiss."

Her pulse quickened. "You know I never back down…" So why had he challenged her, unless…

He wanted her to kiss him as much as she wanted to…

So she closed the distance between them and pressed her lips to his. And that excitement shot through her along with such an intense attraction that she was overwhelmed and awed.

JESSUP OPENED THE door and took a step back with surprise over the identity of his visitor. "I thought you were on your honeymoon," he said.

When the bell rang, he hoped it would be Cash, but he was happy, albeit confused, to see his mother instead. He glanced behind her, looking for Lem. His new stepfather. He couldn't wrap his mind around the idea that his dad was gone. He would have come to the funeral then, but he'd been so sick. And he hadn't wanted to add the stress of his illnesses to his mom's grief.

There was no grief now. She stepped forward and hugged him. "After all those years apart, it was hard to be away from you again."

Tears stung his eyes and clogged the back of his throat. He closed his arms around her and hugged her back. "I know. I'm sorry."

At first he'd been headstrong and rebellious, but after the rebellion had worn off, it had been shame at the way he'd taken off, the way he'd hurt her, that had kept him from returning. And Cash had acted the other night as if he'd been carrying that same burden of shame and guilt.

"I know," she said, and she stepped back and smiled at

him. "And you need to stop apologizing. We can't undo the past, so let's just focus on the present and the future. Have you seen Cash since the wedding?"

He sighed and nodded. "A few days ago..."

"It didn't go well?" she asked.

"I thought it did," he said. "I did what he wanted me to do, but then I didn't hear from him again." He stepped back and escorted her inside the house. "Where's your new husband?"

"We caught up with his son and granddaughter and grandsons first, and I left him there to visit while I checked on you."

"I like Lem," he assured her. "And I really like who you are with him."

Her brow furrowed slightly. "Who I am? What do you mean?"

"You're happy," he said. "But you're also more self-aware, too."

She snorted. "That's because that old fool never lets me get away with anything."

He snorted now. "I doubt that anyone could stop you from doing what you want."

"He doesn't stop me," she agreed with a grin. "But he still calls me on it."

"I love Lem," Jessup corrected himself with a grin.

"And I love you," she said as she followed him into the family room and flopped down into a chair. "And yeah, I kind of a love that old man, too."

"It shows," he said. "Love looks good on you." She was eighty, nearing eighty-one, but she still looked so strong and vibrant, more so than he had been for many years. But he was stronger now, though his heart still hurt. That was over his kids, though. Not his health.

"So tell me what Cash wanted you to do," she said.

Heat rushed to his face. It was time to tell his mom the truth; he'd promised Cash he would tell everyone. He wasn't ashamed of what he'd done, of raising Cash as his. But he didn't want his mom to think badly of Colleen. "Biologically... Cash isn't mine," he said. "Colleen got involved with someone she shouldn't have, someone who took advantage of her vulnerability when I broke up with her. So I really blame myself..."

She reached out and grasped his hand, squeezing it. "Of course you do."

"I don't want you to blame Colleen."

"I don't," she said. "Life is messy. Things happen. It's how we handle them that count."

The heat in his face got hotter. "Handling them is the hard part. Running away is easier." It had been for him and for Cash.

"You didn't run away from Colleen," she said. "You were trying to save her like you tried to save me, from worrying about you, from taking care of you..."

"And I hurt her more by pushing her away," he said. Like he had his mother, and he opened his mouth to apologize again but she shook her head.

"And I already knew about Cash," she said.

"You did?" he asked, and he dropped into the chair next to her. "How? When did you find out?"

"At my wedding," she said. "He told me."

"After the pictures?" he asked. He'd been so touched that she'd wanted Cash and Becca in them.

"Before," she said.

He chuckled. "Because he didn't want to be in them and was arguing with you...he told you the truth," he guessed, and she nodded. "That's what he wanted me to do the other night. Tell his brothers. They didn't know." At least the twins hadn't known. Marsh hadn't seemed all that surprised, which made him wonder…but then Marsh never did seem fazed by much. He didn't run; he handled everything like Sadie did, like Jessup's late brother, Michael, had.

"How did they handle it?" she asked.

"Marsh was Marsh," he said his thought aloud.

And she smiled. She'd already figured out his second oldest son.

"The twins were surprised," he said. "But they're all still walking on eggshells around me, worried that anything they say might kill me. Sometimes I just wish they'd yell at me over all the secrets I kept, like Cash yelled at me the day he left. That he hated me. That he wasn't my son…"

"He is," Sadie said. "I don't care what the DNA is. You raised him. He's your son."

"He's more like me than his brothers are," he said.

She smiled. "I know. Stubborn. Proud."

He smiled, too. "So he's like you, too."

She nodded. "Yup, he's my grandson."

Jessup had never loved his mother more.

"And we'll fix this," she said, squeezing Jessup's hand. "We'll make Cash happy."

"Mom…" he said, as a chill of uneasiness chased down his spine like the tip of a cold finger. "Cash is like me. If you push too hard, he'll run again."

She smiled and shook her head. "He has too many reasons to stay. He just doesn't realize it yet."

And clearly she had a plan to make him realize it.

While Jessup had seen her scheming success with his nephews and his younger sons, he was worried. He knew Cash better than she did. If she pushed too hard, they might lose him all over again.

CHAPTER ELEVEN

"WHAT'S THE MATTER with me, Midnight?" Cash asked the horse as he petted the bronco's long black nose. "What was I thinking?"

He couldn't believe he'd asked Becca for that kiss the other night. No. He hadn't asked. He'd purposely challenged her to kiss him, knowing that Becca Calder never ignored a challenge.

But that kiss...

He couldn't stop thinking about how incredible it had been. How soft her lips were, how warm her breath, how sweet the taste...and the way he'd reacted, his heart pounding, his skin tingling...

"I wasn't thinking," he murmured, "because I must have lost my mind."

Just the hug had affected him; he should have known what a kiss would do. Maybe that curiosity was what had compelled him to find out how it would feel to actually kiss his best friend.

And maybe it was all the years of closeness that had intensified the feelings so much, had made it the best kiss he'd ever had, because it was Becca.

But had it been the same for her?

She'd jerked away from him and stepped back, her dark eyes wide, her face drained of color. She'd been shocked, too.

Because of the kiss? Or because he'd wanted one from

her? And now that he'd had one, he wanted another. But his life was a mess right now. He was a mess.

His brothers suspected that he might have torched their family home.

And his...dad. JJ was his dad. He'd always been there for Cash; it was Cash who'd failed him.

Then there was Shep and his daughter, Cash's sister. And Cash was keeping that secret from her.

As much as he hated secrets being kept *from* him, he hated keeping secrets even more. He wondered now if he'd been keeping one from himself: his attraction to Becca.

Midnight expelled a soft sigh and pushed his head close to Cash's, as if commiserating. The horse really was empathetic. He knew what a mess Cash was, that everything in his life felt upside down right now.

Reconnecting with his family, reaching out to new family... He was definitely struggling, which was probably why he'd been literally clinging to Becca for support and comfort, like he always had. But this time he'd taken it too far.

He wasn't sure he could take it back or if he even wanted to...

He sighed and leaned against the horse. "Maybe you're going to have to be my new best friend," he said.

"Don't let Caleb hear you poaching his buddy," a deep voice murmured.

Startled, Cash stumbled against Midnight, who just stood there, supporting him, instead of reacting to his reaction. "Good boy," Cash murmured in appreciation. Then he looked over the stall door at Sadie, who nodded in approval.

"He seems so much calmer," Sadie said.

Cash nodded. "Yeah..." If only he could say the same about himself...

"So you think Dusty will be able to move him soon to the Cassidy Ranch?" Sadie asked.

Cash nodded again. "Yeah." Then he did a double take at Sadie. "Wait, aren't you supposed to be on your honeymoon?" he asked.

"I'll be on my honeymoon for the rest of my life." She snorted and shook her head. "Look what love did to me. I sound like a fool."

"You sound happy," he remarked. And given everything she'd been through, all the loved ones she'd lost, that was a miracle in itself. She was a bit of a miracle. And he wistfully longed for that real familial connection to her, wished that she really was his grandmother. Then he would possess the resiliency every other Haven had, even those little boys who'd lost both parents in that tragic accident.

Maybe most especially them...

"Have you ever been in love, Cash?"

"No." He shuddered at the thought.

Midnight made a strange noise, like a nicker or even a snort of his own. Like he was laughing at Cash.

"You're my oldest grandson," she said. "And you've never been in love?"

"I'm not your—"

"Stop," she said, her voice sharp enough now that it startled Midnight into pawing at the floor of his stall, kicking wood chips up at Cash.

"Easy," he murmured to the horse, who instantly seemed to relax.

"You are my grandson," she insisted. "Jessup said himself that you're more like him than any of your brothers. And I see it, too."

Cash snorted now. "Why? Because I ran away like he did?"

She nodded. "There's that, but once you ran away, neither of you could figure out how to come home again."

He tensed, and Midnight shifted uneasily next to him. "And I thought Darlene understood me best…"

"Darlene? Have you two been talking?"

"A bit. She wanted to make it clear that she didn't replace my mother. She guessed—rightly—that that's what I'd thought. You see, I came home a few months after I left and she answered the door."

"I didn't know that…"

He shrugged. "She was the only one who saw me, and she didn't have any idea who I was until the wedding. And then she came by my work to explain…" He sighed. "But that was my misassumption. And maybe I jumped to that wrong conclusion because I wasn't ready to come home yet. I wanted to go to school without guilt, become a vet."

"Did you do it?" she asked.

He grinned. "I wouldn't have been working with your animals and with Doc Miner if I hadn't."

"No, I know you're a vet, Doc CC. I meant did you do it without guilt?"

He uttered a long, ragged sigh. "No. And that's why I couldn't figure out how to come home again."

"But you're here now," Sadie said. "Make the most of it. Reach out to your brothers. To your dad."

He sighed again, shortly. "My brothers think I burned down our home."

She laughed, then sobered up when she realized he was serious. "What? Why?"

"Colton found my lighter in the ashes."

Her mouth dropped open a bit. "Oh, that was why he was so anxious to find you…"

"To lock me up," he said with a trace of bitterness.

"Did you do it?" she asked matter-of-factly.

"No," he said. "God, no. I was mad when I first found out the truth, but the only person I've been mad at for the last several years has been me."

She reached over the stall door and squeezed his shoulder. "Cash, you need to give yourself a break. Let it go. Let the anger and the guilt and the shame... Let it all go."

Her insight into him was staggering. She was as empathetic as Midnight was. "If only it were that easy..." But there were still things he was holding in, like his connection to Melanie and the relationship he might have damaged with Becca.

Of all the things he needed to fix, he had to deal with Becca first. Make sure they were okay after the other night...

"Come inside," she said. "Taye and Miller are getting lunch ready. We're having a little last-days-of-summer hurrah before the kids start school again."

"You're having a party for that?"

Her smile slipped away, as did her hand from his shoulder, and she gripped the top of the stall door instead. "They had to finish up last school year at home," she said. "Recovering from the accident. The fact that they're all well enough, physically and emotionally, to go back to school..." She released a shaky sigh now.

"That is something to celebrate," he agreed.

"So join us," she encouraged him.

He thought of Melanie; no doubt she would be there. But maybe that was good; he could see how she was doing. And if she was doing well, he could stop keeping one secret.

As for his secret about Becca...

He wasn't sure he was ready to reveal that even to himself. He needed her as a friend more than ever, and he couldn't risk messing that up. "I'll wrap up with Midnight," he said. "And then I'll head up to the house."

He'd been invited before but had always declined the invitation for a number of reasons. Usually he was too busy. And once he'd found out Melanie was working in the house, he hadn't been sure how to act around her. And then when he'd learned that JJ and his brothers were Havens...

It had all been too much. Still was.

That was why he needed Becca. But he wasn't sure how to reach out to her. The last time he'd tried to make things less awkward between them, he'd made them worse.

"THANKS FOR COMING with me," Genevieve said to Becca as they stood before the front door of the sprawling, two-story Haven house.

Their daughters climbed the steps behind them, chattering to each other about the barns and the schoolhouse. "It's like a whole city, not a ranch," Hope said.

"I know!" Bailey Ann agreed.

It wasn't the first time Becca had been out to Ranch Haven, but the scale of it still awed her. It made Becca's ranch look like a hobby farm, which essentially it was. And it reminded her just how much the Cassidy ranch had been neglected, because of JJ's health issues.

"I'm supposed to walk right in," Genevieve said, but she pressed the doorbell instead.

After a few seconds, there was furious barking and scratching at the door. Becca reached protectively for Hope, stepping in front of her, as the door began to open.

A ball of black fur squeezed through the opening and jumped around Genevieve's and Becca's legs. Hope tried to step around Becca to touch the dog. "Wait," she cautioned her daughter, reminding her of the rule about not touching animals until they knew it was safe and all right with the owners.

The door swung back all the way, and the tallest of the Haven boys stepped out and scooped up the long-haired Chihuahua. The dog stopped barking to lick his chin and face.

"That's Miller," Bailey Ann told Hope. "And Feisty is his best friend. This is my best friend, Miller. Her name is Hope."

"Does your dog bite?" Hope asked. She was more fixated on the animal than the boy, very much like Becca had been at her age.

If only Becca had stayed that way...

"No, she just acts like that because she wants attention," he said. "She doesn't bite." He smiled slightly, and his hazel eyes twinkled. "Except maybe Uncle Jake."

"Speaking of biting," Bailey Ann said, "we better get to the kitchen before Caleb eats all the chocolate chips cookies."

Miller chuckled. "Me and Taye made a big batch this morning. Even he can't eat all of them. There is a lot of other food, too, for the party." He leaned down and released the dog, who tore back through the foyer and down the hall, the little girls chasing after her. He started after them, then turned back. "Come on, Aunt Genevieve, Miss Becca, the party is about to start."

Genevieve drew in a deep breath before stepping inside the house, as if she needed to brace herself.

Becca followed her inside and closed the door. She lowered her voice and whispered, "Uh-oh, why the hesitation? I thought everything was good between you and the Havens now."

The two women had bonded when Becca had helped Genevieve find a house when she'd first moved to Willow Creek, so Becca knew the family history. Genevieve's late sister had been married to Dale Haven, and Miller, Ian and Little Jake were their sons. Genevieve and her sister hadn't been close, so she hadn't found out about the tragic accident until months after it had happened. And then she hadn't known how to proceed.

"Sometimes it's just hard to be here," Genevieve said, "when Jenny can't be…" Jenny was her late sister. Their names were so close because, after their mother had had Genevieve as a teenager, she'd seemed—at least to Genevieve—like she'd wanted a do-over when she had her second child six years later.

Becca slid her arm around the shorter woman's shoulders and gave her a side hug. "I'm so sorry…" For all the pain Genevieve had suffered. Becca really was fortunate with her loving and supportive parents and her healthy and happy daughter. She felt a twinge of guilt over not being honest with them. They deserved more from her after everything they'd all given her.

Cash deserved better, too. Because he wouldn't have challenged her to kiss him if he'd known she'd been keeping a secret from him, too. And he must have wanted her kiss or else why would he have challenged her? She didn't know how to react now. Did she pretend like it hadn't happened, like they had the minute they'd pulled apart?

He'd stammered something about it being late and then, unsurprisingly, he'd rushed off. Running…

She shouldn't have been surprised. But she had been disappointed. It wasn't the first time she'd realized that she and Cash would never have the kind of relationship she wanted. And now she wasn't even sure they had a friendship.

He hadn't called or texted her after it had happened. And he'd looked as stunned as she'd been…

As she still was...

So she needed this distraction today. A party. It wasn't the first one Becca had attended at Ranch Haven; there had been a party after Genevieve and Collin's wedding here, too.

She and Genevieve stepped into the kitchen, which was obviously the heart of the Haven home. The enormous room was abuzz with people and activity. Balloons hung from the ceiling like they had at Sadie's wedding. But the kids weren't trying to catch their strings now. Instead they were gathered around the long stainless steel island, sneaking cookies from the trays that were set out with a punch bowl and platters of sandwiches and bowls of potato salad and pasta salads.

"Wow," Becca said, and her stomach growled. She hadn't been eating much since that kiss. Her stomach was as unsettled as her emotions.

"We might have overdone it a bit," Taye Cooper remarked. Sadie had hired Taye to cook at the ranch the same time she'd hired Katie to help with the ranch accounts, Emily to teach the boys and Melanie to work with Miller as his physical therapist. Ostensibly Sadie had been helping her great-grandchildren, but it was clear she'd had plans in mind for her grandsons, as well. Matchmaking plans...

She'd even employed those plans with the Cassidys now. Colton was engaged to Lem's granddaughter, and Becca suspected that Sadie had had a hand in them meeting just as she had with Genevieve and Collin. She had referred Collin to Genevieve for her legal advice. Genevieve had helped him foster Bailey Ann and had already started the adoption process.

Sadie walked up and greeted her with, "Becca, I'm so glad you were able to get away from your office and join us today."

Becca glanced at Genevieve, wondering if she'd been enlisted in Sadie's schemes. She'd thought, at Sadie's wedding, that the older woman might have intended to matchmake her and Cash. But the invitation to this party had come from Genevieve, not Sadie. Or so she'd thought. Her friend blushed a bit and said, "I wanted to make sure that it was all right to bring you and Hope with us so I called ahead to check."

"And you're home from your honeymoon already?" Becca asked Sadie.

Now Sadie blushed slightly and glanced at her groom, who sat at the end of the long table. The table was positioned between the island and a wall of French doors that opened onto the brick courtyard where Genevieve and Collin had gotten married. The older man, with his white hair and beard, looked like Santa Claus, especially as he had the toddler, Little Jake, curled up on his lap as they looked at a big picture book together.

"You're not going to tell her what you told me in the barn?" a deep voice asked.

Becca whirled around to find Cash standing behind her. How hadn't she been aware of his presence? Or had he just walked in after she and Genevieve had? That must have been it because she was well aware of him now, her face heating up while nerves gripped her.

Hope must not have seen him, either, until he spoke because she exclaimed, "There's my Cash!" And she grabbed Bailey Ann's hand to pull her toward where he stood just inside the doorway between the kitchen and the hall.

"That's Doc CC!" Caleb exclaimed around a mouthful of cookie.

"What did she tell you in the barn?" Hope asked the question that was stuck in Becca's throat.

"She told me," Cash began, and he raised his voice

and looked at Lem, "that the rest of her life is going to be her honeymoon."

Bright red spots appeared on Lem's round cheeks, and he blinked furiously. And so did Sadie, as she blushed an even deeper red than he was.

Ben Haven, who'd been standing in the kitchen, slapped Cash on the back. "I like you. You're going to fit in well around here."

Caleb sighed. "I'm getting sick of this mushy stuff," he said. "There's been way too much kissing around here."

Now Becca's face got even hotter, and Cash's flushed, too.

"Tell me what Midnight told you," Caleb demanded.

Cash chuckled.

"You think our horse can talk now?" Dusty asked Caleb as he and his very pregnant wife walked in through the open French doors.

"Doc CC is the horse whisperer," Caleb said.

"That doesn't mean Midnight whispers back," Dusty said.

Cash crouched down and whispered something into the little boy's ear, and Caleb's big blue eyes widened and twinkled with delight. Cash was so good with Hope and now with this child, who clearly loved horses as much as he did, or at least one particular horse.

"The horse talked to you?" Hope asked, her dark eyes wide with wonder. Then she shook her head. "Horses don't talk or Tilly would have said something to me by now."

"Tilly?" Caleb asked.

"She's my horse," Hope said with pride. She was growing up so fast.

Then the toddler, Little Jake, who'd been on Lem's lap moments ago shoved his way through the other kids to

Cash. "Horsey, horsey," he said. With his big dark eyes and chubby cheeks, he was so adorable.

With all the kids gathered around them, Becca yearned to have another baby. But this time she didn't yearn just for a child of her own. She yearned for a child with Cash.

SOMETHING WAS DIFFERENT between them since her wedding. Sadie watched the way that Becca and Cash watched each other, sneaking glances, quickly looking away if those glances coincided. Something had happened since her wedding.

Cash seemed different, too, and Sadie had figured it was just because of what must have been an emotional meeting between him and his family.

Family...

She took her seat at the table next to Lem, setting the plate she'd filled between the two of them with a handful of silverware, too. He bumped her knee with his under the table, and she blushed, thinking he was being flirty.

He chuckled. "Look up. They came."

And she turned her attention toward the doorway from the hall and watched as Jessup and Darlene walked through with a younger woman and a child around the same age as Caleb, Ian and Hope. The boy seemed shy, his head dipped down so that his blond hair fell across his forehead as he studied the brick floor instead of meeting anyone's gazes.

"That's Sarah and her son, Mikey."

She'd met them once or twice at Jessup's house in town, but she hadn't been able to get them out to the ranch. Any other time that Jessup had been out, Collin had been with them, so Jessup hadn't needed the nurse.

With how well he was doing, how healthy he looked with his new heart, Jessup didn't seem as if he needed any medical assistance. But she figured he needed something else...the same thing so many of her grandsons had found, the same thing she'd found with Lem: love.

But he wasn't going to think about himself or his happiness until he was certain that his eldest son was happy. His eldest son...lost just as hers had been.

She'd thought for so long that he'd gone off somewhere and died because he hadn't had her there, looking out for him, looking over him. But he'd had his wife taking care of him, and he had taken care of her, too, and they'd had their beautiful sons.

And then after Colleen died, Darlene had shown up, and acting out of her guilt and self-imposed penance over her husband's accidental death, she'd taken it upon herself to take care of Jessup and his boys.

They were incredible people. But Sadie wasn't sure they were meant to be together. That they might truly be just friends.

Unlike Cash and Becca...who actually blushed when they caught each other sneaking glances. They weren't just friends anymore.

Something had happened. And suspecting who might know, Sadie patted Lem's hand and went to greet the new arrivals. She spared her son and Darlene a quick hug, and while she warmly welcomed Sarah and her son, the woman seemed as shy as her little boy.

"Thank you for having us here," Sarah said. "I hope it's not too much trouble."

Sadie laughed. "The more the merrier..." And she certainly was. That old fool Lem had been right, like he always was: everything and everyone they loved was right here.

Now to just make certain that everyone she loved was as happy as she and Lem were. She slipped away from Jessup and the others to approach the island, where a little dark-haired girl stood, studying the trays of cookies. Taye had made an assortment, including chocolate chip, of course.

But there were also some chocolate ones with thick buttercream frosting sandwiched between them. There were sugar cookies with sprinkles on them, and there were also snickerdoodles.

Sadie reached over Hope's head and took one of those from the plate. She broke it in two pieces and handed one to her. "This is my favorite," she said. "And no matter what Caleb says, they are the best."

"This party is the best," Hope said, smiling. "There are so many people."

As an only child, the crowd and chaos in the kitchen could have been overwhelming for her, like it clearly was for Sarah's son. But Hope seemed intrigued rather than intimidated. She was definitely her mother's daughter.

"And there's so much food," the child continued. "I didn't know what to try." But she happily took the cookie half and popped it into her mouth. Then her eyes sparkled and she nodded. "Yup, Caleb's wrong. These are the best."

Sensing a kindred spirit, Sadie smiled. "You and I are going to be very good friends."

"Like my mommy and Cash?" Hope asked. "They're best friends. Bailey Ann says she's my best friend now, too."

"You're not sure?"

She shrugged. "I like having friends, but…"

"There's something else you really want?" Sadie guessed.

The little girl nodded. "A daddy." And her gaze shifted beyond Sadie, who turned and followed it, to Cash.

Sadie nodded. Hope was definitely a kindred spirit.

CHAPTER TWELVE

CASH HAD KNOWN that coming up to the house was a mistake. He didn't have a child to celebrate summer ending and school starting. And he wasn't likely to have one anytime in the near future; he didn't have a wife or even a girlfriend. And after that kiss the other night, he wasn't sure that he had Becca anymore.

She'd barely been able to look at him since he'd walked into the kitchen. She'd just glanced at him from time to time and then glanced away. Usually she would have walked right up and started talking to him, teasing him...

And he would have done the same. He'd started to when he'd walked into the kitchen and found her standing with Sadie. But when she'd turned and looked at him...all he'd been able to think about was that kiss. And he'd wanted to kiss her again.

Fortunately Hope and Caleb had distracted him, and he'd been able to focus on them. Now every time he looked at Becca, he had to look away immediately.

Had he messed up his friendship with her like he'd messed up so many other things in his life? With one impulsive action...

Like when he'd stormed off the ranch, hurling insults at the man who loved him most, the man Cash had loved most but hadn't been able to help.

JJ was here now with Darlene, and a younger woman with a boy in tow. He guessed they were the home health nurse and her son. While JJ looked better than Cash ever remembered him looking, medical complications with his heart must still be a concern.

Cash was concerned, too, especially because his brothers weren't there. Were they angry with their dad after learning the truth? Had Cash caused more problems with his insistence on no more secrets?

And if revealing that secret had caused problems with his brothers, how would revealing his secret affect his biological sister?

Melanie seemed fine now as she bustled around the kitchen, helping clean up the empty plates and bowls from the feast.

"Sit down," Taye Cooper, the cook, urged her. "You're not supposed to be on your feet this much. You need to rest."

Melanie shook her head and smiled. "I'm fine. You all worry too much."

"With good reason," Dusty muttered. He stood next to Cash. "Let the guys clean up the mess," he suggested. "And all you lovely women sit down and relax." He met Taye's gaze, and they exchanged a look.

Taye put down her dish towel, then grabbed a plate of cookies and another one of fruit. "Ladies, let's go out to the patio and leave these guys with the mess."

"Thanks a lot," Baker grumbled, but he was grinning as he headed to the sink. Then he tossed the dish towel at Dusty. "Since this was your idea, you can dry."

"I'll help," Cash said.

"You're not billing us for your time, though," Dusty said with a teasing tone. "Now that we know you're family, are we going to get a discount on our veterinarian services?"

"Yeah," Baker, the new foreman of Ranch Haven, said. "The family discount would be nice."

JJ was standing near Cash, close enough that Cash could feel his body tense, could tell that he was bracing himself for Cash's denial that he was a Haven. But Cash didn't feel as defensive as he'd once been; maybe he could figure out how to take Sadie's advice and let it all go.

Except for Becca...

He had to find a way to get back on normal footing with his best friend.

But now he just chuckled in response to his new cousins' teasing. "I don't think my partner would go for that given that half our clients are probably 'family.'"

"So when is Doc Miner retiring?" Jake was the one who asked the question. "He keeps threatening, but he stays on."

"I hope he never retires," Cash said. "We're so busy." That hadn't bothered him when he'd first started working with the older man. But now...being here with all the Havens, seeing what it might be like to have a family someday...he didn't want to just work all the time.

"Speaking of busy," Jake said. "Have you had a chance to evaluate Midnight for moving him out to the Cassidy Ranch?" He glanced at his brother, who sighed and held up his hands.

"I want that, too," Dusty said. "I just don't want to set him back. He's been calming down quite a bit thanks to the horse whisperer."

"Yeah, what did you tell Caleb that Midnight said to you?" Jake asked curiously. "Hopefully to never try to ride him on his own?"

Cash nodded. "Well, words to that effect. That Midnight is ready to retire from the rodeo and start a family."

"Just like Uncle Dusty," Caleb chimed in as he swiped a chocolate chip cookie from the tray on the counter. He wrinkled his nose in disgust. Not at the cookie obviously, which he greedily shoved in his mouth, but over the idea of starting a family.

Jake chuckled. "So Midnight doesn't want to be ridden anymore."

"No. He wants a wife," Caleb said and sighed his disappointment. "Do horses kiss?" He grimaced and shook his head. "Forget I asked. I don't want to hear about kissing." Then he grabbed another cookie and ran off.

"Thank you," Jake said. "I'd been trying to end his obsession with that horse but had no idea how to do it. Maybe you're the kid whisperer, too."

"Like Taye and Emily," Baker said. "And Old Man, I mean, Grandpa Lem."

"And Sadie," Cash added thoughtfully. He'd seen the older woman talking sweetly with Hope like they were already best friends. At the thought of best friends, he looked around for Becca, but she must have slipped out to the patio with the other women.

Hope bounded in through the open French doors and ran up to the counter. "The snickerdoodles are the best, Cash," she told him as she grabbed one from a tray. "Grandma Sadie says so."

He swallowed hard. "Grandma Sadie…"

"She told me to call her that," Hope said.

"She'll want you to call her that, too," JJ said, his voice soft as he leaned close to Cash.

Cash nodded. "I know."

"So can you move Midnight out to the Cassidy Ranch soon?" Jake asked. "Like today?"

Dusty sighed. "I don't even have possession of the place yet."

"I told you it's yours," JJ said. "The insurance should settle things soon, and then the paperwork can go through. But to me, it's already officially yours."

If the insurance hadn't been settled yet, that meant Marsh was right. There were concerns that it had been arson.

"I've taken you up on that," Dusty assured him. "Cash and I already checked out the barn, and I'm making a few alterations for Midnight. We'll be able to move him there soon."

"*You* were out to the ranch?" JJ asked, his dark eyes filled with concern as he looked at Cash.

He nodded. "Yeah, I was out there with Dusty earlier this week."

"Did you see the cat?" JJ asked.

"Cat?" Hope asked, her voice breathy with excitement. "Where's the cat?"

"A stray cat started coming around my old ranch a few months ago," he said. "I put out food for her, but I'm not sure how long that would have lasted…"

Hope gasped. "We need to go find her and make sure she has food!" She loved animals as much as her mother did, as much as Cash did.

"I didn't see a cat," he said.

Dusty shook his head. "Me, neither."

"She's probably hiding," JJ said. "I think she's feral or…"

Maybe she had been abused, but he was too sensitive to mention that in front of Hope.

The little girl ran around the long island and grabbed Cash's hand with her small one. And despite its small size, it felt like that hand was wrapping around his heart, too. He loved Hope like she was his own.

Like JJ loved him…

"Can we go find her?" Hope asked. "Please? She's probably so hungry and scared."

"I wouldn't mind taking a ride out there to check on the

progress in the barn," Dusty said. "We can make a family trip of it."

"Yes, a family trip," Hope said with a big smile and a certain sparkle in her dark eyes. "Mommy has to come, too." And she dropped Cash's hand to run back out to the patio.

JJ chuckled. "Now I know who she reminds me of…"

"She's the spitting image of her mother," Cash said. Maybe that was why he'd always had such a deep connection to her.

"I was thinking more of my mother," JJ said, and he chuckled.

Cash's uneasiness returned. That was probably just over having to interact with Becca after that kiss. Chances were that she would say no to Hope, though, that they had something to do. And even if they didn't, she might make up something if she felt as awkward as he did over that kiss.

But as awkward as he felt, he didn't really regret it—and part of him hoped to do it again.

SHE SHOULD HAVE said no. She'd intended to say no the minute that Hope had asked. They'd ridden with Genevieve and Bailey Ann out to Ranch Haven, so they should leave with them. And Bailey Ann had had a doctor's appointment, so they weren't able to go on the excursion to the Cassidy Ranch.

Other people had jumped in with offers to drive them home after, and Hope had pleaded so much, her big eyes glistening with tears of concern for this missing kitty. And as an animal lover herself, Becca couldn't say no. She wanted to make sure that the stray was safe and taken care of, as well.

But she wasn't certain how she and Hope had wound up riding in Cash's truck with him. Hope sat in the back seat of his pickup, in a booster seat, and she was animatedly chattering away. She usually didn't talk this much, but maybe she'd sensed the awkwardness between Becca and Cash and was determined to fill the silence. Or maybe she was just that excited over the day they were having.

First a party and now a rescue mission.

Hope gasped. "Wow! That's what everybody was talking about..."

Becca's eyes widened as they started down the driveway toward the farmhouse. It was just a blackened skeleton.

Bailey Ann wasn't the only child who hadn't been allowed on this excursion. Baker and Taye had nixed the other kids going; they'd used the excuse that they had to go school shopping. But they probably weren't sure it was safe for curious boys to visit the ranch yet. Baker, as a former fireman, would know how unstable that structure was. The other child, Mikey, hadn't wanted to come back, probably because he'd been here when the house had burned down.

"What happened?" Hope asked.

"There was a fire," Becca replied. And she glanced over the console at her best friend. This had once been his home. But now that it was gone, he could never really go home again.

Poor Cash...

She wanted to reach for his hand or touch his arm. But she knew what would happen if she did; she would feel that little zap of energy, of awareness. And after the kiss, she wasn't strong enough to ignore it as she had in the past. Or had at least tried to ignore it.

"Yeah, but what happened?" Hope asked. "How did it catch fire?"

"Nobody knows for sure yet," Becca said. "Probably just something electrical or mechanical..."

"Or..." Cash murmured, his voice gruff.

"Or what?" Hope asked.

He shrugged. "Nothing." And he drove past the house to the barn, which already looked better than it ever had.

Dusty had taken JJ up on his offer of possession before closing on the property, and he'd replaced the roof and re-sided it.

"It looks brand-new," she said as Cash pulled the truck up to the big double doors and parked.

"Is the kitty in there?" Hope asked.

Cash shrugged. "I don't know. I didn't see her when I was here a few days ago."

"Maybe the construction scared her away. We might not find her," Becca cautioned her daughter.

Hope unclasped her belt and clamored over the console and across Becca's lap to open the door. "We gotta find her, or she'll starve."

"Honey, she survived on her own out here before Mr. JJ started feeding her," she said. "She found things to eat then, and I'm sure she has been finding things now."

"Like what?" Hope challenged her.

"Mice. Birds."

Hope grimaced. "Gross." Then she opened the door and ran from the truck to the barn, her hair flying behind her.

"I don't know what's gotten into her," she murmured.

"Snickerdoodles," Cash replied.

Becca pressed her palm to her forehead. "Oh, of course. She usually doesn't eat many sweets."

"There was so much good food at the ranch," he said, and he patted his flat stomach before unclasping his seat belt.

"I was surprised to see you there," she said.

"Surprised or disappointed?" He pushed back his hat and turned toward her.

"Surprised," she said. "That's all."

"Then you're not feeling as awkward as I am about the other night?" he asked.

Heat rushed to her face. "I'm sorry," she murmured.

"*You're* sorry?" he asked. "I goaded you into it. We both know you can't turn down a challenge."

"Then why did you challenge me?"

He shrugged. "I don't know, Becca. I'm a mess. What can I say…?" He pointed out her open door to the burned-out structure of his family home.

"I know you didn't burn it down," she assured him.

"I wish Marsh and the twins believed that," he said. "But I think they have their doubts. They didn't even show up today."

"It's a weekday," she said. "I'm sure they're busy with their jobs." She stared out that door at the house and sighed. "It's sad that it's gone."

"It doesn't matter," he said. "Dusty and Melanie weren't going to live in it. They'll build something of their own here someday."

"Does that bother you?" she asked.

"Why would it?"

"It's supposed to be yours, isn't it?" she asked. "You being the oldest son and all?"

He shrugged. "I don't want it."

"Do you know what you want, Cash?" she asked, and she was talking about that kiss.

He shrugged again. "I don't know. I don't feel like I really know anything anymore."

Then he glanced out the back window at the other vehicles pulling into the driveway. His sister and her husband were in one, Melanie's mother and JJ in the other. JJ, the man who Cash had believed, for the first eighteen years of his life, was his father.

"But that's not an excuse or the apology I owe you," he

said. "That's what I can say. I'm sorry. I always dump all my problems on you. But I can't lose you, Becca. I don't know what I would do without you."

He was talking about friendship. Just friendship…

But she wanted so much more, and so did Hope. That was the problem. She could handle him breaking her heart, but she didn't think that Hope could.

JESSUP HADN'T BEEN out to the ranch since the fire, and he hadn't particularly wanted to go. He'd had an excuse not to, as well. Sarah had to sign Mikey up for school in Willow Creek, so she couldn't go.

Mikey hadn't wanted to come back here anyway. When Hope had asked him about helping to find the kitty, he'd shaken his head. Had the kid said anything to anyone at Ranch Haven?

Jessup knew it could be overwhelming. *They* could be overwhelming. But it had seemed like more than that with the little boy. Ever since the fire, he'd been so quiet.

It must have scared him.

It had scared Jessup, too, especially when they hadn't been able to find him. And Jessup had gone back inside the house…

He shuddered as he stared at the burned-out structure of the home where he'd lived for so long, where he'd raised his sons, where he'd lost his wife…

Juliet Shepherd was staring at the house, too, or rather, at the pathetic bits that were left of it.

Juliet, who was staying at Ranch Haven because of her daughter's pregnancy, was worried about Melanie's health. She'd wanted to come along, but since Dusty just had a two-seater truck, Juliet decided to drive her own vehicle. And she'd offered a lift to JJ.

He glanced over at her. She was probably nine or ten

years younger than he was. Given her flawless skin and deep auburn hair, he might have thought she was even younger if she hadn't had a daughter who was probably close to thirty.

"Are you okay?" she asked now.

"I'm fine," he said.

"I mean…about the house…being back here," she murmured.

"Yes," he said. "No lives were lost and the injuries were minimal."

"Injuries?" she gasped.

"I had some smoke inhalation," he said. "And so did my son Marsh. Collin got burned the worst." He flinched, thinking of his cardiologist son's wounded hands. "But he's healing now."

"And how is everyone emotionally?" she asked.

"He and Colton are doing so well. They each found their soulmates, thanks to my mother's meddling."

Juliet smiled. "Sadie is a force of nature."

"Yes, she is."

"What about you?"

He chuckled. "I'm not a force of anything."

"I meant, how are you doing?" she asked. "Physically and emotionally? You lost your home and could have lost your life, too."

"I had already sold the place…to your son-in-law." He grinned. "And that was before I even realized the great Dusty Chaps was my nephew."

Juliet let out a little giggle. "What a name. But what a man. When Melanie married him on their first date, I was so afraid that she'd made the mistake I had with her father. But she got lucky. Dusty is a good man."

Jessup nodded, glancing toward Melanie, where she reclined in the passenger seat of the truck. "He is." And he felt a pang of regret that he'd never gotten the chance to know Dusty's twin, Dale.

"What about Cash?"

They turned their attention to the two men who stood in front of the barn doors. Dusty and Cash. Becca, holding her daughter's hand, was standing beside Cash, where she usually was...

Where she belonged, if only she and Cash would realize that they should be more than friends.

He groaned. He was becoming just like his mother.

"What?" she asked with alarm. "Isn't he okay?"

"I wasn't groaning about Cash," he assured her. "Not anymore, though I have worried about him over the years. His mother and I kept a secret from him that nearly destroyed him when he found out."

"That he's not your son," Juliet said.

"My mother told you?" he asked with surprise.

She shook her head. "No. I know who he is."

Jessup put it together, saying, "You probably saw him when Cash was working as a vet with the rodeo. Didn't you travel with your husband?"

"Ex-husband," she corrected him. "And not enough to keep him in line. And now... I don't even know why I bothered trying. I wanted this happy family home life for Melanie, but she never had it. She always knew. And I know that Cash is Shep's son."

Jessup sucked in a breath. "Shep was your husband?"

She nodded. "Yes. I'm the woman who was stupid enough to marry him."

"I hope you know that Colleen had no idea he was married, or she wouldn't have gotten involved with him."

"I didn't travel much in those early years of our marriage. Every one of my pregnancies was so difficult..."

"You have more than Melanie?"

She clenched her jaw and shook her head. Then she released a shaky sigh and said, "No. That's why the pregnancies were so difficult. I was lucky that I carried her to term."

And all the while her husband had been acting like a single man. He reached across the console and touched her arm. "I'm very sorry."

"We all make mistakes," she said.

"I wasn't talking about that," he said. "You've been through so much…"

She smiled. "Haven't we all?" she asked. She rested her fingertips on his hand. "Some more than others."

She was a very sweet woman. And Shep Shepherd had been a fool.

"He hasn't told her," Juliet said.

"What?" He'd been thinking about her, about her hand on his…

"Melanie knows she has half siblings, but she doesn't know who they are. And Cash hasn't told her that he's her brother," Juliet clarified.

"Do you think he knows?" Jessup asked.

She nodded and lifted her hand from his to point through the windshield at Cash standing awkwardly near Melanie's open door. "Look at the way he looks at her."

"He will tell her," Jessup warned her. "He hates secrets."

Juliet sighed. "Don't we all…"

CHAPTER THIRTEEN

CASH DIDN'T WANT to disappoint Hope...like he'd disappointed her mother. Becca mightn't have told him she was disappointed with how he'd taken off all those years ago, but he knew it was true. Even though she'd continued to talk to him...

And he should have known that, despite that kiss the other night, she would continue to talk to him. While she hadn't actually accepted his apology, she'd seemed to understand what he'd been trying to say. Like she always understood him.

And nothing ever seemed to really faze Becca. Her husband left and she couldn't get ahold of him. She just raised her daughter on her own, without complaint.

She never complained. Not even about coming out to the Cassidy Ranch when she probably had a hundred other things to do. But she didn't want to disappoint her daughter, either.

So she was helping Hope search for the cat, along with JJ and Melanie's mom, Juliet. While they all searched for the cat, he and Dusty quickly assessed the barn's readiness for Midnight. Dusty was particularly quick because he had convinced Melanie to wait in the truck with the air conditioner blasting to combat the heat of the late August day.

"Midnight's ready," Cash assured him.

"Not a minute too soon for Jake," Dusty remarked. "Too bad we didn't have you relay that message from

Midnight to Caleb sooner. You would have saved us all some trouble."

Cash chuckled. "I don't know how much that will discourage him from trying to ride him, though. And even though Midnight is calmer, he was trained to buck off riders. So it's probably a good idea to bring him over here."

"You're a natural with kids," Dusty said. "I saw you with Becca's daughter, too."

"Hope's a sweetheart. And your nephews are really good kids." He'd talked to Bailey Ann a bit, but he wasn't sure how much his brother Collin would let him be involved with his little girl. If Collin didn't trust that he hadn't burned down the family home, he wouldn't trust Cash with his daughter.

"My twin was a really good dad. He was a natural, too. I'm not sure how good I'm going to be at this…" He stood in the doorway to the barn staring out at his truck, looking more afraid than Cash had ever seen the champion rodeo rider before, and Cash had watched him ride bulls.

The horn on his truck tooted, and then the passenger's door started to swing open. And Dusty rushed to his truck. Cash followed, his heart thumping with concern that something could be wrong with Melanie.

"Are you okay?" Dusty asked.

"Just getting impatient," she said. "I need to stop in town, too. Pick up a few more things for the babies."

"After that shower Taye and Emily and Katie gave you, you must have everything you need for the babies," Dusty assured her.

"I don't feel like I'm ready yet. I'm sure there is more… something we're not thinking of…" She patted her belly, as if soothing her babies.

The babies he would be an uncle to. Cash swallowed hard as he considered that. Would she allow him to be part of her children's lives? Would she be able to accept him? Or would she prefer to never know about, let alone associate with, her father's indiscretions?

"Cash!" Hope called out from the barn. "We need you!"

Melanie smiled at him. "You're needed, Doc CC. Maybe they found the cat."

"I hope so," he said. "She won't be able to sleep unless we do. She's exactly like her mother, so in love with every animal she sees. Or in this case hasn't even seen."

"You and Becca are close," she said, a twinkle in her brown eyes. The same twinkle he'd glimpsed in Sadie's eyes when she'd insisted that both he and Becca be in her family pictures at her wedding.

A matchmaking twinkle.

Dusty chuckled as he saw it, too. "You've been spending too much time around Sadie, my love. Cash and Becca are just friends."

But Cash thought of that kiss. And he knew they weren't just friends anymore.

BECCA WISHED THEY had found the cat…alone. But the small gray tabby lay in a bed of old hay with six tiny kittens snuggled up to her.

Cash was leaning over them, carefully checking on the kittens and the mama without scaring them. The mama blinked her amber eyes at him in that slow blink that indicated trust and affection.

The same look she'd given JJ when they'd all climbed up into the loft. They'd found the kittens and a stash of food for her up here, as well as some little race cars and plastic horses. "Mikey's fort," JJ said with a smile. "So I wasn't the only one feeding her."

"Which was good since she wasn't eating for one," Cash remarked.

"Mommy, can we keep them?" Hope asked, her brown eyes wide and beseeching as she stared up at Becca. "Can we keep all of them?"

If that included Cash, Becca might have agreed, but she knew her daughter was asking about the kittens. Or maybe she was talking about Cash, too, after that conversation Becca had overheard between Hope and Bailey Ann.

Not that Becca had lost Cash. While things had been awkward after the kiss, it was clear it would never happen again. He thought it was a mistake, because of everything he was going through, and he'd apologized.

But at least he still wanted to be her friend. If she told him her secret, though, she might lose him.

"Mommy, please..." Hope implored her desperately.

"It would be selfish of us to keep them all, especially since Mr. JJ and Mikey have been taking care of the mama kitty," Becca said.

But JJ shook his head. "I can't have them at the house I'm renting. And since Mikey is staying with us..."

"Well, I'm sure other people would love to have one of her kittens," Becca said, "when they're old enough to be separated from their mommy."

"But I'm sure they don't wanna leave their mommy," Hope said. "I don't ever wanna leave you."

Love wrapped tightly around Becca's heart. "That's so sweet," she said. "And you know so well how to work me..."

Cash and JJ chuckled.

"But one day you will want to leave me," she said with a heavy sigh. "For college and to travel and your career and maybe someday to get married."

Hope grimaced. "Yuck to getting married. But I do wanna go to the same college Cash went to and become an animal doctor just like him."

"I thought your mama might become a vet, too," JJ said. "She's always loved animals as much as Cash."

"But I love sales more. And I was much stronger in my marketing classes than my science ones." Becca grimaced now. "I also can't stand seeing an animal in pain."

"But you can help the animal if you're a vet," Hope said.

"You're so smart," Becca praised her. "And I'm sure you will do everything you set your mind out to do. So you see you're going to move away from me one day."

Hope rolled her eyes in a dramatic fashion befitting a teenager rather than a six-year-old. "That won't be for a long time."

Becca hugged the little girl. "Promise?"

Hope giggled. "Mom, if you're worried about missing me, you could keep all the kittens, then you'll never be lonely."

Becca smiled. "You're pretty good at sales, too," she said. It could have been worse; Hope could have suggested she get a husband instead of the mother cat and kittens.

But then the little girl added, "Or you and Cash could get married."

JJ laughed hard. "I thought I saw my mother talking to you," he said to Hope. Then, over the little girl's head, he mouthed *Sorry* to Becca.

"Your mother would probably rather keep the kittens," Cash remarked with a chuckle of his own.

"Can we, Mommy? Can we?" Hope pleaded.

Becca was afraid to answer now because she wasn't certain what the little girl wanted. The kittens or Cash? Probably, just as Becca herself had been thinking moments ago, all of them.

"Their eyes are fully open, and they're very active," Cash said as he picked up one and it wrapped itself around his big hand. It was black with white paws and a white chin. Once he picked it up, the other kittens began to move around, as if looking for their sibling. "I'd say they're probably three to four weeks old."

JJ nodded. "So she gave birth right around the time the house burned down."

"That must have been so frightening," Juliet murmured, and she reached out and touched his arm.

She was a very sweet woman. And Becca felt a twinge of pity for her, for what she'd endured with her philandering husband. She caught Cash looking at Juliet in almost the same way, but there was guilt as well as pity in his expression.

Like any of what had happened was his fault...

She stroked the kitten he held, touching his hand, as well, to offer him comfort. She felt that little zip she always felt when she touched him. And his blue eyes widened, as if he felt it, too.

"Ow," he said, grimacing. He moved his hand, and the kitten clung to it with claws sunk deeply into his skin.

Pain was the reason for his reaction; it wasn't like hers. It had never been like hers.

Hope giggled as the other kittens climbed onto her, looking for their sibling. Or for attention. She was all too willing to give it to them, petting and cooing over them. "They're so cute, Mommy. Please..."

The mother cat stood up then, as if anxious that her babies were in danger. She sniffed Cash's jeans where he was kneeling in the hay. Then she brushed up against Becca's arm, and Becca felt her thinness, the bones all too obvious on her sides and back.

"We can bring them home after Cash checks them out and gives them the vaccines they need," she relented. She petted the mother cat who purred, but even her purr seemed weak, as if she didn't have much energy left.

"Yay!" Hope exclaimed.

"But we're just going to foster them until we can find them good homes," she said. "So don't get too attached to them."

"Bailey Ann is being fostered," Hope said. "But Miss Genevieve and Dr. Collin are keeping her."

"You are too smart for six," Becca said. "That is why I told you not to get attached."

"But I love them already!" Hope exclaimed. And she picked up a little tabby that looked as much like her mother as Hope looked like Becca, kissing its furry head.

Cash leaned close to Becca and whispered in her ear, his breath stirring her hair and making her skin tingle. "Sucker. You never could turn away a stray."

She closed her eyes at the sensations washing over her. He was the stray she'd wanted to keep, all those years ago when he'd shown up heartbroken at her house. That was the moment when her feelings for him had changed. But he hadn't stayed then. And even though he kept coming back, checking in with her, he didn't stay. That was why she couldn't trust him not to run if she ever told him the truth.

She opened her eyes and met JJ's gaze. He was looking at her as if he knew and understood. And he probably did understand Cash better than anyone else did.

"Let's find a box or crate to put them in for the ride into town," JJ suggested, and he helped disengage the kittens' claws from Hope's clothes. As he took them off the little girl, he handed them to Juliet, who cooed over each one of them like she was a little girl, too.

"They are very cute," she said. She held up a black-and-white one that had a bit longer fur than the others, and she pressed her cheek against it. "Oh, you're not going to have any problem getting rid of these," she whispered reassuringly to Becca.

Hope was far enough away, with Cash and JJ helping her down the ladder from the loft, that she hadn't heard.

The mother cat must have decided to trust them with her babies because she climbed onto Becca's lap and curled up. While she kept her amber eyes open just a little, she relaxed and began to purr again. And Becca ran her hand over her soft fur. "It's okay, Mama. We're going to help you. You don't have to take care of all these babies on your own any longer."

Juliet smiled. "No, you are."

Becca shrugged. "I'll have a lot of help."

"From Cash?"

Her tone made it clear she was wondering what their relationship was, like all the Havens had wondered at the wedding.

"Sadie might have other ideas, but Cash and I are just friends."

"So you're a single mom?" Juliet asked.

Becca tensed a bit, startling the tabby into opening her amber eyes and staring up at her with concern. This was why she'd made up the whirlwind wedding and annulment. She wanted to avoid any judgment against single mothers.

"I am now," she said, which wasn't necessarily lying since she was only implying that she hadn't always been. "But I have a lot of help from my parents."

"I was married, and I was a single mother," Juliet said. "Or at least my now ex-husband thought *he* was single then. I stayed for Melanie's sake, but I know now that it would have been better for her and for me if I'd just done it on my own."

"I really wanted to be a mother more than anything," Becca said.

"Me, too," Juliet said. "I had so many miscarriages before I had Melanie. I blamed myself, but I realize now that it had probably been stress." Her brow furrowed, and she held the furry kitten closer, as if for comfort.

Becca reached out and touched her arm. "I'm so sorry."

Juliet smiled. "I have Melanie. And she is everything to me, just like Hope is to you. I'm so happy for my daughter, for Dusty and the life they're going to build here at the ranch. But…"

"But what?" Becca asked, and she tensed again. This time she was worried about Cash. Did Juliet know about him? That he was her daughter's brother?

"I don't want to rely too heavily on my daughter for my life," Juliet said. "I want a life of my own now. A job. A house. I know you're a Realtor. Would you mind helping me find something in Willow Creek? I want to be close to my daughter, but I don't want to be one of those interfering mothers-in-law or grandmas."

Becca smiled. "Like Sadie?"

"I wish I was like Sadie," Juliet said with obvious envy. "I wish I was as strong as that woman is."

"Don't we all…" Becca murmured. Because then she wouldn't have worried about what anyone thought of her. She would have told the truth about Hope's conception, and she wouldn't have cared if anyone had a problem with her choice.

But now that she'd lied, she didn't know how to tell the truth…without making everything so much worse than if she just kept silent.

AFTER A DAY of family and food, Sadie was happy to retreat to her suite and join her new husband. Lem and Feisty had already settled into their chair in the sitting area, and while the TV played some news program, the man and the dog both had their eyes closed.

Reluctant to disturb them, she softly shut the door to

the hall and nearly tiptoed to her chair. As she settled into it, Lem asked, "How was your day?"

She laughed. He was always more aware of what was going on than she'd ever credited him for. "You were with me the entire day. What do you think?"

"Pretty spectacular."

"Yes…"

"You don't sound convinced," he said. "Cash was here. Jessup showed up with Darlene and Sarah and her little boy." His brow furrowed a bit beneath the lock of white hair that had fallen across it.

She reached out and pushed it back. His hair was so soft, like his enormous heart.

"That child is a little too quiet," he murmured with concern.

"We can be overwhelming," she admitted.

"You can be," he agreed. "All kids love me."

She snorted, but she couldn't argue with him. Kids loved him. So did she…

"So if you're not worried about the boy, what are you worried about?" he asked.

"Jessup."

"He looked great, and he and Cash seemed to be getting along well," Lem said. "I think they're on the mend."

"What about Jessup's heart?"

"He looked great," Lem said, his voice louder as if he figured she hadn't heard him. And Feisty growled softly, warning him to hush.

Sadie smiled and petted her little dog. "I know health-wise he's doing well. But he's so alone."

"He has a houseful of people, too," Lem said. "He's not alone."

"His wife has been gone a long time," she reminded Lem. "He's been alone a long time."

"He's had Darlene."

"As an angel of mercy," she said, and she felt a pang of regret that Darlene had thought for so many years that Sadie and her own sons hated her, that they had blamed her for the accident that had taken Michael away from them. That poor, sweet, misguided angel…

Lem patted her hand, as if he'd felt what she felt.

"He and Darlene are like brother and sister," Sadie said. "They have a deep bond. But it's not romantic at all."

"That's what everyone says about Becca and Cash," he reminded her. "In case that's who you've intended to match up next. Their friendship might be a line they can't cross."

Sadie remembered the way they'd kept looking at each other and then looking away. "I think that line might have already been crossed."

But what would they do now that they were on the other side of it? Run back the other way? Run away from each other? Or run to each other? Because the one thing that Sadie knew for sure about Cash was that he was capable of running…

Just like his father.

So she had to be careful not to push either of them too far or too fast, or she would push them away. And as happy as she was, she wasn't sure that was a loss she could bear again.

CHAPTER FOURTEEN

CASH CHUCKLED AS he leaned against the doorjamb, watching Becca check on the kittens and mama cat "just one more time" before she went to bed. Just like her daughter, who had finally gone to sleep a short while ago.

Hope had been so excited over the kittens that she'd fought to stay awake, but eventually the long day had taken its toll and she'd passed out where Becca sat now, on the floor next to the mama cat and her babies. Not only had there been the party at Ranch Haven and the trip to the Cassidy Ranch, but he'd had to bring them back to his office so that he could give the kittens their first shots and a deworming. He'd also given the mama cat some vaccinations. And Hope had acted as his assistant the entire time, holding the animals, helping him fetch things. So it was a wonder that she'd managed to stay awake as long as she had. Once she'd fallen asleep, he'd picked her up and carried her to bed for Becca even though she'd insisted that she could handle her.

And she usually did.

He'd heard what she'd said in the loft to the mother cat. *You don't have to take care of all these babies on your own any longer.*

And his heart ached that she had to.

He'd also heard what Juliet had said. While JJ and Hope had gone off to find an empty crate or a box, he had unabashedly eavesdropped on that conversation. His heart ached for Juliet, too.

And for Melanie...

They would both probably hate and resent him as a constant reminder of how selfish and uncaring of their feelings Shep had been.

While JJ...

Cash had definitely had the better man as a father figure. And he'd deserted him when JJ had needed him most. Yet JJ had no anger or resentment for him. Or suspicion like Cash's brothers had.

He watched as the kittens all snuggled up together in a squirmy, furry ball. They took comfort and security from each other's presence as much as their mother's. He and his brothers had once been like that, so very close even when they squabbled.

They'd still always been able to count on each other. Becca had been an only child, just like her daughter. That idiot of a husband of hers had denied her the family she'd always wanted. That she deserved.

But she had Hope. And she would obviously deny her daughter nothing. Like the kittens...

Cash could have kept them at the office; Dr. Miner often brought in stray animals to foster on the premises. That was why their office was in a barn, so that there would always be room for strays, no matter their size.

But if he'd kept the felines there, he would have disappointed Hope, and he'd also suspected Becca was as enamored of the kittens and their mother as her daughter was. She sat now next to the bed stroking the mama cat's chin. The tabby rubbed her face against Becca's hand.

"She has some bad teeth I'll need to treat soon," he said. But he hadn't wanted to put her through any more trauma tonight. The cat was already in an unfamiliar environment, but she seemed very content and happy in Becca's presence.

He could relate. She had always calmed and comforted him, too. Until that kiss...

"I'm sorry," he said again. He felt so badly about challenging her like that, about testing the limits of their friendship with that kiss. And he'd already put her through so much with how often she'd been stuck between him and his family.

She snorted. "Yeah, right. You knew I would wind up bringing them home with me."

"I didn't know there was a them," he reminded her. "I thought there was just the one, and I wasn't even sure we would find him or her."

"She's definitely a her," Becca said. "A little mama." She petted the cat again then started to shift around on the ground, as if she was about to stand.

Cash stepped forward and held out his hand. She hesitated before she took it, and he felt that little jolt that he had when she'd touched him in the loft earlier that day and when she'd hugged him that night after his family meeting. And most especially when they kissed. No. That had been more than jolt.

That had been entirely more than that.

She tugged on her hand, as if trying to pull it away. And he realized he'd just been standing there, holding it. So he used it to help her up from the floor. But when she was standing, he didn't release her hand.

"I wasn't apologizing about the cats," he said. "I was apologizing about the kiss."

"What?" she asked, her forehead furrowing beneath her wispy black bangs.

"The kiss," he repeated, and heat rushed to his face.

"What kiss?" she asked, her dark eyes wide with feigned innocence.

"Becca..." He wasn't in the mood to be teased about that, not with how it had affected him.

"I know," she said. "You explained. You're a mess. It was a mistake. You've already apologized."

"But I feel like an apology isn't enough," he said, because it hadn't made everything go back to the way it had been. At least not for him...

She didn't seem at all affected by him now, not like he was by her. His pulse pounded fast and hard, and he was breathing faster, too.

"Cash, you need to stop getting so hung up on the past," she said. "With your family and with me. Put it behind you and forget it."

She said it like it was so easy. Like she'd already forgotten about that kiss.

And it was all he'd thought about; she was all he'd thought about. How could that kiss not have affected her? Maybe he needed to kiss her again to see if he'd imagined his reaction...or if she was downplaying hers. "Then consider that apology for what I'm about to do now," he said.

She cocked her head in that challenging way she'd always had and arched her eyebrows. Her dark eyes were bright with what he hoped was anticipation. Or excitement. "And what are you about to do now?"

"I'm about to kiss you again..." And he lowered his head and covered her mouth with his.

BECCA DIDN'T WANT this kiss to ever end because she was afraid that if it did, she would wake up and realize it had all just been a dream.

Another dream...

She'd dreamed before of Cash kissing her. But even in her dreams, it had never been like this. Perfect.

He tasted a bit like cinnamon and nutmeg, from the snickerdoodles he'd shared with Hope in the truck on the way home from the Cassidy Ranch. And he felt like home.

She'd once thought that kissing him would be awkward or it would feel wrong after all the years of friendship. But it felt so right. He felt so right.

She was the one who was wrong. Who'd kept a secret from him. Who'd lied to him...

And if he knew that, he wouldn't be kissing her. He probably wouldn't even be her friend. But now she wasn't the only one who would miss him if he ran away from her; Hope would miss him, too.

Tears stung her eyes at that thought, of losing him so completely when he had just finally begun to see her as more than a friend. And while she tried to blink them back, they slipped free and trailed down her face.

And Cash, who'd cupped her chin in his hand, must have felt it because he jerked back as if she'd shoved him. "Becca..." he murmured, his voice gruff with concern.

And that concern, that she didn't deserve, was her undoing. And she couldn't fight the tears any longer; they kept trailing down her face as she was overwhelmed by the enormity of what she'd done.

Of the lie she couldn't unsay...

Of the damage she couldn't undo...

"Becca," he said again. "I'm so sorry. I didn't mean to upset you." He held his hand against his forehead, as if his head was pounding. "I don't know what's wrong with me. I can't seem to stop myself from messing up the relationships that mean the most to me."

"Cash..." She tried to speak, but the tears were clogging her throat.

"My relationship with you—our friendship means more to me than anything else," he said. "You mean more to me…" Now his eyes, so blue, glistened with unshed tears. "I never meant to upset you. That's the last thing I would ever want to do…"

"Cash—"

"I'll get out of here," he said. "Give you some space…" And he turned and rushed out of the room, leaving her alone before she could stop him.

Before she could explain…

That she wasn't crying because of what he had done. She was crying because of what she had done.

DARLENE HAVEN DIDN'T know who she was anymore. At a young age she had become Michael's wife, and then a mother to Jake, Ben, Dusty, Dale and Baker. And those were roles she'd lost too soon.

She still blamed herself for that, even though no one else did. At least not for Michael's death. But she wasn't sure they really understood how she'd felt thinking that they all hated her. How that had been more unbearable even than losing her husband.

Jessup had understood immediately all those years ago when she'd showed up at his door, desperate to find him and bring him back to his mother.

As if he could replace the son she'd lost…

As if anyone could ever replace Michael…

But, as sick as he'd been, Jessup had refused to reach out to his mother. She'd just lost Michael, and he hadn't wanted her to suffer another loss so soon.

But Jessup was alive.

No. He wasn't just alive. He was thriving now.

She glanced across the patio table to where he sat in his chair watching the fireflies flit across the yard. She remembered, all too well, how hard it had been for him to stay awake for just a few hours a day when his heart had been failing. Everything had taken so much effort for him that he'd slept most of the day and all of the night.

So he had needed Darlene then. And she had taken on the role of caregiver to him and to his boys, who'd needed her far more than she'd thought her own children had. Her kids had had Sadie and their grandfather. Jessup and his sons had had no one after Colleen died. But his sons had grown, and now Jessup was well. He didn't need her anymore.

And she felt restless...

"Are you okay?" he asked, as if he'd sensed her stress.

She sighed. "I don't know," she admitted.

"Didn't everything go well today with your sons and grandsons?" he asked.

Love warmed her heart, and she smiled. "Yes. They were all amazing." Forgiving and warm. "Sadie did such a good job with them."

Like she'd known the older woman would. Sadie was so strong and supportive, so determined and fierce to care for those she cared about.

"You did, too, Darlene," he said. "They have so much of you in them."

Her smile slid away, and she shook her head. "I see more of Michael. And Sadie." Her smile twitched again. "Especially in Ben."

Jessup chuckled. "Yes, he certainly turned the tables on her by setting her up with her arch nemesis."

She laughed now at the thought of sweet Old Man Lemmon being anyone's arch nemesis. But he had been Sadie's. Darlene remembered from her days on the ranch the times that Sadie had gone off to town to yell at some decision the "idiot" mayor had made. Lem had been that "idiot" mayor.

Now he was her husband. And she was so happy. So happy that Darlene selfishly yearned for that happiness herself. For so many years she'd thought she hadn't deserved it.

That all she deserved was suffering.

"Ben did good," she said. "Sadie and Lem are soulmates." Then she realized what she'd said and hastened to add, "Not that she and your dad weren't very happy, too. Maybe a person can have more than one soulmate."

That thought had never occurred to her before. She'd just figured that after losing Michael, she was destined to be alone the rest of her life. That was actually what she'd thought she deserved. To be alone...

But now was the first time she felt how alone she was... because until now she'd been so busy.

Jessup suddenly sucked in a breath, and Darlene shot forward in her chair. "What? Are you all right?"

"I'm fine," he said. "I just didn't think... I just thought... Well, I never really have let myself think about the future before." He pressed a hand to his chest. "But now I realize I can."

She smiled again and leaned back in her chair. "Yes, you can." And so could she...

Jessup glanced around and then leaned across the table and whispered, "So how was Mikey after you left the ranch? Was he excited about signing up for school?"

She shook her head. "No. He's been so quiet since the fire." She leaned forward, too, and whispered, "I think he should talk to the counselor my grandsons have been seeing, but I don't know how to bring it up to Sarah."

Jessup sighed. "That's not the only thing I probably need to bring up to her..."

"You don't need her anymore," she said. "I think Sarah is well aware of that. And so am I..."

"What do you mean? I don't want Sarah and Mikey to leave. I'm very fond of them."

The little boy had been a welcome addition to their home, a great distraction from the fear they'd felt over Jessup's heart condition. But maybe they'd done more harm than good to the child.

Just like Darlene had done with her own kids.

"I know," she said. "But you don't need her anymore. And you don't need me anymore."

He sucked in a breath and leaned across the table. "But, Darlene, I don't want you to go, either."

"I know," she said. "You and I are like war buddies." Ones who'd connected after the biggest battle losses: their spouses. "We've been through a lot together." A lot of fear and uncertainty for the future.

"But we can both retire now," Jessup said. "We can relax."

She snorted. "You've met Sadie, right? We can't relax."

"What do you mean?"

"I'm afraid that once she gets done messing in her grandsons' love lives, she might turn all her matchmaking energy on us."

Jessup gasped. "On you and me?"

He sounded so horrified that Darlene laughed, completely unoffended. "No. I think she knows that we're just friends."

Jessup reached across the table and touched her hand. "We're more than friends, Darlene," he said. "We're family."

Warmth flooded her heart. "Yes, we are." Then she sighed. "And speaking of family, how did it go with Cash today at the Cassidy Ranch?"

Jessup tensed for a moment then nodded. "Well, I think. He's not angry with me anymore."

"I don't think he was angry with you," she said. "I think he was angry with himself. For reacting the way he did all those years ago…" And not knowing how to fix what he felt he'd broken. She knew that feeling all too well.

And even though she hadn't done as much damage as she'd feared, the relationships with her children would never be what they could have been.

"He found his biological father, too, you know," Jessup said. "And he has a sister…"

"Really? Has he met her? Does she live nearby?" Darlene asked.

"Yep. She's your daughter-in-law."

She gasped now. "Who? Which one?"

"Melanie."

"Oh…" She smacked her forehead and then shuddered. "Shep." He'd hit on her back in the day when she'd been a barrel racer. He'd hit on her before she'd married Michael. And then when she'd rejoined the rodeo after Michael's death, in order to find Jessup, he'd hit on her again. And while she'd been single both times, he hadn't been. "Poor Juliet…"

"She's a sweet woman," Jessup remarked.

Darlene smiled. "Don't let your mother hear you say that."

He chuckled. "I am well aware of how to handle my mother."

"By running away?"

"Hey!" he protested. Then he laughed. "I'm too old to run now."

She sighed. "Me, too."

"Cash isn't," Jessup remarked.

"I thought things went well," she said. "What are you worried about?"

"Sadie's not done with my sons yet," he reminded her.

"And while Marsh will deal with her the same way he deals with everything, Cash's way is the same as mine."

"You think he'll run," she said. "That would be a big mistake on his part." He had so many reasons to stay. He had his veterinarian practice with that interesting partner of his. But she suspected Becca and her daughter were his most compelling reasons...

CHAPTER FIFTEEN

THE LAST TIME Cash had seen Becca cry was when his mom died. But even then she'd quickly dashed the tears away and forced a smile for him. Which broke his heart. She'd loved his mom, too. Loved hearing her talk about her barrel racing days with the rodeo and about how she'd fallen in love with a young, fearless bullfighter during those days. His dad. JJ.

Last night Cash had seen Becca cry again. And knowing that it was because of him had kept him awake the rest of the night. So he was in the office early, checking over the animals he and Doc Miner were keeping in the barn so they could monitor their recovery from illness and injuries.

They all seemed to be recovering well. Better than he was from the night before.

What had he been thinking?

He hadn't been. He'd just wanted to challenge her claim that the first kiss hadn't affected her when it had affected him so much. That was his only excuse for kissing her again. But he'd made her cry...

He'd felt like crying, too, when he'd seen the tears rolling down her beautiful face. And he knew he'd made a huge mistake. But what was the bigger mistake, kissing her last night? Or relying on her so much all these years, leaning so heavily on her that he was surprised he hadn't crushed her?

He tried to reciprocate in their friendship, in helping

out with Hope and with her ranch. But it wasn't nearly enough. He knew that, but he wasn't sure how to make up that disparity to her.

Obviously it wasn't in kisses.

Because now he had to make it up to her for kissing her and upsetting her. And he didn't think an apology would do it this time. He wasn't sure what would...

He wasn't even sure why she'd gotten so emotional. Was she still in love with her ex-husband? She never talked about him. Cash didn't even know the guy's name. He'd never asked many questions, hadn't wanted to upset her. Now he wondered if he'd avoided finding out more about her husband because he'd been jealous.

Had he always had feelings for Becca that were more than friendship?

Maybe that was why none of his other relationships had ever lasted...because his girlfriends had actually had every reason to be jealous of Becca. Because his love for her wasn't as platonic as he'd always thought it was.

"Hello?" a soft voice called out.

Too soft to be Becca's. She had the tendency to bellow, which was why she'd always been so effective in quelling arguments between him and his brothers. He could have used her help now with Collin, Colton and Marsh.

But they weren't arguing with him. They weren't even talking to him.

And after last night, Becca probably wasn't talking to him anymore, either.

"I'm in here," he called back, but he stepped out of the stall of a miniature horse they were monitoring. She was pregnant, but due to the size of her fetus, she was going to need help to deliver. That made him think of the stray from the Cassidy Ranch who'd had no problem delivering all of her babies on her own. She wasn't alone now, though; she had Becca, who would take good care of her, just as she took good care of Hope.

She was a wonderful mother. And the best friend he could have ever asked for...

He closed his eyes as the fear that he'd screwed up that friendship overwhelmed him.

"Are you okay?" that same soft voice asked.

He opened his eyes to Juliet Shepherd's concerned face. As if he hadn't been feeling guilty enough...

"I'm fine," he said. "Is—is everything all right?" He couldn't imagine why she had come to see him. Unless... "Did Dusty ask you to come see me?"

Maybe the former bronc riding champ was too busy to reach out himself. Maybe...

"Is everything all right with Melanie?"

She reached out and touched his arm. "Everything's fine," she assured him, and then she smiled.

And he could tell that she knew...

"Did Shep tell you?" He leaned heavily against the stall door.

She shook her head. "I heard that he had a son." Her throat moved as she swallowed. "That you sought him out years ago and then turned up around the rodeo, working as a vet."

"So you knew...?"

"Not right away, but when I saw how you look at my daughter..." She nodded and sighed.

He groaned. "You must hate me..."

"I don't hate you," she said, and she squeezed his arm gently before releasing him. "I don't even hate Shep. I just know who he is. You must know that now, too, after you talked to him."

Cash nodded. "Yes." And his stomach churned at the man he'd found.

"I'm sorry."

"You're sorry?" he asked. "Why? He was married to you when…when I was conceived. But I swear my mother didn't know."

"I know," Juliet said. "Shep behaved like he was single." She smiled. "Now he is."

"Good for you," he said. "You deserve better."

She nodded. "Yes, I do. And so did Melanie for a father. I wish…" She trailed off and shook her head. "No. There's no changing the past."

Cash groaned again. "I wish there was." For so many reasons.

She smiled. "Me, too. But it's pointless. All we can do is focus on the present and the future. Make better choices from now on. Obviously you have a choice to make now."

He tensed and jerked away from the stall. What was she talking about? How could she know about last night? Then he nearly laughed at his paranoia. "You're talking about Melanie."

"Of course. She's always been my priority," she said.

"I don't intend to make any trouble for her, or to upset her," he assured the woman. "Especially now…"

"Because she's pregnant?"

He nodded. "I don't want to cause any problems. I know she's had a difficult pregnancy."

"That might have been more about her situation with Dusty than with the twins," Juliet said.

He furrowed his brow. "They seem very happy."

"They are," she agreed. "They just fell in love before they really knew each other. Kind of like how I did with her father. But she got lucky. She found out how good a man Dusty is while I found out her father, your father, is a very insecure man who needs constant validation to feel better about himself. While I think he loves Melanie and maybe even me, too, in his own way, he'll always put himself before anyone else."

"I'm sorry," he said again.

She shook her head. "Cash, none of this is your fault. You have no reason to apologize."

"But I feel so guilty," he said. "And I don't want to cause anyone any discomfort." Yet he didn't seem to be able to stop himself from upsetting people no matter how much he wished he wouldn't.

She narrowed her green eyes a bit. "I'm not so sure you're talking about me or Melanie right now. And you looked very distressed when I walked in. Are you all right?"

He nodded. "Yes, I just have a lot on my mind." Becca and those kisses.

"I know there have been some issues between you and your family," she said, and her face flushed with color as she added, "And I know that it's none of my business, but I just have to say that what you have, with Jessup as your father, is so much better than what Melanie had."

He flinched over how he'd treated his father. His real father: JJ Cassidy also known as Jessup Haven. While he'd kept secrets, he'd always been there for Cash and his brothers. But the secrets…

"I just felt so betrayed when I found out the truth," Cash said. "And I don't know…" He didn't know how to get back to what they'd once had, who they'd once been, with JJ or with his brothers.

And now he'd made the same mess with Becca.

"Forgiveness is hard," she agreed. "I know that all too well. Sometimes it's easier to run away. And sometimes it's harder to leave when you should." She sighed. "Listen to me getting all philosophical. And that's not why I came here."

"Why did you come?" he asked.

"I just wanted you to know that it's okay," she said. "That you have nothing to apologize for to me or to her."

They were the only two then.

"And you should tell her that you're her brother," Juliet said. "Melanie always wanted a sibling, but I had such a difficult time carrying a pregnancy to term. I've always said she was my miracle baby."

This poor woman had endured so much that Cash wanted to hug her, wanted to console her; instead she'd offered him comfort.

"Are you sure it won't be too stressful or shocking for her?"

Juliet shook her head. "As Sadie has convinced her, she's stronger than she thought she was. Much stronger." She lifted her chin then and smiled again, brightly, sincerely. "And so am I."

Cash let out a wistful sigh.

And she smiled again and encouraged him, "You are, too, Cash Cassidy. You're stronger than you think you are."

He wasn't sure about that. He'd always gotten his strength from Becca. He had to fix their friendship. But how could he do that without her support?

BECCA HAD CHOSEN to close the real estate office for the day. Mostly because she hadn't slept at all the night before. But even now, as she washed the dishes from lunch while her mom and Hope played with the kittens, she kept checking her cell phone that sat on the butcher-block countertop next to the farmhouse sink.

She wasn't looking for texts or voice mails from Cash but from clients. She didn't expect Cash to contact her after last night, after how she'd sobbed all over him. He probably thought she'd lost her mind.

And she must have…

To imagine they could ever have anything more than friendship. They couldn't have more with her lie between them, but their friendship wouldn't endure if she told him the truth. She was stuck.

Those kisses had been so bittersweet because they'd showed her how it could have been between them. If she'd been honest with him about everything…

But it had all changed anyway. Maybe she should risk coming clean now. Somehow, realizing he was keeping a secret of his own made her feel for the first time that he might understand. But it was much too easy for him to cut the people out of his life who loved him, like he'd cut out his brothers and his dad. She'd take a friendship that had grown awkward with him over nothing at all.

The doorbell chimed, startling Becca. Was it Cash? Usually he just walked right in with a perfunctory knock as he opened the door. But after last night…

He might have decided it was wiser to ring the bell. She dried her hands on a buffalo-checked dishcloth and headed toward the door. A shadow darkened the glass. Whoever was at the door was tall. Like Cash…

Or it could have been one of his brothers, too. Or JJ…

But when she opened the door, she found Sadie March Haven Lemmon standing on her front porch. Sadie had bound her long white hair in a braid, and she looked more like a girl than the octogenarian she was. That had more to do with the brightness of her eyes and her smile than the braid, though.

Becca smiled back at her and mused, "You look so happy."

"I am," Sadie said. "How about you?"

Becca gasped at the question then stammered, "Well, yeah, of course…" But she wasn't. Cash thought he was the one who'd made a mess of things, but this mess was all hers.

Sadie cocked her head and studied her face. Then she shook her head. "I don't think so…"

"Who's here?" Hope asked, her footsteps coming up fast behind Becca. Then she stepped around her, clapped her hands together and exclaimed, "Grandma Sadie!"

"Grandma Sadie…" Becca muttered, though she was relieved that her daughter had saved her from having to reply. "That happened fast."

Sadie smiled. "All the other kids call me that," she said. "She should have that right, as well."

The other kids were her actual great-grandkids. Becca kept that thought to herself, though. "That's up to you what you'd like her to call you," she said. She just hoped that Hope didn't get her heart set on becoming part of the Haven family like the little girl had her heart set on Cash becoming her father. She didn't want her daughter's heart breaking like hers was bound to break.

"Grandma Sadie," Hope said as she took Sadie's hand. "Come see the kittens."

"I'm sure that isn't why Grandma Sadie came all the way here from Ranch Haven," Becca said. The older woman must have stopped at her office in town, like she had before, and seen the note on the door that Becca was working from home today.

"Actually it is," Sadie said. "I was so happy to hear that the mama cat and her kittens had been rescued. And—" she held up a plastic container "—I brought more snicker-doodles. There weren't many left yesterday to send home with you."

"And Cash ate those," Hope said.

Sadie glanced around the foyer and asked with what sounded like idle curiosity, "Is Cash here?"

Becca shook her head. "No."

"But he'll come over later probably," Hope said. "He comes over all the time. He should just move in." She glanced at Becca, who could feel heat rushing toward her face.

"Cash has his own place." It wasn't much, though—a studio apartment attached to the barn out of which he and Dr. Miner ran their veterinarian practice. As many times as she'd offered to help him look for something else, he insisted that it was all he needed. That was another reason she hadn't trusted him to stay because he'd seemed reluctant to put down permanent roots.

"And I don't think he'll be over later," she cautioned her daughter.

"Why not?" Hope asked.

"I'm sure he's busy," Becca said. "And I'm sure Miss Sadie is, too, so you should show her those kittens."

Sadie chuckled slightly. "My day is wide open. I have plenty of time to play with kittens."

"Then please, pick out one to take home with you."

Hope gasped. "Cash said they're too little to be away from their mommy yet."

"She can take it when it's ready then," Becca said.

Hope lowered her eyebrows and glared at her. "You're trying to get rid of the kittens!"

"I told you we can't keep them all," she reminded her daughter. "We're just fostering them." And she was too tired and stressed to deal with her argument right now.

"Hope, why don't you take me to the kittens now," Sadie suggested, as if she'd sensed that Becca was at the end of her rope.

"Hello, Mrs. Haven… Mrs. Lemmon, I mean," Phyllis Calder, Becca's mom, sputtered as she stepped out of the room where the kittens wrestled around their weary mother.

"Sadie," Sadie told her. "Call me Sadie, Phyllis."

Becca's mom glanced at her, as if checking to see if it was okay. Becca shrugged. "You know, Mom, since you're here with Hope, I think I'll go into the office for a bit and make some calls. And I need to check to see if Ben's signed and returned those agreements so I can get those properties listed."

Sadie smiled. "I am so glad you were able to help Ben out with those. That will be a relief to us both to have those sold. We are so busy now."

And thanks to Sadie, Becca was busy now during what had been a slow time. "I very much appreciate the business," Becca said even though she had no doubt Sadie had an ulterior motive for using her as the Realtor. Just as she had an ulterior motive for showing up at Becca's ranch today.

Since she had a pretty good idea what that motive was—matchmaking—Becca could not get away fast enough. And she finally understood now why Cash had chosen to run from conflict instead of dealing with it.

But just as Cash had discovered, running only put off the inevitable. Because eventually conflict was going to have to be dealt with...

SADIE SMILED AS Hope almost reluctantly handed her a kitten to inspect. It looked like it was wearing a tuxedo with its black-and-white fur.

"Careful of their nails," Hope cautioned her. "They're super sharp."

The kitten's claws scratched Sadie's skin, but she felt no pain. "My hands are like leather," Sadie remarked. "Feels and looks like I'm wearing gloves."

Hope giggled, and Phyllis Calder smiled at her. "Those are hardworking hands," Phyllis said.

"Not anymore," Sadie said. "But it's fine with me to take it easy." Now that she had someone to take it easy with...

Although Lem had had to go into City Hall today for meetings with Ben. He was still deputy mayor. But Ben was going to have to find someone else to run with him for the next term, so that Lem could truly take it easy with her. Neither of them was totally capable of sitting back and letting others do everything around them, of course. They would pitch in with committees and with their families.

"Are you going to adopt a kitten?" Hope asked almost anxiously.

Sadie shook her head. "I don't think Feisty would like the competition for my affection." Or more likely for Lem's; he was her favorite person now. And Miller was second. The little dog must have forgotten how Sadie had saved her years ago from certain death in a hot car.

"So you just came here to see them?" Hope asked.

Sadie nodded. "And to bring the cookies. Us snicker-doodle lovers have to stick together."

Phyllis chuckled. "These cookies are all I've heard about besides the kittens."

Sadie settled the kitten down next to its mama and then popped the top off the container of cookies.

"That's not all I've been telling you, Grandma," Hope said to Phyllis. "I told you about the kisses."

"What kisses?" Sadie asked. She faked a stern look for Hope. "Who have you been kissing?"

"Ew, not me," Hope said with the same disgust Caleb showed about kissing. But then she added, "Mommy and Cash have been kissing." And she didn't sound disgusted at all; she sounded hopeful. Clearly Sadie wasn't the only one who wanted Cash and Becca to be more than friends.

Sadie arched an eyebrow. "Really?"

Maybe she wasn't going to have to work much harder to get Cash and Becca together.

Hope nodded. "But both times they acted all weird and Cash left right away. Do you think he'll come back?"

"If he doesn't on his own, we'll have to figure out a way to get him back here," Sadie said. "And I think if we put our heads together, we'll come up with an idea."

Phyllis sighed. "Becca isn't going to like this…"

"So you don't think it's a good idea?"

"Oh, no," Phyllis said. "I think those two belong together. I just know how stubborn my daughter can be. And how stubborn Cash is."

He was definitely Jessup's son and Sadie's grandson. And because he was, Sadie knew they had to be careful or their meddling might keep the couple apart more than bring them together.

CHAPTER SIXTEEN

CASH WAS COMPELLED to drive out to Ranch Haven right after Juliet left. He trusted her opinion that telling Melanie wouldn't put her or the babies at risk. Cash had already carried this secret longer than he'd wanted to, so he wanted the truth to come out as soon as possible.

And if he stuck around the office, Doc Miner was going to keep teasing him about his female visitors.

"No wonder I can't find anyone my age to date," he'd said. "They keep coming here to see you."

"It's not like that," Cash had assured him. Juliet and Darlene felt like family through the relationships they had with people who were Cash's family.

The door to the farmhouse opened, and Caleb stared up at him. "Did Midnight tell you something else?" the little boy eagerly asked him. "Did he change his mind about having a family?"

Dusty, coming up behind the boy, chuckled. "I hope not. I intend to make a lot of money off Midnight's babies."

Caleb gasped. "You're going to sell them?"

"After I train them for the rodeo," Dusty said.

Caleb's blue eyes sparkled with excitement. "Can I help you? Can I help you?"

"Your school starts soon," Dusty reminded him. "You're going to be busy all day."

"Are you going to help him?" Caleb asked Cash. "Are you going to whisper to Midnight's babies, too?"

The kid was so utterly charming that Cash smiled. "I don't think your uncle Dusty is going to need my help." And he might not want it if Cash upset his wife.

"Caleb!" Taye called from the kitchen. "You're on KP duty. You need to come back and help Ian with the dishes."

Caleb sighed but turned around and headed down the hall.

Taye popped her head out into the hall and said, "There are a lot of leftovers from lunch if you haven't eaten yet."

His stomach roiled at the thought of putting food into it, and Cash shook his head. "No thanks."

"And if Sadie was here, she'd tell you to stop ringing the doorbell and just come on in," Taye added.

Dusty chuckled. "She really is a lot like Grandma. Baker and the boys are lucky Grandma brought her here." He patted his stomach. "We all are. Sure you're not hungry?"

Cash shook his head again.

"What brings you by?" Dusty asked. "Midnight update or do you need to see Baker or Grandma? She and Lem left pretty early this morning. I don't think they have any idea how to actually retire."

"I know Lem is deputy mayor, but I thought Sadie had retired."

Dusty chuckled. "Oh, that will never happen. She doesn't work the ranch anymore, but she's always working on something. Usually our personal lives. You and Marsh better be careful or you'll be getting married soon, too."

Cash shook his head so hard this time, his hat slipped down over his eyes, and he had to push it back up. His hand shook a bit then when he did. "That's not going to happen." Not after his kiss had made Becca cry...

Not that he intended to marry her. But he couldn't imagine marrying anyone but her.

"So if you're not here for ranch business or Sadie's matchmaking hustle, what do you need, Cash?" Dusty asked.

"I'd actually like to talk to your wife," Cash said.

Dusty cocked his head to the side. "Melanie?"

He nodded. "Yeah, is she feeling all right today?" he asked.

"You're a veterinarian, not an obstetrician," Dusty said. "So I don't think you can help her. But yeah, she's doing great. She actually has tons of energy. I think she's weeding the flower bed on the patio, which reminds me that I should bring her something to drink. It's hot out there. And I don't have Juliet as backup today to get her to take it easy. She headed to town before Sadie and Lem left."

"I know," Cash said. "She came to see me."

"My mother-in-law came to see you?" he asked, and now he sounded completely dumbfounded. "What's going on, Cash?"

"I'll explain it to Melanie," he said. "But I'd like you to be there, too." Just in case she wasn't going to take the news as well as her mother thought she would.

Expression tense, Dusty led the way through the kitchen. Taye must have overheard their conversation because she said, "I already brought a pitcher of lemonade and some glasses out to her."

"Thanks," Dusty said, and he headed out the open French doors to the patio where Melanie was alone, plucking weeds from a raised flower bed.

Cash closed the doors behind him in case Melanie didn't want the news he was about to give her shared.

"Hi, Cash," she said when she looked up. Her face was shiny with perspiration, but she was also glowing with happiness and vitality.

"You need to take a break and have some lemonade

before all the ice melts," Dusty said, and he led her over to the patio table where the pitcher sweated condensation down the sides onto the tabletop. "And Cash has something he wants to tell you."

She glanced at Cash again. "You do?"

He nodded and advised her, "You should sit down."

"What is this about?" she asked. With Dusty's help, she settled onto a chair.

"Shep," Cash said.

"What has my dad done now?" she asked.

"Is that why Juliet went to see you?" Dusty asked.

Melanie gasped. "He's not giving my mom a hard time over the divorce, is he?" Her forehead creased. "I know you know him from the rodeo, but are you still close to him?"

He shook his head. "No. I was never close to Shep." He wasn't even sure if familial closeness was what he'd been looking for when he'd tried to figure out who his father was, or if he'd just wanted no more secrets in his life. And because he still wanted that, he had to tell Melanie the truth. "But he's my biological father, too."

Melanie's mouth dropped open in shock. And then tears began to roll down her face.

And Cash felt like he had the night before when he'd made Becca cry, like he was getting punched in the gut. Then he braced himself, expecting Dusty to punch him for upsetting his very pregnant wife.

Juliet had been wrong; her daughter wasn't happy at all to find out she had a brother. Or maybe she just wasn't happy that he was that brother.

BECCA WAS HAPPY she'd gone into the office, after all. Juliet had showed up just as she'd been unlocking the door. While she hadn't taken her to see any houses, she had talked to her about what kind of properties she was interested in seeing.

"Someplace with enough room for grandchildren to stay and a yard for them to play in," she'd said, smiling as she thought of the twins that would be born soon.

And Becca had felt that yearning inside her again to have more children. That yearning had been so intense before she'd had Hope that she hadn't been thinking rationally when she'd come up with her elaborate cover story. She was definitely the one who'd made the mess of her relationship with Cash, not him. But she had no idea how to clean up that mess.

She'd considered asking Juliet, but the woman had had an interview in town for a job at the local diner and had had to leave. Becca had hung around the office for a while longer to make sure that Sadie would be gone before she returned home. She was, but that didn't stop Hope and Becca's mom from talking about her.

And from the glances they kept exchanging, Becca knew something was up. Then Hope asked permission to spend the night at Grandma and Grandpa's, since school was starting soon and Becca didn't allow sleepovers on school nights.

"The mama cat and her kittens need to stay here," Becca said. "Moving them again so soon would be too much of a disruption."

"That's okay, Mommy," Hope said. "You'll take good care of them." She hugged Becca before heading off with her grandmother with a bag she'd already packed for the night.

They were definitely up to something.

But what?

She opened the door to the room where she had sequestered the mama and babies, just to make sure they were all right. That Hope hadn't smuggled them out in that little suitcase she'd packed for her sleepover.

The mama cat lifted her head and peered at Becca. The babies were nursing, kneading each other as they all struggled to feed at the same time. "You poor mama," Becca said. "You have more than you can handle."

Sometimes Becca felt like she didn't have enough, like when Juliet had mentioned the twins earlier, and Becca had felt that pull inside her, that yearning.

But she didn't just yearn for more children. She yearned for Cash. For him to be the father instead of some anonymous donor.

But that wasn't going to happen.

She settled onto the floor next to the bed where the mama and kitties were nestled, and she petted the mama's soft head, offering comfort and support while she sought it, as well.

She closed her eyes as she leaned back against the wall. And the door creaked open again. She smiled and said, "I knew you wouldn't be able to stay away."

"You asked me to come," a deep voice said.

And she opened her eyes to find Cash standing in the doorway. "I didn't..."

"Well, Hope did," he said. "She said something was wrong with the kittens..." He was looking at them nursing hungrily from their mother.

"I didn't ask her to call you," she said. But now she knew what her daughter and her mother had been exchanging looks over, and it hadn't been the sleepover. "Sadie was here earlier today..."

He groaned. "Oh..."

"I'm sorry," she said. "I knew they were up to something. I should have gotten them to spill, so I could have saved you the trip out here." After last night this was probably the last place he wanted to be and she was the last person he wanted to see.

"I was already on my way here," he said, "to apologize again."

She tensed. "You have no reason to apologize," she assured him.

"Yes, I do," he said vehemently, so much so that the mama cat let out a faint warning hiss.

Becca petted her head. "It's fine."

"Are you talking to her or me?" he asked with a slight grin.

"It is fine," she said. "You don't owe me an apology."

He took off his hat and shoved his hand through his hair, which was mussed, as if he'd done that already. And he had dark circles beneath his blue eyes, as if he hadn't gotten any more sleep than she had.

As always concern for him filled her, and she patted the floor next to her. "Sit down. You look exhausted."

"You do, too," he said.

"Why, thanks," she murmured. "Just what a woman wants to hear, how tired she looks..." Especially from the man whose opinion mattered most. She wanted him to think she was beautiful.

He dropped onto the floor next to her, his shoulder bumping against hers. And they both tensed at the contact. "You said I looked exhausted first," he said.

"And we both know you're not vain," she said.

"You're not, either," he said.

"Then maybe you don't know me as well as I thought." Because she wouldn't have made up the cover story for her pregnancy if she hadn't cared what people thought.

Especially what he thought...

"I have a feeling you're right about that," he said. "I don't know why you cried last night."

"It wasn't because you did anything wrong," she assured him. She was the one who'd done something wrong, who'd lied and kept a big secret.

"That's what Melanie said."

"What?"

"You're not the only woman I made cry in the past twenty-four hours," he said. "I told my sister that she's my sister."

"And that made her cry?" she asked.

"She blamed the tears on her pregnancy hormones and assured me that she's not upset that we're related…"

But clearly he wasn't sure if he should believe her.

"I wasn't going to tell her till after the twins are born, but her mom figured it out and encouraged me to," he said, and the tension drained from his body, making his shoulders slump so that the one next to her touched hers again.

And she nearly shivered in reaction.

"It was good to get rid of the secret," he said with a sigh. "That was the last one now. No more."

She drew in a deep breath, bracing herself to confess. The final secret he didn't know about.

But he continued talking. "I'm not sure my brothers believe that, though. You're probably right about that. After all the years of having no contact with them, that I'm the one who needs to reach out to them again."

"I'm always right." She gave him the reply he was expecting, but she knew it wasn't the truth. She had been very wrong.

He chuckled, though. "I need to tell them that I was wrong to leave like I did all those years ago. And last night… I was wrong to leave like I did, especially when you were crying."

"Those tears weren't your fault," she assured him.

"Then what were they about, Becca?" he asked. "I'm

always dumping all my problems on you, but you haven't shared any of your problems with me."

That wasn't all she hadn't shared with him.

"I do have something I need to tell you," she admitted. And it was time that she finally came clean. "But I need to tell Hope first." This would affect her daughter the most, especially if Cash reacted the way Becca was scared he would.

But she knew how hard it was for him to forgive and how hard it was for him to come back after he left.

"It's about her father," he said.

She nodded. "Yes…"

"You know you can tell me anything," he said. "I'll be here for you like you've always been here for me."

She wanted to believe that, but she knew that when she shared her secret with him, everything would change between them. That he would feel as betrayed as he'd felt when he'd found out the truth about his own paternity.

EVEN THOUGH SHE sat quietly in the chair next to him, in her suite—no, their suite—at the ranch, Lem could almost hear Sadie's gears grinding. And he could feel the excitement radiating from her.

She'd unbound her hair from the braid she'd plaited earlier that day, and it lay in waves around her strong shoulders. She was so beautiful that he couldn't help but stare.

She caught him when she glanced over at him, and her dark eyes met his gaze. "What?"

He would have told her she was beautiful, but she would snort like she did every time he complimented her. That wasn't going to stop him, though. He knew how short life could be, especially for people their age. So he was going to make sure she knew how much he loved and admired her.

"What's up?" she asked again when he remained silent.

He wriggled his eyebrows at her. "I can tell that you've been scheming."

She cocked her head. "Are you mad at me?"

"It's probably what I love most about you."

"I know you wouldn't be mad at me for scheming," she said. "But you might be mad that I've done it without you."

He nodded. "Oh... I've been replaced."

She reached across the space between their chairs and took his hand in hers, entwining their arthritic fingers. "You are irreplaceable, Lemar Lemmon."

"So are you, Sadie March Haven Lemmon."

She let out a sound that sounded like a girlish giggle. "Then we are perfect for each other."

"Yes, we are," he agreed wholeheartedly.

"Just like Becca and Cash."

"Ah, and who's helping you scheme to get them together?"

"Hope."

At first he thought she meant the emotion until he remembered Becca's daughter's name.

Then she murmured, "Hope..."

And he knew that she was definitely referring to the emotion now. She hoped that Cash and Becca would find the same happiness together that he and Sadie had found. That was all they wanted for their family.

Happiness...

CHAPTER SEVENTEEN

CASH WAS GOING to find out what had made Becca cry. He just hoped he would be able to handle it. If she was still in love with her ex-husband...

He would be supportive. He would be the friend to her that she had always been to him. But his heart ached at the thought of hers belonging to another man. And he couldn't figure out why that hurt so much, unless he wanted her heart to belong to him.

"You look pretty miserable," Colton said. "And you're the one who asked to meet us here."

Here was Colton's apartment, which was in a refurbished warehouse, complete with brick walls and open ceilings. It was a nice place. His younger brothers had done well for themselves. Collin had come right from the hospital and wore his white coat. And Marsh had his badge on his shirt, as if he was still on duty.

"Thanks for letting me come here," he told Colton. Then he couldn't help but add, "I promise I won't burn the place down."

Colton snorted, but his mouth curved into a slight grin, too.

"And I promise I didn't burn down our childhood home," he continued. "I don't know how my lighter got into the house, but I didn't put it there." He studied their faces, checking for skepticism or outright suspicion.

"You kind of burned it down when you took off like you did," Colton said. "Nothing was ever the same after that."

"Darlene showed up," he said. "I met her when I came back later that summer, before I started college."

Collin sucked in a breath. "You came back?"

He nodded. "But then I saw her…"

"And assumed Dad had already moved on," Marsh finished for him. He snorted now but with no amusement. "Mom's been gone nearly twenty years, but he still hasn't moved on. He's still in love with her."

Was that the case with Becca? But her husband wasn't dead. He'd just moved away.

Like Cash had…

"I'm sorry," he said. "I'm sorry I took off like that, that I left you all to deal with Dad's health on your own."

"Dad?" Marsh was the one who picked up on that change.

"I know he isn't biologically my father, but he is my dad. The one who taught me to ride a bike and a horse. The one who encouraged me to pursue my dream of becoming a vet."

"And you did it," Collin said.

He nodded. "Just like you became a doctor, just like you said you would. I'm very proud of all of you. But I'm ashamed of myself, of the way I acted, the way I treated Dad."

"He's the one you need to apologize to," Colton pointed out.

Cash nodded. "I know. And I will. But I wanted to apologize to all of you, too. Do you think you can forgive me?"

"I understand why you were upset," Colton said. "When we found out that we're Havens…" He released a shaky breath. "When we learned about the secrets he was keeping and then there was another one…"

Cash shuddered. "I don't know how he did it all these years," he admitted. "I've been keeping one myself, and it's hard."

"What secret?" Marsh asked, and he tensed.

"You know," Cash said. "That my biological father is Shep Shepherd."

"The old rodeo champ?" Colton asked.

He nodded.

"That's Dusty's wife's dad," Colton said.

He nodded again.

And Collin expelled a breath this time. "Wow. So she's your sister? That's the secret you're keeping?"

He just kept nodding.

"So Dad's not the only one who's kept a family secret," Marsh pointed out. "Kind of hypocritical of you…"

"I didn't want to upset Melanie while she's carrying twins," he said defensively. But with as hard as he'd come down on their dad for keeping secrets, he knew his defense was weak, which was probably what his brothers considered his apology.

But at least they didn't refuse it, like Becca had last night. Because she had something to tell him…

His stomach churned over what that could be. He'd always thought he and Becca knew everything about each other. But she clearly had secrets, too. Secrets he wasn't sure he wanted to learn.

BECCA HAD SPENT the morning talking to everyone but Hope. She'd talked to Baker Haven about the child psychologist his orphaned nephews saw.

She'd talked to Genevieve, too, who'd insisted that being "open and honest" was the best policy. Then she'd talked to the school psychologist, who had advised her to keep it simple and relatable.

Simple and relatable...

She drew in a breath and pushed open the door to the feline sanctuary. Hope lay on the floor with the kittens crawling over her while the mama cat watched through half-slitted eyes. She trusted the child with her babies.

Hope would never hurt an animal, not even accidentally. She was such a sweet and loving child. And the thought of hurting her, even accidentally, hurt Becca.

"What's wrong, Mommy?" Hope asked as she met her gaze. "Is it time to give the kitties away?"

Becca shook her head. "Not yet..."

"Are you still mad about me calling Cash last night?" she asked.

"I wasn't mad," Becca assured her. "I was disappointed that you would lie and trick him like that." And yet she had done the very same thing herself.

Even though she'd meant to reassure her child, tears glistened in Hope's eyes. "I'm sorry, Mommy," she said. "I know it's not right to lie. I just wanted to make sure Cash came over so you could kiss him again."

Becca sucked in a breath with the shock. "You saw us kiss?"

The little girl nodded.

And Becca had been so unaware during those kisses that she hadn't even noticed her daughter watching them. "I can understand how seeing that must have confused you," she said. Because she'd been confused, too.

Cash had kissed her without knowing the truth.

He deserved to know and so did Hope.

Open and honest...

"And what I'm going to tell you now is probably going to confuse you, too," she said. And she knelt down in front of Hope.

Hope sighed. "I know. You and Cash are just friends. That's all you ever say. But I don't kiss *my* friends."

A smile tugged at Becca's lips, but she refused to give in to it in case it encouraged the little girl's matchmaking. "What I need to talk to you about has nothing to do with Cash," she said.

Hope sat up and gathered the kittens all close on her lap, as if to protect them from Becca. "You said it wasn't time to give them away yet."

"It's not, honey." Although the longer they kept them, the harder it would be to give any of them away.

"Then…is it about school? It's still starting next week, right?"

Becca nodded. Hope loved school because then she could play with other kids; she wasn't alone like she was as an only child. Becca had always loved school for that reason, too.

"Yes, school is starting next week," she assured her. "I want to talk to you about your father."

Hope's little forehead furrowed with confusion. "What about him?"

"You don't really have a father, Hope."

"I know."

"No, what I mean is that I wasn't married, so I didn't go about having a baby the way married people do."

"How do married people have babies?" Hope asked with innocent curiosity.

Becca swallowed a groan over the can of worms she'd opened. "Well, that's a discussion for another day," she said. "Today I'm telling you how I made you. Usually mommies and daddies make babies together. But I made you on my own. I went to a special doctor who helped me get pregnant with you with the contribution of genetic material from a man I never met. I never met your father, Hope."

Hope shrugged. "I never did, either."

"But you won't be able to," Becca said. "Because he's just an anonymous donor so that people like me, who really want to be a parent, can make a baby."

The furrows in Hope's forehead deepened. "Anon…"

"It means I don't know his name," Becca explained. "I just know his medical history. That he's really healthy. But I have no way of contacting him."

Hope shrugged again. "I know. You already told me that a long time ago."

"But I'm trying to explain…"

"I get it, Mommy," Hope said. "I'm like the kittens. They don't have a daddy, either."

Hope was taking this way better than Becca had worried she would. But maybe she was just too young to fully understand.

"I didn't want anyone to know that you didn't have a daddy, though," Becca continued. "So I told a lie to people about being married when I wasn't."

"Why?"

She sighed. "Foolish pride, I guess. I thought people might think badly about me being a single parent."

"Why?" Hope asked. "Bailey Ann didn't have even one parent before she went to live with Miss Genevieve and Dr. Cass. And Mikey just has a mom."

"Mikey?"

"He was at the party at the ranch, too," Hope reminded her. "He was really quiet."

"Oh." She nodded, remembering that Mikey was the home health aide's son. "You're right, there is nothing wrong with having just one parent. What was wrong was me lying about it. But I didn't know if people would understand how much I loved and wanted you before I ever met you. I loved and wanted you so much that I couldn't wait until I found a daddy for you. I just wanted you all to myself."

Hope smiled. "I'm big now, Mommy, so there's enough of me to share. And now I can choose the dad I want like Bailey Ann did. She chose Dr. Cass, and I choose Cash."

Becca wanted to choose Cash, too, but she doubted he would understand and forgive her for lying as easily as Hope had. And just as she'd feared, Hope's heart was set on Cash being her father. If he took off, her daughter's heart would be broken. And so would her own...

Since she'd moved to Willow Creek, he'd helped her so much with her daughter and with the ranch. He'd been such a good friend to her, but in her heart, he'd always been more than a friend. He was her soulmate, like Sadie had found hers with Lem.

"Bailey Ann only got to choose Dr. Cass because he chose her, too," Becca pointed out. "Cash isn't looking for a family, Hope." She wasn't sure if he had even mended his relationship with the one he already had.

"Can I ask him?" Hope asked.

Becca shook her head. "No. I need to talk to him first." And she wasn't sure if they would ever see him again once she did.

Marsh walked Cash out to his truck, leaving the twins inside the apartment to sort their feelings. Marsh had already sorted his; he loved his older brother no matter what he'd done.

"Do you think they'll forgive me?" Cash asked.

"For what?" Marsh asked.

Cash groaned. "I did not burn down the house," he said. "So stop doing your thing."

"What thing?"

"That thing," Cash accused. "Where you keep asking vague questions and play with your words until you get your suspect to confess."

Marsh snorted. "It still works with the twins. That's how I got Colton to tell me about the lighter."

Cash laughed, then the grin slid from his face. "God, I've missed you guys."

Marsh snorted again. "You should have come home sooner."

"The longer I stayed away, the harder it got to go home," he said. "Darlene said something to me about guilt being paralyzing. And that's how I felt. Stuck. Unable to make a move..."

"Is that your problem with Becca, too?" Marsh asked.

Cash tensed. "What do you mean?"

"That you got stuck in this friendship with her, and you don't know how to make your move," he explained, but as he did, he studied his brother's face.

A face that suddenly blushed, nearly as pink as the setting sun.

And he chuckled. "You did make a move." He clapped his hands together. "About time..."

Cash shook his head. "No. I think it's too late."

"Because she has a kid?" he asked.

Cash sucked in his breath. "No. Hope is great. I already love her like she's mine."

"Like Dad loves you," Marsh pointed out.

Cash closed his eyes, but not before Marsh saw the tears shimmering in them. "I know..."

"I know he kept a lot of secrets from us," Marsh acknowledged. "And I hate that, too, but he had his reasons. Or at least they were reasons in his mind. Worries. Fears.

Whatever made him keep the truth from us… But I can forgive him. Can you?"

"It's not just him…" Cash murmured.

"What?"

"Nothing," Cash said. "It's getting late. I better go…"

And he jerked open his driver's door and hopped in his truck, as if he was as desperate to run off as he'd been all those years ago.

But Marsh couldn't stop thinking about what he'd said and wondered why he thought it was already too late for him and Becca.

CHAPTER EIGHTEEN

IT WAS TOO LATE. And Cash was too emotionally wrung out to reach out to Becca again. Or even to open the text she'd sent him...

He left it unread. For now...

Then he dropped onto his bed in the studio apartment attached to the barn. Doc Miner lived in the house on the property. It was a big house, so he'd invited Cash to move in with him. Cash had refused, claiming that he preferred to live alone, that he preferred to be alone.

But he realized now that he'd never really been alone; he'd always had Becca. Even when they'd been on different campuses, at colleges hundreds of miles apart.

He'd always had her as a friend. And that was all he had considered her, at least consciously. Maybe the women he'd dated had been right, though, that his friendship with Becca had always gone deeper than mere friendship.

The guys Becca dated hadn't been threatened, though. Not that Cash had met many of them. Now that he thought about it, Becca hadn't seemed to date that much. She'd claimed she was too busy to date. That was certainly the case for her now.

That she had her ranch, her business and Hope.

But Cash kept circling back to what she'd said the night before, that she needed to talk to him about Hope's dad. The man she'd married and had a child with. She must have loved him in a way that she had never loved Cash.

And that nausea filled his stomach again, making him realize how jealous he was.

He wanted more than friendship with Becca now.

Could she love Cash like that? She knew him better than anyone else; she knew the mistakes he'd made.

Would she risk her heart on a man like him? And could he ask her to? His life was the mess he'd warned her it was. His brothers, at least the twins, suspected he might have burned down their family home. And while he knew he hadn't done it, his lighter had been found in the ashes.

Could that get him in trouble?

And even if it wasn't enough to arrest him, it was enough to tarnish his name, his reputation in Willow Creek. And by association, it could tarnish Becca.

And Hope…

He'd told Marsh the truth. He loved Hope like she was his, and he wished she was.

HE HADN'T OPENED her text. It had been late enough last night that he might have already been in bed. But today…

Becca had waited the entire day for a response from him. And for one from her parents. At least from her mom.

When she'd told them her secret the night before, after Hope had gone to sleep, her dad had chuckled. It hadn't mattered to him. He hadn't thought any less of her. "I don't care how she got here, I'm just grateful we have Hope," he'd said. Then he'd hugged Becca.

While her mother had nodded in agreement, she hadn't offered a hug. Then she'd quickly rushed off to their house with the excuse that she had to get up early. Even though she had showed up at the office this morning, she had yet to even look at Becca, and it was edging toward afternoon.

So Becca knew she'd hurt her mom. And she understood because she could imagine how she would have felt had Hope ever kept that kind of secret from her. Had told her that kind of lie...

She would have been devastated.

She stood in front of the reception desk now, waiting until her mother finally looked up only to look away immediately. "Mom," she said. "I am so sorry."

Phyllis's lashes fluttered as she furiously blinked. "Your father is right. It doesn't matter how we got Hope, just that that perfect little girl is in our lives."

"It matters because I hurt you," Becca said, "because I wasn't honest with you."

"You've always told me everything," Phyllis said, her voice cracking with emotion. "So I was shocked when you claimed to have married a man you never even mentioned before let alone introduced us to. That was so unlike you in so many ways."

Becca had never been impulsive, and even the decision to have her child the way she had hadn't been made quickly. "I know."

"I couldn't imagine you marrying anyone else when you've always been in love with Cash."

"I wanted a child," Becca said. "So much."

"You wanted Cash."

She still did. "But I couldn't keep waiting for him to notice me as more than a friend. I wanted to have a child before I turned thirty because I'd hoped to have even more. And in case I didn't get pregnant right away, I knew I needed to try for her."

"You didn't have to keep waiting for Cash," Phyllis surprisingly agreed, but then she added, "You could have told him how you felt about him."

"Why? To humiliate myself?" Becca asked. "If he'd felt the same way, he would have told me." Because Cash was always open and honest. And she hadn't wanted to put any pressure on him or make their friendship weird. She'd known Cash since they were little kids; he wasn't just part of her life, he was part of her. And losing him would be like losing part of herself.

Phyllis shook her head. "What? The same way you told him? Maybe he was waiting, too. You're both too proud and too stubborn."

Becca couldn't deny that. She had been proud and stubborn then. "But he never looked at me the way I looked at him, Mom," she said. She would have noticed if he had because, since their kisses, she could see that he looked at her differently now.

Phyllis sighed now. "I know. But that must have changed." Her face flushed.

Becca narrowed her eyes. "What do you know?" And then she remembered. "Hope saw us kissing, and obviously she shared that news with you."

Phyllis smiled. "With me and with Sadie Haven."

Becca groaned.

"So everything has changed," Phyllis said. "While I'm glad you didn't wait because I can't imagine our lives without Hope, maybe you could have moved things along if you'd spoken up all those years ago."

Becca shrugged. "I will never know. It might have just ruined our friendship then because it would have made everything awkward." As awkward as it had been since those kisses, since that line had been crossed.

Phyllis emitted a wistful sigh. "If only you'd had Sadie Haven in your lives then…"

But Cash hadn't known then about his connection to the Havens. She wasn't sure he considered himself related to them even now.

Her mother brightened. "But Sadie is involved. She'll

help you and Cash work things out, so you can finally be together."

Becca knew that there was little hope of her ever winding up with Cash once he learned that she'd lied. Fear over how he would react fluttered inside her. Would he be as angry with her as he'd been with JJ?

"Think about how you feel over me keeping this secret from you," she said to her mom. "Cash isn't just going to be hurt. He's going to be furious."

He would feel so betrayed that whatever chance she might have had with him would be gone. She doubted that he would even consider her a friend anymore, let alone trust her with his heart. But then, considering how he took off when people made mistakes…she hadn't been willing to trust him with hers, either. Maybe that was the biggest reason she'd never admitted how she felt about him.

DARLENE HAD TALKED to Cash about how paralyzed she'd felt for so many years. The guilt had been so heavy that she hadn't been able to reach out to her children. But things were better between them now.

JJ was doing better now, too. He didn't need her like he once had, and neither did his boys, who were grown men. Nobody needed Darlene but Darlene. She needed to find herself, and she needed to find a place of her own.

She'd never had one before. She'd gone from her parents' home to her husband's, moving to Ranch Haven after their wedding. She'd traveled with the rodeo, too, before her marriage and after.

But she hadn't had a home then, just a camper on the back of the truck that had hauled her horse trailer. She'd met Michael at the rodeo, when he'd been looking for his runaway older brother. He'd found her instead.

And he had been her home.

After he'd died, everything had changed for Darlene. She had changed.

And she didn't even recognize herself anymore. She wasn't sure who she was, but she knew that she needed to find out. And the first step was in finding a job. Then she would talk to Becca Calder about helping her find a place to live that would be her own home.

But first the job...

She drew in a deep breath, then walked through the open barn doors of Willow Creek Veterinarian Services. When she'd first sought Cash out at his place of business, the barn and the setup had impressed her.

It was not a clinical environment, although she had glimpsed the surgery suites back behind the reception area in the building attached to the barn. As she'd done the day she'd spoken with Cash, she bypassed the reception area because nobody was sitting behind the desk again.

And she wondered, like she had then, if that position was open. "Hello?" she called out.

Horses neighed and shuffled their hooves against the ground. She smiled and breathed in the smell of fresh hay and wood chips. A barn always felt like home to her. She loved the scents and sounds.

Her heart yearned a bit for missing Sasha. She'd inherited the horse from an old rodeo friend who'd believed Darlene would take good care of her. She'd done her best, but Jessup had been so sick then. And even after he'd received his new heart, there had been so many bills.

And so little money coming in...

Years ago her father-in-law had found her and Jessup, but things had been so precarious with Jessup's health that he had decided reuniting his wife and her oldest son would have been a mistake. He'd given them money to help out, but Darlene wondered now if Big Jake had known his wife as well as he'd thought.

As well as Lem knew her...

While Darlene had once envied her in-laws' marriage, she realized now that Sadie's second marriage was probably healthier than the first. Lem would have known that Sadie was strong enough to handle anything. Darlene should have known that, as well.

Darlene was stronger than she'd thought she was, too. Because after everyone she'd lost, she was still standing...

Still getting out of bed in the morning.

But now she needed somewhere to go when she did.

"Hello?" she called out again.

A door opened somewhere in the back of the barn, and Cash appeared in the aisle between the horse stalls. He looked disheveled, and there was blood on his jeans.

"Are you all right?" she asked.

He nodded. "Yes, I just helped Little Miss Molly bring her baby into the world," he said. He gestured toward a stall where a miniature horse stood with a tiny foal lying next to her in the hay.

"Aw," she murmured. "They're beautiful."

"I was in my apartment about to change my clothes when I heard you," he said, and then his blue eyes filled with concern. "Is everything all right? Is... Dad all right?"

She smiled that he'd said it, that he was back to thinking of JJ as his dad, and nodded. "He's great," she assured him. "In fact he's so good that he doesn't need me anymore. So I'm actually here about a job."

"A job?" another voice chimed in with the question as the silver-haired man she'd seen the other day walked into the barn. "You're hired."

Cash chuckled.

And Darlene gasped. "You don't even know what position I'm applying for."

"We need someone to handle the desk and phones," the older man said.

Despite his silver hair, his face was unlined and quite attractive. He probably wasn't much older than she was.

"I saw that there has been nobody at the desk."

"We had a college student," Cash said. "But he went back to school last week."

"And we've both been too busy to place an ad or interview anyone," the guy said. He held out his hand. "I'm Forrest Miner."

She placed her hand in his and felt a sudden rush of warmth. "Darlene Haven. And don't you want to interview me? Get a résumé?"

He was still hanging on to her hand. "I feel the calluses. You're a worker. You'll do." Then he dropped her hand and hurried off somewhere as quickly as he'd appeared.

Darlene's mouth dropped open. This guy was something else, almost as big a force of nature as the Havens were.

Cash chuckled again. "That's how my interview went, as well."

"But you're more than an employee," she said. "You're his partner."

Cash nodded. "Now I am."

"So it's not just his decision whether or not to hire me," she pointed out a little uneasily. "I can understand why you might not want me to work here."

Cash pushed back his hat and furrowed his brows. "Why not?"

"The whole situation with our families…"

"Which situation is that?" he asked. "That you live with my father?"

She smiled again that he was freely calling Jessup his

father. "That's why I want a job. To get my own place," she said. "And to support myself."

"You've supported him for a long time," Cash said. "I really appreciate that you did that for him and for my brothers."

Her heart warmed.

"But that's not our only situation with our families," Cash said. "You're also the mother-in-law of my sister."

"I know. Does Melanie?"

"She knows," he said. "I told her. She cried but insisted she was happy to find out," he said, but his shoulders slumped, as if he was carrying guilt over it.

She knew all too well how that felt. "You can't blame yourself for what her father did," she said. "And I'm sure she wasn't crying because she was upset with you."

He sighed. "I don't know. I just feel bad for making her cry. And…"

"And what?" she prodded when he trailed off. "Not that it's any of my business. While I love Sadie, I don't want you to think that I'm like her, that I meddle." But she wished she was like her in other ways, like having strength and courage. She'd survived great losses and was brave enough to try for love again.

A slight smile curved his lips. "I think you understand…probably more than anyone," he said. "You got that whole feeling paralyzed thing…"

She shuddered. "I hate that feeling. Still feel it sometimes…"

He sighed. "Me, too." And he pulled out his cell and glanced at the screen. "I need to have a talk with someone, and I'm dreading it."

"I do understand that," she said. "Why are you dreading it?"

"I just feel like everything's going to change and that there will be no going back…"

"Is there any going back without the talk?"

He tensed for a moment and shook his head. "No."

"Do you want to go back?"

"I want my friend," he said. "But I also want more."

"That's the feeling I have right now," she said. "It's why I want this job. I want a life of my own."

"The job is yours," Cash assured her.

"But you don't even know what my qualifications are," she pointed out again.

"You work hard," Cash said. "That's all we need."

"Sometimes hard work isn't enough," she said. She'd been working hard for years, but there had to be more. "Sometimes work isn't enough."

He nodded now. "You're right." He glanced at his cell phone again, but she didn't try to see what he was reading.

None of it was her business. So she started backing away from him. "I'm going to go man that desk and those phones," she said. "But, Cash? I've done a lot of things I regret, and what I regret the most are the things I didn't do."

He glanced up at her. "Thank you, Darlene," he said. "For everything…" Then he sighed and focused on his phone again. "I know you're right about this, too. But I have this feeling, this dread, that this isn't going to turn out well."

"You will never know unless you try," she pointed out.

He started typing something on his phone, so she turned away to give him privacy.

She was worried that maybe she'd given him bad advice. He knew his situation better than she did. So his instincts were probably right. Whatever he was about to do, to risk, might not turn out well.

CHAPTER NINETEEN

CASH READ BECCA'S text finally, asking him to come and talk to her as soon as possible. The urgency of her message intensified his dread.

But Darlene was right. Things wouldn't be the same between them no matter what now...

They'd crossed a line with those kisses. And he didn't want to uncross it, even if he could. He wanted to kiss her again. But whatever she had to tell him...

He knew he wasn't going to want to hear it. He steeled himself and texted her back. **Where and when?**

What works for you? was her reply.

He had to go out to the Cassidy Ranch. Midnight was being moved to his new premises this afternoon, and Cash had promised to check in on him. Make sure he was all right. Her ranch was on the way there, halfway between Willow Creek and Moss Valley, which were the areas she covered as a Realtor.

Your barn. An hour.

He was probably asking a lot. It was early afternoon, so she was probably at the office. But she replied with a thumbs-up.

Within the hour, he found himself walking into her barn as he had not so long ago when he'd asked her to be his plus-one to Sadie's wedding.

Was that the day that everything had changed for him? Or had he always had feelings for her that he hadn't acknowledged because he hadn't wanted to complicate his already complicated life?

"Becca?" he called out.

"I'm here," she said, and she stepped out of the shadows. She was dressed in one of her business suits. The slim skirt, the light jacket and the high heels were totally impractical for the barn.

And for his peace of mind...

She looked so very beautiful that he wanted to kiss her again. And he wasn't sure he would be able to resist the temptation.

"You could have changed," he suggested. "You don't want to get your clothes dirty."

She shrugged. "It doesn't matter..."

As beautiful as she was, Becca had never been vain or overly concerned about her appearance. He'd always appreciated that about her. He'd appreciated everything about her. How had he not realized how he really felt about her?

"I'm sorry I didn't answer your text last night," he said.

Her lips curved into a slight smile. "Or this morning..."

"This morning I was delivering the foal of a miniature horse."

"Little Miss Molly had her baby?" she asked, her dark eyes shining.

She remembered everything he told her about his day. She was the one who always listened and was interested.

He nodded. "Yes."

"Are they okay?"

"Great," he said. "It went better than expected."

"If you need to get back to them..."

He shook his head. "I do have to go out to the Cassidy

Ranch soon and check on Midnight, though," he admitted. "He's being moved out there now."

"We can do this another time," she offered.

He realized she was reluctant to have this conversation, too. "What is it, Becca?" he asked. "What do you have to tell me?"

"Something I should have told you a long time ago," she said, then expelled a heavy sigh.

She was definitely dreading this conversation.

"We don't have to do this," he said as panic pressed on his lungs, making it harder for him to breathe. "We don't have to change anything."

"Hasn't it already changed?" she asked.

"Because I kissed you…"

"I kissed you first," she reminded him with a flash of her old competitive spirit.

"I goaded you into it," he reminded her in turn. And he stepped closer, wanting to goad her into it again. No. He just wanted to kiss her.

"It didn't take much goading," she said.

"You wanted to kiss me?" he asked, his pulse quickening.

She sighed again. "You have no idea…"

"You've been attracted to me?" he asked with surprise. "You, more than anyone else, know all my faults and shortcomings."

Her lips twitched as a small smile crossed her face then disappeared. "But you don't know mine."

He snorted. "I know everything about you, too, Becca."

But she shook her head. "No. You don't."

"You said this is about Hope's dad, that you had something to tell me…" His stomach muscles tightened. He didn't want to talk about the man she'd married, the man she must have loved. Jealousy ate at him. "Have you been in contact with him?"

She shook her head.

He drew in a deep breath, bracing himself, then asked, "What is it then, Becca? What do you have to tell me?"

"A secret," she whispered. "I've been keeping a very big secret…"

IT HAD BEEN hard enough to tell Hope and her parents. But telling Cash…

Her heart hammered so hard with fear that she trembled a bit. She could tell that he was already upset. And she hadn't even revealed the secret yet.

She knew that what would bother him most was that she'd kept one. But that hadn't been all she'd done.

"I lied, too," she said.

And he made some noise, like a gasp, or a strangled cry like he was in pain. And she wanted to reach out to him. But she curled her fingers into her palms instead.

"What…" he rasped out the word. "What did you lie about?"

"Hope's father…" She groaned and decided to just get it over with. Even if it cost her this friendship.

"I didn't get married," she said.

Instead of looking horrified, Cash sighed. "Becca, if you're embarrassed or ashamed about that, you shouldn't be. This isn't 1950 anymore. Things happen. Accidents happen."

She bristled then. "Hope isn't an accident."

"Of course not," he agreed. "She's a blessing, but you shouldn't be embarrassed that her father walked out on you."

"Her father is a sperm donor."

He sucked in a breath. "That's a little harsh. I'm sure he must have meant something to you…" And he tensed, as if bracing himself to hear what.

A laugh slipped out of her mouth, an almost hysterical sound to it, but the situation was so ridiculous she could almost see the humor in it. "No. He was literally a sperm donor. I was artificially inseminated. I chose to have Hope on my own."

He laughed for a few seconds, too, before the humor left his face, and he narrowed his eyes. "Why lie about that? Why claim you were married?" His throat moved as he swallowed hard. "Why lie to *me*?"

She shrugged. "I don't know. I guess I was worried that everyone would think I was pathetic. That I couldn't find a husband. And I didn't want Hope to get teased about how she came into the world."

"It's not 1950," he repeated.

"In Willow Creek and Moss Valley, it sometimes feels like it is," she said. "People are judgy. I didn't want to be judged, not when I was starting a business here. And I didn't want to make Hope a subject of gossip or anything else."

He released a shaky breath. "Okay, I know how protective you are of your daughter, so I get that…but why not tell me?" He swallowed again. "Did you think I would judge you?"

She closed her eyes for a moment, fighting against a sudden rush of tears. She knew she had to tell him everything. "I didn't want you to think I was pathetic."

"Becca, I would never think that…" He touched her now, his fingertips sliding along her jaw.

And she opened her eyes to find him close. He was so close now, but he'd probably be further out of her reach. Because along with his concern and understanding was confusion and betrayal…

She could see the hurt in his eyes. "I am pathetic," she

said. "I've been in love with you for years, and I never told you."

He sucked in a breath now. "What?"

"You never looked at me as anything but a friend," she said. "Your buddy. I got tired of waiting for you to notice me. I wanted a child, and I didn't want anyone else if I couldn't have you, so I decided to start my family on my own."

He shook his head. "I never knew…"

"I know," she said. "And I didn't want you to know."

"But, Becca…" His voice trailed off in a rasp, and he shook his head.

"You didn't feel the same way about me," she said. She waited a moment, hoping that he would deny that, that he would suddenly profess the unrequited love he felt for her all these years.

But he said nothing.

"And now," she continued, "what I feared would happen is going to happen. That you won't be able to understand. But once the lie was out there, I didn't know how to take it back, especially the longer it went on. And I didn't want you to know why I said it, how pathetic I was to have this crush on you for so many years."

He shook his head again. "You know how I feel about secrets and lies and yet you weren't honest with me. And if you really loved me, as a friend or as more, you wouldn't have lied to me."

Tears stung her eyes, but she blinked them back. "Sometimes people lie because they love someone so much they don't want to lose them. And after how you took off on your family…" She hadn't trusted him not to do the same thing to her.

But she knew now that it was too late. Even before Cash turned and walked away, she knew she'd lost him.

Sᴀᴅɪᴇ ʜᴀᴅ ɪɴᴛᴇɴᴅᴇᴅ to drive out to the Cassidy Ranch more than once. But fear had kept her from making the trip, fear that her oldest son was dead. Then, when she'd heard that the house had caught fire, her heart had literally stopped beating. If not for Baker and Taye getting it going again, she might not have made it.

To her wedding.

Or out here…

The house was a total loss, just ashes and random blackened boards standing in sharp contrast to the recently renovated barn. The barn was ready for Midnight, but everybody at Ranch Haven was struggling with him going. Especially Caleb.

She had assured the little boy that she would make certain that Midnight liked his new place and report back to him. It wasn't safe for the kids to come along for the move, in case Midnight reacted badly and got loose.

Dusty hadn't wanted Melanie to come, either, but she'd insisted on riding along with him. Like Lem had insisted on riding along with Sadie.

She reached across her truck console and patted his arm. "You didn't need to come."

"No, but I wanted to," he said. "That horse has caused a lot of trouble. And it's probably not going to be happy about this move."

Lem wasn't the rancher that she was. The only animal he really interacted with was Feisty. But she had no doubt that he intended to put himself between Sadie and Midnight if that bronco got out of control.

She smiled. "He's probably not going to be happy that he's not going to get carrots every day like he has from Caleb. But the mare is here, and he might be very happy about that."

Lem smiled, too, and his blue eyes twinkled. "You think love will mellow him out like it has us?"

She chuckled. "I don't think either of us are mellow." They'd just had a fierce Scrabble match the night before. She'd been so certain that fjordic wasn't a word. But Lem, as usual, had survived her challenge and won the game. She was still a little salty about that.

Lem chuckled. "Mellow would be boring," he admitted.

And that was why they were perfect for each other.

"There's Cash," she said as the pickup with Willow Creek Veterinarian Services on it pulled up next to the barn. "If anyone can mellow Midnight, it's him. The horse whisperer."

When Cash pushed open his driver's door and stepped out, his shoulders were slumped, though, as if he was carrying the weight of the world on them. And the expression on his face...it was one of devastation.

"Looks like someone whispered something to him he didn't want to hear," Lem remarked.

"Looks like he lost his best friend," Sadie murmured, but she hoped that wasn't so...

That Cash and Becca's friendship wasn't over.

CHAPTER TWENTY

CASH COULDN'T QUITE remember how he'd gotten out to the Cassidy Ranch. Maybe it was that he instinctively knew the way home.

But his brothers weren't here. Or his dad.

Not even Darlene this time.

She was at his work, though. A part of his life now that he never would have envisioned. And he never would have envisioned this...

That Becca had lied to him, had kept a huge secret from him, even knowing how he valued truth above everything else. She wasn't the best friend he'd thought she was.

And this ranch wasn't home anymore.

It was Dusty and Melanie's.

And Midnight's...

He was here for the horse. He had an attachment to that bronco and to this town and to his family and friends. So even though the old Cash would have run about now, the new, mature one wasn't going anywhere. He forced himself to rally, pulling away from the side of his pickup where he'd been leaning while he found the strength in his legs again. Then he headed toward the barn, which was eerily quiet.

Maybe Midnight was still in the trailer he'd seen out front. That wasn't all he'd seen, though, from Ranch Haven. Sadie and her sweetheart were here.

She and Lem followed him into the barn. "You all right?" she asked him.

Of course she would notice how he was feeling. "Do you ever miss anything?"

She smiled and patted his cheek. "You would be surprised."

He shook his head. "No. I don't want any more surprises." He still didn't know how to deal with what Becca had told him. That she was in love with him. That she'd lied about Hope's father.

But why lie to *him*?

Why not tell him the truth about her feelings and, most especially, about Hope?

"Are you okay?" Sadie asked, her deep voice even deeper with concern.

He nodded. "Yeah, I'll be fine."

"You look like you lost your best friend," Lem remarked.

Cash gasped.

"What's going on?" Sadie asked. "Did you and Becca get into a fight?"

"Not a fight…" He wasn't sure what there was to fight about or to fight for right now. Not when he knew he couldn't trust her. "But speaking of fights…" He drew in a breath and looked around. "Where's Midnight? Is he still in the trailer?"

A soft nicker drew Cash's attention to Midnight's stall. Cash walked over to it to find the bronco inside, nibbling on a bunch of carrots. "Caleb here?" he asked.

Sadie shook her head. "No. He sent those with Melanie, though." She glanced around the barn now. "Where are Melanie and Dusty?"

A scream rang out then, so intense that Midnight reared up and answered it with a cry of his own.

"Help!" Dusty yelled, and his head rose above the wall of another horse stall. "Melanie's in labor. She kept telling me they were just more Braxton Hicks. I should have—"

And another scream rang out, so full of pain that Cash winced.

"I'll call for an ambulance," Lem said as he pulled out his cell phone.

Cash shook his head and whispered, "It won't get here in time." He knew those cries were too close together. There was no time to get Melanie to the hospital. She was in active labor.

"You'll have to deliver them," Sadie whispered back at him.

"I'm a vet, not an obstetrician," he said. But he knew there was no other option right now, so he rushed over to the stall where Dusty had popped up, and he pulled open the door to find Melanie lying on a blanket over a bed of hay.

She screamed again.

"We've got this," he said, even though his heart was racing, too. "We've got you. We'll get those babies safely into the world."

And hopefully they would stay safe from heartbreak and disappointment and loss…if that was even possible…

BECCA HADN'T CHANGED out of her business suit before talking to Cash because she had an appointment later that afternoon. She hadn't canceled because she'd suspected that he would react to her revealing her secret exactly the way he'd reacted.

That he would run off.

"I'm sorry," Becca said, and as she did, she wasn't sure she'd said those words to Cash. Had she apologized for lying to him?

Or had she just tried to justify it?

He would never see or accept her reasons, though. She knew that now.

"What are you sorry about?" Juliet asked as they arrived back at the office.

She was sorry about so many things.

"I wish I'd had more places to show you," she explained. "But there's so little on the market right now."

Juliet smiled. "That's not your fault, Becca. I just have such a vision of what I want in my head." Her smile slipped away. "But we can't always get what we want."

"Isn't that the truth?" Becca murmured.

"I think it's also a Rolling Stones song," Juliet said and laughed. "And the story of my life…"

"Mine, too," Becca said in commiseration.

Juliet's cell vibrated, and the older woman pulled it from her purse. "Hello? Dusty? What? Oh, my God…" All the color drained from the woman's face.

And Becca reached out, holding her arm to steady her in case she fainted.

"But Melanie is okay?" she asked. "And the babies, too?"

Becca gasped. Melanie Haven had had her twins.

"I'll meet you at the hospital," Juliet promised. Then, with a shaky hand, she dropped her phone back into her purse.

"Melanie went into labor?" Becca asked.

"She had the babies," Juliet said. "A boy and a girl. They're all right…"

"That's good," Becca said. But she could tell there was more to the story.

"She had them in the barn at the Cassidy Ranch."

Becca thought fleetingly of Cash. He'd intended to go

there. Had he made it in time for the birth of his niece and nephew?

She pushed thoughts of him aside and said, "Let's get you to the hospital then, Grandma."

Juliet laughed and looked a little wild-eyed. "I don't know if I can find it right now."

"I'll drive," Becca assured her.

But she regretted that when she walked into the hospital ER and nearly collided with Cash.

She didn't know how to act. Like nothing had changed between them? Or like they were strangers?

That was how he was looking at her, like he'd never seen her before.

And her heart broke, just as she'd been scared it would.

Sadie and Lem rushed up, and Lem hurried off with Juliet to show her to her daughter's room while Sadie stood there, staring at the two of them staring at each other.

"What's the matter, you two?" she asked. "This is a cause for celebration!"

Becca cleared her throat and said, "Congratulations on your new great-grandchildren."

Sadie grinned. "They're beautiful. Well, they will be once they get cleaned up a bit. What a mess… I'm not sure what would have happened without Cash here."

"What do you mean?" Becca asked.

"He delivered them."

He had delivered his niece and nephew.

"Congratulations," she said to him. And she wanted to hug him, to offer him whatever he needed from her.

But he clearly didn't need her anymore because once again he turned and walked away.

This time she wasn't having it. She wasn't going to just stand there and watch him leave. So she rushed out the automatic doors after him. "Running again, Cash?" she asked. "Are you going to keep doing that every time life gets complicated or messy? Are you just going to take off instead of dealing with your feelings?"

He stopped and turned toward her. "Like you care about my feelings," he scoffed. "You wouldn't have lied to me if you did."

"That's *why* I lied to you," she said. "I didn't want to lose you like your family lost you. I didn't want you to cut me off like you cut your family out of your life."

"Because of secrets and lies," he reminded her.

She flinched. But she still refused to back down. "Nobody tried to hurt you," she said. "They did it so they wouldn't hurt you."

"That might be true about my dad and mom," he agreed. Surprisingly. "But *you* were protecting yourself, not me."

All her self-righteous indignation drained away as she realized how right he was. How selfish she had been...

When he turned and walked away again, she didn't try to stop him. The thing she'd feared the most had happened; she'd lost her best friend.

WITH A GRIN spreading across his face, Jessup clicked off his cell phone. Darlene had called to share the news about the birth of her new grandson and granddaughter with him. She'd never sounded so happy.

Twins, like his own. Thinking of Colton and Collin brought Colleen to mind. He still missed her so much. Like he'd missed Cash for so many years.

Maybe he should join everyone up at the hospital. He grabbed his keys from the table and started toward the front door, but when he opened it, he found an unexpected visitor standing on the front steps.

"Cash..."

Cash lifted his face, and there were tears shimmering in the blue eyes that were so much like his mother's.

Jessup opened his arms, and Cash stepped into them, hugging him close.

"I'm so sorry, Dad," he said. "I'm so sorry..."

"What? What happened?" Jessup asked with alarm. He pulled back. Had something happened to those babies? Or to someone else they cared about?

Cash shook his head. "Nothing..."

But Jessup could see that was a lie. "Something happened. What are you sorry about?"

"I'm sorry for the things I said, for running away," Cash said. "I'm so sorry I wasn't a better son to you. A better brother..."

Jessup pulled him inside the house and closed the door. "Cash, none of that was your fault," he assured him. "I know it was all too much for you, and then how you found out the truth..."

Cash shook his head. "That wasn't the truth," he said. "I understand that now. The truth is that you are my father in every way that counts. You always were. You were the one who was always there for me."

Jessup smiled. "Me and Becca. And I'm glad she was there for you when I wasn't. That you've had her all these years."

Cash shook his head again, and he looked even more miserable than he had moments ago.

Jessup continued, "I know you two never lost touch over the years. You've been so close ever since you were little kids."

"She lied to me."

And Jessup sucked in a breath with sudden understanding of why Cash looked so devastated. "Sometimes people lie."

"Why did you lie to me?"

He sighed. "It never seemed like a lie," he admitted. "I always loved you like my son."

"But when I got older, why didn't you tell me the truth?"

"I didn't want to hurt you," he said.

Cash nodded. "That's what Becca said…"

"Why did she lie to you?" Jessup asked.

Cash grunted and clenched his jaw before saying, "To protect her pride. To save face."

Jessup snorted. "Becca?" He shook his head. "No. That girl's never worried about saving face. She probably did it for the same reasons I did. She didn't want to hurt you or she didn't want to lose you."

Cash's mouth dropped open with a soft gasp, and he murmured, "She didn't trust me…" He blinked as more tears brimmed in his eyes. Then he added, "Just like my brothers…"

"Your brothers what?" Jessup asked. He hoped they weren't still giving him a hard time. "They love you," he insisted. "And I know Becca does, too." He grasped his son's shoulders. "Just like I love you."

"I'm home now," Cash said. And he hugged him again. "And I'm done running."

Maybe from his family, but what about from his best friend?

Jessup wasn't his mother, though. He knew when to push and he knew when to back off. And right now was the time to back off.

Cash would come around with Becca. Jessup only hoped that it didn't take him as long as it had with him. That he wouldn't let two decades pass before he forgave Becca.

CHAPTER TWENTY-ONE

WHEN CASH WOKE up in the morning, on the couch of the den in the house his dad was renting, he had a text from Becca on his phone.

I'm sorry. You're right. I was selfish.

"What was she selfish about?" a deep voice asked.

Startled, Cash nearly dropped his phone as he snapped his head toward where his brother Marsh stood behind him. "I never could get any privacy from you guys," he murmured.

"You had your privacy for the last seventeen years," Marsh pointed out. "Except for Becca. You always shared everything with her."

"Yeah," he said, "but she didn't always share everything with me." He was beginning to understand why he had and she hadn't. He'd trusted her, but she hadn't felt the same about him.

"Is that what she was selfish about?" Marsh asked. Then he snorted. "I can't imagine that. Becca always dropped everything for you when we were kids. She helped out around the ranch and in the house when our parents were sick. She took on more responsibility than a kid ever should have."

"We all did," Cash reminded him.

"But it was our lives," Marsh said. "Not hers. She didn't need to pitch in like she did. And it didn't look like much changed when she showed up at Sadie's wedding with you, even knowing how awkward it would be."

"She did that because she knew how awkward it would be," he said. And she probably hadn't trusted him to handle it with maturity or patience since he hadn't displayed a whole lot of that before.

"She's always been there for you, Cash," Marsh said. "Selflessly. I wish I had someone like that."

"Why don't you?" Cash asked.

Marsh shrugged then sighed. "Because he took off seventeen years ago."

Cash's stomach hurt like his brother had sucker punched him like he used to, but Cash had obviously hurt more people than had hurt him. It was no wonder Becca hadn't trusted him not to hurt her, too.

"I'm sorry," he said. He was the one who'd been selfish. Not Becca. He saw that now.

"I know."

"An apology isn't enough, though," Cash said.

"From you or from Becca?"

"I don't know..." Did Becca owe him an apology? Or did he owe her one like he owed his family?

Marsh sighed. "It's not possible to undo the past. It's already happened. You can apologize for it and move on."

"But it'll never be the same," Cash said.

"No," Marsh said. "But maybe it'll be better."

He wasn't sure if his brother was talking about Cash's relationship with him or with Becca, and Marsh walked away before he could ask.

Then he realized Marsh couldn't answer that question. Only Cash could...

And Becca...if she would give him another chance... and he could prove himself worthy of her trust. And her love...

BECCA HAD SENT Cash that last text days ago. And she never got a reply. Not that she'd really expected one.

Their friendship was done.

He would never trust her again.

And she couldn't blame him.

She could only blame herself.

"Mom!" Hope called out.

The cry startled Becca so much that she dropped the glass she'd been washing. "What's wrong?"

"The kittens got out!"

"What? How?"

"They must've pushed open the front door," she said. "I can't find them."

They were still too little to be separated from their mother. Tabby would probably find them on her own, but Becca had promised the mama cat that they would help her take care of her babies.

"I'll help you look," she said. She quickly dried her hands to head out with her daughter to search the yard around the house.

"There's just one missing yet," Hope said, as she held an armful of fluff. "I think it's in the barn."

"In the barn?" Becca glanced across the yard toward it. "That's a long way from the house."

"You better catch it before one of the horses steps on it," Hope said.

"I doubt the kitten's in the barn," she said. But she couldn't take the chance that the little thing might get crushed. "You get them back to the house," she said as she rushed off to the barn herself.

When she stepped inside, she heard the soft cry of the kitten right away. "Here, kitty, kitty…" How in the world had it made it that far that fast?

But then a shadow fell across Becca, and she realized

the kitten hadn't made it that distance on its own four legs. Cash held it against his chest.

She pressed a hand to her madly pounding heart. "You scared me!"

"I'm sorry," he said. "I've been doing that a lot lately."

"What?" she asked. "Scaring people?"

"Apologizing," he said. "I apologized to my dad and my brothers for running off, for not being there for them."

She smiled. "I'm glad you've made up with them."

"How do you know they forgave me?" he asked.

"Because they love you."

"Do you still love me?" he asked.

Her breath caught in her throat. "Cash..."

"Becca..." He stepped closer to her. "I'm asking because I love you. So very much..."

Hope warmed her heart, but then she reined it in because he was probably talking about as a friend. That he just loved her as a friend...

"Do you still love me? Enough to forgive me?" Cash asked. "And to trust me?"

Tears stung her eyes. "I was the one who screwed up."

"I'm glad," he said.

"What?"

"For once it wasn't me who made the mess," he said.

She laughed. "That's true."

His expression grew serious. "I get it now. I know that it was my fault. You didn't trust me to handle the situation without overreacting like I've done before, without running."

She sucked in a breath. He understood. "And I wasn't worried just about me getting hurt. Hope loves you, and I didn't want her getting hurt."

"I know," he said. "I don't want to hurt either of you."

"Can we get past this?" she asked. "Can we go back to what we had?"

"I don't want to go back to what we had," he said.

"You don't want to be my friend anymore?"

He held the kitten out to her. It was the fluffy black-and-white one, but now it had a red ribbon around its neck. It chewed on one end of the ribbon. But it wasn't just the ribbon around its neck.

There was a ring hiding in that soft kitten fur.

"What is this?"

"My mother's engagement ring," Cash said. "Her rings survived the fire."

"That's good…" She hated to think of everything else that had been lost in it, all the mementos.

"I want you to have it, Becca," he said. "I want you to wear it."

"I… I don't understand… I thought you were mad at me."

"I was," he said. "And then I remembered that there is no way you could ever be selfish. You're the most loving, supportive, selfless person I know. And I realized why you didn't share your secret with me. The same reason that I didn't tell Melanie I'm her brother right away. You didn't want to hurt someone you care about. And you also didn't want to get hurt—I gave you every reason not to trust me about this. You thought I'd hurt you, and Hope, too, like I hurt my family."

"Cash…"

"I don't want to be just your friend anymore," he said. "I love you as more than a friend. I have for a while now. I was just scared, too, because you're the last person I want to lose. I want to be your partner for life, for the rest of our lives, for forever." He dropped down to one knee. "Will you marry me, Becca?"

"Oh, Cash…" She couldn't see him now as tears flooded her eyes.

"Do you still love me?" he asked. "Can you forgive me? And can you trust me?"

"You didn't do anything wrong," she said. "I was the one who messed up."

He stood and cupped her face in his hands. "I messed up because I didn't realize sooner that you're not just my best friend. You're my soulmate, and I love you so much, Becca Calder. Will you marry me?"

"I love you, Cash," she said. "And yes, I will marry you."

He kissed her then, and it was just like their first kisses. She lost all sense of self and time until she heard applause and turned to find they had an audience.

Hope and her parents. And JJ, with Cash's brothers and Sadie.

"You were pretty sure of yourself," Becca said.

"I was Hope-ful," he said with a grin.

Her little girl ran up to them, and Cash picked her up and swung her around. She squealed and locked her arms around his neck, hugging him. "She said yes, so you're going to be my daddy."

"Yes, I will be your daddy," Cash said.

Becca's heart had already been full of love for them both, but it seemed to swell even more now. She had more love to give to Hope and to Cash and to the children they would have in the years to come.

"So you're the last man standing now…"

Marsh looked uneasily around him. "What?"

"The only single one of our family left," his dad said with a teasing grin.

Marsh shook his head. "No. I'm not, Dad. You're single, too."

And that grin slipped away from his father's face.

Marsh chuckled. "And I'm not worried about Sadie's matchmaking schemes." Grandma Haven Lemmon had her work cut out for her if she had any plans to get him married off. He was too focused on his career and his family. He'd rather risk his life in the line of duty than risk his heart...

Not that his life was in danger in Willow Creek. While he wasn't sure if the fire at the ranch had been deliberately set, he wasn't too worried. It may well have been an accident. So his life was safe, and as stubborn as he was, his heart was safe, too, from his grandma's matchmaking...

* * * * *

WESTERN

Rugged men looking for love...

Available Next Month

Redeeming The Maverick Christine Rimmer
The Right Cowboy Cheryl Harper

....

Fortune's Secret Marriage Jo McNally
Home To Her Cowboy Sasha Summers

....

LOVE INSPIRED

His Unexpected Grandchild Myra Johnson
His Neighbour's Secret Lillian Warner

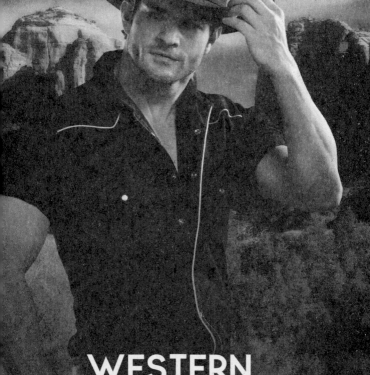

brand new stories each month

WESTERN

Rugged men looking for love

Keep reading for an excerpt of a new title
from the Special Edition series,
A SMALL TOWN FOURTH OF JULY by Janice Carter

Chapter One

Where's Jake?

Maura Stuart dropped the pitchfork of hay into the stall trough, muttering at the same time. Stomping down the length of the barn to its opened doors, she stood for a moment, shading her eyes from the early-morning sun. No sign of him anywhere. *Great. Just what I needed today.* And no sign of Maddie, either. Too much to hope that she'd gone looking for Jake—the enticing aroma of coffee was probably just now luring her out of bed. She took a deep breath. Giving in to this constant frustration would gain her nothing, especially if they continued to be business partners. But there were moments—plenty of them—when Maura silently questioned her decision to bring her twin sister on board. Yet there'd be no business at all if she'd had to manage on her own.

She scanned the property, from the two-story farmhouse straight ahead and its adjacent garage, to the shed on the far side of the garage. It was closed up, so no Jake there. She knew the chicken coop behind the barn and the small, fenced riding ring next to it wouldn't be a draw for Jake. Thankfully, he wasn't trotting down the long gravel drive out to the road. Then her gaze drifted east, to their neighbor's fields, overgrown with weeds. No sign of Jake, but she suddenly caught a glimmer of red through the thicket of vegetation separating the two farms.

Maura walked across the drive to the row of cedars along the property line and pushed through them into the adjacent land. She and Maddie used to come this way when they were kids, but the cedars had been newly planted then and only waist-high. Now they were taller than her shoulders.

Stepping onto what was once the Danby homestead felt strange. The elderly owners, Stan and Vera, had passed away several months ago, but the farm had been left derelict since their admission to a nursing home in Rutland two years before. When Maura and Maddie took over their own family farm a year ago, the Danby place was already run-down. The neighboring families had been close when the girls were growing up, but that gradually changed after the sisters left for college.

It was only natural, Maura knew. People aged, withdrew from community and old friends due to health or mobility issues, and lost touch with one another. She and Maddie had experienced a similar loss of contact after being away from Maple Glen for so long. But thankfully, they'd been able to reconnect with former schoolmates and other neighbors since their return.

Maura waded through the field toward the Danby farmhouse, realizing as she got closer that the flash of red was a car—a fancy sports car. When she reached the drive, she could hear the low rumble of a male voice. She paused for a second, debating whether to retreat or continue looking for Jake. The voice pitched nervously as she was rounding the back end of the car to see Jake standing between it and the closed barn door, his stocky frame blocking the object of his interest from Maura's view.

"He won't bite," she said, stifling a laugh as she drew near. "He's just curious."

The man splayed against the barn door grimaced. "Maybe call him off?"

She closed in on Jake, wrapping an arm around his neck and gently pulling him away from his attempt to nuzzle the man. She recognized him then, despite the passage of years and his transformation from teenager to adult.

"Welcome back, Theo." She kept her eyes on him, fighting to ignore the sudden throbbing at her temples, then turned Jake around, slapped him on the rump and ordered, "Home, Jake."

Theo Danby watched the donkey amble off. "Thanks... uh... Maura?"

The fact that he was slow to identify her irked. "Yes," she snapped.

He moved away from the barn door and unzipped his windbreaker. "Warmer than I remember," he mumbled.

So he's going for small talk. "Yeah, climate change and all that. Plus, it's the middle of June." She shifted her attention away from the well-toned chest muscles emerging through his short-sleeved shirt—muscles that the Theo she remembered hadn't had. She felt her cheeks warm up as a trace of a smile crossed his face.

"Are you visiting your folks or...?" he asked.

"No, Mom died about three years ago and my father, last June."

"I'm sorry." His face softened, and she peered down at the ground, hiding unexpected tears.

"We moved back here more than a year ago," she went on.

"We?"

She raised her head, meeting his dark brown eyes again. "Maddie and I."

"Ah."

"So…you're here to…" she continued.

"Have a look at this place before I sell it."

Of course. She'd been expecting that from the day she and Maddie first returned home and had seen that the Danby homestead had been left to ruin. Though she couldn't figure out why it had taken Theo so long to return after his aunt and uncle passed away. She was about to ask him more about his plans when a slamming door and a young voice got her attention.

"Dad?" A boy who looked to be a preteen was standing on the farmhouse veranda, his face wrinkled in disgust. "This place is a dump!" He caught sight of Maura and hesitated before descending the porch steps and walking their way.

Maura shot a glance at Theo. He flushed slightly as he said, "My son."

Maura scolded herself for automatically assuming that Theo might still be single, too. The boy heading their way was a near replica of a young Theo—same thick dark hair and eyes. He sidled up to his father but kept his eyes on Maura.

"Uh, Luke, this is Maura—" The last part of his introduction dropped off, as if he were unsure of her current surname. "Her family owns the place over there." He gestured to his right, though the boy kept his attention on her.

"It's Maura Stuart. Nice to meet you, Luke." She held out her right hand, and after an elbow nudge from Theo, the boy shook it. "My sister and I knew your father years ago, when he used to spend his summer vacations here, with his aunt and uncle."

"Dad told me about that, but he made it sound more interesting than—"

"What you see here?" Maura smiled. She resisted glancing at Theo, but thought she heard a faint sigh.

"Yeah." He looked at Theo and asked, "So now what?"

"Well, uh, I thought after we looked around, we could go into Maple Glen for some lunch and then talk about our plans."

"*Our* plans? It wasn't *my* idea to come here."

Maura took in the disgruntled face and voice. Time to head back to the farm, she decided. "Okay, well, nice to see you again, Theo and Luke… The bakery in the village sells sandwiches and pizzas, but if you want anything substantial, you'll have to drive to Wallingford."

Theo's smile was strained. "Thanks, Maura. I think a bite to eat will help us both. And…uh…is there a place to stay? It's been a while since I was last here."

"Maybe you remember the Watsons? Bernie used to manage the gas station at the junction to Route 7, but he bought the old Harrison place about ten years ago and turned it into a B and B. The Shady Nook. I hear it's quite nice. If you're planning to stay in the area for a few days, of course." When Theo failed to respond, she added, "Unless you'd rather stay somewhere with more to offer, like Rutland or Bennington." Theo was staring, and she realized she'd been babbling. "Okay, well, I better go."

She was about to turn around when he finally spoke. "Thanks, Maura. Um, my plan is to stick around until I can make a decision about my aunt and uncle's place. A few days, anyway—maybe more." He shot Luke a quick look. "Nothing definite yet. But maybe we'll see you around. And Maddie, too, of course. Say hi for me."

"Sure." She managed a smile and headed off, taking the same route across the weed-filled field and through the cedars, feeling two sets of eyes tracking her. Her mind buzzed with random thoughts and questions. *Theo Danby is back. He has a son. Presumably he's married. Or was.*

But the important question was, how long would he be around?

The very thought of Theo spending any amount of time in Maple Glen made Maura's stomach churn. Was it too much to hope that Theo Danby would just drop out of their lives again, as he had twenty years ago, and never discover her secret?

By the time she reached the barn, Jake had instinctively headed for his stall and was munching the hay she'd deposited. She took a moment to inspect the stall door and noticed the hasp was loose enough to give way with a solid push. A small thing to fix, but one more item on the long list of jobs. The other two donkeys, Matilda and Lizzie, were too busy eating to give her more than a half glance, their long ears twitching as she walked by their stalls.

Maura decided that after the encounter with Theo—and his son!—a second cup of coffee was definitely on the day's agenda and headed for the side door of the farmhouse that led through a tiny mudroom into the kitchen. Maddie was sitting at the table eating cereal and skimming through yesterday's Rutland newspaper. She looked up when Maura entered the room.

"What's up?" she immediately asked.

They'd always been good at reading one another, Maura knew. Even though they were nonidentical twins, there was still that inexplicable twin connection. At least, until the summer they'd turned eighteen, when they'd withdrawn from one another and begun new, separate lives.

Maura sighed. There was no point postponing the inevitable. "Jake got out of his stall—it's okay," she quickly put in, seeing Maddie was about to ask how. "I've figured it out. We have to fix the stall gate. Anyway, he'd wandered over to the Danbys', and I followed him." She paused. "Someone was at the house."

Maddie put her spoon down. "Who?"

"Theo."

Their eyes locked for what seemed ages. "He's come to get the place ready to sell," Maura added. "And he has a son who looks to be about eleven or twelve."

Maddie's impassive face revealed nothing. "Okay," she said and resumed eating.

That went well, Maura thought. Clearly her sister was still unhappy with her after last night's disagreement over the ongoing plans for the business, as well as finances. She poured herself a coffee and sat across from Maddie, whose head was still bent over the newspaper. The kitchen filled with the silence that had fallen between the sisters seventeen years ago, and Maura hoped it wouldn't last five years this time around, too. *Not if you do something about it right now*, she told herself.

"Look, Mads, Theo is ancient history. We were all teenagers the last time we were together, and presumably—" she attempted a half laugh "—we're a whole lot smarter now. I got the impression he and his son are here only long enough to sell the farm. Then he'll be gone."

Maddie finally looked at her. "I'm not worried about any of that, Maura. Like you said, that last summer is ancient history. I've moved on, and I hope you have, too."

Maura felt her face heat up under her sister's penetrating gaze. She bit down on her lower lip, quelling an instant rise of hurt. She wasn't going to be drawn into a debate they'd both sworn to put behind them. "Okay," she mumbled. "You're right." She got up from her chair and rinsed her coffee mug, letting the tension seep out. "So, who have we got riding today?"

It *had* to happen. Theo parked the car in front of the Shady Nook B and B and sat, unmoving. He'd known from the start that meeting up with the Stuart sisters—or at least one of them—was a possibility, but he wished fervently that it hadn't happened under such humiliating circumstances. Trapped by a donkey, for heaven's sake! Only to be rescued by one of the sisters. Worst of all, for a second he couldn't recall which was the redhead and which the raven-haired. They weren't identical twins, so it shouldn't have been so difficult. When he was a boy and then a teen, he'd never have made such a mistake.

"Are we going in or what?"

Luke's grumble finally registered. Theo blinked. He was back in Maple Glen. Thirty-six years old, divorced and on leave from his job. With a twelve-year-old son he barely knew who didn't want to be there any more than he did. He sighed. Those few minutes back at the farm with Maura had been a cold-water-shock reminder that time didn't change everything. Her stony expression and clipped voice took him immediately back to his last summer in Maple Glen countless years ago.

"Dad? Jeez!"

"Yeah, yeah. C'mon. We'll leave our stuff here until we know if we can get a room."

"Why don't we go back to the highway? I saw some motels there. Maybe we could get one with a pool, like we did yesterday."

Theo ignored Luke's plaintive tone, which had been incessant since he'd made the decision to take a road trip to Maple Glen and finally deal with his inheritance. Reconnecting with his son was meant to be part of a new, postdivorce direction in Theo's life, but he had a sinking feeling he'd already taken a wrong turn somewhere and now was lost. Like the rookie hikers on the nearby Appalachian Long Trail that the locals used to complain about.

At least the B and B looked like a welcoming place,

with its smoky-blue clapboard siding, white gingerbread-trimmed veranda and wicker chairs and tables. Theo vaguely recalled the original Colonial-style home had been painted white, but any memory of the people who'd lived there—the Harrisons, Maura had said—escaped him. Though come to think of it, had there been a boy roughly his own age?

"Well?" Luke was staring up at him from the bottom porch step.

His expression was a mix of frustration and concern, which made Theo feel a tad guilty. He hadn't been paying full attention to him since leaving Maine. Perhaps their road trip's destination should have been somewhere more exciting than a small place like Maple Glen, Vermont. He reached down and tousled Luke's hair. "C'mon," he said and opened the screen door.

Theo's eyes were adjusting to the cool darkness inside the entryway when a voice called out from somewhere farther inside. "Give me a sec!"

The interior gradually took shape, from the hall table with a vase of flowers and a small display of tourist pamphlets, to the staircase straight ahead. There were rooms to the left and right off the entry, and Theo spotted tables and chairs in one of them. A good sign, he thought. Even if there wasn't a room available, maybe they could get a bite to eat. Breakfast had been early, at a fast-food place on the highway.

Luke was fidgeting beside him, but at least he wasn't complaining. Not yet. Theo was about to reassure him that the next town, Wallingford, was only minutes away and they could always get some lunch there when a large, gray-haired man wearing an apron over baggy pants and a T-shirt emerged from a room at the end of the hall and lumbered toward them.

"Had to pop my bread rolls into the oven," he explained, his big, welcoming smile shooting from Theo to Luke. "What can I do for you folks?"

"We'd like a room, if you have one."

"Aha! That I do. You came at the right time—it's Sunday and I've just had two checkouts, plus the Fourth of July holiday is a couple of weeks away. How many nights are you thinking?" Before Theo could reply, the man headed for one of the rooms leading off the hall and, after a second's hesitation, Theo and Luke followed.

The room still exhibited its early days as a parlor, with a cluster of seating arrangements and an impressive bow-legged table with a Tiffany-style, stained glass lamp in the center of the bay window that looked onto the veranda. The man—Bernie Watson, Theo assumed—was rifling through a drawer in the table. Pulling out a small ledger book and pen, he swung around to say, "Here we go. Have a seat there—" he gestured to a chintz-upholstered wing chair "—and fill in the information I need while I go check on my dinner rolls."

Theo grasped the book and pen that were thrust at him and, casting a quick grin at Luke, sat where he was told. He wrote his name and address on the page headed with the day's date, hesitated over the "length of stay" column before jotting *2-3 nights* and hoped Luke, now standing at his elbow, hadn't noticed. He had yet to tell the boy that his plan was to fix up a couple of rooms in the farmhouse for them until the meeting with the Realtor.

Despite Luke's disparagement of the house as a "dump," the place had been dusted and aired only the week before their arrival by a company from Rutland that Theo had hired. The Stuart sisters obviously hadn't noticed the recent activity there, though the weeds in the fields between the two places could have hidden the cleaning agency's vehicle. Maura's search for her donkey had likely been the only reason for her to discover he was back. A donkey! Theo was pretty certain the Stuarts had never had animals larger than goats.

"Dad? I'm hungry." Luke was pulling on his arm.

Theo roused himself from thoughts that were leading nowhere. He was hungry, too, and the heavy footfalls along the hallway were reassuring. They'd be getting a room and, hopefully, lunch as well.

"Excuse my bad manners," the man was saying as he reentered the room. "I'm Bernie Watson, the owner, general manager as well as cook here."

Theo shook his hand and passed the sign-in book to Bernie, who peered down at it.

"Good heavens," he exclaimed. "Theo Danby!" His beaming grin faltered immediately. "I was sorry to hear about Stan and Vera."

"Thank you," Theo murmured. Luke shuffled impatiently, and he added, "Is it possible to get some lunch?"

"Definitely. Go get your things from your car. It'll be okay parked out front for now. I've got a small lot behind where you can move it later. As for lunch, I don't have any other patrons at the moment, but I can rustle something up for you two." He turned to Luke. "How about a grilled cheese sandwich with fries? I can even manage a chocolate milkshake, if you're up to it."

The smile on Luke's face was the first Theo had seen since the motel with pool they'd stayed at. "I think he's up to it," he said.

Don't miss out!

Limited edition commemorative
Anniversary Collections

In honour of our golden jubilee, don't miss these four special Anniversary Collections, each honouring a beloved series line — Modern, Medical, Suspense and Western. A tribute to our legacy, these collections are a must-have for every fan.

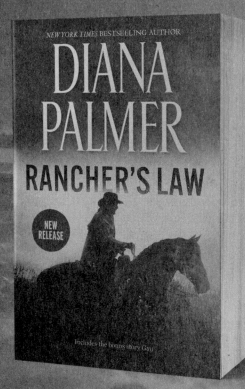

NEW RELEASES

Four sisters. One surprise will.
One year to wed.

Don't miss these two volumes of
Wed In The Outback!

When Holt Waverly leaves his flourishing outback estat
to his four daughters, it comes to pass that without an
eldest son to inherit, the farm will be entailed to someor
else…unless all his daughters are married within the yea

May 2024   July 2024